Clouds of Ecstasy

by

Jakob Aalborg Solvang

Clouds of Ecstasy
ISBN 978-82-303-3270-2
Copyright © 2016 Jakob Aalborg Solvang,
All rights reserved.

Cover design by Jakob Aalborg Solvang.

Printed and bound in the USA.

Published by Lulu Press, Inc.
3101 Hillsborough Street
Raleigh, NC 27607

Clouds of Ecstasy

CHAPTER ONE

Perched on the longest branch of a large dead oak tree sat Tucker and cawed 'fucker' at his owner Brandy Rabinow, who struggled headfirst uphill against a vicious coastal wind. As she neared the tree the wind weakened and ceased in less than a second, and in leaning so much forward, she promptly tipped over and fell, with her face landing in a small puddle. Tucker flew down to her and landed atop her head as she got back up on her feet.

"Fucker!" he cawed mockingly.

"You little bitch you." Brandy said. "You keep up that attitude and I'll sell ya to KFC."

"Fucker." Tucker repeated.

"I'm not kidding. They'll take your kind. You think that stuff they got is real chicken? They'll take crow any day, y'know."

Tucker hopped down from Brandy's head and onto her right shoulder.

"Fucker." he said in a more muted tone.

"I'm just fucking with ya." Brandy said and scratched her crow friend under his beak. "I'm pretty sure what they use at KFC is magpie."

The two of them approached the tree, situated atop a convenient vantage point with a splendid view of Brandy's new town of residence, the city of Riverside.

Far larger than any other town in America that shared its name, Riverside, New Hampshire was distinct for its almost renaissance-style architecture. With the exception of a few new skyscrapers built mostly in the business district in the south-west, all the city's buildings remained the same as they were before the American Revolution, and it did resemble a medieval European town more than any American one.

1

As the sun seared Brandy's back from the east, it cast a pleasant warm golden glow over Riverside as she and Tucker gazed at it from their hill on this bitter October Monday. Once again, a burst of chilly wind assaulted Brandy's face. Her olive green cardigan, a holey husk of its former self, flapped and fluttered with the gale, it being many sizes too large served more the purpose of a coat over her gray over-washed blouse. She grabbed hold of her umber Basque beret to keep it from blowing off the bush of jet black unruly hair she had thread it upon.

An irritating burning sensation returned to the left lower part of Brandy's abdomen. She rubbed the area trying to subdue the pain, and then she checked her watch.

"Well, it's still an hour till my doctor's appointment." she said to Tucker. "That's enough time for a little refreshment or two, don't you think?"

Tucker did not reply, but instead scratched Brandy's right temple with his beak.

"Why don't we head down to the O'Caiside, y'know? Get to rest my legs and shit."

Brandy descended the hill towards Riverside, with Tucker firmly attached to her shoulder. He did finally let go as Brandy left the zig-zagged paved road, and started running straight down the grass, doing a sloppy somersault towards the bottom, before landing on her feet, standing still in wait of her crow to re-enter his place on her shoulder. So he did.

She walked down the little street leading to the outer rim of urban Riverside, making her way towards the O'Caiside Irish Pub, one of her favorite drinking dens in the city, partially for its friendly staff and cozy atmosphere, and partially for its lack of avian discrimination. Many establishments in the US still prohibit birds from entering, even after the end of segregation laws, but the O'Caiside held a policy of welcoming all species. Alternatively, maybe their employees were paid too little to care about birds within the perimeters.

The door bell rang as Brandy opened the door to the pub and was immediately welcomed by its familiar damp air and basil green walls covered in framed monochrome photos from old boxing matches.

"Another mojito?" the bartender asked upon catching sight of her. "You bet." she replied. "And some peanuts for Tucker, please."

The bartender, a big gruff bodybuilder type of person, bald with a blond soul patch under his lip and tattoos of Chinese dragons all over his arms, started mixing Brandy's drink as she leant on the counter in anticipation, looking randomly around the room.

"Oh tit cunt motherfucker!" she exclaimed. "Some dipshit marauder took my spot!"

She looked towards her usual favorite seating, the booth in the corner at the far end, with a lamp convenient for reading hanging straight above. It had now been occupied by an older man. A lanky slick-haired man with a pencil thin moustache above his puffy wide anglerfish lips, sitting there in a navy blue business suit with a white shirt but no tie, reading a newspaper with his beady small black eyes with thick dark eyebrows above and thick dark bags beneath.

Brandy scowled at him sipping from his tiny coffee cup with his big lips.

"You want me to ask him to find another seat?" the bartender asked.
"No... No. No, that'd just be embarrassing." Brandy said.

She hopped up on the nearest barstool and received her mojito along with a small bowl of peanuts, and flicked a ten-dollar bill at the counter. Tucker hopped down from her shoulder onto the counter and started pecking at the peanuts. Brandy sucked eagerly from the straw of her drink and looked around the tavern. Only five people there, including her and the big-lipped booth occupant.

As usual, the O'Caiside was sparsely populated, as would be normal at one thirty in the afternoon. But only this time had someone claimed Brandy's regular corner, and someone who also looked nothing like the place's general clientele, but rather someone who would belong better in a restaurant at the top floor of the D'Orleans Tower in the business district, Brandy thought, negotiating some deal with the representative of some Japanese company over cups of Chai latte and plates of vegan croissants, looking out of that phallic glass skyscraper across the city and the New Hampshire forests, imagining where in that landscape to build the next factory. Perhaps he was an out-of-town accountant or similar on a business trip who had received poor road directions and ended up in this little blue-collar district in the outskirts, and sat down at the closest thing he could find to a coffee shop, and is now awaiting a call from his boss or whoever to give proper directions to the D'Orleans Tower, or another one of those buildings. He did look rather confident and relaxed though, quite smug in fact. And he looked far too old, Brandy thought, for an occupation that would have him chased around on such poorly organized trips.

Brandy then decided she was only giving him so much thought out of bitterness for losing her regular seat, and so scratched Tucker's neck and took another deep sip of mojito. The bartender saw that she was still a tad downhearted, and, having no other customers to serve, approached her.

"So what have you been up to today?" he asked.

"Well, uh, I woke up." she answered. "Had me some stale Lucky Charms and Mountain Dew for breakfast. Still have that sugary yucky taste in my mouth, really. Was pretty quiet at the complex, much better than usual."

"Oh, they make noise there even in the morning, usually?"

"Like fucking hell they do. Shit's a fucking warzone twenty-four seven. There's only like, every fourth or fifth day maybe, that things go quiet there, for a couple of hours. Feels nice, really. Not such a bad place to live when it's quiet."

"Yeah. I remember when I was a student. My roommate kept me up all night every day of the week. Couldn't even pay attention in lectures, I was so fucking exhausted from his bullshit."

"Oh I'm fucking grateful to God almighty I don't have a fucking roommate."

"What did you say you were studying again?" the bartender asked.

"Oh, um, economics, I guess."

"You wanna become a stockbroker or something?"

"Well, I dunno. It was my parents' idea. I was pretty decent at math, y'know, and they thought there would be a lot of money in the, uh, the money business. You can't really fault that logic. Plus, my guidance councilor in High School said I had a natural talent for working with numbers and finances, which really was kind of an anti-Semitic thing to say, I think, like, not in a hateful way, just, y'know…"

"Say, does your little raven friend want another helping?"

Brandy saw that Tucker had eaten all his peanuts.

"He's a *crow*. And I s'pose the little fella would. How's about it, Tucker?"

"Fucker!" Tucker chirped gleefully.

4

The man in the corner booth threw a puzzled glance at the bird, which Brandy noticed and grinned.

"Yeah, he would like another batch." she said, and slurped up the remnants of her mojito. "And I think I'll have a bottle of Bud, while we're at it."

The bartender served up Brandy's order, and she took a greedy chug of her beer as Tucker started pecking away.

"Boy, that guy over there sure takes his sweet time with his coffee." Brandy said throwing him another glance. "Pretty sure it's gone cold and yucky ages ago. He's probably not even drinking it. Pretty sure you could throw him out."

"Sorry, no can do." the bartender said. "It's not nearly crowded enough for that yet."

"You said you could make him move his ass, like, just a few minutes ago!"

"Yeah, I could ask him to move to a different seat, for your sake. Making him leave altogether is a bit different though."

Brandy took another chug from her bottle.

"Ah, alright. Never mind." she said.

"I *could* ask him if he wanted something more." the bartender suggested.

"Oh no. Please don't. Doesn't matter anyway, I gotta go once I'm done with this one. Doctor's appointment."

A couple more patrons entered, whom the bartender quickly attended to. Brandy returned to stroking Tucker's neck and let her eyes idly wander around the bar, her unfocused gaze gliding between the photographs and old posters framed around the walls until she reached a large copper plaque which she had passively noticed on previous visits but never given much attention. It contained the sculpted image of a stern-looking man with a bushy beard, and it read:

LYNDSEY LAZARUS D'ORLEANS

1909 – 1968

Founded in 1946 D'Orleans Industries LTD.

along with its first venture,

the D'Orleans Industries Asbestos Factory on Hamilton Street,

the first of its kind in Riverside.

Passed away, on January 26th 1968,

and left his estate to his widow Monica Taylor D'Orleans.

Brandy drank down the last drops of beer while reading the plaque. Tucker swallowed his last peanut, and flew back up on Brandy's shoulder as she hopped off the bar stool.

"You know what?" she said to her bird. "I know you've totally filled up on nuts, but I could certainly go for some lunch after the doctor check-up. Just hope it doesn't take too long."

She scratched the sore spot above her waistline once more, though doing so helped very little.

"See ya soon." she told the bartender before leaving the perimeters, and he silently waved back.

II

"Congratulations, Miss Rabinow, it's a girl! Have you decided on a name yet?" Doctor Herbert Walker said in his usual affable demeanor.

"Oh-ho-ho, you're so fucking hilarious." Brandy said as she lay on the doctor's bed staring at the ultrasound image of the demonic centipede-like abomination squirming around inside her ovaries.

"Oh come on, we all need a sense of humor in this day and age."

"Easy to say when you don't have a… what even is that fucking thing?"

"We call it a '*Tidak Nyata*'." Doctor Walker explained. "It's a sexually transmitted parasite native to Malaysia. It's initially microscopic, but rapidly grows within its host, until after a few weeks it's swollen to the inch long worm you see before you."

"Oh god." Brandy moaned, feeling increasingly nauseated by each word the doctor spoke.

"So, pardon me for asking, I know people can be uncomfortable discussing these things, but have you had any recent sexual partners you might have contracted this from?"

Brandy looked up at the ceiling.

"There, uh, was this guy I met a couple of weeks ago. Lucas. He said he'd spent the past year or so backpacking around Asia and Polynesia."

"Well, then that must certainly be our culprit!"

6

"Really cute guy. Never heard from him again though. He did have a weird hook-shaped dick, actually. I thought it was just a birth defect or something. It felt oddly good though."

"Oh no, to my knowledge the Tidak rascal doesn't cause outwardly deformation like that. He must have gotten it very recently though, given that he wasn't in excruciating pain."

"What, the bent dick?"

"No, the Tidak! When that thing grows to full size inside a male host, the pain can become extremely intense."

Brandy scratched her lower stomach where the Tidak lay, and watched it react on screen.

"But um, is this shit any dangerous, or…?"

"Well…" Doctor Walker removed his glasses and wiped them on his sleeve. "Right now it only feeds on blood, in tiny quantities. You'll notice your menstruations diminishing after a few months, and occasionally you'll feel a little dizzy. It's already more or less completed its natural growth, but as time goes on it'll grow fatter, and eventually burst your ovaries from the inside."

"Wh-what?!"

All color drained from Brandy's face as she bit tightly on her lower lip.

"You have about a year, a year and a half maybe, before things go really haywire. And it won't be a quick death, you'll suffer some simply fantastic internal bleeding."

"You fucking call that 'fantastic'?!"

"I meant 'Fantastic' as in 'overwhelming'. It doesn't have to be positive."

"Look, we're not gonna start a fucking semantics argument while some fucking vampire caterpillar is eating me alive, okay!"

"I understand you're upset right now, but listen here. We can easily have this removed surgically. It's a simple procedure, no fuss, no sweat. And only about five people in America get afflicted by this each year, so there's no line or waitlist or anything."

"Fucking surgery? What's that gonna cost me?"

"Probably not much more than fifteen thousand dollars."

"And… Probably how much less?"

"Not much. Fifteen thousand is about it."

7

"Fucking fifteen grand?! I can't afford that! I don't even have a job right now. I'm a student!"

"Well, what about your parents? Maybe they can chip in a few?"

"Aw no, doubt it. They spent their whole fortune getting me into college in the first place."

The doctor sighed.

"Well, the only thing I can tell you is to come back if you find a way."

"But aren't there, like, alternative methods? Can't we just flush out the fucker or something?"

"No, I can't think of any such methods that would not also kill *you* in the process. And I assume you wouldn't want to sacrifice your own life just to destroy the little rascal. That would just be spiteful."

Brandy took another gander at her unwanted guest, crawling restlessly about, making the little strains of hair on its sides look like legs.

"Holy shit." she said. "Does that fucker have teeth?"

"Those fang-like antennae at its head are used to scout for non-blood nutrients. Semen would be a typical type of such matter."

"Seriously? That thing eats jizz?"

"If any should enter, yes. Which means you're not any likely to get impregnated before you remove it."

"I'm as good as infertile?"

"Yes. Very much so. Very much so."

Brandy moaned.

After Brandy had gotten dressed and left the hospital, she found her trusty crow waiting on a tree branch outside. As he landed on her shoulder she felt her whole stomach twisting into a pulsating knot, her former feeling of hunger turning into a desire to puke. She rested herself onto the tree by her forearm and stared at its root, waiting to vomit. Never before in her available memory had she wanted so much to vomit, just to maybe ease the overwhelming sensation of dread and nausea. But nothing came up. After several minutes of coughing and straining her guts, her system was still in limbo. Tucker soon started pecking at her neck. Brandy soon gave up and stood up straight, wiping her mouth as if there was anything to wipe.

"The air ain't fresh enough." she said. "I feel like I'm still inside."

"Fucker?" Tucker responded.

Brandy sighed heavily.

"Y'know what? I don't really feel like it now, but maybe it'd help if I got some food in me. Whaddya say?"

Tucker endearingly stroked his head against Brandy's cheek.

"Some food would be good, huh? We'll go find a nice spot, alright. Have ourselves a really solid lunch, and then afterwards I'll call dad, or maybe mom. Tell them what's up and see if they can spit in a few."

III

Nearly half of Riverside's restaurants, diners, bistros, and taverns were located on Mapplethorpe Road, a long stretch of venues in different price ranges. The restaurants serving what was allegedly the highest tier of gourmet cuisine received a so-called 'D'Orleans Seal of Approval', a big hexagonal gold-tinted plaque which they proudly displayed on the most viewable wall within their perimeters, as well as a similar-looking sticker, which they plastered on the window or wall by the entrance. Even if the seal was only a local sign of recognition, receiving one was still a high honor, especially since Riverside had not yet been recognized for evaluation by the Michelin guide. The restaurants usually given this badge of honor were the priciest, snobbiest venues around, which always enforced a strict dress code and served highly experimental dishes presented in the manner of meticulously crafted abstract art. Yet the plaque had also, to the surprise of many, been awarded to 'Greez-Burger', a local fast-food joint proudly advertising their willingness to deep-fry any of their menu items. Several of the other Mapplethorpe venues, as well as venues across town, had voiced displeasure with this decision, even going as far as suspecting bribery or other types of foul play to have been conducted under the table. Yet, the gesture had never been retracted by the D'Orleans estate, and Greez-Burger still retain their little plaque, proudly displayed above their condiment shelf with the ketchup dispenser and paper-wrapped straws.

Wandering down Mapplethorpe Road, Brandy pondered on exactly who gave away these hexagons. They were obviously acting on behalf of the D'Orleans estate, a name she had learned to acknowledge since moving to this town from her native

9

Philadelphia, an estate which seemed to own a share of everything in Riverside. Through her now two months of staying here, Brandy had still not quite grasped what this D'Orleans company was doing. They had their name stamped on several factories, hotels, one real-estate agency, a shopping mall currently out of business, and now they also judged restaurants. 'But hell' Brandy thought to herself, 'if a truck tire company can do that, why not these guys?'.

Eventually Brandy and Tucker found a decent establishment. 'Shokuchudoku', a middle-range sushi bar with ample seating and a vast selection of Japanese beers. The prices were fairly reasonable, and Brandy's wallet was still thick with bills. Sushi was the type of food Brandy felt the most comfortable eating when feeling less than well, due to its lack of grease and its lean consistency.

"Fucker!" cried Tucker.

"What? No." said Brandy. "Look, I know we should try to save as much money as possible. I know that's the most obvious thing to do right now. But even if we had all our meals at the soup kitchen the next twelve months we still wouldn't be able to afford the surgery just like that. I mean, we can afford this now. We'll just keep going like normal, and try to score some serious stack of moolah on the side, right. Hopefully my parents will shove in a portion. I'm sure they will. Let's just enjoy ourselves for now, okay?"

Tucker scratched his head under his wing.

"Yeah, you get me, alright."

They went inside.

The Shokuchudoku was quite spacious, with a seating area rooming up to one hundred and seventy people, separated into four smaller venues connected by the bar in the center. The décor was overall cold and dark, with black ceramic tiles covering nearly every wall, and a wide waterfall lit by blue spotlights between the men's and women's rooms. The place was furnished with round tables scattered around the venue floors and booths with U-shaped crimson Naugahyde cushions dug into the walls. Not far from the entrance was a particular booth with no table by it, with a plaque above with the word 'Reserved' etched into it. Apparently, this seat rooming about six people, with no table, was under permanent reservation.

Brandy approached the bar, located about five yards from the entrance, with the intention of sitting there. Before she arrived, the chef behind the counter, busily chopping up a filet of tuna, threw her a disapproving glance and quit cutting.

"You get that bud out of here now!" he shouted angrily while pointing his Santuko knife at her with a slight stabbing motion.

"Huh?" Brandy responded, and paced closer, despite the threatening knife gesture, to allow for a quieter conversation.

"Don't go any closer, you hear!" the sushi chef shouted just as loud as before.

"Alright, alright." Brandy said, and stopped in her track with her hands raised before her.

"Now get that dirty bud out of here!" the chef continued.

His speech was noticeably accented, though with mostly flawless diction.

"You don't have to shout, alright. You can hear you just fine!" Brandy said back, raising her own voice.

"You get that bud out now, or I'll call the police!"

"What 'bud'?" Brandy asked. "What are you even talking about?"

"The bud on your shoulder! We don't want that dirty shit in here! It will ruin the hygiene!"

"Aw right, I see." Brandy looked at Tucker. "But this little fella is totally domesticated, alright! He's housebroken and everything."

"I don't care! The health inspector will tear our asses apart if he sees another bud in here!"

"Yo, come on, bud. Buddy. Pal. Whatever. What's the chance you'll get a health inspection today?"

The chef wrathfully struck his knife into the cutting board.

"This is not a discussion! You leave now!"

"Alright, alright, asshole! Jeez." Brandy said and plodded out.

Tucker looked back at the chef, who was sternly observing their exit. "Fucker!" he cawed at him.

IV

"I wasn't really that hungry anyway." Brandy said leaning her back against a light post, scrolling through the contact list on her cell phone. "That piece of shit can go fuck himself, though. Motherfucking saggy-ass cunt."

"Fucker." Tucker added.

It was not particularly unusual for Brandy to be disallowed into places because of Tucker. It depended on a given establishment's policies but also on the attitudes of its employees. Many people employed in the service industry in Riverside were too jaded to care about quirks like pet birds, but there was always those whose principles eclipsed their hospitality. Taking the agency and average level of cynicism of the employees into account, Tucker had an estimated chance of three to five of being allowed entrance, and in that event, a chance of four to five of receiving service like a regular customer.

Brandy's thumb circled reluctantly around the call button to her mother's number. Informing her mother of a recently contracted STD was embarrassing by itself, but to then also ask for fifteen thousand dollars seemed like a bulletproof way to get herself disowned on the spot. She had pondered on who of her parents would be softer on her, but could not land on a solid conclusion, and so flipped a dime which land heads up on the sidewalk by her shoe.

She quickly tapped the call button, and felt a gallon of blood rushing up her neck. The phone rang for well over a minute. Her mother had always been slow to pick up. It continued to ring for another whole minute before it gave up.

Brandy went on to call her father, less hesitant this time. As she tapped the call button, her stomach began to tighten up again. It rang for over a minute also this time. Then another minute. Then the phone gave up again.

Brandy sighed, and tried once again to call her mother. Again the phone rang for a whole minute without answer. Then another minute. Then sounded a click.

"Hello?" said a very nasal voice. "Sweetheart? Are you okay, muffin?"

Brandy took a deep breath.

"Hi, mom. How're you doing?"

"Aw, I'm doing fine, sweetheart. I'm watching Ellen DeGeneres. It's a rerun, y'know, but it's one I haven't seen. She's got these little kids on, y'know. They're twins. Aw, and they're so adorable. They sing acapella together, cover Elton John and the stuff. You really oughta see it, Brandy. I wish you could've been here."

"Great. Sweet. Well um… yeah."

"So why did you call, sweetheart? Something the matter?"

"What? No. No, well, uh. Yeah. Sort of. Uh… well…"

"C'mon, sweetie. It's okay. You can tell your momma anything, y'know."

"Alright. Well, here goes. Uh… I… Sort of need to have this… uh… this surgery."

"Aw what? Come again? You need surgery?"

"Yeah, it's… nothing *that* serious, I guess. It's just…"

"Sweetie, you're not telling me you want a nose job, are ya?"

"What? No. Of course not. It's not like that."

"Look, sweetheart. Your nose is beautiful just the way it is, okay."

"It's not… It's not *plastic* surgery, alright. It's not a cosmetic thing. It is health related, alright?"

"So what kinda surgery is this?"

"It's… well, I got this sort of… infection in my stomach, this thing. And I need to get it out. It's not doing a number on me right now, per se, but it could get like, genuinely bad over time, y'know. Like, the doctor said I should act as soon as possible."

"Aw, that's terrible."

"Yeah, it is kinda bad, actually."

"Well, how're you gonna pay for the operation?"

"Well, uh, to be frank, uh… The bill will total out at about… uh… twenty thousand grand."

"Thousand… grand… You mean twenty million?"

"What? Oh, no. I meant Twenty grand. Twenty thousand. Twenty triple-Oh. Two and four zeros."

"Twenty thousand dollars, then?"

"Yes. That's right."

"So how're you gonna get that money?"

"Well, that's… I was hoping, maybe you and dad could, maybe, like, possibly spit in a few?"

"Aw, sweetheart. We're practically broke back here. We spent your father's whole lottery winnings just getting you into college. Heck, we keep spending it just to keep you from starving."

"But you don't have any… additional assets? This is really serious, y'know."

"Sweetheart. You know I'd do anything for you, within my ability. It's just we're practically living hand to mouth here. Your father's repair shop ain't doing that hot lately. People don't drive cars as much as they used to, I s'pose. We got just enough for food and barely enough to pay the bills. We can't have expenses like these flying our way every day."

"Look, this is just a one-time deal, alright."

"It's one time too much, I'm afraid."

"Well, what about… What if you just pay for part of it? That's kinda what I asked for to begin with. Like, maybe fifteen little grand?"

"How much is a 'little grand'?"

"No, fifteen grand. Fifteen thousand."

"Aw. But, I'm sorry. No can do. We couldn't even spend a single little grand no matter what we tried."

Brandy's phone arm dropped down to a sloppy hanging position, barely holding the phone, as she stared into the clouds with moistening eyes.

"Brandy sweetheart? You still there?"

Brandy waited a few seconds.

"Yeah, mom. Still here."

"Look, don't be upset, muffin. We'll still send ya the regular flow. Y'know, why don't you go look for a job? I'm sure there's plenty of people hiring up in New Hampshire. You got a good résumé too, so you could probably demand a little more than minimum wage. Just try to find something that doesn't interfere with your studies too much. We don't want all that money going to waste now."

"I… I s'pose."

"Yeah, you figure it out, don'tcha. You're always good at figuring stuff out."

"Alright. Okay. I'll… I'll try, I guess."

"Yeah, don't you give up, now. That's what *my* momma always said, 'never give up' she said."

"Well, uh… Thanks anyway, I s'pose. Thanks for your time at least."

"Yeah, but actually, Ellen's almost over now. So if there weren't anything else, I'd like to watch the end bit now, okay."

"That's fine, mom. I'll call you back, maybe."

"Yeah, call me back when you found a nice job, won'tcha."

"Okay, I will."

"Well, bye-bye, sweetheart."

"Bye."

After hanging up, Brandy noticed Tucker had perched atop the lamp post she was leaning on.

"Come on, Tucker." she said, wiping her eyes.

Tucker gently fluttered down on Brandy's head, attaching his claws to her beret.

"You know what? I'm still not very hungry, but I really, really need a solid drink right now."

CHAPTER TWO

In Roland's private quarter, to which only he held a key, by his master's admission, he had placed on his work desk a small hickory casket inherited through his bloodline for three generations, highly resembling a classic cigar box, but indeed originally created with his usage as its original intention. Opened by yet another key only he possessed, it contained a family heirloom, a pair of gloves in authentic tawny antelope leather. Worn through innumerable trials and hazards, the pair had still not attained a single noticeable scratch. Yet, when not in use, Roland had like his father before him treated them like sacred porcelain. Only when fully thread over his hands could he use them as normal articles of clothing, and still then with an inherent underlying sense of respect and gratitude. He never used them at home, but never left the property without them, as they were, in his father's words 'required equipment for maneuvering through the world, but never should they be misused in a domestic setting'.

It had been a ritual for all of his career as butler at the D'Orleans estate to, after breakfast with the master family, lock himself in his private quarters for just a few minutes, open the casket, and embrace his family pride with his eyes, maybe touch them slightly, every single morning. But if any of the three D'Orleans family members had requested the day before an excursion for any reason, or he himself had requested such, Roland would have to put the gloves on, slowly, delicately pull them down over his fingers and palm, left hand first then the right hand. Always left hand first. No deviations could be allowed.

Today was such a day, as the family daughter Olive D'Orleans, with whom Roland had spent the majority of his professional time, had a few days earlier requested a ride down to the latest hot restaurant on Mapplethorpe Road, along with full assistance.

After Roland had fully applied his gloves, he only had to twine his fingers and crack them, and the ritual was complete. He knew after that to be efficient with his preparations, in order to keep his masters from getting impatient.

II

A small blue bird had landed in the opened windowsill above the entrance door of the D'Orleans Manor foyer, chirping loudly and gleefully through the room. Down in the foyer, right next to the double entry door, on a sturdy re-enforced bench built especially for her, sat Olive D'Orleans, dressed in her tailor-made buttoned cerulean blouse and sangria red velvet vest, idly combing her black hair with her fingers, a short Eloise haircut with two shark fin bangs pointing forwards on each side. While she waited for her butler to escort her to the limousine, she observed the little bird, infatuated by its pleasant sounds and endearing appearance backlit by the morning sunbeams.

Olive D'Orleans required assistance and surveillance with most of her daily activities, for she was quite impaired by her now extreme weight. She was indeed a colossus of obesity, her low-hanging belly the size of a yurt, legs thick as manatees, arms like seals, breasts like watermelons, neck obscured by a collar of flab, her whole body wider than tall when sitting down, which she did almost exclusively. Leaning on her thigh was her trusted cane inherited from her grandfather, a polished ebony staff with tip and handle of silver, the handle sculpted into the shape of a wild hare's head. She needed it to walk the very short distances she still could manage, though she had with increasing frequency taken use of her wheelchair instead.

This particular Monday in late April was one of great excitement for Olive. Disinterested in her family's ventures, Olive had instead for many years pursued her great passion for the culinary arts, primarily as a reviewer of restaurants, having her first critique published in the local newspaper when she was seventeen. She had since gained much respect for her expertise on food, to the point that receiving a positive review from her became the highest honor one could get in lieu of a Michelin star, at least in Riverside. Soon her father ordered uniquely crafted plaques to be awarded those who attained her approval. Now restaurants considering themselves ready for her judgment would invite her over for a scheduled feast, after which she would take a few days before submitting a verdict. Today she was appointed such a feast at the La Bulle, a French gourmet restaurant which opened last year at the north end of Mapplethorpe Road. Since she received the invitation last Thursday Olive had barely been able to sleep from the anticipation, as the venue had received overwhelmingly positive feedback online. Olive's, however, would be the first formal review of the establishment.

Down the stairs descended Roland into the entrance hall, holding up his gloved hands, with the required brought along equipment hung around his arms, and a brown plaid flapcap on his head. About ten seconds after him followed Olive's father, Reginald Lazarus D'Orleans, in his casual scarlet silk blazer, which he wore on schedule-free days, carrying his set of golf clubs over his shoulder.

"How do you do today, lady Olive?" asked Roland.

"I'm doing great!" replied Olive with a big smile. "Thanks."

"It seems you neglected to bring your purse, my lady." Roland then said and handed Olive her little black leather purse with the chainmail strap. "I took the liberty of fetching it for you."

"That was so kind of you." Olive responded and hung the purse on her elbow pit.

"Would you say we are ready to leave now?" Roland asked.

"Well, I just need to say goodbye to father first."

Reginald was about to leave through the living room when he heard himself mentioned.

"Of course. Shall I assist you up?" Roland asked.

"Yes, please."

Roland grabbed Olive's hands and pulled her towards him, as she tried to raise her legs. Once Olive was up on her feet Roland handed her the cane. She turned to her father with a loving smile. Reginald approached her for a farewell-hug.

"Goodbye, father." Olive said. "I'll be back in time for dinner."

She then kissed her father lightly on the cheek, trying to avoid his meticulously combed moustache.

"Yes. Take care, now." Reginald said, and left through the living room.

Roland opened up the double door, as the blue bird flew away.

"Do you require assistance down?" he asked.

"No, I'm sure I can do it." Olive said with some strain.

"Very well."

Roland proceeded down the stairs to the driveway, opened the garage, where the limousine stood parked, and wasted no time getting it started and driven up to the bottom of the stairs, to minimize the walking distance for Olive and ensure she would not have to wait. Half the stairs had been covered by a long gradually descending ramp reaching into the driveway, for Olive to walk down and up, for climbing stairs had become too fatiguing and risky at her size. By the time Roland had parked the car, Olive was only halfway down the stairs, looking more exhausted by each slow step. Roland stood by the opened back door and observed her closely as she waddled down, prepared to act if she should fall or absolutely needed to rest before she reached him.

When Olive finally made it all the way, Roland helped her climb into the car one leg at a time. Once she was inside he helped her strap up. This limousine's back seat area had been modified to accommodate Olive's size and limitations, the seat made as a curved sofa with two opposite-gendered seatbelts on each side meeting in the middle. The area also had three regular seats opposite Olive's, on the rare occasion that guests accompanied her.

Once Olive was properly seated, she withdrew a silk handkerchief from her purse and wiped away pearls of sweat from her forehead, before taking out her Japanese Sensu fan, which she waved frantically at herself until the carmine coloration in her face faded away.

"We aren't expected at the La Bulle for over an hour, my lady." said Roland, now having taken his position behind the staring wheel. "Shall we take a detour on the way?"

"Oh, yes." Olive said as her breath was starting to return. "Can we drive past the Governor's Plaza? I love the architecture there."

"Splendid idea, my lady."

"And maybe we can stop for ice cream there as well." Olive continued, her fatigue not diminishing her enthusiastic tone.

"As you wish, my lady."

III

Olive and Roland arrived outside the La Bulle at one PM, where they were awaited by the restaurant's manager, who stood outside the entrance along with two female chefs in full attire. They had stood there for almost half an hour as he frenetically combed his waxy hair and straightened his tie, and tweaked on the position of each of the chefs' hats as if it would make a difference.

After he had nervously watched Olive being helped out her car, and debated in his head on whether or not he should offer his assistance, he quickly approached Olive as she stood fully erect with her cane planted on the sidewalk.

"It is truly an honor to have you here, Miss D'Orleans. To have you here as our guest, it is truly, truly an honor." he said reaching out to shake her hand.

"Aw, that's so sweet of you to say." Olive responded and gladly shook his sweaty hand.

"Now, if you please, we would like for you to come inside. Everything is prepared."

He and the chefs then placed themselves in a row on the entrance's left, awaiting for Olive to enter before them. As Olive waddled up to the entrance, which she had to walk through diagonally, the chefs and the manager gently nodded at her in sequence, all with wide fixed smiles.

Once inside, she was met by a waiter, a young tall man much more handsome than the manager, who directed her to her designated booth only a few feet away. She sat down, wiped the manager's sweat off her hand, and greeted the waiter while flapping the Sensu at herself.

"My name is Bernard. I will be your waiter today."

"It's so nice to meet you, Bernard. I like your earring."

"Thank you." Bernard replied politely. "I will bring you the menu immediately. Would you like a drink as well?"

"Oh, yes, please. Could you make me Sazerac, please?"

"Right away, miss."

Two more waiters arrived with Olive's table, complete with a white tablecloth, and placed it as close to her as possible without digging into her stomach, before a third waiter put down a red wax candle and lit it. Afterwards, the manager came in, staring at Olive with wide open eyes as he rubbed his hands, looking as if he had something of grave importance to tell.

"Well... Enjoy." he said, and marched to the kitchen.

Olive leaned back in the Naugahyde booth, resting her arms on her belly, tapping it in anticipation, and sucking back saliva. Soon Bernard returned with the glass of Sazerac along with the menu. When he tried to give Olive the menu, she abruptly snapped it away from him, and flipped through the pages with childlike enthusiasm, reading certain items out loud.

"Foie gras of goose? With eggplant purée?"

After having scanned through the menu, Olive put it down and closed it.

"That was awe-inspiring, Bernard." she said. "I will have one of each, please."

"That's a total of twelve meals then, ma'am."

"Yes. And I'll also have all the vegetarian substitutes served alongside their meat-based counterparts." Olive added and sipped her Sazerac.

"So that's a total of…" Bernard took the menu and began scanning through. "Well, very well. What will you have to drink with that?"

"You know, I think I'll have a glass of wine for every serving, a different wine for each. I'll let the kitchen decide which. Then a cup of mocha latte with cinnamon and brown sugar in addition to a glass of cognac for the dessert items."

"A new mocha and cognac for each?"

"Well, no, just one mocha in total. Too much caffeine makes me nervous and jittery. And just bring a whole bottle of cognac with the first dessert."

"Very well." Bernard frantically wrote down the order. "Is that all, ma'am?"

"I'm pretty sure it is?" Olive chortled.

At the time Olive and Roland had arrived, there were no other patrons present as it was an hour before La Bulle's regular time of opening. However, as she ate her way through the menu, more people arrived, mostly white collar business men discussing work over lunch. By the point when she received her sixth course, a wild boar knuckle with rutabaga purée and broiled shallots, paired with a dark red Shiraz, half of the restaurant's tables were occupied, many by patrons who could not help themselves but stare at her. She was not bothered by any of them, however, as she was far too enthralled with her dining to even detect their presence. Roland on the other hand saw and heard all, or at least very much. He stood watchfully besides her, waiting to act in case she were to choke on something, but his attention soon shifted over to the reactions she received from the regular patrons.

One woman demanded to be re-seated to somewhere obscured from the view of Olive since the mere sight of her triggered the woman's gag reflexes. Two men, one fairly young and the other more middle-aged, with nearly identical haircuts and dressed in nearly identical business suits, eating the same item of lobster sandwich with a knife and fork, seemed to also take offense with her, particularly the young one.

"That thing right there is the fucking fattest bitch I've ever fucking seen." he whispered to the older one, who reacted by slapping him hard across the cheek.

"You *work* for her *father*, you moron!" he said.

Roland recognized them both.

Bernard was quick to pick up Olive's empty plate.

"I will bring your next course in just a couple of minutes." he said, and Olive nodded.

"*Ooh.*" she exclaimed to Roland. "You should have tasted that boar, Roland. Just perfectly grilled, and with that subtle rosemary rub. It was absolutely exquisite."

"I would imagine." Roland replied.

Olive drank up the last remnants of the Shiraz, and stared out into the room, where she noticed several persons staring back at her. She smiled and waved at one particular couple, who, without responding to the gesture, began looking at each other while trying to conceive an empty conversation. Just to their right sat another couple, older than the first, who gave her a meanly condemning look, and upon making eye contact, snorted spitefully and reverted their attention to their menus, before one of them looked back up to send her a final vicious glare.

Olive was left with a sense of rejection. A feeling of not being welcome came creeping into her brain. Her shell of security thinned down to nothingness in a matter of seconds. She looked around her and found more people staring, with contempt or shock or both in their eyes. She started feeling less like a guest and more like an intruder in a world of beings unlike herself, and she clenched her hands into tight fists and squeezed them against her chin as her heartrate jumped into a frenzy.

"Is anything the matter, my lady?"

"It's… no, it's… it's nothing." Olive lowered her hands, attempting to outwardly seem calm, and patted her lips with her napkin. "When is the next meal coming?"

"My lady, it has barely been a minute."

"Well, how long is it going to take, Roland? What, am I just supposed to sit here?"

Roland waved in a nearby waiter.

22

"Could you serve the madam a drink while she waits?"

"Certainly. What kind?"

"An old-fashioned Bloody Mary should do."

"Certainly."

"Did you hear that, my lady? I just ordered you a Bloody Mary. How about that?"

Olive gave him a polite smile with her mouth.

"That was kind of you, Roland. I really do appreciate your diligence."

Less than ten seconds later, her Bloody Mary appeared, simple, with only a sprig of celery for garnish.

"You are the best, Roland." she said as she sipped down on the drink, only looking at the drink, and the table, not wanting to engage with the resentful faces populating her surroundings.

By the time Olive was just about to finish her drink, Bernard arrived with the next course, duck confit with rowanberry sauce, caramelized apples and pan fried red thumb potatoes.

"What took you so long?" asked Olive, trying to restrain any impression of her inherent frustration.

"I know it was a little longer than a couple of minutes. The chefs wanted to make sure it was perfect before serving."

Olive had already commenced eating before his sentence was finished.

"Well, it's… time well spent." she mumbled through the duck meat in her mouth. "This *is* delicious."

Time went on, and a little over six PM Olive had reached her final dessert item, a large cherry soufflé with grated dark chocolate and lime zest. She poured herself a final glass of cognac, and punctuated the soufflé with her spoon.

"It's a bit tart." she noted. "Could benefit from a little more sugar."

The dinner crowd had begun to fill up the premises, although many of them had re-decided to just having drinks upon seeing Olive, then promptly leaving. Others gazed with slacked jaws at her gargantuan anatomy and seemingly eternal inhalation of food.

"How can she possibly eat that much?" asked one woman.

"Oh, she looks like she's got plenty of space." retorted her date.

After Olive had eaten the final few crumbs of her soufflé she gulped down her cognac glass like a shot, and then cleaned her lips. Immediately Bernard rushed down to her.

"Was everything to your satisfaction, ma'am?" he asked.

"This was a… 'scuse me, this was a lovely… a lovely feast." Olive said, politely trying to repress an onslaught of little belches.

At that point the manager arrived, along with the trio of waiters from before, who now commenced the removal of Olive's table.

"We at the La Bulle hoped you enjoyed your stay here, in our restaurant." he said.

"Oh I… I did. I would in fact… like to personally show my gratitude to the wonderful chefs."

"Oh, well, some of them, in fact, all of them are very busy preparing the other guests' orders at this moment." the manager said as his face visibly heated up.

"Oh? Okay then. But I'd like to thank you guys at least."

"You're very welcome, ma'am." said Bernard, and nodded.

"Come here, now." said Olive and opened her arms. "Give me a hug."

Bernard politely obliged.

"It was indeed a pleasure to serve you, ma'am." the manager said and reached out his hand for a shake. "We'll be looking forward to your review."

"I will have it published by the end of the week." Olive said, and shook the manager's hand, before immediately reaching for her handkerchief. "But could I have the check now?"

"Oh no, no, ma'am." the manager said and showed her his sweaty palms. "It's all on the house."

"Don't be like that, silly. I can obviously afford it."

"No, we insist. Really. We really do insist."

"Well, I suppose I have to respect that. Though you know were to address the bill if you re-decide." Olive leaned forward a little with a grunt. "I suppose I will be leaving now."

"Shall I fetch the wheelchair, my lady?" asked Roland.

"Yes. I don't think I can walk much right now." Olive said patting her stomach.

IV

Olive gazed out at the sun setting behind the residential blocks of the West Cedarbrook district and the tall Catholic church in front of them, while she idly waved her Sensu fan at herself.

"Why, I take it you found your visit satisfactory, my lady." Roland hypothesized.

"Yes. It was lovely." Olive said, unable to disguise a somberness in her tone.

"Pardon me, but you do sound bothered, my lady."

"It's nothing."

"Are you certain of that?"

Olive looked down over her breasts on her belly and patted it with both hands in unison.

"It is… nothing, Roland."

"Has the food perhaps given you a belly ache again?"

"No, I don't get that anymore."

Olive looked out the window again. Roland remained silent for a while.

"Perhaps you've had an overly stressful day, lady Olive." he finally said. "When we get back, shall we listen to some classical over cups of hot cocoa together, and let the conversation flow? After dinner, I mean."

"That would be nice." Olive said.

"How about something by the splendid Dvořak, perhaps? Maybe the New World Symphony."

"Yes. That could work. That would be nice, yes. Thank you."

"Excellent choice."

CHAPTER THREE

In the West Cedarbrook district, currently the biggest low-income area in Riverside, one Doctor Isaac Manson, psychiatrist and entrepreneur, founded in nineteen twenty eight the Doctor Isaac Manson's Asylum for the Criminally Insane, commonly just referred to as the Manson Asylum. Through the years, the institution received numerous complaints of poor sanitary conditions and overly lenient hiring policies, as the employees were frequently accused of incompetence, as well as neglect or abuse towards the patients. After Manson's own death in nineteen forty seven his sister Gabrielle Manson inherited the estate, and to many people's surprise did an even worse job running it, allowing high positions to personal friends and even a few convicted felons, including one who had escaped prison and was on the lam, none of whom had the slightest competence or experience within the field of psychiatry. The facility only descended further into disrepair, especially after the whole sanitation department were fired for budgetary reasons, and soon mold, moisture damage and material decay ran rampant, until one inspector declared the building unfit for human inhabitation. Many more accusations of mistreatment of patients followed also, until the night of the fourth of July, nineteen seventy one when a patient was found dead in his room, having committed suicide by stabbing himself eight times in the back with a scalpel. The incident even made headlines in the local newspaper.

The asylum was shut down later that year, and afterwards repurposed as a cheap apartment complex. Only the bare minimum of required alterations had been conducted in the transition, although one janitor was eventually hired. The place still received negative reviews from the government inspectors, though it was now also allowed more lenience, due to not having to meet the same standards as a medical institution.

The building's interiors were characterized by their moldy cracking pale green concrete walls and noticeably uneven floors all covered in dusty crimson wall-to-wall carpet, all illuminated by the buzzing sickly green-tinted fluorescent light pipes in the moist ceiling, of which only half worked at any given time. This aesthetic extended to the many tiny one-room apartments, of which one belonged to Brandy Rabinow.

Having applied too late for student accommodation on campus, Brandy was forced to seek residence elsewhere, and due to limited funds and hasty research, ended up in this former mental asylum that largely still resembled one, with noisy neighbors, rampant and frequent destruction of property in the hallways, and even occasional bursts of violence, with one particularly heinous knife assault on the first floor, the first week of Brandy's stay, with the bleeding victim painting the lower half of the wall red as he leaned onto it in pursuit of help, turning it into the ugliest rendition of the Polish national flag in known history. He died before the ambulance showed up.

Brandy lay in her little spring heel bed in her apartment, sipping from a can of lukewarm Budweiser. The apartment was sparsely furnished, with a wardrobe, an IKEA bed stand, a kitchen table with an old laptop, two chairs, a tiny stove with one hotplate, a maple tree branch nailed to the wall for Tucker to sit on, with a waste basket underneath, and a small fridge she bought at a flea market, but which she had considered unplugging due to the worrying noises it had been making the past few weeks, in addition to its inner temperature having been terribly bouncy, hence the lukewarm beer.

The walls she had decorated with a wrinkly '*Sullivan's Travels*' poster and a framed fifteen-by-twenty-four copy of a Hieronymus Bosch painting which she had never learned the title of.

As Brandy stared aimlessly around the room, deep in her own worried thoughts, Tucker sat on his little branch, his little crow brain free of any care, and nonchalantly defecated into the basket beneath him.

As was to be expected in this place, the momentary relative silence was very soon interrupted by exterior noise. This time from directly above, on the third floor, when that apartment's resident turned on their television to what sounded like a sports broadcast. The commentary and loud cheering from the game itself was only mildly annoying, But the commentary and loud cheering from the watching resident was an entire other matter. His hoarse baritone voice thundered through the ceiling as he screamed, cheered, moaned and growled at a near constant. Had Brandy bothered to pay close attention, she thought, she could from his voice alone actually follow the match perfectly informed, so detailed was his unnecessary input.

She had always had a low level of tolerance for audial disturbance, but this evening she was in a particularly sour mood, and this cacophony of unruly passion above her rubbed right through her skin. She grabbed the broom by her side, an item she had never used to clean but often used to try and silence her upstairs neighbor. The effects of her attempts were still debatable, but the mild catharsis of banging the broom tip into the ceiling and yelling 'shut up' along with a chain of profanity made it at least feel worthwhile. And Brandy banged her broom harder now than ever, dents forming where it hit, some starting to deepen, which would have lowered the property value had there been any. Usually she gave up after about seven or eight knocks, but this particular time she was far too angry. She refused to accept such a loud obtrusion on this already rotten day. She did not deserve this, and any sensible interpretation of theology would agree. God, or the gods, or the titans or the elves, whichever deities were the true ones, would never allow, let alone impose, so much suffering onto her poor soul in such a small timeframe, at least if they wanted to remain worthy of her worship.

She stood on her bed and kept knocking and shouting, until clouds of concrete particles descended down in her face, but to no avail. All she had achieved was making the man turn up the volume on his television, and seemingly on his own vocal cords. Brandy was now so strained with anger that a plump blue vein looked ready to pop on her carmine face, while her bite was so tight her teeth were on the verge of breaking each other. Tucker had taken notice of her mood and behavior, and flew down to the bed, to comfortingly rub his head against her left shin.

Brandy hopped down from her bed, and Tucker flew away with the bounce, and perched atop the wardrobe.

"Wait here, Tucker." Brandy said stepping into her slippers. "I'm gonna settle this face to face. Gonna tell this goddamn freak exactly how I feel."
"Fucker." Tucker replied.
"Yeah, that's exactly what he is."

Brandy slammed the door hard behind her, causing another cloud of concrete to emit from the ceiling. She stomped up the stairs with tightly clenched fists, and then

28

towards apartment three-three-seven with the unstoppable determination of a Mongol warlord, dead set on silencing the insensitive sports obsessed baboon, even if it meant killing him, killing him with a plastic spoon, if necessary.

She slammed her fist repeatedly at the door.

"Open up, you fucker!" she yelled.

The door opened, and there stood the resident in question, the one who had disturbed her many times before, but especially this evening.

"Yo, listen, you goddamn little fuck-tard! I'm fucking sick of your goddamn noise, alright!"

Only when Brandy finished that sentence did she first gain the lucidity to realize what she was talking to, and her rage turned to humbled fright. Before her stood a gigantic gorilla of a man, twice her height and thrice her width, with a low-hanging forehead featuring one thick unibrow, and a cartoonishly large chin and disproportionally prominent underbite. He looked like an ancient barbarian, or an oversized Neanderthal, forced through a nineteen forty's make-over, for he was dressed in a tight-fitting white buttoned shirt with a big crimson bowtie and matching suspenders and gray striped suit pants, his black shiny hair carefully combed backwards with gallons of pomade. King Kong dressed as a ventriloquist dummy.

"Was I disturbing you?" he asked in a gentle and benign tone.

"Well, uh, yes." said Brandy much less aggressively than before. "I was very disturbed. Had a bad day, you see, been a little edgy this evening. Needed some rest."

"Well, I deeply apologize, little lady." the man said. "It's just so very exciting. You see, the Toucans are playing the Bengals tonight, and I'm really not sure what I'd do with my life if they lost."

"Is it football you're watching?"

"Yeah, of course. Major league."

"Alright, so… Toucans?" Brandy asked. "Is that like a local team or…?"

"Yeah, the Riverside Toucans! The best team of them all!"

"Riverside's got a Major League football team?"

"Of course they do! The best one! How come you haven't heard of them? You like football, don't you? Are you into football?"

"Go Iggles." Brandy responded and half-heartedly raised her fist in the air.

29

"Oh, the Eagles, yeah. You're from Philadelphia?"

"Yeah I am. Frankford, Philadelphia. You been there? Been to Philly?"

"No. I've never left the state. But would you like to watch the rest of the game with me? It's only about fifteen minutes left." The man suggested, bending down towards Brandy.

"You know what. Sorry. I'll be honest. Not all that hot on football. Or sports in general. Not my kinda thing, actually."

"Well come on in then!" the man said, as if he heard a different answer, and grabbed her by the arm with his gigantic hand, which width across the palm was the same as the length of her bicep, and forcefully pulled her inside.

"My name is Denis, by the way. Denis Burke."

"I'm, uh, I'm Brandy. Brandy Rabinow."

"Say, that reminds me... do you like rye? I have some rye whiskey, if you want some."

"Oh, yeah. Yeah, sure, I'd love to have some of that, yeah."

Denis pulled a quart of rye out from the cupboard under his television. The bottle was opened, but only a few sips had been drunk from it. He handed Brandy a red coffee mug with a joke about bees written on it in a bold cartoony font. For himself he found an orange mug with Garfield's face on it. While he poured the rye into Brandy's cup, she looked down and saw that he wore Garfield slippers, the biggest Garfield slippers she had ever seen. She sat down in the little kilt-patterned sofa in the middle of his apartment, and he sat down next to her, leaving not a single inch of free space.

The television in front of them had impressively loud and clear sound given that it looked like it was manufactured during the Eisenhower era, with a wooden cabinet and a blurry hazy screen no wider than a foot. The décor of the whole apartment seemed in fact to consist solely of furniture, electronics and ornaments that pre-dated the Civil Rights movement.

Brandy shuffled into her corner trying to lessen the amount of body contact with Denis, turning herself at an angle and swinging her arm over the back of the sofa to make more space, but found this position to be even more awkward, so she soon returned back to the former one. The sportscast announcer babbled on about various players and stats and such that Brandy had no familiarity with as the match was nearing an end.

"So you said you didn't like football?" asked Denis.

"Well..."

Brandy regretted her statement on the matter, fearing Denis would react violently to an elaboration, in which case he could easily tear her into a hundred pieces in seconds. The police would be unable to even identify her, and the autopsy would be an endurance test of a jigsaw puzzle.

"To be totally frank, no. I'm not a huge fan of sports." she finally murmured. "Oh I am, though. I'm a ginormous fan of football." Denis responded.

'You're ginormous, alright' Brandy barely restrained herself from saying out loud.

"But why aren't you interested in football?" Denis continued. "Or sports in general? I thought everybody liked sports at least a little."

"I have watched a few games with my family, but I've always fallen out, y'know, couldn't keep up my attention. The reason I even bothered after a while, is just to have an excuse to drink with my parents, or my brothers."

Brandy took a big sip of rye, and then another. She had gotten her mug filled up almost to the top, so there was plenty to go.

"My brother wasn't into football, either." Denis said. "He liked hockey. I never understood hockey. It's too chaotic for me. Just folks fighting while a black little biscuit floats by."

"The way I see it, to be totally honest, sports are just mostly a type of war surrogate. People use it to get the catharsis of winning a war, or just fighting a war, or at least the romanticized idea of fighting a war, in, y'know, within a safe environment, relatively safe environment." Brandy started haranguing, as the rye was beginning to boost her confidence.

"A 'war surrogate'?"

"You see it quite a bit in America. Though in South America it's especially prominent, especially with soccer. And fucking Europe, man, especially the Balkans and the British isles, them motherfuckers got issues to vent on that there field, y'know. I've read about it."

Brandy did not know why she inexplicably applied a southern drawl to her speech.

"Could you please try not to cuss under my roof, please?" Denis said in a slightly strict tone.

31

"Aw, sorry. I'm very sorry."

"I don't know about that 'war surrogate' thing you're talking about. I know I don't like war. My pop fought in the war, you see."

"Oh? Which one?"

"Both of them."

"Both?" Brandy asked with a puzzled face. "Whaddya mean 'both'?"

"Both the wars."

"Which two… I mean, what are… Never mind."

"He died in war too. Really gruesome death at that. You see, Charlie got him. Captured him. And those gooks tortured him really bad."

"Aw, the Vietnam war."

"Yeah, the last one."

"The las… I mean, sorry, please go on. If you want to. I mean, whichever."

"It was pretty bad. By the time they got him back, he had no skin left on his back or butt. None at all, it was all gone."

"Oh, they tried to flay him?"

"Yeah. And it got so infected in the jungle that he died before they could send him home."

"Shi- sh- shame that, really. Can't imagine a worse way to go."

The game was over, and the commercial break had commenced. Denis chugged down his last bit of rye, and went up to fetch the bottle for a new helping. He poured his cup full, and poured the rest of the bottle into Brandy's, without asking, then he sat down in a wicker chair not quite big enough for his figure, and leaned back, facing Brandy from a forty-five degree angle.

"Oh, there are worse ways to go." he said, and took a sip.

"Okay?" Brandy said, and spread out a little, taking advantage of the extra space.

"You could be force-fed with whole live bullet ants, you know, forced to swallow them whole, and let them bite around inside you."

"Could you, like, die from that?"

"Maybe. It would hurt like heck, at least."

"Well, I've read it's possible to die from pain alone, actually. Like, it makes you produce so much adrenaline that your brain Oh-Dees. Like, lethal overdose from naturally produced chemicals."

"Yes, it would probably kill you, I think."

"What about getting nitric acid funneled up your butthole?" Brandy slurped.

"That could be pretty painful, yes."

"Or getting your tongue nailed to a rack or something, in the middle of the desert, so then you have to just stand there, with a nail through your tongue, with your mouth open and tongue out and then you die from dehydration." Brandy said sitting up more straight.

"I know one." Denis leaned forward. "Drowning in a tank full of instant noodles. Drowning. Boiling hot. Smelly. Noodles getting stuck in your throat."

"What about getting force-fed till you explode? Like, your stomach just pops."

Denis covered his eyes and giggled.

"What about…" he said. "What about getting flayed, starting with the penis."

He blushed a little at his remark, but still continued.

"So, it starts like a circumcision, of sorts, but then it just keeps going, until it reaches the bottom of the shaft, and then it keeps going, until all your skin is gone."

"So… just flaying?" Brandy asked.

"Yeah, but starting at the penis."

"Alright." Brandy leaned forward. "If we're gonna go with gender-specific ones, I got one for ya. You're hoisted upside down, like a caught fish, a fish caught by a fisherman, he's hung you on a rack and poses with ya for a photo, all proud he caught the biggest fish, y'know. Actually, fuh-forget that, forget the whole fish analogy. You just hang upside down, and you got your legs spread apart, y'know, then they pour molten cement, boiling hot, down into your cooch."

Denis blushed. "Well, how about they inject molten cement into your penis. Through a needle."

"Can you even do that? Like, is it possible to thin out cement so much that it flows through a syringe?"

"It's not about thinning it down, it's about refining it enough. You grind it until you make a super-smooth purée. That should work."

"Well, I've read about these quack doctors, quack plastic surgeons, injecting cement into butt cheeks. I assumed they just sort of cut a slit underneath the cheek and shoved the cement up with a spoon or something, though I s'pose actual injection could work."

Brandy then chugged down the rest of the rye.

"Do you want anything else?" Denis asked, seeing Brandy's empty cup.
"Oh, I, well, whaddya got?"

Denis opened up his little cherry red fridge, and took out two whole six-packs of bottled Samuel Adams.

"We could share some of these, if you like."
"Yes, we could." Brandy said. "Let's."

About another couple hours passed by.

As the two drank their way through the six-packs, they conversed about an array of topics, personal, political, and cultural, their dialogue gradually growing more inane by the bottle. By the time the beer was gone, Brandy figured it was time to get back to her apartment.

"I think it's time I get back to my own crib." she said.
Unfortunately, the alcohol had swollen her head to twice its weight, and when standing up it was impairing her balance to a noticeable degree.

"Jesus Jehovah, I think I better go get some sleep." she said.
"You don't look so well." noted Denis. "Maybe you should spend the night here."
"Seriously? I live like, straight below you."
"You do?"
"Straight fucking below. If I stomped hard enough I could crack the floor and fall through and land in my own bed, right where I stand."
"Better not do that, though." Denis said sincerely.

Brandy burped.

"Well…" she said. "It was surprisingly nice to meet you. Maybe I'll see you again, sometime, y'know."
"You sure you're going to make it down the stairs? You might trip and break your neck."
"I'll be fine. I'll be so very fine."

Brandy left through the apartment door, and smacked into the wall on the opposite side, before venturing down the hallway, and tumbling down the stairs.

When she returned to her apartment, Tucker sat calmly on her bed, waiting for her. She made her way to the bathroom, and upon watching herself in the mirror, realized she had been wearing only a tank top and her underpants the whole time. Too breezy to genuinely care, she drank some water from the faucet, and then threw herself into her bed, where Tucker had already perched on the pillow, inches from her face.

"Wake me up before noon, won'tcha Tucker." Brandy mumbled with her eyes closed.

Tucker patiently observed her as she descended away from consciousness.

II

And only that's when it's okay to say you belong, as is, believe me. Where are you going? Where are we going? We are hopping aboard the Continental Express, we are. It is very much a good train, one that never leaves, but always arrives. And when you go aboard, you get a free beer. Did you remember your ticket. They're gonna stamp the tickets now, better have your ticket ready. If you don't have your ticket, you cannot get aboard. Or you can get aboard, sort of, but only slowly. Getting flayed alive, would you do such a thing? Where are you? Here we are, getting our tickets stamped, nicely and orderly. Did you have your ticket? No, I did not. I don't have it. Don't have it still. Then you won't get your free beer. Ever. You see it? You see its frothy golden head? It's not for you. You won't get to drink it. Not before you cough up a ticket. Her ticket was stolen. It was an accident. I know, thieves, man. It was stolen. Anyway, come aboard. Really, it's okay, they don't care. They do care, but I don't. I don't care either. Where were we? Alright. Alright, your beer. You won't get to have it. Not yet. My friend, Lucas, who I'm sure you are acquainted with, wants to play a song he has on his song list. It is called something Polynesian, something of that language. It is about poop. Hear them sing about poop in Yiddish. Poop, poop, poop, and so forth, I s'pose. We are all dancing. Even Imogen is dancing. She never dances to songs about poop. Yet here, within us, within this building, she dances to a song about poop in Yiddish. Buckle up, we're heading for the big building the Wayne manor. The great phallic tower made of glass, exploding glass, shoved up your butthole, don't choke, ahead of you, in the grand central district, here in Riverside, where you belong, where you are. Where we are. Look outside the window, we're riding up the countryside, by the river, towards the great

35

David Letterman farm. Can you believe it? He finally fulfilled his dream of becoming a dairy farmer. He is one, right now. Look, driving by his barn, it reads 'David Letterman Dairy Farm and Friends and Hostel Everything is Welcome' in big capital letters. It makes me cry very much. I cry, till my eyes are deep red craters of tears. The tears tear into my face, it's getting sore. Too sore. Dad is here, though. He'll fix it very good, as he always does. Don't be afraid, it'll be alright. Alright. Alright. Relax. Even Imogen is dancing to the poop song. Dad will make it alright, if only Lucas could leave. Lucas, why are you here? Get your pants up. What happened to your crotch? It's a vagina there now. Why? What happened to your crotch? Where is your vagina? What happens if you poke inside it? Will the worm come out? Please be responsible. Please tell if someone bothers you. You can do that, right? Aboard the Continental Express you can. It is very efficient. Very safe. Only thing is, this little rascal here, this mister Grendel, this monster, he thinks he's a spy, a very good one, but in reality we are the spies. We observe him, and wait for him to make one lousy move. When he walks to the left with the briefcase, we have chiseled several markings into the fence besides him, and when he's gone, we'll paint over all of those, so that when he returns, we'll know the chisels are gone, and so, we can follow him to the airport, because we have proof he got there because of the paint, and then we can arrest him for high treason and fraud. Do you follow? Do you like this plan of mine? I like your nose. It has a pleasing shape. You should keep it. Don't listen to mother, you are fine and dandy, and Lucas likes you very much, that little rascal. Nobody believes a word your mother said to you when you first met her. Flayed alive. Don't believe a word the people you know are speaking, you are not a bone in the system. We are all free in some capacity. Don't worry about the saggy-ass China-man and his excuses. He is very mad at you, you should apologize. What if he disrespects you. I am very happy about this town. Too bad it isn't made of clay. It is not good to keep the China-man waiting. He might flay you alive. He has the knife for it. There is a sick sensation within us all. Did you hear that? It must certainly be a bomb. It is going off very slowly. So slowly that you still have time to save yourself, if just that annoying tapping would stop. It's hitting you face. It's hitting my precious face. Stop it, Tucker. Stop it. Stop it, you dastardly fool, the police will search my saliva. Stop it, Tucker. Tucker, stop! Tucker, Stop! Damn it, stop!

"Alright, alright, I'm awake. Alright?" moaned Brandy.

36

III

A Bloody Mary appeared on the table before Brandy, and she eagerly started sipping from the straw. She shared a booth at this place, Skimpy's Diner, a run-down gaudy fake fifties diner right outside of campus, with her friend Imogen Olson, and incidentally also Imogen's half-sister Dori Olson, their shared father being the owner of the Olson Naugahyde Furniture Store down on Brouwer Avenue in the Dreamville district, over breakfast and some catching up, even though Brandy was in a poor mood for such at this moment.

"You're gonna start with the booze this early?" asked Imogen.
"Y'know, seriously, lay off." Brandy responded. "Got a bad little conflict in my belly right now, gotta get old sister Mary come and settle a peace treaty."

Imogen and Brandy became associates on the day of Brandy's enrollment when Imogen had helped her get through the many intricacies of the college's bureaucracy. They had since hung out at various point, usually meeting for breakfast or lunch. Imogen was recognizable for her curly hair dyed completely zaffre blue, her face filled with a varied array of piercings, and her arms overcrowded with tattoos amalgamated from various religious and cultural sources, such as the god Vishnu centered within a circle of Celtic scripture on her left bicep. She also had a big one on her whole back, which was shown to Brandy at a previous instance, a tattoo formerly depicting her now ex-boyfriend but later modified to resemble RoboCop instead.

"You know, we don't really see you on campus all that much. Just sayin'." Imogen said, adjusting her big Steve Urkel glasses.
"So?" Brandy said. "That whole area is fucking boring as fuck. You wanna experience this town, you gotta go around in the weird little places outside."
"You mean like, the weird little bars?"
"You guys." interrupted Dori. "Wouldn't it be nice if we didn't bring out such negative vibes over the breakfast."
"I'm not being negative." said Imogen.
"I'm not bringing out anything." said Brandy.
"Brandy, dear." continued Dori. "It is so nice to finally get to meet you, Imogen told me a bunch about you. You don't really strike me as an economy student, to be frank."

"So what do I strike you as?" Brandy asked, hugging around her chalice of Bloody Mary, with her lips sealed around the straw.

"Oh, nothing. Just thought you'd be more... I kind of imagine economy students as being a bit mousy, to be honest. Sort of dry, nerdy types. You're not like that, though. You have this almost Bohemian quality to ya."

Dori was in fact two years younger than Brandy, yet looked and behaved like anyone's middle-aged aunt, with her tall orange hairdo and purple nylon sweater, and the long red nails on her long pasty fingers clambering around her cup of herbal tea.

"Look, Brandy, is something the matter?" asked Imogen. "You look a little... Off. Like, do you have some emotional baggage you wanna vent, or...?"

"It's just..." Brandy slurped down the lower half of her drink on one big go. "I think I need a job right now. Or very soon. It's kinda... Y'see, I got this thing I gotta pay for. This thing that I'm not really all that proud of."

"Oh, it's something private? Like, is it a drug deal, or?"

"No, it's not something of that sort, no. It's a medical thing, y'know. It's like, well, it's a surgery of sorts."

"You're gonna have an operation done on ya?"

"Yeah. Hopefully. If I can afford it in time."

"What kind of surgery is it?" asked Dori. "Are you getting a nose job?"

"What?" said Brandy. "No. Why... why do people just assume I want a nose job?"

"Look, sweetheart." Dori said. "We're not judging you."

"Look, it's not plastic surgery, alright. It's medical stuff, like, health-related."

"Oh, so it's kind of more serious than a nose job?"

"Yeah! Why, seriously why, do people think I want a nose job, specifically?"

"Brandy, sweetheart." Dori lay her hand over Brandy's one that lay idly on the table. "We're not judging you. If you really *want* to have a nose job, that's fine, but you totally don't need one. Your nose is perfect just the way it is."

Brandy did not respond verbally, but instead looked confusedly at Dori.

"It's just good to have a little ethnic character to your appearance. Be proud of your Jewish features?" Dori continued.

"Like, fucking seriously?" Brandy asked. "You're calling me a hook-nose?"

"I'm saying you shouldn't be ashamed if your nose is a little big. You shouldn't be ashamed of your Judaism. It's who you *are*!"

Brandy pulled her hand away from Dori's touch.

"You know what?" she said and slammed her palms on the table. "I don't take very kindly to be taught self-acceptance by someone whose understanding of Judaism comes from the works of Joseph Goebbels!"

"Jeez, that's a bit harsh, Brandy." said Imogen.

"Who's Joseph Goebbels?" asked Dori.

Brandy did not respond, but took another sip of her drink, and a small handful from her bowl of home fries.

"Anyway…" Dori continued. "Don't take it negatively. I'd die to have some ethnic traits like that."

She took another sip of her tea and sliced off another chunk of her pancake stack.

Brandy looked at her with exasperated confusion. "How can you—waiter! 'Nother B-M, please."

The nearest waitress nodded affirmably passing her by.

"You're gonna have another one?" asked Imogen. "Really?"

"Look, things are a little rough now, alright."

"That's like two drinks *for breakfast*. And what *is* your breakfast? A bowl of home fries?"

"Home fries are good. Mom used to make some really good ones. These aren't *that* great, but they are alright enough, I s'pose."

Brandy grabbed a lump off her bowl of home fries and ate it.

"I'm sorry if I was being a tad culturally insensitive, but I was just saying you look good the way you are, and that you shouldn't change yourself out of insecurity or anything." Dori said.

"Y'know what, shut the fuck up, Dori. Nobody gives a fuck what you're saying." Brandy said.

A brief silence followed.

"Well, then." said Dori. "I really better get my butt in motion, got to reach my sociology lecture in time."

Dori stood up, and withdrew a zipper bag from her satchel, and poured the remnants of her pancakes into it.

"See you later, sis." she said.

Then she left.

Imogen said nothing, and continued on with her scrambled eggs and pomegranate juice.

"Fucking Christ." Brandy said, just as her drink arrived.

"You know, Brandy…" Imogen said with her mouth half-full of eggs. "The local post office is hiring these days. There's either that, or McDonald's maybe, if you want a job. Post office probably pays better, though"

"Thanks, but I already had a paper route back in my youth." Brandy replied. "It doesn't pay that well."

"Well, you have a driver's license, don't you? I'm sure they'll pay you a bit more if you drive, or, maybe, I dunno, really, but you know, it's something."

"To be honest, I don't have anything else to go by, really, so might as well check it out, as long as I get more than minimum wage."

"So how soon do you need to have this surgery, if you don't mind me asking?"

"Soon as possible, really. Any money I can get I'll take, I really need to squeeze every penny, y'know."

"And you still order several Bloody Mary's for breakfast?"

"Well, I don't need to squeeze that hard."

Brandy took another sip of her drink.

"This is just the second one, y'know, and, I mean, I gotta eat and drink on a regular basis, right? Can't straight up kill myself trying to save myself. That would kind of defeat the purpose, y'know."

"Well, suit yourself, I suppose. Just remember you should probably go for that post office gig if you're really so desperate. Just try to submit an application before they fill the position, might not take too long, there's a lot of people in this town looking for jobs." Imogen said.

She took a big swig of juice.

"Hey, um, seriously, I don't really have, like, a 'Jew-nose', do I?" asked Brandy.

"Look, don't take anything sis says too seriously, okay. She just likes to babble a bunch of bullshit through her opiate highs." Imogen said cutting off another slice of vegan bacon. "Did I already tell you she's a pill popper? Don't think I did. Got herself an illegitimate Valium prescription. Other stuff too. Stuff I'd never even heard of before. Some I'm sure is straight up illegal."

"Seriously though, do I look like a Nazi propaganda caricature or not?"

"You don't have a Jew-nose. It's a normal size and shape. Looks just like mine."

"Thanks." Brandy said and ate some more home fries, one bit at a time. Imogen took another sip of juice.

"You've got major Jew-brows, though." she said.

"I do not."

"You do. Some big-ass caterpillars you got crawling up there."

"Are you just trying to piss me off? 'Cos I'm already in a bit of a bad mood right now."

"They do look good on you though." Imogen tried to restrain a little taunting smirk. "Makes you look more intelligent, you know. Less doe-eyed."

Brandy tossed her drink's straw on the table, and downed the remaining half in one big gulp.

"Seriously, not in the fucking mood, alright." she chucked the last five bits of fries in her mouth, and waved at the nearest waitress. "Check please!" she said upon getting her attention.

"I gotta skedaddle anyway." she continued. "Got stuff to do."

"Shit." Imogen moaned. "Dori just left. We have to pay for *her* orders too."

"That damn cunt." Brandy commented.

"Hey, don't call her that!" Imogen responded. "She's my sister!"

"Doesn't make her any less of a cunt."

"Hey, show some respect."

"You just babbled on about her pill abuse, like, totally unprovoked. Your own sister. Then you're telling *me* I need to show her more respect?"

"Goddamn, it's, like, okay. I'll admit it, she kind of is a… you know. She's pretty immature, irresponsible, a little mean sometimes."

"Like hell."

"But it's like, *you* can't call her that word. Not in my presence, anyway."

"Why not, if we both agree?"

"It's like, how would you feel if I, like, called one of your brothers a… you know."

"A cunt?"

"Yeah, what if I called him a cunt?"

"Which one?"

"Uh, does it matter? The oldest one?"

"Oh, Brendan? He totally is a cunt."

"You know, forget it."

CHAPTER FOUR

The D'Orleans compound had an extensive garden behind it, nearly as big as some parks in town, with a vast array of somewhat exotic plants spread around its numerous ponds, some of which had built-in fountains and sculptures. The garden was overgrown enough with trees and bushes that one could, by venturing far enough inside, completely obscure oneself from the view of the mansion, even if one were Olive D'Orleans.

Olive took much pleasure in traversing the garden on sunny summer days, being pushed around the trails in her wheelchair by Roland. She rarely left the estate when not explicitly invited somewhere, and even within the mansion she had become confound to the first floor. The structure of the old house did not allow for installation of elevators, and the stair lift soon became unable to withstand her increased weight. So Olive spent most of her time in her own private quarters and elsewhere on the first floor, but utilized every opportunity to depart into the garden when the weather allowed it, usually to arrange a picnic with Roland by one of the particularly scenic spots.

On this cloudless Saturday in early May, Olive had picked for their picnic location a flowery plot of grass under a large old oak tree, atop a small hill with the view of a pond surrounded by ferns and filled with lilies, which at this point also had a lone peacock walking around it. The hill was by no means particularly tall or steep, but Roland still struggled severely with pushing Olive up to the top, rubbing his feet into the ground behind him, all the while she idly scanned her surrounding landscape while eating hazel nuts from a paper bag. The moment they finally reached the top, Roland dropped himself on the grass behind her to catch his breath, letting go of the extensive travel backpack he had been carrying. 'I might possibly be getting too old for this job' he thought to himself, not daring to let Olive hear it.

"This is the place." Olive said. "Could you maybe turn me towards the pond a bit more, please?"

Roland stood up, and obliged her.

"Of course, lady Olive." he said.

After that, he removed the portable TV-dinner tray strapped to the front of the backpack, placed it in front of Olive, and covered it with a small white tablecloth whipped up from his breast pocket. Then he opened the backpack and removed several Tupperware containers filled with food: potato gratin with parmesan, a whole grilled chicken, baked asparagus wrapped in bacon, buttered boiled green beans, coleslaw, Greek meatballs, béarnaise sauce, as well as shakers of pepper and salt.

For himself he had brought his tin lunch box with a turkey rye sandwich and a lump of the same coleslaw.

Olive had her food served on paper platters, starting with the gratin and the meatballs, and ate it indulgently while observing the peacock, anticipating it to possibly display its train, even if it was alone.

"It's a marvelous day today." she said. "Don't you think so, Roland?"
"It is quite marvelous, yes." replied Roland.

Olive withdrew a bottle of Chianti from the satchel on the side of her wheelchair. She poured a glass for herself.

"How many peacocks do you think we have in the garden?" asked Olive.
"It's difficult to say, lady Olive. I would assume at least a dozen. It could possibly be as few as half a dozen though, to be perfectly honest." Roland said with a slight cough at the end.
"I haven't seen any of the pelicans in a while." noted Olive. "They've been getting scarcer every year, and I haven't seen *one* since last fall."
"Your father actually wanted emus in the garden." Roland said. "He wanted to have them wander freely about. It turned out they were far too aggressive, so we had to make due with peacocks and pelicans."
"I would love to see a live emu up close."

When Olive had finished her first portion, Roland stood up and withdrew from his inner pocket an envelope.

"Pardon me, lady Olive, but before we commence the rest of the meal, I would like to bring this letter to your attention."

He handed her the letter.

"I had taken the liberty of reviewing its contents beforehand. As you can see the envelope has been quite sloppily re-sealed. I hope you won't take great offense with my actions."

Olive read that the letter was addressed to her, and quickly removed the letter from the envelope. It read:

> *To: Olive D'Orleans*
> *1123 Vermogend Drive*
> *Riverside, N.H. 035168*
>
> *Dear Ms. Olive D'Orleans,*
>
> *We represent the Michelin Guide, and are currently considering the possibility of releasing a guide in your town of residence, Riverside. Given your proven expertise within the field of culinary arts and your prolific career in gastronomical critique, we would greatly appreciate if you spoke on Riverside's behalf, defending its right to the honor of an official Michelin guide, at the upcoming Michelin Culinary Convention at the Thomas Jefferson Plaza Hotel & Conference Center on 516 Herring Street, Riverside, on Wednesday May 12th, at 02:00 pm.*
>
> *Responding to this letter will not be necessary should you accept the offer. Should you decline, please notify us in due time.*
>
> *Sincerely,*
> *Samuel Jackson Snead*
> *Rep. of The Michelin Guide*
> *Dept. 354*
> *1700 Broadway*
> *N.Y., N.Y. 10019*

Olive shook the letter feverously in her hands. She gulped down her wine and wiped sweat from her now chalk white face, and touched around her chest for her overworked heart, now beating so rapidly it could break her ribcage.

"Lady Olive, are you quite well?" Roland asked worriedly.
Olive breathed like she had just escaped fatal suffocation.

"Lady, please do respond!" Roland squatted down in front of Olive, anxiously looking into her eyes.

"Oh, Roland." Olive finally said, as her breathing gradually calmed down. "This is the happiest I have been in many years. I don't know what to even say."

Roland emitted a sigh of relief.

"The Michelin Guide has recognized my writing! Just think about it! They might inspect our city's restaurants *because of me*! Isn't that fantastic?!"
"Yes, quite, lady Olive." Roland said, standing up again. "Though I must remind you that if you ever experience chest pain or similar worrisome sensations, let me or someone else know immediately."
"I know, I know, Roland, you've told me hundreds of times, but I'm not in pain. Just really, really excited!"
"Very well." Roland said and turned away to check his own heart.
"You know what? I think I'll have that chicken now, please."
"Yes, naturally, lady Olive."

Roland lay the chicken before Olive, and she pulled off a drumstick. As she ate her attention undecidedly switched between the letter and the view of the pond, where the peacock still had not left, and still had not displayed its train.

CHAPTER FIVE

"So you don't have any previous experiences in the postal service?" asked Mister Charles Humphrey.

"I had a paper route until I was fifteen." answered Brandy. "And I delivered pizza for a couple of years. A year and a half, there-about."

"Yes, I've read your résumé." Mister Humphrey rested his head in his left palm scratching his temple with his index finger, staring at Brandy sitting opposite him in his office.

"Though you didn't write on it that you were laid off from both jobs. Or that the same happened with that other job you had, down at the repair shop."

"Where did you get that from?"

"I asked your references over the phone."

"Oh. Well, I'll take full responsibility with the paper route one. I was a bit of a lazy teenage bum. The pizza one though, that was a fu—fat conspiracy on the manager's part. I can't prove it, it's just I knew he was after me. Held a grudge against me. Probably didn't like me as a person. Like, tons of stuff happened, but in short, he fired me for illegitimate reasons, is what I'm trying to say."

"And the repair shop one?"

"Oh, that one I was just not really qualified for. Don't understand car mechanics or mechanics in general. Don't care, to be honest. Only got the job 'cos dad gave it to me. It wasn't a good decision on his part really."

"Mm-hm. It didn't say on your résumé when you got laid off here though. From the repair shop."

"Oh, I was about nineteen, I would say."

47

"And how old are you now, if I may ask?"

"I'm twenty one."

"I see." Humphrey said with pouted lips as his forehead wrinkled up.

He put on his round little glasses and looked over Brandy's résumé again. He then cast another glance at Brandy, leaned back a little too comfortably in her chair and letting her gaze drift freely around the office when not spoken to. She casually cracked her fingers to his annoyance and he saw she was wearing ravaged wool gauntlets matching the rest of her outfit, the oversized wool cardigan, the buttoned beige shirt, the old leather satchel hung over her shoulder, and the purple bandana tied around her throat. Upon first entering she had removed her beret from her unkempt hair and clenched it between her fingers like she was a Depression era street child begging for food or money.

"Look, miss..." Humphrey said. "It's Miss, right? The résumé didn't mention any marriage or..."

"It's Miss, yeah."

"Okay, look, miss... You seem like a nice kid and all. In the long run I probably wouldn't mind having someone like you on the staff. I'm sure you would be capable of doing your job. It's just that I honestly don't feel comfortable hiring someone who shows up to a job interview smelling like tequila."

"You can't smell that!" Brandy protested and smelled her breath. "I had half a box of Tic-Tac's right before I got here."

"You can't disguise the scent of tequila that easily, I'm afraid. I've been to Tijuana, you know. I know the smell."

"Well, I can promise you I won't drink and drive, if *that* is your problem. I can stay totally, utterly, completely, absolutely dry till the shift is over, you got my word on that."

"And how much is your word worth to me?"

"A paycheck? I mean, whaddya mean, 'worth'? I don't have to prove my worth to you!"

"Well, yes, you actually do. That technically is the purpose of a job interview in the first place."

Brandy had no clever response to that, or any response that was not embarrassing.

Back at the O'Caiside, Brandy had allocated herself to her favorite booth with a tall mojito in her hand and Tucker by her side. The frustration from the failed job interview was still lingering in the back of her cortex, but she hoped her drink would burn that feeling away and let her move forward with her life, perhaps find another, even better job. Any profession would suit her now, she thought. Getting a job at McDonald's could work after a little wage negotiation. Even performing fellatio behind a McDonald's would be within her willingness at this point. Only thing that mattered was the money. Perhaps this is how greedy people felt all the time. Perhaps it was never a matter of selfish lust for wealth with those people. Maybe all the corporate magnates in the one percent of the one percent were all motivated by fear of vicious evils inside them unknown to the public. Brandy was certainly uncomfortable discussing the specifics of her health problem, maybe that was the case with those fellows as well. They behave like parasites and cancer cells because they literally have those inside them. Or maybe their ailments were delusions, diseases of the mind, or self-imposed delusions created to justify their greed. What, Brandy thought, if that was the case with her as well? What if the Tidak Nyata inside her was simply imagined? Was she in the first stages of becoming a greedy capitalist? Was extreme greed a mental disorder? Was Donald Trump and Rupert Murdoch and the rest of the lot mentally ill? Was Brandy mentally ill?

Realizing her train of thought was speeding towards a ditch, Brandy whipped up from her little satchel her book to put her mind on a more relaxing track.

'*The Undying Man*' by C. Novel Turner, a small pocket novella with browned water-damaged pages, purchased for a single dollar from an odd little book store on Hamilton Street which name she could not recall, where she had found it in a dusty cardboard box in the corner. She had initially been intrigued by the book cover's colorful depiction of a tall vaguely demonic woman ripping a man's skeleton out through his mouth, drawn in a minimalist style reminiscent of the works of Saul Bass. She just thought it was quite amusing that the cover of a book called '*The Undying Man*' showed on its cover a man definitely dying. Also amusing was that it came with its own bookmark, a hot pink calling card for a brothel called 'Nights of Perfume' located on Rosemary Avenue down in the Capricorn district. Brandy had once, upon wandering down that street, checked the cited address out of curiosity. It was a Starbucks now.

Before Brandy could begin reading, however, she needed to get herself another mojito, and also another bowl of peanuts for Tucker.

When she approached the bar to place her order, she saw a familiar face; on the same barstool she herself had sat on her last visit sat now the man who had taken her booth last time. Same suit, same tiny coffee cup, same newspaper (might as well have been), same massive lips. As Brandy ordered her drink, the man threw her a slimy gander. She attempted to look neutral and dethatched as their eyes met, trying not to show the hair raising creeps his face gave her. When she returned to her booth, she saw that the man was still looking in her direction, before returning to reading his paper. Reading seemed like the best thing to do for her as well.

So this man was apparently not just a traveling salesman or the likes. He had not simply come to town and wound up in this place from unfamiliarity with the local geography. He actually chose to spend his leisure time at the O'Caiside, seemingly fairly frequently. Some people do apparently enjoy time away from their natural habitat. Perhaps the sterile, squeaky-clean white-collar environment bored him, even if he fit perfectly in. Maybe he hated himself. Actually, he *could* fit in at the O'Caiside if one interpreted his appearance as that of a corrupt lawyer collaborating with drug dealers or mobsters. He could fit very well in in a mafia film, as the conniving attorney planning to bribe the judge to dismiss all charges on the recently arrested mob kingpin, then he would be killed towards the end, revealed to have disloyally played both sides for profit or something, shot in the head after begging for mercy on his knees in the mud. That was the kind of character he could be.

Brandy had now stared into the pages of the book for minutes, but had started constructing the plot of a hypothetical crime film in lieu of actually reading. Her concentration had not been its sharpest lately. She began reading at the fifth chapter, trying to remember what had happened so far in the story.

Before she had read any more than fifty words into the first paragraph, however, she was confronted by a stranger.

"Hello." he said in a friendly tone. "May I sit here?"
"Well... I guess." Brandy said with some doubt in her voice. He sat down in the booth opposite her.

The man looked much more at home at the O'Caiside than the suited fellow with the coffee cup. This was a pale unkempt fellow with a worn-out trench coat, a stained indigo baseball cap with the Riverside Toucans logo on it, and a gray wool scarf similar to one Brandy owned, and would wear on colder days. His gaunt unwashed face was riddled with acne and an prominent three-day stubble, and conjoined eyebrows bordering on a proper unibrow above his bulging blue bug eyes. He also had a third eye tattooed on his forehead. It looked unfinished.

"Listen." he said. "I saw you at the post office. You didn't get the job, did you?"

"What?" Brandy said. "First, that was really fucking abrupt, to just jump into that topic just like that. Not even introducing yourself first."

"I prefer to get straight to business." he responded.

"Well, alright, but…" Brandy rolled her eyes. "Second. What the hell do you know about anything at the post office? You don't know what I did at the post office, unless you're a fucking stalker, in which case, fucking idiotic to confront me here, in broad public. You can't kidnap me here. These folks'll see ya. They'll call the cops on ya."

"I'm not a stalker." he said. "You can trust me."

"Well, can I?" said Brandy. "You're either making wild fucking assumptions, or you've been paying creepily close attention to me. Criminally close attention, I'd say."

"I saw you enter the manager's office. You didn't look like someone who already worked there, the way you were dressed. You left looking angry, and disappointed. They have been hiring for a few weeks, advertising such with big posters all over the entrance. So yeah, it was an assumption, but not a particularly wild one."

"So what exactly is the point you're getting at here, anyway?"

"Well, I would have gotten to it sooner, had you been a bit more inviting." the man leaned back.

Brandy's doubts only increased for every second she looked at him, and more so for every word he spoke.

"What I was trying to say is, I represent someone who wants to offer you a job."

None of his words improved Brandy's impression of him. What decent job had ever been offered in the corner of a bar? Brandy tried to imagine how this could have a happy ending, how the story that began here would conclude on a good note, and all she

51

could think of was something along the lines of '*I successfully escaped the sex trafficking ring*', and the implied journey up to that point was simply not worth it.

"Thank you, but no thanks." Brandy said dryly and politely, hoping the man would leave soon.

"It's not what you probably think." he said. "I understand that you might find this a little suspect, but... You know, here's our card."

He flipped out a card from the breast pocket of his coat and placed it on the table. It was an ivory white, elegantly designed business card, with bold black print in a serif font, reading the alleged enterprise's name, 'The Helping Hand Company' on top, with the address and contact information of a 'Crispin Dodd' in smaller letters underneath, and the company's logo, an open hand with two feminine eyes in the palm, imprinted in bronze on the side. It looked like a legit business card, but Brandy knew such cards could be purchased online fairly cheaply.

"What kind of a job is this, really?" Brandy queried, mostly just to humor the man.

"Postal delivery." the man answered. "It's a private enterprise."

"Sort of like FedEx?"

"Very much in the same vein, yeah."

Brandy observed the card some more. "So why exactly do you want me?"

"You're looking for a job, right? In postal delivery?"

"I am... well, I was just applying at the post office 'cos they were hiring. I don't have any real competence or interest in post related stuff in particular."

"But you *are* looking for a job?"

"What's it do you?"

"I am offering you a job."

"Well, yeah, but this is just kind of a weird way to go about it, don't you think? You do seem really, like, overly eager to give me this job."

The man finally stood up. "Well, I can't force you to accept, I understand that. Just hang on to that card. Maybe you'll re-decide one day. Just so you know, though, the offer don't stand forever."

Brandy only looked at him in silence as he left the establishment. He had to her knowledge not bought anything here, not even a soda.

52

III

The next day, Brandy had returned to the doctor's office with a seething and worrisome stomach ache she feared was caused by the Malaysian gremlin worm.

"Are you sure it's not just gas?" asked Doctor Herbert Walker.

"I know what gas feels like. This ain't that." answered Brandy. "This is like a burning stingy sensation, y'know, like being bitten by an ant, only on the inside and much bigger."

"I suppose we better have a look then." Doctor Walker said.

So they did.

Doctor Walker stared somberly at the ultrasound image.

"The Tidak seems to have grown quite a bit." he said. "Nearly doubled in size. That is a much faster development than I've ever seen before."

"Before? How many of these have you exactly seen, really?" asked Brandy.

"Coincidentally, I spent a summer as a foreign exchange student in Bali, Indonesia, back in the day. Early nineteen seventies, I think it was, seventy two or three maybe. They have the Tidak Nyata there too, don't you know, almost as common there as in Malaysia. I didn't treat those patients myself, but I certainly learned a lot about it, saw many cases. Hideous disease really, if you do nothing about it. Saw a man whose whole scrotum had exploded. Just a fleshy crater where his genitals used to be. Ghastly sight. Thought I'd never see the Tidak again once I returned to America, but lo and behold, here you are. Small world after all, don't you think?"

"Um, yo, doctor..." Brandy said. "Normally I would really love to hear the story of Mister Crater-dick and all that; but I'm kind of *in a lot of fucking distress right now, AND I'M ABOUT TO FUCKING DIE AND IT'S PAINFUL AS FUCKING HELL!!*"

"Oh, I'm so sorry. Well, I suppose we need to locate the reason for this abnormal development."

He looked over Brandy's chart, deep in hard thoughts.

"Tell me, how often do you drink?" he asked.

"How frequently I drink?" Brandy paraphrased the question. "I never start until after breakfast. Well, almost never, there's been a few exception. I have maybe one or two drinks around lunch time. Some drinks for dinner, some in between the two, maybe, if

I'm bored, then see what I feel like having in the evening, maybe a little nightcap of some kind before bed."

"Every day?"

"Yeah, sure. There's a little variation, but that's basically the norm."

"Had any today?"

"Took a couple of mojitos while I waited for my appointment, yeah."

Doctor Walker observed the charts some more. "Well, hate to break it to you, kid, but that might very well have contributed quite a bit."

"Are you just being mean now?"

"No, I'm quite serious. You see, when you consume alcohol, the liver reacts by producing a specific type of enzyme that happens to have a fattening effect on the Tidak Nyata parasite. It's honestly very technical, it's all very hard to put in layman's terms, but let's just say every alcoholic beverage you consume is like a little BigMac to the parasite, and if you were to eat fifteen BigMacs every day, you would probably get a little chubbier pretty soon."

"But, uh, hasn't it been just a little over a week?" asked Brandy.

"You shouldn't underestimate the effect of a BigMac. Believe me." Doctor Walker said and clapped his beer belly.

"Okay, so if I keep going like I do with the drinking, how much time do I have left?"

"Well, first of all, if you quit drinking today, I'd give you about a year. Not likely a year and a half anymore, but definitely a year. And by 'quit drinking' I mean completely cold turkey. No wine, no beer, no cocktails, not even a glass of port for Christmas." the doctor removed his glasses and wiped them on his sleeve. "If you keep going like you do now, however, I would give you about a month or so. Month and a half, possibly."

Brandy covered her face with her hands and rubbed it hard.

"So, wait. Is it possible to pay for the operation, like, after the matter? Like, I don't care if it puts me in debt, I just wanna live, y'know."

"I'm very, very sorry, kid." the doctor said. "That's not in this hospital's policy, I'm afraid. You could look online for hospitals that both provide the Tidak Nyata removal surgery, and has that kind of policy. I can't name any off the top of my head, but it definitely could exist. You certainly shouldn't exclude the possibility."

IV

Brandy left the doctor's office, and sat down on a chair in the waiting room. Before she left, she was given a prescription of mild pain killers, that could soothe the pain from the parasite if nothing else, but was strictly not to be mixed with alcohol or other drugs. She crumbled the printed prescription and tossed it on the floor, and stared vacantly at a pair of posters about vaccination on the wall. Some of the others in the room looked momentarily up from their magazines to cast confused glances at her.

The parasite, that wicked heinous lousy little segmented genital wart, it so agonized the body and the mind in equal measure, now heating Brandy's intestines to a furious white volcanic boiling point. Her belly became a seething black hole of death.

Three mojitos, a diet coke, and the remnants of a chewed-up teriyaki chicken Subway sandwich torpedoed out Brandy's mouth and onto the hospital floor. She did not even feel nauseated at this moment, yet now she spewed like a fire hose, forming a little lake of vomit stew around her feet. And she kept spewing, till nothing but acidulous bile was left inside her, then a little more, until she was drained dry and empty.

Spitting out the last morsels of bile, she thought about whether the hospital's sanitation department got a high enough salary to justly tolerate this mess. Her fellow patients did not seem to tolerate it, and they were not even expected to interact with it. They could block all their senses from its existence if they tried really hard, none of them carried any responsibility to have it removed, yet they insisted on expressing hyperbolic vocal and visual reactions of revolt and repulsion. Their exaggerated responses slightly tickled the annoyance center of Brandy's now numbed brain as she staggered out, into the cold fresh outdoors.

V

The blood on the wall from the stabbing incident at the Manson Asylum had finally been almost completely washed away, after only two months of hard procrastination and three days of relaxed work, though there was still a distinctly darker complexion on the wall's lower half. Perhaps it would always stay there, at least until the impending day when the whole building would collapse from its own rot.

Upon entering the asylum, Brandy automatically checked her mailbox, to find nothing but advertisement. Denis Burke did at that point walk by on his way out, now

55

dressed as a Noir-detective with a beige trench coat and a matching fedora. He tipped his hat to Brandy with a cheery grin on his wide face.

"Lovely day today, huh?" he said. "Haven't seen sun like this in weeks."

"Yeah, it's pretty neat, I s'pose." Brandy said back. She did think of quipping something about solving a murder to Denis, but her mood was not in the right place.

When he left, she noticed some crude red graffiti on the wall above the mailboxes reading 'BEWARE THE COCK', which had not been there the day before, and to her memory, not this morning either.

"You remember this being here before, Tucker?" she asked.

"Fucker." cawed Tucker.

"Me neither. Some little twerp must've done it in broad daylight."

The pain from the parasite had been easing significantly since she left the hospital, but its mental impact not so much. After she arrived at her apartment, Brandy had tried to smoothen the emotional edge by downing a bottle of cheap merlot, which took her twenty three minutes. She paired it with a small bag of Cheetos, her second meal this day, which Tucker also gladly ate from.

While drinking, she scrolled through her cell phone's contact list, looking for anyone to converse with, whether about her current crisis or anything else. She called Imogen, who did not answer; her mother, whose line was occupied with another conversation, same case with her father. And then she came to her ex Ryan. He would understand. Brandy had once caught him trying to hang himself, and after she managed to save him, the first thing he did was offering to take her out for hotdogs. Surely he would gladly return the favor, she thought, regardless of the breakup. So she called him, but then remembered he had changed his number. After that, she considered calling either of her brothers, Brendan or Brad. Brendan did not answer, as was typical of him. Brad, she remembered, had lost his cell phone to the lion's cage at the zoo back in July. Unable to receive social consolation, she instead decided to open another bottle of wine, the same brand as the last one, but this time drink it in a more dignified manner, with a plastic stem glass.

Halfway through the second bottle, Brandy had brought Tucker into the hallway, where she sat leaning against a wall, refilling her glass between gulps and listening to a randomized playlist on her cell phone that lay on the floor.

"Here's to you, ya little bitch gremlin." Brandy said and toasted her belly. "Have some more fatty booze, ya fucking leech. Hope you get a fucking cardiac arrest, ya fat fuck."

She chugged down the remainder of her half-full glass. Tucker skipped down from her head and into her lap, where he consolingly rubbed against her stomach with his head. She appreciated the gesture, but she still felt alone in her heart. '*Alone*' by Heart was playing, and she knew the lyrics by heart. At least in fragments.

"*Till then! I always go by on my own! A-dibby-doobie cared until I met you!*" she howled throughout the halls, to the bother of likely nobody. Loud disruptive mania was commonplace in this complex.

Once the bottle was empty, she went back inside. the little business card Brandy had been given lay lonely at her nightstand, its bright sharp whiteness contrasting the whole rest of the room. As Brandy collapsed into bed, it was the first and only thing that caught her fading sight. She picked it up and idly read through its inscriptions once more. A full address was declared on the bottom. She let it slip out of her hand, and let her mind drift into more pleasant thoughts than what had occupied her day. The alarm clock was still ticking away. It was only ten past eight. The ceiling light was still turned on, but seemed to darken by the second. It is indeed a beautiful day today, and here at the beach everything is so shiny; but we need to go. In order to enter the palace one must insert the golden key into the cat's butthole.

CHAPTER SIX

Turning east on the lower side of Harmony Square, one would venture into Bloomberg Alley, a very narrow pedestrian zone, only about a yard and a half wide, mostly a residential block with one little café at the beginning. But one entrance, which one could easily miss, had a discrete door bell with a name tag reading '*The Helping Hand Company*'. '104 Bloomberg Alley' was one address Brandy passed several times before properly discovering. She was almost certain of the street, but could find no reasonably fitting entrance until she spotted that one little doorbell on the side of what seemed like the backdoor to a strip club. When she rang the bell, a voice sounded from the intercom above it.

"What do you want?" said the hoarse cigarette-ravished voice of an older woman.

"Uh, I am here to apply for a job." Brandy said. "At the, uh, the Helping Hand Company."

Dead silence followed for at least ten seconds.

"Hello?" Brandy said.

Suddenly the door made a clicking sound. She opened it, and hesitated for a short while, thinking about whether she really wanted to do this.

That hot sharp achy feeling was swirling around inside her. The pain was intensifying again. She figured if this was any kind of scam, she would die in a single month anyway. Even if they intended to kidnap her, at least she could not suffer for a particularly long time before the parasite did her in. Her upcoming death would be her blissful escape from any hypothetical deviousness, and if this truly was a proper job, with a solid enough salary, then all her troubles would cease to be, possibly. There was however still a small part of her mind that screamed for her to turn back, as she slowly stepped into this lawless, heartless territory. There would be no rights and no expectations, only a free fall with one possibility of a cushy landing, and one of a plummet into spikes and fire. Which one was the bigger, she could not say.

What met her upon entering was a single staircase up a passage of browning gray concrete walls filled with cracks and elaborate graffiti, distant rat squeaks echoing between them. As she reluctantly climbed the wooden stairs, each step creaked furiously as she touched them. If any staircase in the world could collapse under her weight, this one would be it. The banister wobbled as she grabbed, and seemed barely attached. The only light in here came through the mostly broken small windows, one for each floor.

When she reached the second floor, she was met by a barricaded door with the handle removed. This was probably not the right door, she thought. She then braved up to the third floor, nervous step by nervous step, where she was met by an empty doorframe blocked by a moldy old sofa. When looking inside, her eyes were met by a mostly vacant apartment, with bits of trash and broken office furniture scattered wildly about.

Finally, at the fourth floor she was met by a more normal-looking entrance, and with '*The Helping Hand Company*' written on the doorbell's nametag. The previous doors did not have doorbells at all.

Brandy rang the doorbell, and waited, somewhat anxiously. After a few seconds, someone on the inside unlocked the door, but refrained from opening it. After a tiny bit of hesitation, she opened the door herself.

Inside was what seemed to be an old two-bedroom apartment repurposed for professional purposes. The entrance room, the living room, now served as a waiting room, with two rows of five chairs, a poster on the wall about the importance of flossing seemingly taken from a dentist's office, a rack with various brochures, and even a table with old magazines, but no reception. There were two locked doors on opposite sides of the room, one with a taped-on sheet of paper reading '*bathroom*' in red magic marker writing, the other one blank. There was not a single person present. Whoever unlocked the door must have then fled into another room. 'Fucking rude', Brandy thought.

She sat down on the chair by the magazine table, and picked up an issue of Parade from nineteen ninety six with Bob Dole on the cover, idly scanning through its pages while waiting for someone to reveal themselves.

59

Reasonably soon, the blank door did slowly open with a loud creak. An older woman stuck her head out of the small opening, a droopy-faced tired being with gray leathery skin, wearing a flower-patterned gown and a tall curly sweet potato orange wig, having a smoking cigarette butt dangling from her pink pouty lips.

"The boss wants to see ya, kid." she said with her recognizably raspy voice.

Brandy stood up and went inside.

"Here's the gal ya wanted, boss." said the old lady to the little man sat behind the large desk at the end of his office.

"Thanks, Ermintrude." he said.

Ermintrude returned to her little desk covered with several full ashtrays in the corner by the door, where she proceeded to work with her late nineties IBM computer.

"I take it you're Crispin Dodd?" Brandy said.

"Yes, most certainly." Crispin Dodd replied. "As it says on my desk sign."

Brandy looked on his desk and saw an expensive-looking desk sign by Crispin's computer, with his name engraved in gold letters on a dark green felt cloth within a wooden frame. It was likely the most expensive object in the whole building, possibly more expensive than the building itself.

"Please sit down, ma'am." he continued.

Brandy sat down on a wooden chair opposite Crispin Dodd. He was a small puny narrow-shouldered man with large brown bloodshot eyes like a stray puppy, with dark Velcro eyebrows and a flimsy graying comb over. He sat in his chair struggling to keep his torso above the desk while forcing a smile against his heavy puffy cheeks.

"I presume you're here about the job offer, yes?" Dodd said.

"Well, yeah. There was this dude at this bar that said he had a job for me, and gave me a card directing me here, so I take it I've come to the right place."

"Oh yes, this is very much the right place." Dodd chortled slightly creepily. "I take it you have experience in the field of postal delivery, yes? You have the discipline and the work ethics and the sense of loyalty required, yes?"

"I guess so, yeah." Brandy said.

"Yes!" Dodd exclaimed. "And I presume you have some knowledge of our operation, yes? You are to a certain extent familiar with The Helping Hand Company?"

"Don't know shit, I'm afraid." Brandy admitted. "Some, uh, FedEx type of deal, I guess."

60

She looked around bashfully, slightly insecure in her response, hoping Dodd would not take it too harshly or find it offensive. Though, in sincerity, she thought, comparing this operation to FedEx would only be insultingly generous.

"Oh? I see." Dodd said as his eager attitude deflated. "Well, I suppose it is my responsibility, my duty, of sorts, to explain our business. I take it you're not wearing a wire, no?"

"What?" Brandy reacted. "Of course not. Why would I…? Like, no. No, I'm not wearing a wire."

"Good, very good." Dodd said. "It'd be a shame if you were. We really need to establish a solid foundation of trust, do we not?"

He leaned forward towards Brandy, resting his whole upper body on the desk.

"Now, what we essentially are is a delivery service for those who may have reasons to not trust the regular postal service, or any of the mainstream private companies for that matter. To put it one way, we are some people's last resort. Not that I would call our clients desperate or anything. They just have certain unique needs, if you understand."

"What kind of people are we talking here, exactly?" Brandy asked. "Criminals?"

"Oh, we don't like to judge our clients like that." Dodd answered. "Whatever reasons they may have to seek us out we don't care to find out. We value privacy and discretion above all else."

"Well, if you say so." Brandy rested her elbow on the backrest. "So exactly what is it you want me to do?"

"Deliver packages, whenever we tell you to. You'll be a courier. In return you get a ninety percent, no wait, I'm sorry, eighty percent cut of what the clients offer us. There's an eighty dollar minimum per client, that is eighty dollars for you. So, a hundred dollar minimum, eighty of which you get. Yes. Some of these cases range up to a thousand dollars, though. Eight hundred bucks for one delivery, doesn't that sound swell?"

Brandy's interest grew as she heard the proposal.

"And how often do these deliveries occur? How many do I do in, like, one day?"

"Depends. Sometimes two or three per day."

"*Sometimes*? And then what about other times?"

"Other times, well, maybe four or five… yes?"

Brandy knew to remain a little reserved even if what she heard sounded tempting.

"So…" she queried. "Even on a slow day, or say a slow week, where every day I get only one client, and each of those only give me eighty, that leaves me at five hundred and sixty at the end of the week. And one hundred and forty for you, if you take twenty per client. And how big a crew do you have here? How many couriers do you have working for you?"

"I don't think I'm at liberty to say, I'm afraid."

"Rough estimate? Double digit? Twenty? Thirty?"

"Let's just say we have enough to get by, yes."

"So, if I were to take this job, and I assume you're actually offering this job, right? It's my call if I want it or not?"

"Yes. So far I've discovered no reason to reject you."

"Alright. So… if I were to take this job, how much would you estimate me earning this week alone?"

"I have absolutely no way of telling. You said yourself the least would be five… hundred and…"

"Sixty."

"Sixty, yes. And that's the very least."

"Well, it is already Thursday, so…"

"Yes, but still, very least. You should expect to have made possibly at least a thousand by Sunday."

"Well, that sounds pretty sweet, I have to admit."

"Yes, it is a very sweet profession, this. I wouldn't be working here if it wasn't."

Brandy leaned back with her finger twined in her lap.

"So, maybe I actually *will* do it." she said cautiously. "Yeah, you know what, I actually will take the job."

"Yes, yes." Dodd nodded. "Well, the trial job at least."

"The trial what?"

"The thing is, we give you your first courier gig, your first client, right away, and if you don't screw it up, we'll keep you on our payroll, or, well, we'll keep you employed. If you do screw up this first gig, you're terminated. Got it?"

"Well, yeah, or course, I don't expect you to let me fuck up constantly and still keep me around. I have *some* sense of responsibility, y'know."

"Oh, we'll be a bit more lenient on you afterwards, I mean, we have to tolerate a *few* errors from our employees. It's just that this first one will be a bit like a trial, and you just have to pull this one off perfectly, or we can't risk keeping you, if you understand."

"Well, I'm perfectly fine with that. You just tell me when my first gig will be. Tomorrow, maybe?"

"Tomorrow? No, no, no. Right now. We have a package that needs to be delivered at the Waterfront district at four PM sharp. You can do that, can't you?"

Brandy found herself a tad overwhelmed by this immediate imposition of work.

"Yeah, sure, alright, I s'pose. I can do that."

Dodd handed her a small neatly tied package the size of a lunch box.

"The southern end of Winchester Promenade, Waterfront district, outside the KFC, at four PM sharp. Not a second late, not a second early. You will see a middle-eastern looking man in a brown sweater and a Toucans cap. Quickly approach him, hand him the package, receive an envelope with four hundred bucks, then walk away. If you're even a minute late, he will leave, and don't try to follow him, he will refuse to talk to you after that. And as I said, don't just show up half an hour early, either. Don't draw attention to yourself. Our client might frown upon that kind of unprofessionalism and refuse to hire us again. Do you understand?"

Brandy received the package.

"Winchester Promenade, outside the KFC, four PM, yeah, I got it."

"Good. Here's your first half in advance." Dodd handed her four hundred dollar bills in a bundle, tied with a rubber string. "I presume you have a functioning and precise watch already, yes?"

"Holy hell, I get eight hundred for this? Sweet." Brandy said. "And yeah, yeah. I got a good watch. Trustworthy as fuck."

"Yes. Now, don't spend that money before the job is done. If you fail, we *will* come and take it back, you see."

That comment struck Brandy as a bit horrid, almost threatening, but she figured it best to ignore it.

"You have two hours. Should be plenty of time." Dodd added.

"Don't you worry, Mister Dodd." Brandy said and stood up, jokingly giving him a military salute. "I won't disappoint you."

"Good luck, love." Ermintrude said through a cloud of smoke before Brandy exited the office.

II

On the way to the Waterfront district, Brandy knew of a particularly pleasant tavern called Billy's Barricade, which served delicious food and played mellow, easily ignorable folk music on vinyl. Their prices were a bit stiffer than those of the O'Caiside, and Brandy had usually no other reason to roam the area, but every now and then, she would find herself nearby and could think of no reason to not come in for a refreshment.

She went inside with Tucker on her shoulder, because Billy's Barricade was also one of the good ones that did allow him entrance. She grabbed a pamphlet with the menu from the bar, and checked her watch to find she had an hour and a half until her scheduled delivery, and decided a light lunch would be in order. The bartender, a plump and jovial red-haired girl, took her order of one mojito, one glass of rosé wine, a bag of peanuts, and a bowl of lentil soup with cilantro, before Brandy found her seat at a booth near the entrance, where she whipped up 'The Undying Man' and, with her mojito in hand, commenced reading.

III

Brandy lay plenty of tip in the tip jar before leaving the bar. Once outside, she checked her watch again. Five minutes to four. That seemed about right. She strolled down to the harbor, where she glanced out at the ocean, as Tucker flew in circles above her and landed on the roof of a jewelry store. The designated KFC was a few hundred feet to her left. When she looked in its direction, she saw no man of the description given by Dodd, and hoped he was only a very precise man, and not one who had bailed or was lousy at keeping appointments.

'What if he's the one who's late?' she thought. He could have missed a bus, or the bus might have been late, or he was being stalled by the police. There were naturally numerous factors outside his control, and maybe he really was just a victim of circumstances and really could not help it if he was late. But then what? Should Brandy wait for him? Leave just as he would? She would then fail her job, but it would by no means be her fault. Could the company really blame her?

She checked her watch again. One minute to four. It was time to act. She walked over to the spot, trying to look as casual as possible. She was so naturally casual just a minute ago, yet now she struggled to be. She struggled to play herself from a minute ago. 'Acting is tough' she thought.

Right outside the KFC, not a single person fitting the given description was in sight. Brandy checked her watch, four PM exactly, and she felt her nerves acting up. Where was this man? Was he late? Had he synchronized his watch properly? Had Brandy synchronized her watch properly? She checked it again. Four PM exactly. She pulled up her cell phone, to see if it was off by anything.

Five PM, exactly. Her phone read Five PM.

"Hey, 'Scuse me." she asked an old man sat at a nearby bench. "Do you have the time?"

The man checked his own hand watch.

"Five o'clock, ma'am."

"You sure it's five?" she asked.

"Yeah, look for yourself. Five sharp."

Brandy looked directly at the old man's old watch, and saw that, indeed, it had its short hand placed directly above the V, and the long one above the XII.

"But I was supposed to meet someone here at four." she said.

"Well, you're definitely late for that." the man chuckled.

The reality dawned on her, that she had missed the scheduled meeting by a whole hour. Brandy buried her face in her palm and moaned loudly. Tucker, who had been spying on her from the rooftops since they first came to the waterfront, flew down and perched on her shoulder.

"Oh, Tucker, dear Tucker." said Brandy. "I think I just fucked up royally."

"Fucker." said Tucker.

IV

There would most definitely be no second chance, no point in even going back. Only thing that could happen was Brandy getting yelled at and having her four hundred bucks forfeited. Better stay low, she thought, keep the money, look for a job elsewhere, assume the threats of retrieving the money were hollow, merely chest inflation. Dodd seemed like the type of person who would try to intimidate people just to boost his own self-esteem. What army could he possibly possess? What means could he have for not only tracking Brandy down, but effectively force the cash out of her? Who could he hire to do that? He held office in a building so run-down he probably paid a negative amount in rent, and even then he seemed to only be able to employ vagrants and addicts and other societal outcasts, and Brandy.

She thought about it, and while the possibilities of a career in a shady courier service seemed to have evaporated, at least she was now four hundred dollars richer for absolutely no work. Not that she was much closer to pay for her surgery, but a profit it still was.

On her way home, Brandy took a detour to the O'Caiside, where she ordered a large margarita to soothe the embarrassing impact of her failure. She found her seat in her regular booth and held around her drink like it was the only heat source in a frozen wasteland. After a few intense slurps she felt more at ease, and reached into her satchel for her book, only then to pull out the package, which she at this point had almost forgotten about. She had certainly given the job and the company a good deal of thought on her way here, but the package at the center of all this seemed to have slipped her mind.

She started wondering what to do with this thing. Nobody wanted it anymore, or at least they could no longer accept it. She could give it to the police, but if its contents were not outright illegal, authorial knowledge of it was at least undesired. As Brandy lay the package on the table her curiosity for it grew rapidly. What could it contain? Who was it from? Who was it for? Given the need to involve the Helping Hand Company, it certainly must have been something interesting. As she made her way further down the margarita, Brandy's fingers started itching to tear it open.

Looking around the bar, she found no one watching her. Not even the unsettling suit-clad fellow with the lips, who was indeed still sitting on the same stool, intently reading his newspaper.

The best way to go about it, Brandy thought, was to be very discreet while also trying not to come off as trying to look discreet; to look like she was in the legal right and purpose to open this package, yet try not to call attention to it. No loud rips or tears.

66

There was however a slight hesitation. What, she thought, if it contained something highly incriminating, like narcotics? Or something outright dangerous, like a bomb or anthrax? In that case, she thought, she would at least die a news sensation, which is more than most could hope for, and at least the Malaysian parasite would be denied the satisfaction.

She slowly ripped off the paper, and lifted the lid of the white box within. The first thing to catch her sight inside was a smaller cream-colored box, long and slender, a third of the outer box' width. Within that one was a rainbow of macarons. Twelve delicious-looking macarons placed in a row, forming a gradient from blue to red to green. Underneath the macaron box was an envelope. Brandy pulled it out for inspection and saw it bore a red wax seal. She tore open the envelope and removed the letter inside. A letter written on a typewriter in what looked like a foreign language, in the Latin alphabet but full of unfamiliar letters and accents. The words resembled no language Brandy knew of, and after having feebly tried to read the first few sentences, she gave up.

She looked around a second time to double-check her seclusion, only to realize that the creepy lip-man was now staring at her, as he had done before. He could not possibly know what she was doing, she thought. He just liked to stare regardless. Had she sat there buck naked or snorting cocaine or eating roadkill, his staring face would still have been the same. She told herself this was the case as she looked further, and saw a separate letter in the same envelope. A hand-written letter, written in black ink with an elegant and disciplined calligraphy. It read:

> *Dear Glorious President, Eternal Guide to the Grand National*
> *Revolution of the Republic, Dzargonin Dzarban.*
>
> *It warms my heart that you have found interest in our project. Your*
> *contributions, financial and otherwise, will be greatly appreciated, and*
> *we welcome you to take part in the process at your own will. It was to*
> *my understanding the latest alterations of the mission statement that*
> *ignited your enthusiasm, and so I am glad the changes, in frankness*
> *brought on by necessity, have indeed not come to compromise the*
> *project's integrity, but rather had the opposite effect. I was truthfully in*
> *doubt, questioning whether my new plan might have become over-*

ambitious. Your support has truly re-enforced my confidence in the project. I hope to meet you in person in the future.

I do hope you do not take offense with the manner in which I address you, for as I must confess, I am not sufficiently acquainted with the social norms of your culture, and have little experience with addressing political leaders. I do also hope my assistant Mr. Wilkes has done an adequate job of translating this letter. For reference, accompanying this letter is the English original, as written by hand by yours truly.

Glory to the Republic and the Revolution

Sincerely,

And then followed a gratuitously extravagant and totally incomprehensible signature that covered the whole bottom quarter of the page.

Brandy sat there looking at the two letters in total confusion. She thought to eat one of the macarons, but they could easily have been poisoned for all she knew.

"Fucking hell. What do *you* make of this?" she asked Tucker.

"Fucker." said Tucker.

After having put everything back into the package, and put that in her satchel, Brandy figured it best to go home, and forget everything she had just seen, perhaps dispose of it for good measure. Burn it, maybe.

As she went past the bar on her outside, she noticed the creepy lip-man had left before her, yet left his newspaper behind, and his little cup of coffee completely full.

V

Back at the Manson Asylum, the janitor had been in the process of removing the 'beware the cock' graffiti in the reception, but decided at this point to call it a day. The graffiti now just read 'be the cock', which he considered more than satisfactory progress for today.

"How do you do, miss?" he said politely, wringing red liquid from his dirty cloth.

"Good, how are you?" Brandy responded with the same automatic politeness.

"Been better."

68

Brandy opened her mailbox to find it empty, not even a single ad inside.

"By the way, miss, somebody came by looking for ya."

"What?!" Brandy exclaimed as her face heated up.

"Yeah, some fella wondered what apartment you lived in. I told him the second floor somewhere. Go to the second floor, and follow the smell of bird poop, I told him."

"Dude, you can't just direct random strangers to my place. What if it's a serial killer or something?"

"Look, miss, it wouldn't have been a problem had ya cleaned up your bird's mess, like I told ya to. Now, this is all on you, lady, for your lack of hygienic maintenance. You gotta take some responsibility if ya want to rent an apartment, don't ya know. I know this ain't the Boston Hilton, but..."

"Look, listen!" Brandy interrupted him. "Did he say what he wanted?"

"Nah. Looked like a busy fella, though. Could've been from the IRS or something. Better hope it's nothing too serious."

Brandy rushed upstairs. Once she got there she looked around in both directions. Not a single person in sight. She slowly approached her own apartment door, trying to make each step as quiet as possible. Once she reached the door, she slowly withdrew her keys from her pocket, and slowly placed one inside the keyhole. She turned it around, slowly, making sure to not make a single sound.

"Fucker!" cawed Tucker.

"You goddamn..." Brandy exclaimed at too high a volume. "Be quiet, alright." she whispered. "We got a fucking stalker freak on our tail. He's probably roaming the complex right now, looking for us. Don't make a fucking sound, alright."

She unlocked the door quickly, and rushed inside so fast that Tucker slipped from her shoulder. He nonchalantly flew in after her, as she stressfully waved him inside and slammed the door shut behind him, and locked it. She then threw herself in the bed like a ragdoll. She lay there on her stomach, immobilized from mental exhaustion.

"What a fucking day, Tucker." she mumbled.

A man walked out from Brandy's bathroom, buckling his belt.

"Good evening, Miss Rabinow." he said, sitting down on one of the apartment's two chairs.

Brandy jumped up in bed and screamed, a high-pitched childlike shriek, as she saw the person now sharing her space. He was the creepy lip-man from the O'Caiside, and he now sat in her chair with his legs crossed and his hideous lips forming a smug smile.

"Don't be hysterical, miss. It would serve you well to keep quiet, and listen when I speak." he said.

Brandy crawled to the back of her bed, up against the wall, not for a femtosecond averting her eyes from the man, or even blinking.

"What the fuck are you doing in my crib?!" she yelled at him.

"As I said, it would serve you well to keep quiet." the man said and pulled a small handgun out from his inner suit pocket.

"Oh fucking shit." Brandy gasped.

"Now, let us go through a few ground rules, shall we?" the man said. "If you try to reach for the door, or the window, I will shoot you. If you try to reach for your cell phone, I'll shoot you. If you make any sudden or broad movements, I'll shoot you. If you scream again or make any loud obnoxious noises, I will definitely shoot you. I may not shoot to kill, but I cannot guarantee I won't. And of course, you know as well as I that the sound of a gunshot won't alert anyone in this complex. There are bullet holes next to the soda machine here, for Christ's sake. Now, do you understand?"

Brandy nodded slowly.

"You are free to speak of course, provided you don't interrupt me." the man stretched his free arm and scratched his nose. "Now, I suppose you know why I'm here." he continued.

"Yeah." Brandy said in a defeated tone. "You're from the Helping Hand Company."

"What?"

The man's grin turned to a disgusted frown.

"No. Heavens, no." he said, seeming to have taken genuine offense by the notion. "Do I look like I work for those buffoons? Well yes, I'm not wearing my best suit today, and it has been a while since I had it cleaned, but I… never mind, I certainly do not work for the Helping Hand Company. They were hired against my opinion. It was Roland, that lousy nigger, who insisted we use them as our dark net for long-distance communication. I didn't trust them myself, and today my presumptions turned out to be correct."

"I'm not really sure what you're talking about here, man." Brandy said, still unable to exhale. "Were you one of their clients or something?"

"Yes. I was. We were. I and the ones I represent. And I probably should introduce myself. My name is Mister Wilkes, and I represent the... well, it doesn't matter. What matters is that you, *you*, were the one who failed us. All we needed was someone to deliver a package on time, but because the Helping Hand Company, God how I hate that name, are run by Neanderthals, we got the drunken little floozy I'm conversing with right now. That is you, by the way. You're the drunken floozy who ruined everything. Not only have you set the project back several days, not only do we risk having upset President Dzarban and thereby having lost crucial funding and resources, but now we also have an inconvenient witness on our hands."

"Look, Mister Wilkes, sir. I know I fucked up, you have the right to be upset, y'know, but I, well, I did read the letters, but tell ya the truth, I didn't understand any of it. I don't know the context. If there was anything incriminating in there, I wouldn't know, I just wouldn't. You have nothing to be afraid of when it comes to me, alright."

"Oh, you know enough. You may not understand the context, true, but you certainly know enough to witness in court, should the day ever come. Of course, your testimony probably won't be the nail in the coffin, but I've been in this business long enough to know not to let loose threads simply hang."

"So, you're gonna snuff me? Is that it?"

"What, kill you, you mean?"

"Yeah."

"Oh no, no, no, no, no. Not necessarily. Not if you behave, like a nice little lady, and co-operate. Personally, I dislike killing people on the job. Sometimes, of course, I don't have a choice, you understand, but generally corpses only complicate matters further, and I just abhor it when matters get unnecessarily complicated."

Brandy tried to gather her thoughts and remain level-headed, fighting the desire to scream and run and generally have a manic breakdown.

"So, what do I do?" she asked.

71

"Not much, for now. In fact, until further notice, I want you to do exactly nothing. You will not tell anyone about the package. You will not tell anyone about the, ugh, the Helping Hand Company. You will not tell anyone about me, or this encounter, or anything I've told you. If anyone asks you about any of this, you deny everything, and admit nothing. Furthermore, you will work for us. Now, I can't say if you're useful for anything, actually all evidence so far points to the contrary, but if I should one day decide I need you for something, you will do it, and you will do it for free and without protest. Until then, I want you to stay in town. You're not permitted to leave Riverside until I say so. Should you ever defy these instructions, I won't hesitate to hurt you, kill you, make you a pretty little corpse. Do you understand?"

Brandy nodded sheepishly.

"That's good. It's good to deal with polite and co-operative people. In my business I've often had to deal with some horribly rude little brats."

Wilkes stood up, and walked over to the exit.

"Well, maybe we'll one day meet again."

He unlocked the door, and left, gently closing the door behind him.

Brandy sat still in bed for a while, like frozen fast. For up to a minute she did not even breathe. Upon finally moving, gently climbing down to the floor, she felt her legs shake uncontrollably, as did her hands. Tucker flew down and perched on her shoulder as she opened the fridge to grab a warm can of beer. She struggled with pulling the tab of the can from the severe shaking. Tucker endearingly nibbled at her ear. Once the can finally opened, she chugged down half its contents, indifferent to its temperature, as the tears streamed down her cheeks, and she then crouched into a ball on the floor.

CHAPTER SEVEN

The upcoming culinary convention at the Thomas Jefferson Plaza Hotel and Conference Center had ever since Olive received her invitation tied her nerves in a knot from the immense anticipation. The whole day before the event had she spent figuring out how to dress for the occasion, being uncertain of whether business formal or celebratory formal would be the most appropriate. Contacting Michelin about the details, in regards to dress code or anything else, had yielded no reply, so she decided intuitively on a business formal outfit, figuring the two PM timeframe implied that to be the most appropriate. Her obsession with perfecting her appearance had made it necessary to spend breakfast, brunch, and lunch all in front of the mirror, working meticulously on her hair and make-up while Roland put on her clothes. Her bangs pointed forwards like hooked knives from her shiny Eloise cut after the applied whole can of hairspray had settled, and when finally satisfied with her eyeshades, she proceeded to smear skin lotion over her double chin to make it as smooth and silky as possible.

Roland strategized how to go about buttoning her Italian silk blazer, considering whether he should begin at the bottom or the middle, and whether it would matter if all the buttons were done, and also whether the tailor had made faulty measurements, or if indeed, as he suspected, Olive had grown the past month after it was made, for properly applying the blazer proved almost as challenging as the pants.

"Does it matter if the blazer is completely closed?" he asked Olive.
"It depends. I think you'll have to decide, honestly, how does it look from your perspective? What is the most aesthetically pleasing approach, do you think?"
"As a matter of fact, I think you would be the most aesthetically pleasing were you to be at your most comfortable. But of course, it is your call, lady Olive."

"Why, if you think I could be both the most comfortable *and* presentable at the same time, I certainly wouldn't mind shooting two birds with one gun."

"Then I believe only doing the one middle button would be the least restrictive to your ventilation and circulation."

"That won't look too casual, will it? I need to appear as serious as possible, you know. They must get the impression that I'm quite sincere about this."

"Could you please try to suck in your stomach while I do this?"

Olive obliged as Roland pulled each side of her jacket together, forcing the button through the hole.

"Do you feel well, lady Olive?" he asked.

"It's a bit tight." Olive said short on breath.

"Yes, I do suspect the tailor may have committed a few errors in his work."

"I suppose things like that happen from time to time. How do I look from the neck down?"

Roland rolled two full length mirror side by side, and distanced them far enough away from Olive to display the full width of her figure.

"See for yourself, my lady."

Olive looked upon the reflection of her entire body for the first time in over a year, and what met her was again the somber reality of her tremendous girth. She took special notice of her mastodon legs, which she had rarely before given any thought, now in direct eyesight, gigantic hams shaped in waves of blubber.

"What do you think?" asked Roland.

"This is who I am, I suppose." Olive said.

"What do you mean?"

"I mean, well, the suit is magnificent, Roland. Simply exquisite. Mistakes or not, I think the tailor did a fantastic job."

"Shall I fetch the black lacquer shoes, then? They would make a splendid fit, in my humble opinion."

"Yes. Yes, those'll work."

II

"Are you sure you don't want to walk the distance to the limousine?" asked Roland, pushing Olive in her wheelchair through the foyer. "The exercise would be quite good for your health."

"I need to save my energy, Roland." Olive answered. "I can't read out my official statement if I'm all sweaty and out of breath. Besides, we're a bit short on time now."

"Ah, yes. We're expected in forty minutes."

"Do I have time to say goodbye to my parents, do you think?"

"Your father is out playing golf again, I'm afraid. And I wouldn't dare disturb your mother at this hour. She is very busy with her writing."

"Still? She spent all yesterday writing too."

"It's a demanding process, I would imagine. Especially when it comes to one's memoirs. So many agonizing memories to reproduce in print."

They stopped at the pick-up point in the parkway.

"I just hope my statement is persuasive enough." Olive said.

"Are you not confident in its contents?"

"I'm a bit nervous. I hope I don't muck it up and say something wrong, or mumble or stutter too much. I've rehearsed every day since we finalized the last draft, and even before that."

"I am certain you will do a terrific job, provided you don't let your nerves get the best of you."

"Maybe I should do some final rehearsal on the ride over, just to be safe."

Olive withdrew the paper with her statement on from her purse, and read anxiously through the first paragraph.

"I hope it's not too short."

"It is just as long as it needs to be." Roland said vacantly on his way to the garage.

III

Olive shut the curtains on the limousine windows on both sides, to block the searing blinding sun from her face.

"It's really hot today, Roland. Maybe I shouldn't have worn so much dark."

"Do you mean to say you intend to change, lady Olive."

75

"Oh no, there's no time for that. Besides, the event will probably be mostly inside, I hope."

Olive folded her statement back into her purse.

"I think I know it by heart now. Ideally I should know it so well I could make it seem improvised. I don't think I'm quite *there* yet, but I hope I still come off as natural enough as is."

"You always sound natural, dear. There is no reason to be so self-conscious."

A minor moment of silence commenced, as Olive let her thoughts freely wander, through fantasies of what foods would be served at the convention. No dinner or other organized meals had been specifically declared in the invitation, but surely some sorts of delicacies would be served, given the event's theme. Perhaps there would be some delicious appetizers upon entry. Rolling into the convention in her wheelchair, presented with trays upon trays of exotic delicacies for her to gorge on along with the top executives of the Michelin guide. They stand around with their wine glasses, chatting, chortling, humoring Olive while she speaks on Riverside's behalf. No. Not humoring. They take her seriously, do they not? They are so tall, and they look down upon her, sat in her wheelchair, floating all over the room. Making her statement, sat down in that wheelchair, gorging on food. Caviar, ostrich liver, sea urchin, filets of antelope, chowing it all down while they look at her, humoring her, judging her, chortling, guffawing, rolling their eyes at the big fat freak. The big fat freak so fat she needs a wheelchair. Cannot stand by her own power.

"Roland, I think I will be going in there without my wheelchair." Olive said.

"You will enter on your own legs?"

"Yes, I just... I must look dignified."

"Why, my lady, Olive, my dear. You do indeed not under any circumstance look undignified. Never. Please do not entertain such ill thoughts in regards to your own worth, my dear, lady Olive. It's simply pure toxicity of the mind for you to have such ideas of yourself as being able to appear undignified in a public setting. I mean, certainly dressing appropriately is to be expected, but..."

"It's like, well..." Olive interrupted. "I think I should stand tall for this occasion. I should stand tall and proud in front of these people and show them, like, a sense of authority, you understand."

Roland gave the idea some seconds to process.

"Why, yes. You are absolutely right. This'll make the whole stratagem easier, in fact. I mean, yes, yes, it makes sense. You should indeed stand tall. It will make you look more authoritarian, and it'll be good for your health too. Just be sure to bring your cane, lady Olive. We'd want to avert any accident, do we not?"

Another moment of silence followed. Olive began to worriedly consider the prospect of there being served no food at all.

"Oowh!" exclaimed Roland. "Do you hear that noise?"

"What noise?"

"From the car, my lady. It's making a worrisome noise."

"I don't really hear anything abnormal."

"Well, pardon me for saying so, my lady, but it might not be easy to hear if you don't have an extensive understanding of the mechanics of automobiles. I, however, have the experience to recognize the nuances of a car engine's sounds. And the sounds our limousine makes right now are quite problematic."

"How so?"

"You see, normally an average engine emits a noise in D minor or D major. That is a fact. This noise, however, is clearly in a C major. And a C major noise usually signals a need for acute treatment, preferably by a legit professional."

"Does that mean we have to stop by a repair shop now?"

"No, we should easily make it to the Thomas Jefferson Plaza Hotel and Conference Center, it is by no means *that* serious. But after I drop you off, I should probably attend a mechanic for consultancy on the matter. That is, of course, if you feel able to attend this event by yourself."

"Yes." said Olive insistently. "I will be fine."

She brushed aside the bottom of one curtain with her finger to peek outside, where she saw streets and buildings of no particular recognition.

"How far are we now?" she asked.

"We'll soon be there, lady Olive. The Thomas Jefferson Plaza Hotel and Conference Center lies within a tricky labyrinth of street corners, you see. I do, however, believe I know the way quite well."

"Do you think they'll be serving food there?"

"Well, it is the Michelin conference, my lady. It would be almost absurd if they did not."

"Oh, they just got to. I'm starting to feel a little rumbling right now. I don't think I could wait all the way until dinner at home. That'd just kill me. Are we nearing now?"

"Just around the corner, my dear. Only a couple more turns now."

Soon they did arrive at the Thomas Jefferson Plaza Hotel and Conference Center.

"I don't think I've ever been at the Thomas Jefferson Plaza Hotel and Conference Center before." said Olive.

"I believe you once made a brief visit back in your childhood, lady Olive. When you were very young."

Olive inhaled deeply.

"Alright. It's time." she said.

After Roland had assisted Olive out of the car, she stood tall and proud in front of the steps to the Thomas Jefferson Plaza Hotel and Conference Center. There were six steps in front of her leading up to the automated glass doors, but the wheelchair route, which she was still forced to use, curved in a long slope, making up a total of at least thirty feet to walk. Olive clenched her hand tightly around the hare head of her cane. She took several deep breaths, accumulating mental strength, before she finally paced up the long track to the entrance, one draining step at a time.

"If you feel you won't require further assistance, I believe I shall get the limousine checked now." Roland said.

"I can do, ugh, I can do this." Olive huffed. "You can... You're free to leave, Roland."

And Roland drove away. Olive kept moving forwards.

She waddled into the reception, and sat in the nearest leather sofa to regain some stamina. The receptionist, tapping away at her computer from behind the desk, noticed the sweaty wheezing gargantuan spread across the three-person taupe couch, and promptly ceased from her current work.

"Excuse me?" she asked Olive. "Can I help you?"

Olive emitted a breathless unintelligibly mumbling reply, so the receptionist decided to walk over to her for a better listen.

"What was it you said you wanted?" she asked Olive, now up close.

"I... hold on, let me... let me catch my breath."

The receptionist waited patiently while Olive filled her lungs and wiped her face dry.

"So what can I help you with? Have you booked a room?"

"No. I am here for the Michelin Convention. I'm expected."

"The 'Michelin Convention'?" asked the receptionist. "Are you sure you're at the right place?"

"Isn't this the…" Olive lost her breath again. "… The Thomas Jefferson Plaza Hotel and Conference Center?"

"Yes, this is the Thomas Jefferson Plaza Hotel and Conference Center, but I haven't been informed of a, uh, Michelin convention happening today."

"I have an invitation. I have it right here." Olive wheezed and withdrew her enveloped invitation from her purse, and handed it to the receptionist.

"I'll go check on the computer." she said.

A long time passed. Olive's nerves began to act up again. Had she made a mistake? Had she gotten the date wrong? Was there another Thomas Jefferson Plaza Hotel and Conference Center in town? Had there been a mistake on their part? Had the people at Michelin given her incorrect information? What exactly was going on?

After a few minutes of frenetic searching, the receptionist came back.

"I'm sorry, I could not find a records of a 'Michelin convention' taking place at the Thomas Jefferson Plaza Hotel and Conference Center." she said. "Or any other venue in town, for that matter. Are you sure you got the date right?"

"I… I'm sorry, did you not see the date on the invitation?" Olive asked. "It says 'May the twelfth, doesn't it?"

"Well, yes, it does, but are you perfectly sure this invitation is legit?"

"Legit? Of course it's legit. How could it not be? It's from the Michelin company."

"Well, yes, I did check up on that. When I googled the contact information, all I got was a deceased golf player and the address of the MAD Magazine editorial."

"So, there is… you don't believe they may be using a pseudonym, maybe? For the sake of privacy, or secrecy? Like father does. He does that all the time when arranging meetings. Isn't that a possibility?"

"Look, I'm very sorry. There is just no proof that the convention you're looking for actually even exists. At all."

79

"At all?"

"At all."

"So, there is just no such convention of this kind, within city limits? At all?"

"No. I couldn't find any evidence or even hint of such an event. Not anywhere, especially not in Riverside."

And then the walls of the quite spacious reception morphed into a tight hot oven around Olive, her heart ascending up her throat as the borders of the boiling breadbox around her shrunk by the second, drawing closer into her extremities, searing and poaching her flesh. Everything closed in, everything became tight. Air ceased to be.

"Ma'am, are you alright?" the receptionist asked.

Olive hyperventilated, little tears mixing in with the hundreds of pearls of sweat gliding down her face. Her sight blackened. This made no sense, it did not fall into place. Nothing fell into place, it all fell apart. Once, many years ago, when she was ten, her cousin had fooled her into stealing a Mars bar from a supermarket, telling her it was free. The feeling when she got caught now rushed back into her carotid arteries, only amplified by a million.

"Ma'am! Do you need any help?"

"I… I need to…"

Olive reached into her purse for her cell phone, but after frenetically scavenging around its content, could not find said phone.

"Ma'am? What is the matter?"

"I think I… it seems like… Seems I have forgotten my cell phone. Could I borrow the phone here?"

"Well, yes, of course you can."

The receptionist went back to her desk.

"Should I come over there?" asked Olive.

"No, no. Just stay there, dear. We have a wireless phone over here."

She soon came back with the aforementioned wireless phone.

"Is there a private number you want to call?"

"Yes. Private."

Olive grabbed the phone and dialed Roland's cell phone number. After a few minutes of ringing there was no response.

80

"He must be busy." mumbled Olive, and dialed her father's number.

Still no response after another two minutes of ringing. Olive sighed and finally dialed the number of her mother, Theodora D'Orleans. The phone rang for one minute and fifty eight seconds.

"What?!" said an irritated voice on the other side of the line.

"Hey, mother." Olive said. "How are you doing?"

"What's this? Don't be calling me when I'm not here!" replied Theodora. "What's this... if you've gotten yourself into something bad, I want no part in it. I'm busy, you understand. Busy."

"Look, I know you're busy, but... I'm sorry to say it, but I think there's been a bit of a mistake in my schedule."

"Yeah, I made many mistakes up in my schedule too, sweetie. Made many mistakes in my life. In fact, tell you the truth, right now..."

"Mother, could you please listen. I know I'm not supposed to interrupt you during your writing sessions. I never do. Never have done since I was a toddler. It's just that Roland has left me here, and it seems I've made a mistake in my schedule, and I'd very much like to get home."

"What, Roland? That dirty old negro. I knew we couldn't trust him. I even said that, the day they hired him, I said to your father, I said 'we can't trust that old negro', I said."

"Look, don't blame Roland. It wasn't his fault. It's just that things got mixed up. I just want a ride home. Could you try to arrange a ride home, somehow? Get one of the gardeners or someone to come in the other limo? Or even the van? I don't mind the van, they can pick me up in the van."

"You know, sweetie, speak to your father about this, okay."

And then Theodora hung up.

"Did it go well?" asked the receptionist.

"I... I think I need to go." Olive said. "Could you help me up?"

"Of course."

The receptionist and Olive grabbed hands.

"How do I do this? Do I pull you towards me, or...?"

"Just pull straight backwards."

She did as instructed, and pulled Olive with all her might.

"Wait, no. I'm not ready. I need to prepare my legs."

They tried again, and this time, after a bit of struggle, they managed to get Olive up on her feet.

"Is there anything else I can help you with?" the receptionist asked, handing Olive her cane.

But Olive just waddled off without a response, hastily leaving the building deep in chaotic thoughts.

IV

Olive's headspace was become a rupturing hive full of cruel prospects gnawing at her skull from within, and flooded by a boiling stew of agonizing emotions. She had taken rest at a marble bench right outside the Thomas Jefferson Plaza Hotel and Conference Center, but the demanding activity in her mind made her unable to lower her heart rate.

Where did her phone go, she wondered. How could she possibly have forgotten it? She always kept it safely in her purse, only taking it out for rare brief usages, always to put it back in. Could she have accidentally slipped it out while searching for something else? Should she not have heard or seen it fall out? Had it perhaps been stolen? Pickpocketed? When? By whom?

And how would she get home? No taxi or bus could fit her, for she knew her proportions required unique vehicular interiors, although an empty van could also work in a case of emergency. This was very much an emergency.

Mentally fatigued, she began to feel a fit of nausea creeping up her intestines, as her vision momentarily blackened for a second. She had become quite dizzy. The sun seared in her face. Could a heatstroke be imminent? What was that, was that a sudden numbness in her left arm? Or was it in the right arm that was supposed to happen? Was she entering a heart attack? Her doctor had warned her numerous times to avoid stress due to her blood pressure. The stress. She was indeed in a heap of stress right now. Stress, distress, tristesse, her heart rate would not settle, her sweating would not cease, her fingers would not quieten. Was this it? Would the infarction hurt? Would she feel it? Would anyone see her and call an ambulance? Any second she would lose all control now. Any second. Any second.

"Don't stare at her, dear, it's rude." said a mother to her little son as they passed Olive by.

"And if you keep eating candy before dinner, you'll end up like that too. Do you want that? No?" she continued, believing to have left Olive's ear's reach.

V

The quarter of an hour had gone by, and Olive was still conscious and breathing. Her heart had shown her mercy for now. Her nausea had also faded, but in its place came an aggressive hunger. It was almost like an old friend had returned. Soon, her need to get home had to fight for attention with her need for food, and deciding which one was the immediately most important proved quite onerous.

Another person walked by. A tall lanky man in a hoodie carrying a backpack and holding a Wendy's bag in his hand.

"Excuse me? 'Scuse me?"

"What?!" said the man irritatedly.

"Do you have a cell phone I could borrow?"

"It's out of power."

"It's just that I think I need to order a van."

"Whaddya need a van for? To ship your fat ass out of town?"

"No. Not that far."

"Fuck off." the man walked away.

"Well, could I... um, hello? Hey?!"

"What?!"

"Could I maybe have one of your burgers? That bag of yours looks pretty full, and I'm very hungry right now."

The man walked back to her, and in lieu of a verbal response, spat a solid yellow lump of phlegm right in her face.

"Fucking fatass bitch." he mumbled to himself walking away.

Olive took out a Kleenex tissue from her purse and wiped away the slime. Not wanting to hold on to it, not tolerating to hold on to it, and seeing no nearby garbage disposal unit, she flung the tissue into the road as if it had electrocuted her, cringing at its existence. Then, as she watched the disgusting little tissue float away with the breeze, her lips began to quiver, and she soon started weeping violently into her hands.

VI

Many hours had passed. The insufferable heat had forced Olive to remove her blazer, which by itself was a small project demanding around thirty minutes of labor and strategy. The sensation of hunger had become so horrendously anguishing it was making her sick, as the whole surface of her belly vibrated at a constant, roaring furiously for nourishments. She could not recall feeling this famished since that one week eight years ago…

Any moment she expected Roland to return, to wait outside for the intended convention to finish. They had not specified a closing hour, but she presumed he would have returned as soon as possible, to stand guard, as he always did.

But he did not come. Nobody came. It had been so long, so many hours. Olive wondered, what if she just tried to walk? Only a short distance, or as long as her legs could endure. There would at least be a bit of progress, a change, something other than sitting still on this one bench. Best case, she thought, she would find a way home, or at least a way to a way home. Worst case, her heart would finally do her in, which at this point, she felt, would at least be preferable to waiting in vain, starving, slowly decaying. Action always prevails inaction, she thought.

It had been well over a year since she last erected herself by her own power. There was no certainty that she could pull it off anymore, for her ample physique had only grown since then, quite significantly in fact, and her sedentary lifestyle had only had the effect of deteriorating her muscles even further, rendering her even more inert. She tried to pull herself up by her cane, but to no avail. Many people had walked by since she first got the idea to walk, but due to her last encounter, she had now lost the courage to call any of them to her attention. Shuffling out to the edge of the bench, she tried to remember how she stood up at a younger age. She leaned her torso forwards, rested her hands on her thighs, let her stomach sag between them, pulled as hard as she could, trying to unseal her rump from the seat. It took about a minute of numerous failed attempts before she finally managed to lift herself up to a standing position.

84

She grabbed tightly around her cane and started waddling down the sidewalk, not knowing where to. Soon something would reveal itself, she thought, something or someone that could help her reach home. Already after crossing half the width of the Thomas Jefferson Plaza Hotel and Conference Center, did she feel unbearably exhausted. 'Can't quit now' she thought. 'Just keep moving until you find something'.

There was a small amount of adrenaline surging through her brain from her ability to stand up by herself.

Maybe, she thought, she could achieve even more, if only she could continue to ignore the pleas for rest screamed by every muscle in her body. As she kept waddling, her vision kept blackening for brief instances, but she no longer cared.

It came to the point that her body just out right ceased to move. Once she had passed the Thomas Jefferson Plaza Hotel and Conference Center building, she stopped in her tracks, not out of her own will, but because her muscles had collapsed from the pressure. They simply would nor could not abide her commands. She stiffened, into a statue. Her legs hurt so horribly she just wanted to sit down on the sidewalk, but refrained, only for awareness of her inability to get back up.

She relieved as much of her weight onto the can as it could take, when she spotted a familiar-looking vehicle approaching from the distance. Olive grew happier by each foot the car drove towards her, for she increasingly recognized it as her own limousine. She even recognized Roland's face from behind the shaded windshield.

The limousine parked besides her, but Roland did not emerge. Instead the door to her seat opened from within, and out came her father, Reginald Lazarus D'Orleans.

"Father!" she yelled. "Oh father, it's you. You've come to rescue me!"
"Are you joking?" Reginald asked, perplexed and frustrated. "This is as far as you've gotten?"
"I told you..." Roland said. "... I told you our search would not be particularly complicated, Master D'Orleans."
"Father, I've been so afraid." Olive squeezed through her limited breath.
"Jesus Christ, this is even worse than I thought." Reginald rubbed his temples with his one hand.
"Father, could you help me get inside?" Olive wheezed. "I can't stand for much longer."
"Fetch the wheelchair, Roland." Reginald moaned.

"I've been terrified, father."

"Oh, hell, suck it up, Olive. This is as far as you've gotten? How long did it take you to walk this far? Eight hours? Unbelievable."

After the long ordeal of moving Olive into her car seat, Reginald sat down opposite her, staring ominously.

"Have you been crying?" he asked her.

Olive wiped trails of mascara off her cheeks.

"Yes. It was awful. I was all alone."

"Your were on your own for less than four hours and you started to cry?"

"There was this really mean man who spat on me, father."

"Oh, really? You cried because of *that*? What are you, six years old? I leave you here for an afternoon, and you start bawling because of *one* mean little guy? You encountered *one* mean person, and *that* made you cry?"

"But why would someone be that mean to me?" Olive started tearing up again.

Reginald looked at her confoundedly.

"I suppose it was at least worth a shot." he said. "Don't you think so, Roland?"

"Everything is always worth at least one shot, master D'Orleans."

Olive wiped her wet eyes with her handkerchief.

"Oh, stop being such a toddler, Olive." Reginald barked.

VII

The grand parlor of the D'Orleans mansion was quite an expansive and spacious one, if not the most welcoming. It had for ages been insufficiently lit by a few candelabras and smaller individual candles. During the colder days of the winter they would often fire up the room's enormous fireplace, which helped enormously with the light, but the rest of the year it was a big cold damp dark void, sparsely furnished and decorated only with paintings of dead relatives recent and ancient, some painted just by guesswork.

It was Reginald and Theodora's favorite room to spend time together, any time, drinking their options from the diverse liquor cabinet, drifting into their own thoughts, occasionally speaking to each other for brief moments. They now each sat in their own quarter of the vaguely swastika-shaped confidante, both sipping from glasses of Leyrat, him staring into the empty void of the fireplace, her into the tall portrait of her deceased father-in-law Hieronymus Lyndsey D'Orleans hung above the mahogany commode.

The door opened. The light from the hallway created a bridge of illumination up to the confidante, upon which rolled a wide wheelchair. Olive D'Orleans, now attired in more casual garments, was being rolled in by Roland, her face bearing a disgruntled frown, a sight so rare it made her mother cough up her latest swig of cognac.

"Something the matter, sweetie?" Theodora said to Olive as Roland parked the daughter in front of her. "Are you still sad because of the conference?"

"The *convention*." Olive said with clenched teeth.

"Yes, the convention, right. You're still bitter because of that?"

Roland fetched a glass of Southern Comfort for Olive without being asked.

"Mother, why didn't you come pick me up, when I asked you to?"

"Sweetie, you knew I was busy."

"You could have sent someone. Were *everybody* busy? The gardeners? The maids? They all had something more important to do than to save me?"

" Oh, now, come on. You're overreacting, sweetie."

"I am not!"

"For Christ's sake, Olive!" barked Reginald.

He stood up and sat himself in the confidante quarter left of Theodora's to better face Olive.

"That was not even half a day, and you started crying like a baby. And you barely walked ten feet. One and a half basketball players, that's how long you managed to walk before nearly collapsing."

"I cried because I didn't know I would survive!"

"You're absolutely pathetic, Olive. We officially failed as parents. We raised our only daughter into an immobile blob with not even the slightest sense of independence."

"Mother, don't let him say those things to me!" Olive sobbed.

"He's right, sweetie." Theodora said through another swig. "I'll be perfectly frank, we've certainly fed you up fat. We could've said 'a job well done' if you were a turkey or a pig, ready to be slaughtered for Christmas. But you're not, so all we can say is 'a job well *fucked* up'. And I'm not going to be gentle, sweetie, you really are a grade-A circus freak, that's how fat you are."

87

Olive stared at her parents in repulsed awe as her face moistened up with tears.

"Honestly, we've been way too soft on you." Theodora continued. "We really shouldn't have given up after the Closet endeavor."

Olive slammed her glass of liqueur into the floor, where it broke into a few dozen pieces. Her face shifted to one of wrathful contempt.

"Retract that." she growled through her teeth.

"There's no reason to be angry, sweetie. Even less so to break property." Theodora responded.

"*RETRACT IT*!" Olive roared. "Roland! Make her retract the… make her retract the 'closet' statement!"

"I am sorry, lady Olive, but it is not my place to take sides in family quarrels."

Reginald sighed, and looked up at the ceiling.

"I was being too optimistic." he said sipping some more cognac. "I thought this little plot would teach you some freedom and independence."

"Those were the values our nation was founded on, sweetie." said Theodora. "Not gluttony and sloth."

"I thought you'd learn to become a bit more self-reliant, but no. Of course not. This project was an absolute failure."

"What are you talking about?" asked Olive, still fairly furious. "What project?"

"Oh heavens, you haven't even figured *that* out yet?" Reginald slapped his forehead. "Are you genuinely retarded? Do you honestly still think there's a Michelin convention in town? Do you expect that to still happen one day?"

"What are you saying?"

"Michelin hasn't even released a guide for Boston. Do you think they'd jump straight to Riverside? You think if they even did that, they'd contact *you* about it?"

"You tricked me? You *tricked* me?!"

"Of course I did. I knew you wouldn't go out on such a fantastic 'adventure' like that voluntarily. Granted, I probably put too much effort into it, given how unbelievably gullible you're turning out to be."

The tears kept flowing down Olive's face, but now she felt nothing. Her being had become a hollow shell.

"Roland…" she said in a fatigued monotone. "I want to return to my private quarters."

"As you wish, lady Olive."

And so Roland began rolling Olive out again.

"And have my dinner delivered there, as well. I will be dining alone tonight."

CHAPTER EIGHT

Another lecture completed, Imogen Olson strolled through the campus of Collin College, on her way to the Barnstable & Kearny bookstore a few miles away, as she had previously neglected to purchase a book elementary to her upcoming exam, which was now only available at that particular store. She had never liked the bus, and since the weather was so uncharacteristically warm and bright on this November Tuesday, she figured she would take a walk through the park.

It was the vast Glengarry Park, connecting Collin College to Mapplethorpe Road and Grant Alley, it leading to Columbia Square where Barnstable & Kearney was. The park was more than two miles across, and the roads within were all curved and bent in order to maximize the amount of scenery being seen by the average passer-through. This was admittedly a quite idyllic park, with wooden white bridges crossing ponds full of lily pads, and the grass covered in a colorful array of flowers both local and exotic.

(While it was probably the prettiest public park in Riverside, it did lack the peacocks and the pelicans of the D'Orleans garden, meaning it was not quite *that* attractive.)

When she entered the park, the first thing to catch Imogen's eyes was one familiar character hung above the ledge of the nearest bridge. It was Brandy, scowling out a thousand miles, one hand full of gravel stones she threw into the pond with the other, one at a time, with her bird sitting by her side on the bridge fence, following each stone intently with his eyes.

"Hey Brandy, wait up!" Imogen yelled, even though Brandy was not moving.

She ran up to Brandy, who looked unfazed by her presence.

"What's going down, Brandy?" Imogen asked.

"Shit." Brandy said.

"What kinda shit?"

"Bad shit."

"Hey, how come I barely ever see you at campus, huh?"

"'Cos I'm not there?"

"Yeah, no kidding. I think I've seen you in, like, *one* lecture. Actually, yeah, I think that's it. You attended the very first lecture, and then nothing. Do you attend lectures in the other classes, then?"

"Nope."

"Okay, so you've just totally given up, then? Already? Like, not even gonna complete the first semester, then?"

"Dunno."

"Like, tell me you're at least gonna be here for the exams, right? You're gonna at least *try* with the exams?"

Brandy turned to Imogen, attaining eye contact. "You know what? I don't think I'm gonna even *be* here by the exams."

"What? You're gonna drop out?"

Brandy reverted to her previous position.

"You could say that, I s'pose."

"What, seriously? You're just gonna give up like, *that* easily?"

Brandy sighed deeply.

"Alright, look. It's kinda complicated, alright. The thing is, it's like, very soon one of two worms are gonna snuff me, either the one inside me or the one with a gun. And all I can do, the only thing I can fucking do is sit here, or there, or whatever, and fucking take it, 'cos fuck me, y'know."

"Okay, I don't understand what you're trying to get at here, like, at all."

"It's like, well… fuck it. Fucking forget it, alright."

"Hey Brandy, do you have like, problems with depression or something?"

"Fuck, I hope not."

"Because, look, if you do, there's nothing to be ashamed of or anything. Like, *all* people can have mental health issues, you know."

"Look girl, I got problems flying at me from the left, right, top and bottom. I don't need shit coming from inside as well. Well, technically it's already… fuck it, you know what I mean. Or you don't, I don't care. And yeah, I don't feel all that hot right now, like, emotionally, but I'm pretty sure what I feel right now is fucking appropriate for the situation."

"Okay, fine. Fine. I won't ask."

Imogen began to walk onwards.

"But, um…" she said and halted. "If you want to, we could go grab a bite. How's that sound? Try the new burrito place over on Mapplethorpe?"

Brandy sighed.

"Sure. Let's."

II

"Oh, hell. Eck." Imogen coughed. "They got my order all wrong. I asked for the mild sauce, and they gave me the hot one. The hottest, probably, the one with the goofy name."

"Yeah, you know a hot-sauce's serious business when it's got a goofy name." replied Brandy, munching on her burrito, while feeding sunflower seeds to Tucker, who was using her hair as a nest. "What was it called again? 'Ass Explosion' or something?"

"I think it was 'The Luchador's Judgment'." Imogen said.

"Y'know, they got my order wrong too, actually. I didn't ask for guac, 'cos it was like, two bucks extra, and I was like 'fuck that', not gonna pay two bucks for that, but I got it anyway. They gave me free guac, girl!"

They both sat on a bus stop on Mapplethorpe Road, only to sit outside and enjoy what they expected to the last somewhat warm day of the year.

"It's gotta be at least sixty degrees out here." Brandy mumbled through the last bit of burrito in her mouth. "Or maybe it's the sun that makes it feel like it."

"It is pretty hot for November, yeah."

Brandy wiped searing hot-sauce off her face, and slurped down on her coke. Imogen was still only halfway through her wrap.

"Seems like you just needed some food to lighten up, huh, Brandy?" she said.

That comment caused the ominous prospects of Brandy's likely imminent death, that she had spent the lunch burying in food and sociality, to resurface to her stream of thought.

"I s'pose." Brandy said stone-faced.

"Hey Brandy. Promise me you won't drop out, okay. I would love to see you next year, you know. Or at least we should finish this one together."

"I s'pose."

"If you need any help with the courses, if *that's* what the issue is, you know, I could totally help you out."

"I dunno."

"So hang in there, okay. We'll complete this semester, and then I'll see you in January. Deal?"

Brandy sighed. "Look, uh… You know what, I really could go for a drink right now. Wanna come?"

"What? It's like, not even two o'clock."

Brandy stood up.

"C'mon, a couple of mojitos will do us good." she said.

"You know, I actually need to be going. Got some books to get."

"Alright, suit yourself."

"You don't think you should maybe, like, cut back on your drinking? Like, whatever issues you have, you'll only make it worse by drinking all the time."

Brandy sniffed.

"Worse? I doubt there's much more worse to make it."

Then she promptly walked away without a goodbye, Tucker flying after.

Imogen sat still in worried confusion. She started wondering if Brandy was suicidal, and then how she would handle the funeral. Would it take place in Philadelphia? Would Imogen have to pay for the traveling expenses? Would she even be expected to show up? Was their relationship at an attend-each-other's-funerals stage yet?

III

Turning east at the south end of Mapplethorpe Road was Fincher Alley, with nothing of note expect a hair salon and the Doberman Bar. It was a run-down establishment in a

93

state of rapid decay, known for offering the cheapest drinks in town, as well as its air of tobacco and far developed alcoholism. Its regular clientele were decomposing zombie drunkards, livers like raisins and brains like walnuts, only barely capable of slurring out semi-audible orders for bourbon and beer from the nests of clothing and garbage they had made for themselves in the booths.

Brandy stepped inside a little hesitantly, being welcomed by a cloud of cigarette stench. Tucker perched on her shoulder, she went to the bar, where an old bearded man with a flapcap and sunshades stood behind the counter deeply invested in a game of solitaire.

"A mojito, please." Brandy said nervously.

"Wuh- what?" the bartender responded.

"Uh, a mojito. Please."

"Oh, oh, sure. Coming up."

The man filled up a pint of Budweiser from the bar's single tap, and handed it over, before resuming his attention to his cards.

Brandy shrugged, and went to find a decent booth. The place was quite crowded, but one booth in the far corner was still vacant. On her way there she bumped into a man who looked like a bloated Freddy Kruger with his nose surgically replaced by an overripe plum. He fell to the floor like a big sack of flour, and there he squirmed around for a while, utterly unable to get back up on his feet.

"I'm so sorry." Brandy said, putting her pint aside to help him up.

She grabbed both his cold hands, and pulled with all her strength. Another man, who looked none the healthier or more sober than the one on the floor, staggered over to help, pushing the man up from behind. Once they got the man up on his feet, he immediately tipped on top of Brandy, who, barely able to keep her standing against his weight, pushed him back, trying to find the right balance where he could stand still.

The man mumbled something unintelligible while clapping Brandy on the cheek, nearly poking out her eye. So intoxicated was he that it was impossible tell if he was angry or happy. He staggered a few feet away from her, where he unzipped his pants and began urinating up against the wall. Nobody reacted, not even the bartender.

Brandy found her place in the booth, where she dipped her face in the beer in an attempt to block out the foul odor of urine that was mixing with the smoke in the room.

94

After a long hefty swig, she put down the glass and pulled out 'The Undying Man' from her pocket, only to discover the bookmark had gone missing. Though she did remember where she last left off, the bookmark itself was a mildly treasured novelty she would have liked to add to her still non-existent scrapbook, that she considered starting just because of it alone. 'Oh well' she thought.

She turned to the page where she last left off, but upon reading her first sentence she nearly spat out her second swig of beer at Mister Wilkes, who had suddenly sat down opposite her.

"Lovely locale you've found for us." he said.

Brandy's heartrate skyrocketed upon the sight of him, and her legs grew numb and shaky, losing their ability to carry her despite her sitting down, somehow.

"What are you doing here?" she asked stutteringly. "What do you want?"

"You thought you could evade me by simply not going to the O'Caiside?"

"I thought I wouldn't have to look at your ugly mug all day, yeah." Brandy immediately regretted saying.

"Watch that tone now, young lady."

Brandy tried to internally calm herself down, to avoid a full out panic attack. 'Be cool' she thought. 'Don't let this dude see you're afraid, be strong, come on, be strong, be aggressive, show him you're not afraid'.

"Look, can I just ask something?" she managed to get out of herself. "Why were you spying on me even before I got that job at the... what was it called again, that company?"

Mister Wilkes groaned with his big lips sealed.

"Do you remember? What it was called?"

"The Helping Hand Company." Wilkes murmured.

"What was that?"

"The Helping Hand Company."

"Alright, yeah, that's what it was. The Helping Hand Company. What a name, huh? 'The Helping Hand Company'."

Wilkes stared at her with squinted baleful eyes.

"Anyway..." Brandy continued. "Why did you..."

"That's not important. Not important at all."

Wilkes then cracked his fingers, twining them together, with his elbows on the table.

"Now then, I assume you're wondering right now why exactly I have sought you out so soon." he said. "Well, before that, I'd like to say I was by no means being sarcastic when complimenting you on finding this locale. It is in fact a perfect place for discussing the matters at hand in confidence, even better than the O'Caiside. Not a single person in this building will have the desire *or* ability to pay our conversation any attention. Heck, even if they did, not a soul of significant authority would possibly believe them. Or understand them, to be honest."

"Well, you know what?..." Brandy rested her elbows on the table, trying to seem confident and unafraid. "That may be true, but tell ya what, I still think they'd notice a gun shot, at least the bartender would. I know he seems a little vacant, but not even *he* could be *that* apathetic." Brandy took another sip of beer, only to discover a dissolving cigarette butt at the bottom of the glass. "So yeah, y'know, pissing, barfing, breaking glass and the occasional psychotic breakdown? Sure, that all's just white noise to these folks. But a fucking gun shot? They'll notice a gun shot."

Brandy then stood up and walked away, confident in her assertiveness.
"That's fine." Wilkes said. "I could kill you in your sleep instead."

Brandy halted.

"Oh yes. Next time you fall asleep could easily be your last. You *could* avoid it by never sleeping of course, though I do believe dying of sleep deprivation will also be quite painful."

Brandy returned to her place. She leaned back in her cushion.

"So then now." Wilkes said. "Are you ready to listen?"
Brandy breathed in. "Alright. Shoot. I mean, don't, I mean, just tell me what it is."
"You see, after some more thorough research, it came to my knowledge that you are a student of economics, and that you have quite a competent brain for economics. In fact, I believe your guidance councilor from your primary education period called you a 'natural talent'. More than meets the eye, certainly."
"Jesus, you're even worse than the NSA. Where the fuck did you find that shit?"
"The thing is, the ones I represent find your skills quite valuable, and so, we would very much like to have you work for us. Financial consultancy."

"You guys don't have accountants and such already?"

"We certainly do, but sadly they are all merely competent, not genuinely *talented*. We want what you have. Natural raw Jewish intuition."

"Hey, what did you say?"

"That magical ingenuity to guide us through what is in honesty a quite delicate endeavor."

"Look, y'know, even if it's a positive stereotype it's still pretty fucking racist."

"Come one now, don't say you find my praise offensive?"

"It is when you put the Jew-thing in there."

"Well, pardon my cultural insensitivity then. I will retract that one word from my statement."

'Doesn't make you any less of a prick' Brandy thought to herself, almost mumbling it out loud.

"Now, normally I would allow you some time to consider my pitch, but given the circumstances I can only expect a 'yes', so I'll move straight to your instructions. Next Monday, you will…"

"No."

"I beg your pardon."

"I said no."

"Well then, did I not make myself clear last time we met? Or again just now?"

"Look, about three weeks from now, give or take, I will die from a swelling parasite that will blow up my nether area. I know that probably sounds odd to you but it's true. So yeah, I will die very soon. I'm scared shitless, I'll admit that, 'cos y'know, I'm gonna die, and that's horrifying, but the more I think about it, whether or not you'll kill me doesn't matter. It just doesn't. I don't care. Really."

Wilkes tilted backwards and stared at her with his chin raised.

"Do you think it will hurt? The parasite inside you? Do you believe it'll be painful when it finally does you in?"

"I reckon it will be, yeah, probably, but I'll either live to experience it, or you'll give me a quick and easy death way before that, and that is if I don't cooperate. So exactly what the fuck do I got to lose?"

97

"Look, sweetheart. Did I at any point tell you it was going to be 'quick' or 'easy'?" Wilkes said and took a hefty swig of Brandy's beer. "What if I told you that you'd have to spend several days, maybe a week, or several weeks, in my, shall we say, 'private quarters'?"

'You're a fucking freak' thought Brandy.

"What if, say, I hung you upside down, like the catch of the day, and filled your nether region with molten cement? And what if that was my way of finally showing you mercy?"

'You're a fucking monster', thought Brandy.

"What if I could make every second of your existence up until your death feel like a decade?" Wilkes licked his moustache. "What if I knew a way to make you constantly feel intolerable agony, even after losing consciousness? What if I told you that while your cooperation pleases me on a professional level, it does disappoint me on a more primal level, giving me what you young ones call 'blue-balls'? Isn't that what you kids call it?"

Brandy did not respond from her lack of ability to breathe.

"Oh, how much fun I've had with girls of your ilk. Boys too. Believe me, before we're finished, I will have taught you how to give birth in reverse, how to excrete on command. Oh, I'm telling you, I will have taught your sphincter to scream."

Brandy farted loudly in terror. She felt like she was about to defecate all her internal organs. The numbness in her legs worsened, as her hands turned into sponges full of sweat.

"So, finally, here are your instructions." Wilkes said. "The upcoming Monday, you will go to the Shokuchudoku Sushi restaurant, at exactly two PM. There you will meet, well, you know what? I might as well tell you right now who I'm working for, it's not like I can realistically distrust you anymore, can I?"

Brandy nodded frantically, without blinking. She had stopped blinking now, possibly permanently.

"Well then. I represent an entrepreneur by the name of Olive D'Orleans. Of course, I know you're from Pennsylvania, and that the D'Orleans name means very little to people down there, but I assume that during your stay here you've been given some impression of how influential that family and their brand is to New Hampshire, particularly Riverside."

There was a boiling mixture of fear and hatred brewing inside Brandy. She felt an immense urge to insult Wilkes for everything about his person, being as unfairly harsh as possible, even physically assault him, punching his smug face, tearing his little eyeballs from their sockets; only the prospect of the ensuing hellish torture kept her quiet.

"So, at the Shokuchudoku, you will be meeting this Olive D'Orleans. You will walk right in, see her, and approach her. You will strike up a chat. Don't worry, she won't find you rude, lewd, or inappropriate, like I do. She will neither bite nor bark. The thing is, you must never mention the project until she does. When *she* says she wants to discuss the project, you follow along, but *you* are never allowed to bring it up, or allude to it in any way. Understand?"

Brandy nodded.

"So then, any questions?"

"Wh-when was it again?" Brandy barely managed to squeeze through her lips.

"Monday, two PM sharp. No delays, no excuses."

"And, uh…" Brandy tried intensely to keep herself from stammering. "And, what does this… Miss… is… this D'Orleans person, what does she look like?"

"Frankly, my dear, she looks quite a lot like you. Well, frankly, maybe a bit heavier. Quite a lot heavier, in fact, I won't lie. I'd say about a metric ton and a half heavier. You two have a bit of a weight difference, certainly, but you have very similar eyes, and hair color. And frankly you both have the same highly charming smile, I must say."

All over Brandy's body, hairs rose from that remark, even where there were none.

"So I assume we have a deal, then."

"Yes. Yes, yeah we do. We have a real deal, yeah." Brandy babbled. "Sure thing we do. A real proper deal. I won't disappoint. No siree. I'll do it. I'll just. I will…I will do it. Just leave me be, let me live. Just let me just see another day in freedom, alright. Don't take me, alright. Don't do… the bad things. Don't. Please don't. Please."

Wilkes then stood up.

"It is good that you are cooperating. Now please, don't let us down."

Then he left the establishment.

99

And Brandy sat still, many thoughts flying through her head, none properly meditated upon. Tucker pecked at her breast pocket for some sunflower seeds.

INTERMISSION

The hit song '*While We're In Paradise*' was written by a to this day unknown person (as they wished to remain anonymous) in 1964. Initially intended for The Cascades, whose agent rejected the song, it was later picked up by The Winged Lieutenants, who made it their first and only hit single in the summer of 1965, and according to their autobiography '*Winged to Win: The Winged Lieutenants Story*', published ten years later, it was received with critical extol and great commercial success, something the band had never experienced with their previous outings (nor would they since).

The lyrics went like this:

> Come and join me in my flight
> Till we reach our Shangri-La
> Come and be my sweet delight
> Throughout the countries near and far
> Let's relieve us of our masks
> Let's remove our shared disguise
> And let's be free
> While we're in paradise

> Leave those poor old sinners be
> Down in their pools of misery
> Come and have a blast with me
> Up in these clouds of ecstasy
> Just allow those petty fools
> To endure their own demise

And let's be free
While we're in paradise

Let me gnaw
Upon your jaw
Let me escape into your bush
Now don't be shy
And don't you cry
Just let your brain turn into mush
Please believe my honest truths
Don't let your head get filled with lies
And come be free
Here in paradise

Years later, The Winged Lieutenants sued Leonard Cohen for melodic plagiarism, but their claims were dismissed in court.

After nearly two decades of making one hit song and nothing else of recognition, they disbanded in 1978, disappearing off the face of the earth.

CHAPTER NINE

Tucker looked down upon the side of Brandy's face as she marched up Mapplethorpe Road. 'Where are we going?' he thought. 'Will there be sunflower seeds soon? Peanuts? Will we get peanuts?'

Brandy, however, was only concerned with not getting flayed alive, or whatever that Mister Wilkes wanted to do to her. Something truly horrible, she was certain. Something gruesome and bizarre and loathsome. Something that, if uncovered by the media, would live on in the public consciousness as a repulsive cautionary tale, or at least a repulsive tale. There was the possibility that Mister Wilkes was lying, only trying to intimidate her. But, in reality, what was it worth to challenge his claim to infamy? While he did not strike her as highly trustworthy, he was very plausibly a person who owned a torture dungeon, and he had also proven to have little to no scruples, likely bearing a few corpses on his dead conscience.

'Where are the peanuts?' Tucker thought, and pecked at Brandy's ear for an answer, but received no response. 'Peanuts here?' he thought when they passed a café called 'The Peanut', which served plenty of peanuts as well as tremendously good coffee and passable club sandwiches.

'Peanuts yeah! Peanuts? No? No peanuts? Sunflower seeds? Pumpkin seeds? No?' thought Tucker.

Brandy walked straight down to the Shokuchudoku. She had only had a single mojito beforehand, just to boost her confidence. One mojito. And a Bloody Mary. Two Bloody Mary's. And a Budweiser, warm, only two thirds of it. The last third, or fourth, or fifth maybe, had to be poured in the sink due to its rancid foulness.

As they stood before the Shokuchudoku, staring at its entrance at three minutes past two of clock, Brandy thought to herself 'maybe this place's prices really were a bit beyond my range'. It did look quite a bit more luxurious than she remembered.

"Fucker!" Tucker cawed loudly in frustration.

"Alright, you spoiled little bastard. I got your grub right here."

She pulled some sunflower seeds from the inner pocket of her cardigan. After Tucker had eaten his seeds, Brandy inhaled deeply and with a puffed-up chest opened the entrance door.

Inside waited the old familiar interior. Brandy looked around after that D'Orleans woman for a few seconds, before her view got blocked by a tall person in a velvet suit. He was an older black man somewhat resembling Scatman Crothers in his facial features, looking down upon her with a cold skeptical expression.

"May I help you, madam?" he asked with a vaguely South African accent.

"Uh, yeah, I am here for, uh, I'm looking for…"

"Are you the economist?"

"Uh, yeah. I guess you could… Yeah, that's me, I s'pose."

The man leaned down to her head level.

"Now, let us be very clear." he whispered in her ear. "You will neither discuss nor allude to the project or your involvement in it. Not while we are here or in public space.

"I understand." Brandy whispered back.

The man stood back up. "Let me show you to lady Olive, madam."

She followed him only a few feet directly to the left, to the peculiar permanently reserved booth with no table, except now a big round table had indeed been wheeled in front of it. What Brandy saw behind said table made her eyes nearly fly out of their sockets.

A mammoth woman of sublime obesity, a sight at once grotesque and spectacular, a body of proportions one would need to observe in person to believe, and even then barely so.

Brandy blinked frenetically as the rest of her body stood stiff as a plank. The enormous woman was too immersed with stuffing her balloon face with sushi pieces to notice her presence. The African man cleared his throat, snapping her out of her shock. Free to move again, she nervously approached the woman and let out a suffocated 'hi'.

104

She got her attention.

"Hello." the woman smiled back, slightly confused.

"I, uh, I take it you're Olive D'Orleans?"

"Oh yes. That's me. I'm Olive D'Orleans."

Brandy walked a little closer, to about an arm's length distance, and reached out her hand.

"Well, uh, my name is Brandy. Brandy Rabinow. I am, uh, um…"

"It's really nice to meet you, Brandy." Olive eagerly reached out to submerge Brandy's hand into her swollen sausage fingers. "Please sit down. Don't tire your legs."

Brandy did as told, and sat down on the eleven inches of free space to Olive's left.

"So, please tell me, what do you want?" Olive asked warmly.

"Oh, well, that guy over there said, um, I mean, I just want to chat, I s'pose. 'Bout nothing in particular."

"No, silly, I meant what do you want to eat?"

"Oh, I'm not really that hungry right now."

"Don't be shy. It's all on me." Olive said swallowing a lean tuna nigiri. "It's all so delicious here."

On the table lay a tray of almost a square yard, covered to the edge with various pieces of sushi, several of them already eaten but still seemingly adding up to a hundred. A cook stood by Olive's right side with a bowl of soy sauce that he brushed each piece with as she lifted them up to him.

"Well, the crab maki was a little characterless in my opinion, but the sea urchin was just magnificent."

"Alright, you want me to just pick a few?"

"Oh no, no. These are mine. I'll have the chef prepare you your own serving."

"I honestly don't think I can take these many though."

Olive chuckled. "Oh no, not with *your* little belly. A single California roll is probably like a full dinner for you."

"Heh, I'm not *that* much of a nibbler."

"Hey, I'm just joking, buddy." Olive clapped Brandy endearingly on the cheek. "Hey, garçon." she said to the soy bowl cook. "Or what is it you people like to be called? 'San'? 'Sensei'? 'Mister Miyagi'?"

"Uh, 'san' will do." he responded a bit nervously.

"Okay, Mike-san, give my lovely little girlfriend here a serving of, let's see… five nigiri; lean tuna, fatty tuna, eel, squid, and crayfish. Four maki; scallop, salmon, halibut, and mackerel. And the sea urchin, gotta have that." Olive ordered and turned to Brandy. "Do you want anything else?"

"No, that'll be plenty, thanks."

"You didn't mind me calling you 'friend', did you?" Olive's face turned more serious. "That wasn't crossing a line, or pushing too fast?"

"What? No. Of course not."

"Will that be all, ma'am?" asked Mike.

"Yes, and give her a cup of the house's sake as well, please."

"Certainly."

"And, um, maybe a beer." Brandy interjected, having grown a tad more house warm. "One of them, uh, Japanese pale ales. Izu… Kizu… something-something."

Mike nodded and left into the kitchen, leaving the brush and soy sauce bowl behind.

"I suppose I need to do this myself now." said Olive, and equipped the brush before moving on to the next piece.

"I like your bird there." she said chewing on a salmon roe roll. "Is that… that's not a raven, that's a crow, is it not?"

"Yeah. He's a crow. A Corvus Monedula jackdaw, in fact. His name is Tucker."

"Is it domesticated?"

"Yeah, he's totally an upstanding citizen. Acting on his best behavior even while he sleeps."

"Wow, that is really cool. This is the first time I've seen a domesticated bird that's not in a cage."

Brandy moved the arm to which shoulder Tucker perched on towards Olive, and he promptly skipped down the path to her wrist.

"You can pet him if you like. He's a real people lover."

106

Olive put down her chopsticks and moved her swollen hand towards Tucker's head, and Brandy began doubting her proposal, fearing the massive claw of flab would hurt her poor bird. Olive stroke Tucker as gently as she could, yet he still seemed aggrieved by the excessive force. Her hand looked like five big bratwursts stuffed into a puffy Cornish pasty about to be slowly devoured by the giant log of blubber that was her forearm.

"You called it Tucker?" she asked.

"Yeah. Don't know why. The name just came to me."

"Can I feed it?" she asked. "Maybe it wants a little salmon nigiri."

"Oh no, don't do that." Brandy said. "Don't give him rice. Last time he had rice he shat like a motherfucker for a week. You should've seen the mess."

The African man cleared his throat in the same manner as before.

"D'aw, the little birdie can't eat sushi?" Olive said staring Tucker in the eyes.

Tucker hastily flew back to Brandy's shoulder, cowering behind her neck. He normally gave little bother to his surroundings, but he did understand when a huge abominable giant gazed upon him.

"It's so cute." Olive said. "Can it do any tricks?"

"I dunno. He can talk, sort of."

"Fucker!" cawed Tucker.

"Oh, that's so dang adorable!" Olive squeed.

Brandy smiled.

"Oh no! Not you! You get out of here!" sounded a voice from afar. "No bud allowed! And you're not allowed either!"

A chef approached the booth. Brandy recognized him as the chef who threw her out on her last visit.

"You're on the ban-list! We've banned you! You're not allowed in here, ever!" he yelled.

"You talking to me?" Brandy asked challengingly.

"Yes! I'm talking to you, and your filthy bud! You're not welcome! If you don't leave now, I'm calling the police!"

The man yelled at the top of his lungs. His face was reddening. A fatal stroke seemed imminent.

"Is he talking to you?" Olive asked.

107

"I s'pose he is."

"Hey, Mister Itto." Olive said to the chef. "Or Itto-san, I think. Is that right? Anyway, what is the problem here?"

"The problem…" Mister Itto said. "… is this intruder, and her filthy disease-ridden bud infecting my restaurant with avian flu, and cholera, and what not! She is a menace! She must leave! Now!"

"Hey, Roland?" Olive said to the African man. "Could you take care of this?"

Roland approached Itto.

"Pardon me, but lady Olive finds your behavior quite irritating, Mister Itto-san." he said.

"I don't care about lady Olive! As long as that girl and her bud gets out of here, I'll be satisfied!" Itto yelled back as loud as before.

"Let me remind you that it is in your best interest to leave lady Olive, as well as her companions, in peace."

"It is in my interest to see this lousy bum and her stupid bud leave here, and never return!"

"Why do we not go and discuss the matter in the kitchen?" Roland asked politely.

"There is nothing to discuss! This girl and her bud leave now, or I'll call the police!"

Roland leaned down to Itto, the same way he did to Brandy earlier.

"You. Will. Join. Me. In. The. Kitchen. This. Instant." he said.

The reddening in Itto's face disappeared, as did all coloration. He walked submissively back into the kitchen, with Roland's hand firmly gripping his shoulder.

"So tell me, Brandy…" Olive said, munching through her lobster maki roll. "What do you do? What is your occupation, or profession, or what you people call it?"

"Oh, um…" Brandy was still a bit distracted by the incident with Itto. "I'm a college student. At the Collin College right past Glengarry Park, y'know. I study, uh, economics. Majoring in economics."

"That sounds fun. I wish *I* could study, on a big school and the likes. My parents had me home-schooled, and then I only pursued further studies via internet courses and books. I've seen the movies, though. Seems like you people have a lot of fun, with the drugs and the sex and the pranks and all that."

"Well, it's not, I mean, sure, I mean, yeah, that's totally how we roll over there. Toking and fucking and pranking all day and night. It's just madness over there, absolutely."

"Oh I bet!" Olive laughed, rice flying out her mouth. "You must be living the dream over there."

"It… It's a lot of fun."

Roland came back from the kitchen alone.

"Mister Itto said he was quite sorry for the inconvenience, lady Olive."

"Oh, that's quite okay."

"Furthermore, he expressed his gratitude for your visit, and he hopes you found his food satisfactory."

"Oh yes. It was absolutely stupendous." Olive said. "I mean, I wouldn't call myself an expert on Japanese cuisine in particular, but what I just ate was simply put a kaleidoscope of flavor and texture. And I truly mean that. It was not only beyond my expectations, but beyond that again. I mean, these guys, they'll certainly be getting my Seal of Approval. Send my compliments to the chef."

"I certainly will, my lady."

At that point Mike came back with a tray of Brandy's meal and sake and pale ale. He looked paler than before, with shaking pupils.

"And how will we be working out the payment in this place?" Olive asked.

"It's all on the house." Mike said. "Your time and your review is all the payment we want. Even if it's a negative review, really."

"Oh, that's so sweet of you guys." Olive clapped her hands. "Remind me to give you a hug when we leave, Mike-san."

"Of course, lady Olive." Mike replied and rushed back into the kitchen.

Brandy rubbed some wasabi over her halibut nigiri, and swallowed it. A tingly little shock swept through her head from the wasabi, reaching the back of her skull, as she twisted her neck and torso in joyous spasms.

"Boy, that sure's some potent wasabi they got here." she noted. "Have you tried it, Olive? The wasabi?"

"Oh no, I can't have that stuff, unfortunately. My doctor says it's dangerous for my heart."

109

"Aw, that's too bad."

"Oh, don't even talk about it!" Olive exclaimed. "I hate it when people tell me what I can and can't eat! They keep trying to control me! If I want to have sriracha on my scotch eggs, that's my decision, dang it!"

Brandy said nothing.

Some time went by, one or two hours. Brandy ordered rows of Sambuca shots for herself and Olive, which they drank competitively, after which they shared a pitcher of mojito, then a pitcher of beer, before their green tea ice cream desserts arrived, all while their conversation floated through an array of loosely connected topics, none too personal for either's liking.

Roland waited patiently while repeatedly checking his Rolex. He was not used to Olive conversing with a third person during their excursions, at least none that were not employed at the given establishment.

The overtly jovial mood was only slightly dampened during each of Brandy's numerous bathroom breaks.

"If you don't mind me speaking, lady Olive…" Roland said during Brandy's fifth break. "I do assert that it would be wise of us to leave quite soon, in order to proceed with business."

"But we're having such a good time, Roland." Olive replied.

"There will always be plenty of time for fun. Believe me, we will keep that girl close by, twenty-four seven."

Olive sighed. "Okay, fetch the wheelchair."

"Hey, you guys, ever had one of those, uh, Irish Carbombs?" Brandy said coming back from the bathroom. "It got a really, really good kick to it, y'know, or like, we could go for some shots, like, I'm down with both, y'know."

"I'm sorry, Brandy." Olive said. "We have to leave now."

"Oh alright, is fine, don't bother me none." Brandy said. "I gots to do, like, stuff, y'know, got stuff to do myself."

"Would that be particularly *important* 'stuff', madam?" asked Roland.

"Sure, important as shit." Brandy said, as Tucker flapped his wings from atop her head. "Gots to go to Mickey Dee, get myself a BigMac."

"Pardon me for saying so, madam, but you appear to be noticeably inebriated." Roland noted.

"What? That's rude! I'm not drunk, no more drunk than you are!"

"Well, it does not matter, madam. You will come with us regardless."

"Come with... what? What're you talking about? I'm going to Mickey Dee."

Suddenly she had Roland's face straight up in hers.

"It would be in your best interest if you came with us, and refrained from resisting any further."

Then Brandy stood quiet for a while. The overtly serene tone of his subtle imposition had a strong sobering effect on her mind.

"Alright." she then said. "Alright. I'll come."

II

Sat in the back of the limousine, faced backwards, Brandy looked out of the tinted window at the behemoth Olive being pushed closer to the car by Roland, whose body seemed much too frail for the task, despite his proud posture.

In the seat to her right sat Tucker, his head snapping from one direction to another in total confusion.

Brandy initially wanted to complain that driving while faced backwards made her queasy, but re-decided upon seeing the seat opposite her was designed exclusively with Olive's physique in mind.

"Can I help?" she asked as she watched Olive getting haphazardly squeezed into the car, with one leg stuck in the doorframe. She looked to be mildly pained and highly fatigued by the procedure.

"No." said Roland. "I doubt you can."

Assumedly, Brandy having tripped and almost fallen on her way out the restaurant had given him a poor impression of her dexterity, and by her own admission, it was far from optimal at the moment. While the euphoric buzz from her inebriation had long passed, the clumsiness and disorientation remained. The only upside to this miserable state, she thought, was that she would likely be much more anxious sober.

After Olive had been properly seated, Roland cast a disapproving glance at Tucker.

111

"Does the bird have to come?" he asked Brandy.

"Yeah." she said. "If he's not coming, I'm not either."

"That, madam, is frankly not for you to decide."

"Well, I'm not leaving without him, fucking no matter what."

Roland snorted and shut the door.

"Hoo, those Japanese." Olive said, rubbing her stomach. "They know how to cook a meal, you know. Didn't they invent the umami flavor? Or they discovered it, or something."

"Hey, uh, exactly where are we going?" Brandy asked.

"You tasted the sea urchin, didn't you? Wasn't that just... indescribable? I can't even think of a word. Beyond umami. I don't think I've ever even had urchin before."

"Hey!" Brandy exclaimed. "Where are we going? What're we gonna do?"

"Oh. Well, I assume you've been briefed on the project, haven't you?"

"I wouldn't say 'briefed', exactly. I only really know it exists."

"Well, that's fine. Luckily, there's going to be this little presentation when we get to the D'Orleans Tower."

"Oh, alright. That's cool, I s'pose. Though could you maybe, like, just go over the basics with me. Like, what is it we're even working on here? Is it a movie, or a bridge, or a political thing? Like, what's the general gist here?"

Olive's head then sunk into the flab collar around her neck like a snail's eyestalk retreating into its body.

"You know..." she yawned. "I think it will be better if you just wait and see for yourself."

She closed her eyes, and started gently snoring.

"Fucker!" cawed Tucker.

Brandy petted his head.

III

Contrary to Brandy's assumption, the D'Orleans Tower did not have a restaurant on its top floor, but rather a confined amphitheater auditorium with at least a thousand seats and a massive cinema screen behind a large round stage, the whole auditorium larger and more lavish than any of Collin College's ones.

Fifty storeys high, the gigantic glass dildo loomed above the rest of the city like an all-seeing watchtower; built in nineteen ninety one to replace the old headquarters of D'Orleans Industries, Harper & D'Orleans Plaza on Dresden Street up in Outer Darlington, which was demolished the same year. All but the first floor was sealed off from the public, only accessed by employees and individuals specifically summoned, as was now the case with Brandy Rabinow.

She was assigned a seat on the front row, right next to the wheelchair space occupied by Olive, who was still phasing in and out of a shallow drowse. By her side sat Tucker in a seat of his own, having been given a handful of seeds to munch on. The inebriation had more or less ceased on the car ride over, and the terrifyingly fast glass elevator lay the final blow, knocking her into clear crisp sobriety, only now with a pressing headache gnawing on her brain. Furthermore, the parasite inside her was acting up again, as it had done on unpredictable occasions the past week and a half, almost once every day, and those sessions of burning stingy pain could last anywhere between ten seconds and ten hours.

The seats were filling up behind them with people, all totally silent, none chatting or coughing or chuckling or moaning. Ultimately only around two hundred people had showed up by the time the lights dimmed.

A projector sounded from the far back. The screen lit up. Sharp imposing white. Then black, with bold white text.

THE FOLLOWING PRESENTATION
IS CONFIDENTIAL, AND ONLY INTENDED FOR A
SELECT, PRIVATE AUDIENCE. ANY ATTEMPTS AT RECORDING OR RE-
DISTRIBUTING
THIS PRESENTATION (whether audio, visuals, or both), OR RE-CREATING OR
DISCUSSING ITS CONTENT BEYOND THE PERIMETERS OF ITS SHOWING,
WILL BE PROSECUTED AND PENALIZED DULY. THIS WILL BE THE ONLY
WARNING PROVIDED.

Then followed another image. A blue one, with the D'Orleans Industries logo on top.

'*A D'Orleans Industries Production, approved for viewing by D'Orleans Industries and relevant associates*' it read underneath.

Then it faded to black. Black and silent. It stayed like this for a short while. Then suddenly a title card flashed on screen, accompanied by loud music, an orchestrated overture resembling the scores from the golden age Hollywood pictures.

D'Orleans Industries

presents

THE QUEST FOR UTOPIA

A Journey To The Promised Land

The title was in big bold golden letters, with a majestic image of a western mountain landscape behind it.

The film faded to black once more in synchronization with the fading of the music. What came next was a clip from a news program, where the host talked about the obesity epidemic. A rapid cutting through various debate shows, talk shows, reality shows and a cartoon, all discussing the same topic.

One doctor being showed was being particularly baleful on the subject. "These fat slobs are killing themselves. They're killing the environment. They don't care about themselves. They don't care about society." he said.

Then the film paused on his disgruntled face, at the precise moment when he was half-way through blinking to give him a quite unflattering face.

"Is it *really* the obese that are society's problem?" said the deep buttery voice of a man with a slight Caribbean accent . "Or is it society that is the obese's problem."

Brandy raised an eyebrow at the remark.

"For centuries, countless obese men and women have made countless significant contributions to the advancements of the human civilization." the narrator continued.

A montage of pictures of, among others, Alfred Hitchcock, William Howard Taft, Solomon Burke, and several fat scientists accompanied his words.

"You could ask yourself: Within the fields of science, arts, politic and industry, where would we be without the valuable contributions of the obese?"

"But society showed to gratitude towards the obese." he continued.

114

Clips of violent protests, lynch mobs, and what was definitely a scene from the original '*Frankenstein*' film followed. The background music was getting really dramatic.

"Instead they have shown nothing but contempt, wrath and mockery."

A clip of Eddie Murphy in a fat suit crushing a chair and falling over played over that last word.

"In society, the fat man has always been second-rate to the thin man."

A dignified portrait of Olive came up, with the written description 'Entrepreneur, philanthropist, writer, esteemed culinary critic, heiress of the D'Orleans estate' underneath her name.

"But there is hope. Thanks to the brilliant initiative of Olive D'Orleans, the long-time campaigner for obese rights in America, a new project shall relieve all obese people from enduring the plights of a thin-dominated society. Presenting to you…"

An intricately detailed illustration of a city appeared on screen.

"Obesiana! A promised land not for the taking, but in the making!"

A picture followed of Olive standing up with her cane in mountainous wilderness, pointing self-seriously up at something off-frame, with three men in suits behind her all nodding approvingly.

A new type of music started playing, a chipper and wholesome tune one could expect to hear in one of those infomercials from the nineteen fifties.

"Deep within the desolate lands of Wyoming, Olive D'Orleans has recently purchased a plot of land twice the size of Riverside, in which to build her urban utopia, designed and constructed specifically with the obese in mind. A city with only elevators instead of stairs, with travelators instead of stationary sidewalks, where all rooms and doorways will be of adequate size."

Several city-planning illustrations depicting what he described flew by in another montage.

"And let us not forget, as a citizen of Obesiana, you will not have to pay a single penny in taxes to the US government. That is because Obesiana will declare absolute autonomy from the United States. That's right, Obesiana will go on to function as its own nation, with its own laws, its own regulations, and its own societal structure."

Then came a clip of a nuclear family of a husband, a wife, three children and a dog, all quite morbidly obese, all carrying luggage with one hand and waving to the camera with the other.

"So if you, and your family, would like to finally break the shackles of the thin man's tyranny, and pursue a new and better life in a land beyond the mountains, do not hesitate. Act now."

Payed for by

the D'Orleans Foundation

for the Support of Young Artists

This production is not to be commercially distributed.

The room lit up again. Brandy's headache had only worsened throughout the viewing.

"What did you think?" asked Olive with moist eyes.

"I was… stunned." Brandy said.

"Yeah, wasn't it great?!"

An older man in a suit, one that Brandy recognized from the picture with Olive, walked on stage to behind the podium.

"Good evening." he said dryly into the microphone. "My name is Mister Sebastian Kenutsen, and I am the project manager for Project Obesiana. Many of you have already made acquaintances with me on an earlier occasion, and I hope you all now understand your position and role on this project. I've had some previous experiences with people misunderstanding their supposed role. It causes a total logistical nightmare, and given the delicate nature of this endeavor, I simply can't tolerate such easily avoidable delays and hindrances. Now then, would the project owner please join me on stage?"

Roland pushed Olive up the stage's wheelchair ramp with the help of another audience member. Once there, she was given a microphone of her own.

"Oh, excuse me." she said, wiping tears out of her eyes. "That film gets me every time I see it."

"Miss D'Orleans, is there anything you would like to tell the audience before we move on?" Kenutsen asked.

"I'd just like to say that, despite what the tone of the film might have implied, I don't hold a grudge on any of you thin people. None of you are individually guilty, necessarily. It's the system and culture at large that is heinous. And anyone helping me with this venture, whether by contributing financially or assisting me otherwise, will be granted status as honorary obeseman or obesewoman, with full honorary citizenship in Obesiana, complete with all the same rights as the regular citizens."

"Very well." Kenutsen said. "On to the matters at hand, then."

"Wait!" said Olive. "One more thing."

"As you wish."

"I would just like to say that after much consideration, I have indeed decided to stick to the name 'Obesiana'. It is not just a production title anymore. It was just so much better than any of the other suggestions. I don't like 'Fat City'. No one would want to invest in that. We're also not going to go with 'Chubby-ville', or 'Portly-Prince' or 'Lard-ass Junction'. 'Obesiana' it is."

"Very well, then." Kenutsen said. "*Now* on to the matters at hand."

A map of a forest area, presumably in Wyoming, showed up on screen, with an orange outline titled 'city limits'.

"This is the plot we've recently purchased, covering two hundred and seventy three square miles. Construction on the city within has already begun, but progressing at an unsatisfactory rate. We are still open for funding from private investors."

"We'll have a fundraising banquette next week." Olive interjected. "All interested can apply for an invitation."

"Yes, quite. But I'm afraid we will not meet our goal in due time without a few creative shortcuts. Fortunately, as I've been informed, Miss D'Orleans has just recently hired a new chief accountant to help us out, namely one Mister…"

He pulled a note from his breast pocket.

"Miss Brandy Rabinow." he read.

"What?" said Brandy.

"Come on up here, Brandy!" said Olive waving her towards the stage.

Brandy hesitantly climbed out of her seat and walked up on stage with Tucker on her head, to moderate applause.

Kenutsen skipped back a little, with an expression of appalled confusion on his face, at the sight of the hungover twenty-something hobo girl with a crow nesting in her bushy hair.

Brandy stepped up to the podium.

"Yo." she said nervously into the microphone.

"Is this a joke?" Kenutsen said under his breath.

"Look, I haven't really actually prepared anything." Brandy said to Olive, covering the mic. "I didn't even know I was gonna have to speak."

"You'll be fine, friend." Olive responded, covering her mic as well. "Just tell us a little bit about yourself."

"Alright, look, I thought I was just gonna be, like, a consultant or something. Fucking chief accountant? I don't have the competence for that."

"Don't be so humble, dear. I've heard you're great. Now just go and say something."

Brandy cleared her throat, and turned back to the audience.

"As I said, yo." she began. "My name is Brandy Rabinow, as previously stated. I will be working on this project as chief accountant, as also previously stated. OW!"

She got interrupted by a particularly nasty sting from the parasite, one of an intensity she had not experienced before.

"Um, looking forward to that." she continued. "I'm sure I'll be able to contribute with a lot of creative shortcuts and such, as, once again, previously stated. Um, so, yeah, that's about it. Peace out."

A couple of audience members clapped.

"Ahem." sounded Kenutsen.

"Should I say anything else?" Brandy then whispered to him.

"Perhaps you should introduce the outlines of your plan." he said.

"*Plan*? I just got the job. I haven't prepared any plan yet."

He leaned down to her, in the same mildly intimidating manner as Roland had done earlier.

"We'll discuss this afterwards." he said subtly threateningly.

118

"So…" she continued to the audience. "I'll be going over the details of my plan on a later occasion. There are still a few… details, yeah, details that I need to be going over… first, before I go over it with you lot. Beyond that, uh… Peace out. Again. Bye."

She then waved to the bewildered audience, before returning to her seat.

"Now then…" Kenutsen continued. "It is time I introduce our most recent collaborator and so far biggest investor, who unfortunately could not be here in person."

A new picture flashed on screen, an older man seemingly of middle-eastern or southern-European descent, with gold-rimmed aviator sunglasses, dressed in an extravagant olive-green military uniform covered in an array of medals; giving a salute in front of a flag of green, white and red horizontal stripes, with golden sabers on the left side of the green area.

"This is President Dzargonin Dzarban, leader of the Sovereign Republic of Ugratistan. Not only has he provided vast monetary contributions, but he is also offering *very* cheap labor, both for construction and for maintenance of the city. He is by far our biggest asset in most respects. A good portion of his workforce has already arrived, with more to come, and they are at this very moment working on construction. However, the lack of funding is already beginning to halt progress, and if he were to withdraw his employment due to dissatisfaction, I am afraid the whole project could easily crumble apart."

The screen turned off. Kenutsen cracked his fingers.

"Is there anything you want to add, Miss D'Orleans?" he asked.

"I just finished the Obesiana Constitution yesterday." she said. "Final draft. We're still working on the National Law, there are some uncertainties regarding funeral practices. Also, not sure if we should define death as the point of cardiac arrest or brain failure."

"Yes, we'll get around to that." Kenutsen said. "Now, are there any questions before we finish?"

There were a boatload of questions Brandy wanted to ask at this point, but was too afraid to. Not only was the nature of the situation rendering critical expression potentially dangerous, but in the case she did receive perfectly honest and open answers, would she really want to hear them?

After the presentation had concluded, Brandy was one of the first ones to leave. She found a chair in the hallway outside the auditorium, where she sat and rubbed her

119

hurting belly while watching the others exit. All men and women in business suits, all looking nearly identical. Three slight variations on each of the two genders, multiplied by dozens. None of them were overweight. They all went quietly to the elevators, not one of them uttering a single word, or making a single sound, just staring blankly ahead.

"So what do you think?"

"Huh?" said Brandy.

"What do you think of the project?" asked Olive, being rolled out by Roland after everyone else had left.

"Oh, uh, sorry I fucked up in there. I didn't get the memo beforehand, y'know, didn't know I was gonna be chief accountant and all that."

"Oh, don't worry about it. You did great. It's really my fault for not informing you well enough first. Actually, I thought you *had* been informed on the nature of your position. But pish-posh, doesn't matter. We'll get you briefed on the specifics of your duties later on."

Then Mister Kenutsen came out, leather-bound documents in hand.

"You know, Miss Rabinow..." he said with a frown. "When I first saw you there in the audience, on first row, I couldn't make sense of it. I knew you couldn't have sneaked in, I have at least that much faith in this company's security. The only thing I could figure was that you were... one of the Ugrati workers. Something akin to a representative, perhaps."

"Yeah, actually, about those workers..." Brandy interrupted.

"Don't interrupt me!" Kenutsen barked. "As I said... Ugrati worker? Possibly. But *chief accountant*? And you dress like that? You come to a summit like this, with that *bird* on your shoulder? And dressed like a vagrant?"

"Hey, don't shame my fashion sensibilities. I dress the way I feel like, alright."

"Miss D'Orleans." Kenutsen turned to Olive. "I must say, in my opinion, hiring this unwashed host of Avian flu in the financial department truly cannot be anything but an error."

"Unwashed?" Brandy said. "I just showered this morning."

"You still smell like bird feces and gin."

"I do not!" Brandy exclaimed. "Hey Olive, do I smell bad?"

"Of course not, friend. You smell *so* good. Like summer during spring."

"Pardon me if this comes off as disrespectful, Miss D'Orleans, but I am beginning to question your judgment." said Kenutsen. "I hope you come to disprove my doubts in the near future, or I will simply have to abandon this project.".

Kenutsen then walked to the open elevator, alone.

"Don't worry about him." Olive said. "If he continues to be so lame, I can easily have him replaced. I have a long queue of potential project managers that can take his place any day."

"Now, lady Olive, you should not burn through project managers so quickly." Roland commented. "Their ranks are indeed numbered. How many more can you afford to hire and fire?"

"A lot more. I have a queue." Olive replied.

Brandy moaned in agony.

"What's wrong, friend?" Olive asked. "You look really pale. Is anything the matter? Are you sick?"

"It's just, if you don't need me anymore, I'd really like to go home now."

"Of course, friend. Where do you live?"

"The Manson Asylum on Franklyn Street, up in West Cedarbrook."

"Oh, poor dear you. You live in West Cedarbrook? That's like living in a third world country. Like Argentina, or… Taiwan or… Finland or… something."

"Or Ugratistan?" Brandy said.

"Or, well, Ugratistan, is that a third world country? They can afford to help us build Obesiana, can't they?"

"Can we maybe take this in the car?" Brandy said. "I don't mean to be rude, it's just that I'm in a lot of pain right now."

"Oh certainly. You go on ahead, in the elevator."

Brandy crawled up from the chair, and ambled over to the one open elevator, bending over from the parasitic pain.

"Aren't you two coming as well?" she asked once inside.

"Olive and I need to ride the elevator alone." said Roland. "Due to the weight limits."

The elevator doors closed. Brandy descended down the tower, with a stupendous view of the million little lights forming nighttime Riverside.

IV

"So, what did you think?"

"Huh?"

"You didn't get to say what you thought of the project, before we railed off."

"Oh right."

The stomach ache had only worsened since Brandy got in the car with Olive, and sitting backwards only added to the nausea.

"Well, what I think is, uh… Well, I think that, y'know, things'll work out, surely. I'm sure it's all gonna be alright, in the end. Y'know, like Bob Marley said."

"Do you have faith in my project?"

"Um, I'm sorry, are we allowed to even discuss this here?"

"Yeah, if I say so, we are."

"Oh, well, sure. Sure, I have faith in this project."

"You have no objections?"

"Well, um, no. A few questions, maybe."

Brandy really did not want to discuss this subject any further. She had no desire to talk, or listen. All she wanted was to take an aspirin and to go to bed, and sleep the pain away.

"What is it you want to know?"

"Oh, well, um, y'know, how does this town of yours, like, deal with manual labor? Like carpenters, and electricians, and plumbers and such?"

"Oh, those will all be occupied by thin people."

"And, okay. Thin people, sure."

"I mean, we might get some ex-pats from America, and possibly Mexico, who would come to Obesiana voluntarily, you know, for work, money. But mostly, we'll rely on Ugrati laborers for all the manual things."

"And the, uh, obese people? What will they do?"

"Oh, the mildly obese will do the regular white-collar work. Accountants, lawyers and such. Then the super-obese, like me, will function as a type of aristocracy. We'll be on top, a few of us calling the shots on things, the others can just spend their time as they please. Either pursue passion projects, or just hang around and have fun."

"So you're gonna have a strict, y'know, hierarchy? Based on weight?"

"Yes. That's the idea. Of course, we'll select honorary obese people; thin people who still helped and supported the project. We do want to reward loyalty regardless of weight class."

"So, still, we're gonna have an old-school class system?"

"A weight class system, yes."

"Okay."

Brandy loosened her seatbelt, and lay down across the three seats on her back. Tucker perched on her chest and started lightly pecking at her face.

"Is there something that bothers you about my project?" asked Olive.

"Look, the only thing that bothers me right now is my fucking stomach, and that goddamn Malaysian parasite."

"What did you say?"

"Oh, it's uh, it's just… I got this Malaysian parasite maggot swimming around in my ovaries. The Tininini-something-something. Real bastard. Gonna kill me one day."

"It's going to kill you?"

"You bet. Motherfucker's gonna pop my innards, fuck my whole system up." Brandy closed her eyes. "The little bastard. Gonna take my organs, turn them into gravy, y'know. Gonna get blood everywhere. Like a fucking massacre. Fucking asshole… Fucking pain… Fucking parasite…"

V

"Fucker!" cawed Tucker.

Brandy awoke in her bed. From what she could recall, she had had no dream during the night. The sun was beaming through the window, straight in her face. A piercing, vicious sun beam forcing its way into her fragile eyes.

"Fucker!" Tucker repeated.

"Shut up, I'm not in the mood." Brandy mumbled and turned around.

The parasite pain was still there, only milder, more tolerable. Brandy still squirmed around under her duvet, clambering around her knees. She had been sleeping in a tight fetal position ever since the diagnosis. All she wanted was getting the parasite out of her.

123

Suddenly, the parasite busted out of her. It was a big fat olive-green worm the size of a frankfurter, penetrating through her lower stomach, making a gaping bleeding hole. The blood flooded all over. The parasite looked straight at Brandy, and hissed, with its huge mouth spreading wide open to reveal a vaginally shaped tunnel into its pit. It roared Brandy straight in the face, it screamed loudly, a high-pitched piercing shriek, like a thousand hungry infants. The sheets were all red. The bed was a pool of blood. It lost all solid form. It was a sea of blood, with a billion frankfurter-sized little maggots screaming and biting. Brandy saw her hands decaying from the blood loss, turning into white withered skeletal claws. Her skin disappeared from all the biting. Her brain melted from the screaming. She vomited her intestines.

"Fucker!" cawed Tucker.

Brandy awoke in her bed, again.

CHAPTER TEN

Snow was falling onto the streets. The sky had been completely cloudless in the morning, but right around noon, white cotton sheets had clogged it all, powdered snow drizzling to the earth, slowly melting under the soles of Brandy's shoes, and obscuring the road ahead of her. She had to walk through four districts just to reach Mapplethorpe Road, and then through Glengarry Park and the college, and then several more streets to reach the O'Caiside; and now doing so through these frosty curtains falling upon her. 'Is it really even worth it?' she thought, 'Isn't there another decent waterhole nearby?'.

There was, in the Bismarck district, an old sports bar called Randy's Spot. In most respects it was about a few notches above the Doberman, and usually less crowded unless there was a big game on the television. Brandy had been there once before, having a can of Pabst one Sunday evening after dinner, before being chased away by a drunken lunatic with a knife who wanted to 'lick ya titties', as he put it. Presumably, hopefully, he was no longer welcome there.

As she passed the bar she figured she might as well drop in for variety's sake, and assuming the probability of another incident was minuscule. She ordered a Bloody Mary at the bar, and was told by the bartender to find a seat and wait for him to bring it over. So she did, finding herself a table for two by the window. There was a little bowl of peanuts at the table, either placed there by the staff as a complementary snack, or more likely left uneaten by a previous customer.

"Have at it." she told Tucker, who gladly dug in.

She soon got her drink brought to her, served in a milk glass, with a single lonely ice cube, and coarsely ground pepper covering the surface. It was the worst Bloody Mary she had ever tasted, without a trace of Worcestershire sauce, and all ingredients likely bought at the dollar store.

She received a text message. It was from Imogen. 'Wanna meet for coffee after lecture?' it read. 'Sure, where?' she replied. 'Dolly's Grinder on campus?' came back. 'I'll be there' she then wrote.

Every little sip of her drink tasted fouler than the last. This thing did nothing to soothe her headache, or stomachache for that matter. Soon she started suspecting the vodka of actually being moonshine. She would not put it below a shabby venue like this to be cheap enough to buy bootleg liquor, and the sharp rancid flavor was oddly familiar.

Many, many years back, four in fact, when Brandy was seventeen, she and a gang of her high school friends spent the summer on a cross-country roadtrip. On their way through the more rural parts of Kentucky, they decided to purchase a little jar of moonshine, just for kicks. That night, camping out in the wilderness, far from artificial lights, while disjointedly gossiping and joking over cans of soda and a shared cannabis joint, they soon decided to pass around the moonshine, each of them getting their sixteen percent in a Dixie cup. They all chugged it down like a shot. The buzz came faster than she was used to, and was of a far heavier kind, weighing her head down, impairing her from properly processing her thoughts into speech. 'Could... maybe... go... no' was a type of sentence she would produce after having fostered the liquor inside her for five minutes. But her mind flew by, a mile a second, just like before. Soon she managed to remind herself that moonshine could easily contain methanol and turn people blind or outright kill them. Was it really this dark outside right now? Were her perceptions failing? Should it be this dark this time of year? Is it darker in Kentucky? Her dexterity in total disarray, she sat there, in her own thoughts, waiting to turn blind, for everything to blacken around her, for her to never see the sunset, or the faces of her loved ones again. It seemed the moonshine had had a similar effect on the rest, as they all soon quit talking and instead stared aimlessly around. Some of them snickered and giggled on occasion. Brandy just needed something to look at, anything, to assure herself that her vision was still intact. But there was so little to focus on. The moon and the stars were obscured by thick clouds. One by one, the others soon collapsed where they sat. She heard a shriek from afar. Whether it was human or animal she could not tell. She frantically turned around in all directions, until she saw it. Sitting on the longest branch of the biggest tree

126

in her proximity, with huge glowing yellow eyes sinisterly observing her with murderous intentions. The infamous Kentucky hobgoblin had sought her out as its next victim. But she had seen it, its cover was blown. It could not yet strike, not now, while she was so vigilantly looking straight at it. She had to fall asleep first, then it was time. Soon she would collapse like the others, soon the moonshine would do her in. It was only a matter of waiting. But Brandy refused to suffer a fate like this. There was no way she would let her life end at the hands of an abominable little murderous elf. No, she would stay awake, the whole night through, until the cusp of dawn. Until that hobgoblin had no choice but to flee, for its skin would melt in the sun.

The next morning she had awoken in a bush from the bite of an ant, still inebriated. As were the others. Yet they drove onwards, hoping the buzz would fade away along the day. Brandy told everyone about the hobgoblin, but was met with grave skepticism.

"There are a lot of owls around these parts." said her then boyfriend Ryan. "Maybe you saw an owl."

"No, it was not an owl. It was definitely a hobgoblin, it had the pointy ears and everything. Like, didn't any of you guys see it? Didn't you see anything unusual?"

Nobody answered.

II

After having finished two thirds of her breakfast drink, Brand ventured further on towards the college. The drink, sloshing around inside her, was beginning to give her a bad stomachache. A second stomachache, of a nauseating variety, on top of the burning stingy one she had been enduring for well over twelve hours at this point, a new personal record.

Once she reached Dolly's Grinder, right by the college entrance to Glengarry Park, Imogen was already there, sipping from a big cup of latte. This establishment did not allow birds inside, so Tucker had to patiently wait atop the nearest lamppost.

"How are things going, girl?" she asked Brandy.

"I guess it could be worse." she replied, swigging from her chamomile tea.

"You know, sorry for saying so, Brandy, but you honestly look like shit."

"I've been getting that a lot."

"No, I mean, you look way worse than last time I saw you, like, you look straight up unhealthy, like, ten years older than last time. I mean, do you have a fever or something?"

Brandy started breathing heavily.

"I don't think so." she said.

"Maybe you should just, you know, quit drinking?"

"Oh, here we go."

"Brandy! I'm serious. Like, I'm not a doctor, but like, your skin is totally white. You look like a bedsheet."

"I… look, it's not that, alright. Don't you remember I told you about that surgery I needed to have?"

"Yeah, the nose job?"

"What? Are you serious?"

"I mean, I don't think you need a nose job, it looks just like mine. And, like, I don't have a big nose, do I?"

"Alright, are anyone fucking listening to me!" Brandy erupted, and slammed her fist at the table, which wound up taking a bigger toll on her stamina than she expected.

"So is it *not* a nose job?"

"No, it's fucking serious shit. A fucking matter of life and death."

"Like, you could *die* if you don't have this operation?"

"Correct-a-fucking-diddely-doo!"

"Like, seriously? Really honest to God seriously?"

"Didn't you fucking listen last time I told you?"

"I must have misunderstood."

Brandy slammed her face on the table. "Fucking hell." she said.

"Well, you know what, if you're really having a condition like that, you really shouldn't be drinking at the rate you're going now."

"Goddamn it, drinking's got nothing to do with it. Why won't you fucking listen?"

Brandy was beginning to cold sweat.

"Ooph!" she moaned, starting to have cramp-like spasms. "Shit, fuck." she exhaled.

"Brandy, are you alright."

Brandy took another sip of tea, but failed to swallow it. She spat it out on the table, and stood up.

"I think I need to use the bathroom again." she groaned at the edge of her breath.

She walked slowly towards the bathroom, hunched over from the pain, coughing and belching.

"I think I need some fresh air."

Then she stopped, and spewed all over the floor, a high pressure garden hose stream of liquid and bile. Everybody in the café looked at her.

"Alright, that's it. I told you not to come in here drunk again." said the barista. "Get outta here!"

"Brandy, how much have you been drinking today?" asked Imogen.

"Shut up. I'm fine."

She stumbled to the exit, and knocked herself against the door to open it. Once outside, she threw up some more on the sidewalk. Imogen followed after, to watch her never-ending stream of puke.

"Tucker… come here, buddy." she mumbled through the barf.

The vomit was changing color from yellow to pink to crimson. She hurled blood.

"Brandy!" yelled Imogen.

Then Brandy descended down to the ground, and landed softly in the puddle of her own creation. She did not feel the impact. She felt nothing. Even the pain from the parasite was gone. It was all gone. Imogen still screamed at her, yet an ocean distorted her voice. All sound floated into the abyss. Brandy's eyes watered up, her vision became blurred and hazy. It all faded away.

Blackness, and silence.

III

Brandy momentarily opened her eyes to see a blurred image of what looked like Doctor Walker spouting something unintelligible…

So much panicking…

Things got clearer, less blurry…

129

That other doctor, she had seen him before too…

Many people, all stressing…

Someone put an oxygen mask on her…

"Ever done this sort of thing before?"

"Anesthesia administered, doctor."

"You're gonna be alright kid."

"I'm not sure if we can…"

"Her kidneys are still prime. If we screw up, I'm sure we could get a decent…"

CHAPTER ELEVEN

Awaking from a deep black void in a hospital bed, Brandy found herself plagued by a splitting headache and a throat like sandpaper filled with tree sap. As she gradually regained lucidity she became aware of the annoyingly beeping heart rate monitor to her right. She also found herself to be receiving intravenous fluid through her hand, urine yellow fluid, from a bag hung on a pole to her left.

Reasonably soon the door opened, and in walked Doctor Walker, smiling as usual.

"How are we doing today, Miss Rabinow?" he asked.

"Could I have some water?" Brandy coughed.

"Oh, no. I'm afraid not. You can't intake any liquid orally for the next five day. Of course, I can let you moisten your mouth a little, but you'll have to spit it out again."

"What, seriously?"

"No, I was just joking."

"Oh, thank God."

"No, I was being serious, actually. The part about joking was just joking. Sorry. You won't be allowed to drink or eat anything until next Monday, at which point you'll be written out, and allowed to leave. Forced to leave, technically."

Walker then took the liberty to pry Brandy's eyes and mouth open, to observe her pupils and tongue.

"How do you feel, by the way? Besides thirst, and light fatigue, do you feel any unexpected pain anywhere? Are you dizzy or nauseated? Any itchiness? Shakiness? Can you move all your limbs normally? Do they respond properly?"

She moved her arms and fingers around, and lightly shook her legs.

131

"I s'pose I feel relatively fine, I guess. Though I still got this pain from the parasite, you remember that?"

"Oh, yeah, you should probably be a little sore around the operation wound."

"Operation wound?"

"Oh yes. Want to take a look at the scar?"

"What are you talking about?"

She flipped away her blanket, and lifted her hospital gown, to see that, indeed, on her lower abdomen, right above the pubic area, there was now a long banana-shaped scar stitched together.

"Like, what? You seriously removed the little bastard?"

"Well, of course we did. The Tidak Nyata is all clear and gone. Why else did you think you are here? This isn't a hotel. And I should know, I worked at a hotel in my youth; as a bellhop, don't you know."

"Like, really? *Seriously?*"

"Oh yes. I was fifteen, and needed a summer job, you see. Pop had fixed me one down at the chocolate factory, but that kind of labor was too monotonous for me."

"No, fuck, not that. I meant the fucking parasite shit. You removed it? It's finally definitely gone?"

"Yes, as I just told you." he said grabbing into his pocket. "Here, look."

He took out a little jar containing a tiny stiff worm creature floating in the middle of what looked like dirty rust-colored brine.

"It's actually sort of adorable, don't you think?"

"That was the thing inside me?"

"Yes, the largest one I've ever seen, to be frank. You've certainly fed it up fat. I could've said 'a job well done' if it was a turkey or a pig, ready to be slaughtered for Christmas. But it's not, so I all I can say is, well, I shan't be vulgar."

He handed the jar to Brandy.

Holding that jar in her hands, Brandy looked in ambivalent awe at the dead parasite. It was slightly smaller than she imagined, about the size of her pinkie, only a bit fatter. There was a tremendous relief in the fact that this cretin that had been festering inside her for so long now lay dead and defeated, pickled in a jar between her fingers. It reminded her of the strings of fat she squeezed out of her zits back in her adolescence, which she for extended periods would keep on her finger for observation, delighting in having exiled them from her body.

She was uncertain what disturbed her the most, the fact that this creature had been living and growing inside her genitals, or that she right now actually wanted to drink its brine out of the immense desperation to quench her thirst.

"I take it you didn't exactly cut down on the glug-glug-glugging?" Walker said, miming drinking from a bottle. "Wasn't particularly smart, now was it?"

'Don't tease me with drinking, you bastard' Brandy thought. 'I'm shriveling up like a prune here, my throat's a fucking desert'.

"Tell you the truth, we got you just in the nick of time." Walker said. "This might not be the best time to bring it up, but truthfully, you were only inches away from dying. I thought you'd have at least two more weeks to go, but it seems the Tidak grew even more rapidly as time went on. I do wonder why."

"Shit." Brandy moaned and sunk into her pillow.

"Yes, you really need some rest now. I'll leave you be."

Walker then walked out.

"Hey doc." Brandy said.

"What is it?"

"What about that whole payment thing? I didn't raise enough money in time. Like, fifteen grand, how am I supposed to get that kind of money in a month?"

"Oh, there's nothing to worry about. It has all been paid for?"

"Paid for?"

"Yeah, some third party took the whole bill. You don't have to cough up a single dime."

Doctor Walker closed the door behind him.

II

The next few hours Brandy had been drowsing off into dreams about liquids. Water, soda, beer, tea, juice, mojitos. All she could think about was moistening her palate, streaming beverages down her crusty throat. Every half hour or so she would wake up and discover she was still as thirsty and dry as ever. One such time she was awoken by a knock outside, followed by voices.

"Do you think you can stand up, ma'am?"

"I should be able to, yeah. Roland, can you hand me the cane?"

"How do you fold this thing… is it… you know what, I'll just carry it in sideways."

"Ready, Roland? Pull me up."

The door opened, and in waddled Olive with her cane, followed by a nurse carrying her wheelchair. Once he sat it down, Olive quickly sat down in it. Roland came in after, standing by her side.

"How are you doing, friend?" Olive asked.

"Oh fuck, I wasn't expecting visitors so soon." Brandy sighed.

"Are you feeling alright?"

"A little tired. Also, thirsty as fucking ass."

"Oh yes. I heard you weren't allowed to eat or drink until Monday. That's a shame. If it were me, I'd probably end myself. I mean, I couldn't go through something like that. You're a real trouper, Brandy. You truly are."

"Thanks, I guess."

"Hope you'll be in good health by Wednesday. That's when we'll be having our fundraising banquette. We'll have a festive dinner over at our compound. I would just *love* it if you'd come. I mean, if you don't feel well still, I understand, but it would still mean just *so much* to me if you came."

"I guess, yeah, sure. Was… was that the reason you came here? To invite me to the… the dinner?"

"Oh no, of course not. We just had to check in on you. We were so worried. When Mister Wilkes told me you had been put in an ambulance after having retched blood, I just knew we had to act. So we came down here, and were told you've been put out for an emergency surgery, so I said to Roland, what did I say to you, Roland?"

"You said we should pay for the surgery, lady Olive." said Roland

"That's what I said to Roland. I said that, and so we did. And we made sure you got a solitary room, all by yourself."

"Only two or three other patients have single rooms in this hospital." said Roland.

"I mean, what risk could we take?" said Olive. "Let you share a room with some strange troglodyte who'd infect you with any kinds of awful bacteria? One cough, and you'd get yellow fever? We couldn't let that happen."

"So wait. Hold on." Brandy said. "You *paid* for this? You paid for *my* surgery? *You*? You paid for this? Paid for my surgery?"

"Well, yes. Of course I did. That's what friends are for, right?"

"I..." Brandy was still a tad overwhelmed. "I... I s'pose. I, um, I don't think I'll be able to pay you back any time soon. It'll take at least a year, actually."

"Oh, no. Brandy. Friend. Don't. Don't pay me back. It wasn't an investment, it was a favor. What's fifteen thousand? Just a drop in the ocean. I've spent more on lunch several times. No, I don't want a single penny in return. All I want is for you to be you, and for you to be healthy. That's all that matters. Health is the most important thing of all."

"Well, thanks a bunch. Much obliged. I guess I... not gonna say 'misjudged' but... underestimated your kindness, I guess. Not that I thought you were cruel, or insensitive, or anything. Just... No one's ever just bailed me out on fifteen grand before. It's just... man. Fuck."

Olive turned to Roland.

"Roland, wheel me closer." she said.

Roland obliged and rolled Olive right up to Brandy.

"And you know what?" Olive said. "I'll give you a little extra."

She whipped up a stack of bills from her purse.

"Just for the fare home, and to treat yourself a little."

Brandy received the stack, and saw they were all hundred-dollar bills.

"Oh no, please, don't. I can't accept this. This is just absolutely horrendously, like, too much."

"No, no, no. You take it. Just a drop in the ocean. I've paid more for a glass of champagne. It's nothing. Just a little boost."

Brandy sighed.

"Alright. If you really insist."

"You're such a sweet little darling, Brandy." Olive said laying her five-pound hand patty on Brandy's forehead. "I hope you get well soon."

III

The next few days Brandy spent bouncing in and out of consciousness around the clock, sleeping for an average of twenty minutes, with hour-long intervals, same at night as day.

All her dreams revolved around beverages. Drinking them, ordering them at a bar, buying them at a store; sometimes grabbing for them in thin air. Oftentimes a bottle of a refreshment would teasingly dangle at her, just out of reach. There were either prison bars separating them, or she would be pulled away by an abstract force. Once she had to wrestle a gorilla who turned into her father and then into Mister Wilkes, and then back into a gorilla. As it slammed her head into the ground she woke up.

In her waking time, she idly watched the television hung on the wall opposite her. It was an old box television circa mid-nineties, with oversaturated bleeding colors and hazy images, with one permanently purple spot in the lower left corner. There were few channels, and there was never anything on except news, reality shows and the occasional sitcom; and it all merely functioned as a distraction from the unbearable drought in her throat.

The first day she had been so weak and reduced that she needed assistance to go to the bathroom, which she did only once during her whole stay. Since there was nothing to consume there was nothing to release.

On the third day two house flies flew in through the window. One sat on the edge between the ceiling and the wall, all mellow and quiet. The other one bounced between the walls like a rabid maniac, buzzing like a rusty old chainsaw all the while. And it never stopped. It kept going at its crazed panic attack for hours, ramming itself into anything and everything at top speed, the impact making a loud *DUNT*-noise each time. Once it even crashed into Brandy's forehead, at which point she attempted to strike it, but did unfortunately not even possess the strength to blow a feather away, let alone hit something, and so the fly continued its aimless rampage for another ten minutes, before, most likely accidentally, flying back out the window. The other fly still just sat there, unflinching, for the remaining days.

IV

Finally, the day had come. It was time to go home. At nine AM, Brandy underwent a final check-up in Doctor Walker's office. Everything seemed to be normal.

"Do you feel well enough to leave, now?" he asked.

"Yeah. As soon as possible." Brandy wheezed enthusiastically.

"Well, that's good. I'm pleased to see you encountered no apparent neurological damages from the procedure. That happens quite a lot with the Tidak, you see."

Brandy kept shifting her eyes in the direction of the office exit.

"So, um, that's it? Can I go now?" she asked impatiently.

"Oh, I just have to write out a prescription for you first. *Nequam Intractabilis*, in pill form. You need to take those from now on. Three pills a day, spread evenly throughout. One after breakfast, one after dinner, and one before bedtime, or at least midnight; that's the usual routine."

"What do I need those for?"

"If you don't start taking them soon, or you abstain for a few days, your blood will curdle up and kill you. I suggest you go pick up your bottle on your way home today."

"Shit, what? I need drugs to live now? Like, just live?"

"Only until you've emptied your first bottle, which should take about twenty days. After that, come back, and we'll determine whether you need to continue the treatment."

"Alright, and if I skip a day or something?"

"I would recommend avoiding that at all costs. Of course, a single day probably won't kill you, or a day where you only take two pills. You would probably survive, but best not push your luck, is what I'm saying."

Walker signed his prescription and handed it to Brandy.

"Oh, and fair warning..." he continued. "Better not mix those pills with alcohol. They'll do a solid number on you if you do."

"Aw shit." Brandy said looking over the prescription.

"The drug doesn't have any common side effects, but in the unlikely case it should cause anxieties, depression, insomnia or psychosis, just give me a call. And you should really get some proper sleep from now on. You've got terrible crow's feet."

"Crow's feet?" Brandy said. "Crow. Goddamn, Tucker. Where is Tucker? I've totally forgotten about him."

During her stay in the hospital, Brandy had only been semi-lucid at best, never once thinking clearly about anything. Through the fog in her mind she had neglected to ask, or even think, about the whereabouts of Tucker.

"Who?" asked Walker. "What are you talking about?"

137

"Like, Tucker. Where is he?!" Brandy said frantically. "Do you have, like, a storage area for pets or something here at the hospital? Is he well? Did you feed him well? Did you get he's not supposed to have rice?"

"Who... what is Tucker? Is it your pet dog or something?"

"No, he's a crow. Y'know, a bird. A black, super pitch black bird. A Corvus Monedula jackdaw. He talks, and he's always loyal, and a real people lover, y'know."

"I don't know of such a thing like that having been reported around here." Walker bewilderedly responded. "Maybe you should ask in the reception."

"Alright, I'll do that. And then I want to leave right now."

A nurse was soon called in to escort Brandy out to the reception in a wheelchair. On the way there, she made her stop by the vending machine, where she bought herself a soda, and chugged it down in one big gulp, then shook the bottle for the last few drops of liquid. She then bought another one, this time savoring it, taking tiny sips with ten seconds intervals, sloshing the soda around in her mouth.

At the reception, she was being told there had been made no record of a crow like Tucker in the vicinity at the time the ambulance had picked her up. She bombarded the receptionist with questions, trying desperately to deduce where he might have ended up. But the receptionist had no further information, and after a while Brandy started repeating herself, at which point she realized it would be better to continue the search somewhere else, and just had the receptionist order a taxi.

On the way home, she stared out a hundred miles in the distance, the snow-clad frosty streets of Riverside passing through her vision. There was nary a person on the sidewalks, nary a car on the slippery roads, and large specks of snow still descended down at a tranquil pace onto the seemingly hibernating city. The taxi driver was a bulky Russian immigrant, 'Fyodor' said his license. His English was rather shaky, and so he spoke very little beyond necessity. Brandy was at the moment not in the mood for speaking either. Instead, they listened to Fyodor's cassette tape of Georgy Sviridov.

Driving through Fightmaster Boulevard in West Columbia, Brandy caught sight of a small black crow flying into an oak tree, perching on its longest branch.

"Stop the car." she said. "Stop it here!"

Fyodor obliged. Brandy crawled out, finding it hard to stand by her own power, for her body had still none. Eying the oak tree where the crow still sat, she slowly limped away, having to catch her balance on a garbage can. She kept limping, closing in on the tree. When she reached the root she needed to support herself against its stem. She looked up to the crow.

"Tucker?" she asked. "Is that you?"

The bird did not respond. On closer inspection, it was far leaner than she remembered Tucker being, and its beak was noticeably shorter.

It flew away.

Disappointed, Brandy limped back to the car, slower than before. Before she reached the halfway, her legs collapsed and sent her headfirst into the snow.

"You need help?" asked Fyodor.
"No, I don't, I'm fine." answered Brandy, trying and failing to get herself back up.
"You need help." said Fyodor.

He stepped out of the car, and pulled Brandy up from the snow to carry her back in his arms.

They continued driving. '*Winter Road*' was playing on the tape. Brandy considered making another stop at the nearest pharmacy to pick up her prescription, but then decided she did not feel like it today. She figured she could either do it tomorrow, or die from blood coagulation before then.

CHAPTER TWELVE

Brandy woke up at eight AM in the morning. It was Wednesday. The night before she had received a text message from an unknown number reminding her to attend Olive's fundraising banquette at the D'Orleans Compound. On one hand, she did not feel like going at all. She remained quite short on stamina from after the surgery. There was practically no energy in her body anymore. Additionally, the emotional void left by Tucker had sent her spiraling into a mild depression since returning home. Or maybe that was caused by the pills. Possibly. Maybe there was a combination. When she woke up the day before and saw Tucker's branch that she had nailed to the wall, she began to weep till her face was naught but a red sore mess of tears and snot. She had never cried for two hours straight before in her memory, but she did then. But she did not cry today. Maybe the pills had begun to dull her senses. They did not cause depression, they repressed it. Maybe. Who could tell?

On the other hand, perhaps attending a party, even one as stiff and boring as this banquette would probably be, could potentially lighten her mood, or in the least put her mind off her missing friend for a few hours. And since this was an Olive D'Orleans arrangement, any greater physical activity would definitely be off the table.

Due to the terribly unstable condition of Brandy's fridge, she no longer dared to put milk in there. Therefore, every morning since mid-October, she had had to eat her breakfast cereal dry, which she really did not mind all that much. Eating Lucky Charms straight from the box with a spoon, and washing it down with a soda of a random temperature had become her morning ritual from which she rarely deviated. Only difference now was she could not share any with Tucker. He used to love the green top hat marshmallows.

After breakfast, she now had to swallow another Nequam Intractabilis with some water. They were some big baby blue oval shapes and much harder to swallow than aspirins, and they tasted offensively bitter, and even if she placed it on the far back of her tongue, that taste would spread to the entirety of her mouth in a second, like an infection. The flavor was so intolerably gruesome it had to immediately be washed away with soda, or beer, or Snapple, or whatever the fridge had in storage. The upside to these pills, besides keeping her alive, was the magnificent effect that manifested when combining them with alcohol. The day before, she discovered that only a single glass of wine mixed with one of these pills would careen her into a state of tranquilized euphoria in less than a minute.

After having swallowed her morning dosage, she opened her half full screw cap bottle of cheap red Merlot, and poured herself a glass which she downed in one big gulp. She looked out the window, where the sun was shining upon the white desolation of deteriorating brick buildings. 'Miller's Deli' said one rusty sign. Said deli had been closed for business since before Brandy moved here.

She opened up a playlist of The Cascades on her phone, and started playing. She tossed the phone on the bed, and lay down besides it, waiting for the effects to kick in.

II

The first twenty minutes or so, the pill and alcohol mixture sent Brandy into a semi-waking coma, where she stared thoughtlessly into the ceiling with smooth pleasant music floating through her ear drums. After that, a state of practical lucidity followed, though everything still appeared like a distant unimportant haze swooping her by as she maneuvered through the corridors of the Manson Asylum, then out to the streets, while The Cascades still played at full volume in her pocket, or maybe not.

Unfortunately, she now required a cane to walk properly, as the recuperation from the surgery was still far from complete. Perhaps, despite Doctor Walker's observations, there had actually been some neurological damage, for Brandy's balance was now significantly impaired. The pills were by no means helping. On Tuesday she had managed to order a taxi over to the nearest pawn shop to buy herself a ten dollar wooden cane that had since already given her a couple of splinters, but was no less reliable to keep her on her feet.

Wandering through the streets with the sun flashing in her face covered with sunglasses, passing an array of cloudy shades of people, she felt remarkably joyous, bordering on ecstatic, as if her worries all faded away into the mist around her. The people who gave her funny looks only made her chortle, for they were funny-looking too, more so than her. People have so many quirks one can only notice by not caring about one's own.

At this point, she desired nothing, missed nothing, feared nothing. It was a new better type of purgatory, a foggy borderland between heaven and an even better heaven.

Then came the third phase, which more resembled regular drunkenness, the tail end of a severe bender, where self-awareness began catching up, surpassing motor skills. The almost magical carefreeness crumbled up, as all the vanished worries came rushing back to form a sudden sensation of anxiety. This was normal. She had experienced it twice the day before. 'Molten cement down your vagina' was a thought that hit her hard. 'That is the mercy kill'.

'Tucker!' she then thought. She had subconsciously imagined him on her shoulder this whole time, but now he evaporated into smoke. Tucker was gone. There was no way around it.

When her dexterity had recuperated to the point that she could confidently communicate with vendors, she bought a submarine sandwich with feta cheese and chorizo at a deli on Bordeaux Avenue in Bismarck, and sat down on a bench right outside where the sun had melted all the snow away, and slowly chewed it with a melancholy stare into the horizon.

On her way home, she received another text message.

'The banquette officially begins at 8, but feel free to drop in before that, just to hang out and chill. Any time is good.' it read.

Brandy thought a little about it. It had been about two hours since she drank that glass of wine, but the effects were still lingering, slowing down her thought process. Eventually, she decided to reply.

'Sure. I'll be there.' she wrote.

Just ten seconds later, she got a response.

'Roland can pick you up at your home in 1 hour. No need to bring anything but a smile.'

142

'Alright, then.' Brandy thought.

CHAPTER THIRTEEN

Sat in the chaise lounge in the mansion living room, attired in her white satin ball dress, Olive glared out down the hill of Vermogend Drive, with a glass of imported Albanian brandy in her hand. The sun was beginning to set over the horizon, as Smetana's '*Má Vlast*' played on vinyl in the background. Mister Wilkes walked into the room from behind.

"Enjoying the view, lady Olive?" he asked.

"I just need a moment to reflect." Olive replied. "I've always done my best thinking when I look out this window."

"I would imagine. You get a decent view of the whole city from here. All those homes. All those people. All that potential."

"Do you have a place you go to think better?" asked Olive.

"Of course I do. I go to the nearest toy store."

"Toy store?"

"Yes. There is an unusual type of serenity to be experienced at the toy store, you see. I feel like I've left reality and found a different plane of existence. Back in my childhood, toy stores were so ordinary, just selling toys, you see. Lately, however, they've evolved into these surreal art galleries of Chinese-manufactured oddities that I simply don't understand what are supposed to be used for. It's like an exhibition of modern art, and unlike any real such exhibition, entry is always free. None of those toys make any sense as children's entertainment, they're way too abstract. Like those cups of slime. Have you seen those? How are those things meant to entertain someone? It makes no sense. And I love it. This nonsensical hellscape. Every item is so bizarre, and they are and so many, so frequent. Just looking down the aisles put my mind in a frenzy, running a mile a minute. I must say, I've always gotten my best ideas visiting a toy store."

"That's nice." Olive responded absent-mindedly.

"Anyway, I came to inform you that Antonio Fregatura, of Fregatura Apparel, will not be joining us tonight. Something about a funeral."

"Oh, no, won't he?" Olive turned around. "He is so fun."

She rested her head on her hand and sighed.

"That's a bummer." she said.

"Of course, I *could* persuade him to re-decide, if you so desire." Wilkes said cracking his fingers.

"No, that's alright. We'll have plenty of guests as it is. And after all, Brandy will be there, won't she, Roland?"

Roland walked in, pulling his gloves over his fingers.

"Of course, lady Olive." he said. "In fact, I am about to go fetch her right now."

"Yay!" Olive swung her glass in the air, squirting parts of the liquor onto the chaise lounge. "I love Brandy. She's so fun. Can't wait to show her around. You think she's in good stand at the moment, Mister Wilkes?"

"Adequately, yes." Wilkes responded.

"That's good to hear. I was so worried about her."

"I believe I should leave now." Wilkes said. "I still have a few errands to run. Perhaps I'll see you at the banquette, my lady."

Then Wilkes quickly disappeared into the foyer.

Olive sighed.

"Roland…" she said. "Do you have a moment?"

"I am not expected to be in West Cedarbrook for forty five minutes, so I certainly have five minutes, or slightly less."

Olive paused a little bit.

"Okay, look." she said after another swig. "Can I tell you something?"

"You always can." Roland answered.

"When I was little…" Olive raised her head to look up at the sky. "… about eleven maybe, I watched with my parents my very first film in the auditorium. It was the first film I ever saw. You remember, we had just installed the auditorium back then, it was just finished."

"Yes, I remember. We re-purposed your grandfather's art studio. Your mother was very against it, as I recall it."

"I remember the quarrels, yeah. The thing is, we were going to celebrate by screening a film in there. We got one of the gardeners to handle the projector."

"Raúl, yes. He was a trained projectionist, I believe. If I recall correctly, he worked at a film theater in Havana before he came here."

"Yes. So we watched this old black and white silent film. I don't remember the title. I don't remember much of the plot either, except it was something about gangsters in the prohibition era, I think. I just remember it was really funny. We all laughed a lot. The thing is, the cast was mostly just very thin people, acrobats almost. The men *and* the ladies. They all had bodies like dumbwaiters. I thought it was a bit strange, actually, that nobody on screen looked like me. And then, finally, one guy showed up that was really big. Properly fat. 'Finally' I thought, 'this is my man, I'll root for him'. It was really good to see someone like myself. He looked a bit kooky, but I didn't mind. And in the first scene what he did was eating a whole cream cake with his bare hands, and mother laughed at it. 'How disgusting' I remember she said out loud. The next time he showed up, he got himself stuck in a manhole, and someone tried to pull him up with a plunger, and then seven guys or so had to come and drag him up. And then later still, he sat down on a park bench and broke it, and fell over, and both my parents roared with laughter. And I had roared with laughter several times before along with them, but I didn't like it when stuff like that happened to that guy. It was so mean how the film treated him. And it did mean things to the other characters too, but it was different. They were, you know, victimized for being clumsy or stupid or evil or just unfortunate. But the fat guy, he got it all because he was fat and nothing else. He was fat, and that was the joke the whole time, like being fat was something funny. And, that was it, I suppose. I don't really know if I had a point with all this, other than I didn't like to watch movies all that much after that, because they kind of make me feel bad. And, maybe, that I suspect that when I go out that people who don't know me start assuming bad things about me, and that makes me feel bad too."

Roland stood still, trying to think of a response.

"My lady…" he said. "I have always believed that people should under no circumstances be judged by superficial attributes. And also…" he paused to think. "I believe… that it is time I get going to pick up your friend Miss Rabinow. We certainly can't let her get impatient, now can we?"

"I suppose we can't."

"Certainly not. So therefore, I'll be on my way then."

II

The D'Orleans mansion was the largest home Brandy had ever seen with her own bare eyes. The plot was the size of a little district, with the warehouse-sized house atop a hill, its entrance a hundred yard distance from the gate. As the limousine neared the driveway, Brandy caught a glimpse of Olive in the window, who seemed to grow an enthusiastic smile at the sight of her arrival.

Roland opened the double door entrance in an overly dramatic fashion, before standing aside to allow Brandy to go inside before him.

"Lady Olive is waiting for you in the living room." Roland said. "To you left, madam."

"Thanks. I think I saw her through the window."

Brandy went into the living room, to find Olive excitedly looking right at her from the chaise lounge by said window.

"How do you do, friend?" she asked, all giddy and energized.

"Oh, good, I s'pose. Still a bit reduced."

"Is that a cane you're using?"

Brandy looked down at the cane she currently supported herself on.

"Yeah, I need a cane to walk now. Ain't as strong as before."

"I have a cane too." Olive raised her ebony cane into view. "Now we're like cane-buddies!"

"Yeah, I've seen your cane before. It's really nice. Mine's just some cheap crap. Probably used by some poor geezer who died a decade ago."

"Oh, that's too bad. We can get you a better cane if you'd like to."

"Oh, wow. No thanks. I mean, thanks for the offer, but you've just done more than enough for me already."

147

"No, no. That's nonsense. Come here, buddy. Don't strain your legs standing around like that."

Brandy did as Olive said, and walked over to her chaise lounge, where she sat down on the seven inches of free space, using her cane to keep herself from tipping off.

"Now you listen, cane-buddy. I'm gonna give you a new cane, because that's what friends are for, you understand."

"Well sure, but there's gotta be a limit to it, y'know. I mean, I don't have a lot to give you back."

"But you don't need to give me *anything*, friend. All I need, and all I want, is your friendship."

Olive then stretched out her arm to scratch Brandy on the neck.

"Because we're best buddies, right?" she said.

"Well, yeah. Of course." Brandy replied.

"And we're cane buddies."

"We sure are."

Olive pointed her cane towards Brandy like a sword.

"Cane buddies." she repeated.

Brandy assumed she wanted them to clash canes together as a form of affirming gesture, and so did just that.

"Yay!" Olive exclaimed, pleased with her reaction.

"Pardon my interruption, my ladies…" Roland said. "But would our guest perhaps enjoy a little refreshment?"

"Sure, yeah." Brandy responded eagerly. "Whaddya got?"

"We do have a fair selection of liqueurs." Roland said. "Or perhaps the madam would want something non-alcoholic?"

"Got any hard liquor?"

"Well, naturally. Would cognac be fine?"

"Uh, sure, yeah. A glass of cognac would be good."

"I shall fetch you a glass right away."

And then Roland left.

Brandy looked around the room. The walls were covered in burgundy wallpaper; one wall decorated with vertical rows of old rifles, separated by rows of Native American medicine shields; another with hunting trophies of various animals' heads.

"What do you think of the view?" asked Olive.

"What?"

"The view. Do you like it?"

Brandy stared out the window, looking over the whole city all the way to the shore.

"It's pretty neat." she responded.

"Yeah? Don't you think so? I always come to look out this window to think better. Ever since I was a kid. And I still do, always gotten my best ideas looking out this window. I suppose just knowing there is an entire city beneath me fills me with confidence. And soon there'll actually be a city beneath me, literally."

"Yeah, that'll be something, I'm sure."

"It'll be so great. I'll sit there, in my high tower, looking down on this fantastic society that *I* have created. And you will be welcome to join me, you know. Of course I'll make you honorary obesewoman."

"That sure would be honorable." Brandy said trying to repress any sarcasm in her tone.

"I mean, I won't be handing out honorary titles all willy-nilly. But not only are you my best buddy *and* my cane buddy, but now that we have you on our team, we can relax in knowing we'll *never* run out of money."

"Yeah, I suppose. Seem like you won't run dry anytime soon, though, judging from this place."

"You like my home?"

"I've seen only, like, two rooms so far, but this is probably the most extravagant place I've been to."

"Oh, I've got to show you around. We've got to visit my private quarters."

"Well, sure, I guess."

At that moment, Roland returned with Brandy's glass of cognac.

"Roland, fetch me my wheelchair." Olive said. "Brandy wants me to show her my private quarters."

III

A section of the first floor of the D'Orleans mansion had been designated as Olive's private quarters. It consisted of a lounge, a work space and a bedroom all tied together, and in addition, a spacious bathroom located right next to the bedroom area. Brandy sat down in the closest sofa in sight, one of three in a circle around a mahogany coffee table, all facing a sixty-eight inch television mounted to the wall over a fireplace, on which mantle stood a line of different Fabergé eggs.

"You may leave us now, Roland, and come back with a Sazerac, won't you." said Olive.

"Of course, my lady." said Roland and left.

"You know you could have asked for a mixed drink if you wanted to." Olive said to Brandy.

"Eh, this cognac here is alright." Brandy took another sip. "Maybe I'll ask for a mojito later if I feel like it."

"So what do you think of my private quarters?"

Brandy looked around the room.

"Well, it's… impressive. Like, it's bigger than the whole apartment I grew up in back in Philly. And we were like, five people. Six, if you count my uncle who lived there almost permanently 'cos he never had any money."

"Oh, that's so sad. You're like one of those children in Africa that they tell us to donate money to on TV."

"It's not *that* bad." chortled Brandy. "Like, we're not starving or anything. And it wasn't that tight, it's just that this place is so, like, ginormous, y'know."

"Well, it gets pretty small once you get used to it."

Brandy stood up, deciding to have a look around the place. She went to a cabinet filled with rows of vinyls, and a gramophone on top.

"This is your LP collection?" she asked.

"Yes. The ones I play frequently, at least. I have a whole stack, hundreds of them, down in the utility room. I never listen to those. They just sit there gathering dust."

"They weren't your style?"

"They bored me, yeah. These ones are all absolute gems, though. Oldies but goodies."

"Yeah, oldies are the best. I've never been one for that modern shit either."

Brandy opened the cabinet glass door and started flipping through the records. The Association, The Beatles, Buddy Holly, Carpenters, The Cascades...

"What kind of music do *you* like?" asked Olive.

"Aw, nothing in particular. Just old stuff. Much the same as you, actually."

"Really? You like the same music as me?"

"From what I can tell from these records, yeah. I got a lot of these folks on my phone."

"You have their numbers?"

"No, I meant, I got playlists and shit of their songs, y'know."

"Boy, I can't believe we like the same music as well. We're just becoming better friends by the second!"

At that point, Roland returned with Olive's drink.

"Here is your Sazerac, lady Olive." he said.

"Thanks, Roland. That'll be all."

Roland cast a bothered look at Brandy.

"I take it you will change into your formalwear reasonably soon." he said.

"What?" Brandy reacted.

"You *did* bring some appropriate garments for this evening, did you not?"

"Nah, didn't have any. Thought I'd just wear my regular threads."

"You intend to wear *that* at the banquette?"

Brandy was once again wearing her regular get-up of her green cardigan, beret, blouse, and now also sun-bleached jeans with holes in the knees.

"Yeah, like, it's all I got. I can take off my beret at the dinner table, if you want me to."

"It's okay, Brandy." Olive intervened. "You can wear whatever you like."

"Lady Olive, I must remind you, we will be having highly important guests at this banquette." Roland said. "Potential investors, whose eyes or honor we cannot risk offending. An attendant representing us just cannot look that obscene."

"She's not obscene. You retract that, Roland."

"I meant no offense, madam..." he said to Brandy. "But for the sake of the project, you simply must dress more appropriately."

"Well, I got nothing else, as I just said, so I either wear this, or I s'pose I got to leave."

151

"Oh no! Don't do that!" exclaimed Olive. "You can borrow some of my... never mind, but maybe you can borrow some of mother's clothes. She has some dresses she's grown out of, hasn't she, Roland?"

Roland groaned.

"I will go and have a look." he said. "I must remind you, though, we expect to have our first guests in only a little over an hour."

And then he left again.

"Good lord." Olive sighed. "So much for a little quality time."

"I hear ya." Brandy said, now having reached the 'T' section of Olive's alphabetically arranged records.

"The thing is, I appreciate Roland's help, and also his friendship." said Olive through a swig of her drink. "To be honest, he was my only real friend before you came into my life."

"Seriously?" Brandy said half-interested, most of her attention still on the records.

"So it's not that I don't appreciate him, it's just that sometimes I wish I had a bit more privacy. These days, he's there all the time, you know. I never get to be alone anymore."

"Yeah, I feel ya. I love being with my own thoughts sometimes, totally indiscreet."

"Right now, I have this button, you see it here." Olive showed Brandy an electronic devise with a red button strapped around her left wrist. "You see?"

Brandy turned around to look at the devise. "Oh, alright. You got a button, yeah."

"It's an emergency button, the kind they give to paraplegics and the elderly."

"Oh, so you press it if you have an accident?"

"No, just if I want to get up, or move anywhere, because I'm too big to do any of that on my own."

"That sucks."

"It *does* suck. And with Roland, it's not his fault either. The problem is that technology, you know, it's developed so fast, we've gotten a man up to the moon, you can chat with people in Bangladesh over the internet, cheese can be bought in a spray bottle; but for some reason *I* still need the help of another person, because technological progress only follows the will of society, and society doesn't care about obese people. I can't do anything by myself, not even move. I can't get this darn wheelchair to move an inch."

"Why don't you just get one of those, y'know, one of those electric wheelchairs?"

"I will, when they invent one that fits me. They're all so narrow, you know. I mean, the one I'm in now was custom-made just for me."

"They should likely have one that fits you still, I think."

"Not that I have ever heard of. If they had such a thing I should have known about it, don't you think?"

"I s'pose." Brandy said with her eyes on a record she had not seen before, '*Paradise Found*' by The Winged Lieutenants. "Yo, who're these fellas?"

"Oh, that's probably one of my favorite records. Well, the first song at least. The rest of them are just so-so, but that first one is just… *Mmmm*."

"You mean the '*While We're in Paradise*' one on the A-side?"

"Oh yes. Want to play it?"

"Sure. Let's."

Brandy put the record on, and carefully lay the needle over its outer edge. She walked back to the sofa. The two of them became perfectly silent in anticipation for the music.

The song started playing. "*Come and join me in my flight, till we reach our Shangri-La…*"

Brandy glared absentmindedly up at the ceiling painting of flowers and plants, tapping her thigh with four fingers to the song's jazzy rhythm. When it reached its interlude, with pan flutes and sitars, she closed her eyes and saw a multitude of smoke clouds of all colors and shapes blowing by.

"*Let me gnaw upon your jaw, let me escape into your bush…*"

She stretched out her neck, rubbed her legs together, rubbed her hands against the fabric of the sofa. It was smooth velvet. The song ended with a twenty-second sitar solo, and she downed the rest of the cognac.

"Wasn't that a beautiful tune?" asked Olive.

"They don't make 'em like that anymore." Brandy said. "I mean, that definitely was one of the better songs I've heard in a long while."

"I knew you'd like it. I liked it, so of course I knew you'd like it. Because we have the same taste in music, you know."

The next song started playing. It had a catchy beat and a similar set-up with sitars, saxophones, pan flutes and electric guitars; but it lacked a certain something. The vibes were all wrong. It was duller, more anonymous. Not annoying or unlikable, just more forgettable.

And then Roland came back, once again.

"Madam, Miss Rabinow, I've found you a suitable outfit." he said, holding a scarlet red silk dress and a pair of black high-heeled shoes. "I must insist that you change immediately. We have very little time."

"Alright, I'll change." Brandy said irritatedly. "I'll just take it in the bathroom over there."

"Oh no. I'm afraid we need to do this in lady Olive's changing room next to it."

"Fine, I'll go there instead."

Roland promptly headed for the changing room with her dress and shoes.

"Uh, 'scuse me. I think I can open the door by myself." said Brandy.

Roland opened the door to the changing room.

"Oh, I will gladly open the door, madam." he said. "What I cannot do is trust *you* to dress yourself on your own."

"What? You're gonna *dress* me? Like I'm a fucking toddler?"

Roland cleared his throat.

"I mean no disrespect, madam, but this banquette is, as you may have understood, *quite* important."

"Can I come too?" asked Olive. "I don't want to be left here all alone."

Roland sighed.

"Very well." he said. "Hold on to these."

He tossed the dress to Brandy, and gently placed the shoes on the ground, before attending to Olive.

"Hey, why did you emphasize the 'you', Roland?" Brandy said. "What's wrong with me specifically?"

IV

"What is this you've put in your hair, madam?" asked Roland. "It is positively malleable."

154

"Just shampoo, balsam. And water." Brandy answered.

"You put an otter in your hair?"

"No. Water, I said."

"Water, yes. And how long has it been since you've washed your hair, exactly?"

"This afternoon. Just finished drying it when you picked me up."

"And you still ended up with, pardon my bluntness, this sticky mess?"

"It's how my hair's always been."

"It's like the jungles of Papua New-Guinea."

"Hey, Roland, remember how my hair was like that too?" said Olive. "Back in my childhood, it was this big mess."

"Ah yes, I remember." said Roland. "How did we fix that again?"

"I just remember I went on this month-long treatment, going to the hair stylist almost every day. I don't know why it was like that either. Mother called it 'kike hair'."

"What did you just say?" Brandy snarled.

"Why don't we just tie it in a ponytail for now?" Roland said, doing just that. "It will not be perfect, but it's the best we can do for now. You don't need to be the queen of the prom, just adequately presentable."

"Thanks." Brandy said sarcastically. "Also, Olive, what the *fuck* did you just say?"

"Did I say something wrong?" asked Olive.

"Manners, madam." said Roland.

"Forget it." Brandy groaned.

"I expect you not to resort to such vile language at the banquette, madam." Roland said insistently. "Need I remind you how important this is, and how intolerant we must be to uncouth behavior?"

"Don't worry, I'll be couth." Brandy half-heartedly retorted as Roland tightened the laces around the back of her dress. "I just cuss sometimes 'cos I get a little angry."

"Are you angry at me?" Olive said sheepishly.

"No, no. I just misheard you, I think. All's fine."

"How do you feel in your dress, madam?" Roland asked.

Brandy stood up from the ottoman with the help of her cane, and looked at herself in the mirror, turning around to see herself from all sides, wanting to do a pirouette, but refrained due to her impaired balance.

155

"It looks nice, really nice." she noted. "I mean, you can tell it wasn't exactly tailor-made for me, y'know. Still a bit baggy in parts, but, well, not complaining, this looks just dandy, really."

"So glad you like it." said Olive. "I remember mother wore it on New Year's Eve in Prague. How long was that ago, Roland?"

"Seven years, lady Olive."

"Seven years, yeah. I was eighteen. We went to Prague, and mother wore that dress at the hotel's New Year's party. And I remember she wore those high heels as well, walking around town on cobblestone in high heels. That was so funny, her tripping all over, still trying to look dignified."

"Now for the shoes, madam."

"You know what, I don't really think I should be wearing high heels. My balance is shitty enough as it is."

"Language, madam."

"Sorry. But seriously, I can just barely walk with a cane, and you want me to wander around on those stilts? I don't think that's, like, gonna work at all. I'll just fall over, y'know."

"I am afraid this is not up for debate, madam. These were all I could find. Lady D'Orleans the elder only wears either high heels or slippers, depending on the occasion. And I doubt you will fit in any of Olive's shoes."

"Alright, find some of her slippers then. I bet they also look all fancy-schmancy."

"I'm afraid none of them are adequately fancy, let alone 'schmancy', simply on account of them being slippers."

"But, y'know, what does it matter? I mean, who looks at what others wear on their feet? Like, could you recall the footwear of the, like, last five people you've met?"

"Yes. Mister Wilkes wore beige suede shoes, right one sloppily tied, left one tied a might too tightly. Henry the cook wore his usual Nike sneakers, white and turquoise, right one slightly dirtier than the left since he probably stepped in a puddle…"

"Alright, fuck it. Shit, I'll wear the fucking high heels." Brandy groaned.

Then Roland slapped her across the cheek.

"What the fuck?" she said.

Roland slapped her again.

"Ow!"

"From this instance, until the end of the banquette, I won't allow a single curse word from you." he said.

"Are you fucking insane?"

Roland slapped her once more.

"Is that understood now?"

"Jesus Christ."

"And don't pronounce His name in vain, either."

"You know what you just did? That was actual physical assault. I could fucking report you to…"

Roland slapped her yet again.

"Ow! Cut it out!"

"I will cut it out when you cut it out."

"Oh, so you think cussing is on par with physical assault?!"

Roland bent down beginning threading on Brandy's shoes.

"It is not assault, it is discipline."

"Some discipline you got here." Brandy commented acidulously.

"Don't worry about it, friend." said Olive. "He doesn't mean any harm. He did that to me all the time when I misbehaved as a child."

"You attacked a kid?!" Brandy asked Roland in disbelief. "Like, physically attacked a kid?"

He stood up, having finished applying her shoes.

"I hope you understand the importance of the situation." he said. "Just to make it clear: no cursing, no blasphemy, no sarcasm, no vulgarities, no lewd behavior, no insults, no disagreements, no intrusively personal questions, and no discussion of inappropriate subject matters, like politics, religion, disease, war, sex, or death. Do you understand?"

"Yes." Brandy said through her teeth. "I understand."

Then Roland grabbed her wrist and started filing her nails. While doing so, he checked his watch.

"Good lord." he said. "I don't have time for this."

He stood up. "Lady Olive, I must implore you to oversee the remainder of Miss Rabinow's preparation. See to it that she files her nails and applies polish adequately.

157

And make certain she adjusts this…" he pointed at Brandy's face. "… amateurish make-up. As stated, she does not need to be the queen of the prom, but she cannot look like a lady of the night either."

Then he left again.

"What was that?" said Brandy. "Was he calling me a hooker?"

"Don't worry about him." said Olive. "Roland's just a bit of a perfectionist. Your make-up looks great."

Brandy started taking off her tight shoes.

"Well, that's enough of this shit." she said. "Do *you* mind that I cuss?"

"Not in private, no." said Olive. "But maybe try to avoid it during the banquette."

"Heh. Right now I'm actually super-tempted to cuss like a lumberjack during dinner, see if that butler of yours tries to bitch-slap me there."

"Please don't, Brandy."

"I know, I won't, for your sake. I know this shit is really important to ya."

Detached left shoe in her hand, Brandy wiggled her newly liberated toes in the air.

"Goddamn, I can't be expected to wear these things all evening. I'm gonna fucking trip over constantly." she said and looked herself in the mirror. "And look at my face. My right cheek's all red."

"What if you slap yourself on the other side, to make yourself more symmetrically rosy-cheeked?" Olive said.

"Yeah, genius idea."

Then Brandy popped off the other shoe.

"How much time till the party starts?" she asked.

"About half an hour." Olive said. "Want to hang out some more in here?"

"Sure thing. We could listen to some other records. Saw you got The Cascades there."

"Oh yes. Let's do that. Would you mind pushing me out, though?"

"Can't you get Roland back in here to do that? Button him back in?"

"No, he seems really busy right now, really nervous to pull this off. But you can do it, right?"

"I dunno. That's kind of a tall order. I can barely push myself forward, to be honest. Got almost no strength left."

"What if you just tried, at least?"

"Well, sure, I guess I could try. But don't get your expectations up too high, though."

Brandy pulled herself up and, supported by her cane, stepped behind Olive, and started pushing.

"Use both arms." Olive said.

Brandy huffed and panted and groaned as she pressed her whole weight against Olive's wheelchair, to no avail. It was like molded to the floor, not budging a femtometer.

In the end she gave up and rested her upper body on Olive's shoulders.

"I got no strength left, y'know." she wheezed. "That operation did a real number on me."

"It's alright, friend." Olive said in consolation. "We can have a jolly good time in her until Roland comes back. I do have a rum bottle next to the bed, if you're interested."

"Really? Why didn't you say so before? As soon as I catch my breath properly, I'll go get it, alright."

After nearly a minute, Brandy did feel strong enough to shuffle over to Olive's bed, past the ramp, and to the bed stand.

"Where did you say it was?" she asked. "In the bed stand?"

"In the lower shelf of the bed stand, yes."

Processing the message too slowly, Brandy opened the upper shelf of the bed stand, where she found a shiny black revolver.

"There's just a gun in here." she said.

"The *lower* shelf, I said."

"Oh right. Got it."

Brandy opened the lower shelf, where she found a half-full bottle of white Selvarey rum.

"Got glasses?" she asked.

"I don't wear glasses." Olive replied.

"No, to drink from."

"Oh yes, we have a few right in here. Just regular water glasses, not proper rum glasses, but you don't mind, do you?"

159

"I wouldn't mind if I had to drink this from a leper's butthole. This is some seriously good shit, I've heard, like, 'legendary' is probably a bit pompous, but y'know…"

"Yes, it is good. I often have a glass or two before I go to bed."

Having returned to the dressing room, Brandy handed Olive the glasses. and poured in the rum.

"Yeah, I love me a good nightcap now and then too." Brandy said and sat down on the ottoman, and took her first sip, savoring the spirit in her mouth. "Used to be maybe a glass of coke and vodka, or a few glasses of wine. Now, though, I just pop one of these pills I've been prescribed, down a single glass of wine or a single vodka shot, or something, and, y'know, that shit sure does a number on ya. I'm kinda glad I got that prescription, get to end every day in, like, fucking euphoria, y'know."

"Yeah, I know exactly how you feel, friend. I've awoken in a euphoric state many times. I don't think I've fallen asleep like that, but I've awoken like it, certainly."

"That reminds me…" Brandy took a bigger swig. "It reminds me that you need to remind me to take another one of those pills."

Brandy got up and went over to her own satchel, from which she withdrew the pill bottle.

"Nequam Intra-something-something. Need these little fuckers to keep myself alive, actually."

Olive began staring into the rum in her glass, swaying it around, observing the consistency of the liquor.

"Got anyplace to put this?" Brandy asked.

"Oh? Well, yes, you can take one of my purses from the wardrobe."

"Thanks, I'll find one later." Brandy said and sat back down.

"So, um, where is your little bird friend?" Olive asked.

"Pardon?"

"You bird. The little raven, or whatever it was."

Brandy paused.

"My crow, Tucker…"

"Oh yeah, crow, right." Olive interrupted.

Brandy took another sip.

"Tucker is gone." she said with a vexed face.

160

Olive understood she had misstepped, seeing moisture accumulating in her eyes.

"I'm sorry." she said.

"It's alright." Brandy sniffed. "I just need to get over it, y'know."

Olive looked around, searching in her thoughts for a different topic to discuss. What did she know about Brandy? What did she want to know?

In the bundle of Brandy's old clothes, she discovered a little book sticking out.

"Is this yours?" she asked, pointing at the copy of '*The Undying Man*'. "This book?"

"Hmm? Oh yeah, totally. That's the one I'm reading on at the moment. Haven't made much progress lately, though."

She picked it up from the bundle, and showed the cover to Olive, who made an intrigued inhalation at the sight.

"Is it good?" she asked.

"Oh yeah, it's really good. Much better than this one, in fact. Really sucks you in once you get to reading it."

"What's it about?"

"Oh, it's about this dude who's, like, really, really afraid of death. He's, like, unable to sleep because of it. Just thinking all the time about, y'know, what'll death be like? Is there even an afterlife, or anything? And it's just tearing him apart, y'know. So he goes to this gypsy woman, y'know, who's like, she gives him this, like, she puts this curse on him, sort of. Or, she doesn't call it a curse, she calls it a hex, and she promotes it like it's a really good thing, and all, and he pays her to do it, y'know. So the curse is all like, he doesn't die. He's become, like, immortal, y'know, invincible, and he lives forever, and nothing can kill him. Except, like, the hook is he can still get injured and feel pain and all that, the only difference is he can never actually die. So he starts getting really reckless, y'know, 'cos he knows he can't die, and so he gets into all these accidents, and, y'know, little after little it all fucks him up really badly, so he becomes like, a paraplegic with constant pain, and then he gets blind, and loses limbs, and, y'know, no matter what happens he can't die. Like, at one point he actually attempts suicide because of all the pain, but that just fucks him up harder. So it's, like, yeah, it's kind of sad and depressing, but it's also really cool, y'know."

"That sounds like a fun read." Olive said. "Is it available for retail, as in, you know, is it widely available? Can I find it easily?"

"I don't know. Don't think so, actually. I found my copy in a cardboard box. I think it might actually be kind of rare."

"Can I borrow it? I mean, once you're done?"

"Sure, I'll give you a call when that time comes, y'know."

"Good!"

They both took a swig in unison.

"So, um…" Brandy said. "What's the deal with the six-shooter?"

"My revolver?"

"Yeah, are you, like, afraid of burglars or something? 'Cos this place seems like a building that would be, I dunno, pretty secured against trespassers. Like, don't you rich people like installing security stuff all over the place?"

"Oh no, that gun is… well, do you want to have a look at it?"

"Oh no. I'm not really into guns, actually. I was just curious why you had it."

"It's a Smith & Wesson Model Ten Caliber thirty eight. I inherited it from my grand father. Actually, my father inherited it from him, but he had an identical one already, so he gave it to me."

"And so you keep it in your bed stand drawer?"

"Yeah, I'm not really into guns either. I don't like putting violent things on my walls, you see. I like to be reminded of nice things when I'm here. Father liked to display guns on the walls, though. He loved collecting old rifles and such, and showing them off to everyone."

Brandy emptied her glass.

"Should we maybe check if your butler is available now?" she asked.

Olive pressed her button a few times.

"If he is, he should be here in twenty to thirty seconds." she said.

She poured some more rum into Brandy's glass, to her eager approval.

Very soon, Roland did show up.

"There is very little time now, lady Olive. We must go and greet the guests. The first ones should arrive quite soon, presumably Mister Repasky and his wife. They always come early."

"Oh, well, perfect. Should I greet them in the foyer this time, or wait for them in the dining room?"

"May I suggest the dining room this time?"

"Very well, then." Olive said as Roland began pushing her out. "And, uh, Brandy, friend, just look in my wardrobe next to the bed. Pick any purse you want. I'll see you in the dining room. You just turn left when you reach the living room."

"Alright, thanks."

And as soon as Olive had left, did Brandy stumble over to the wardrobe, a wide double-doored wardrobe built into the wall. As she opened it she found not a closet, but an entire room twice as large as her own whole apartment, filled with enough clothes for the whole population of Lichtenstein, or at least enough fabric, given the size of each garment. She went over to the pile of Gucci purses in the corner, and picked up the first one she happened to touch, and went on to filling it with her pill bottle as well as her cell phone. She promised herself to take the next pill after the first course. She drank the remnants of her rum in only a few more swigs, and then headed downstairs.

CHAPTER FOURTEEN

The sliced tomatoes were dumped into the seasoned onions sizzling in canola oil, and stirred in as they slowly dissolved.

"It'll take about ten minutes before they dissolve completely into a tomato gravy."

"Then what will you add next?"

"First, I'll drop in a little bit of freshly grated horseradish, and a couple of cloves of crushed garlic. Then some chopped fresh cayenne peppers. Five, I'd say. You know what, maybe six. After that, a few chopped habaneros, equal amount jalapeños."

"With all the seeds, I presume."

"Of course. And naturally, a little tiny splash of this special chili extract, about a lean table spoon of that. This stuff is hazardous to the skin, you know. Direct skin contact and it'll burn straight through to the flesh."

"Fascinating. Now, don't forget the most special ingredient."

"I assume you've managed to acquire it."

"Why, of course. The famous Trinidad Moruga Scorpion pepper. Three of them in fact, all fresh."

"Dump them in. Into this pot, I mean, not that one. This'll be the special one. Sure'll give this dish some real kick, don't you think?"

II

At the far end of the dining table sat Olive in a unique chair designed for her special needs. Directly to her right sat Brandy, as the name tag between her cutlery dictated. A large quantity of people in expensive suits and dresses approached Olive to shake or kiss her hand, and thank her for the honor of being invited, and she in return would thank them for coming. All the guests also greeted each other, and they all greeted Brandy. "Good evening, ma'am. My name is 'duh-dee-duh-dee-duh', I own the 'boobie-doobie-doo', and this is my spouse 'yak-a-dee-yak-a-dee-yak'" they all said. "Name's Brandy Rabinow'" she would quickly reply to them all, forgetting the name of each one within a second after the introduction. "What do you do?" would some ask. "Chief accountant" she would reply, repressing the urge to say something vulgar or crass. She noticed she was by far the youngest one there. Most of the guests, she noticed, surpassed her by several generations, with the exception of a few thirty-something trophy wives hooked around the arms of their retirement-age husbands.

After everyone, about forty in total, had been seated at their designated spots along the long table, Roland began addressing the crowd from Olive's left.

"Before we begin, I would like to say, on behalf of our host, lady Olive D'Orleans..."

"Hello." Olive said gaily to the crowd.

"... and our hardworking staff..." Roland continued. "... I would like to say it is a grand honor to have you all here. And we do hope you will come to enjoy this evening."

Most of the crowd politely applauded.

"When're we going to get our drinks?" bleated a red-nosed old man at the far end of the table.

"Drinks will be served in due time, sir." Roland responded.

"Due time?!" the man exclaimed. "I'm shriveling up like an old grape here. Normally I expect to be served drinks on arrival, as is standard etiquette. What sort of Mickey Mouse nonsense party is this?!"

'You do look like a shriveled old grape' thought Brandy. A servant approached the man, asking what drink he would like.

"Perhaps all should be served a refreshment of their choice." Roland said.

Several more servant approached the table, asking everyone what drinks they wanted.

"Now, then..." Roland said to Olive. "Would you like a drink, then?"

"Yes, I think I'll have another Sazerac. And Brandy wants a mojito. Didn't you, Brandy?"

"Uh, yeah. Absolutely. 'Heeto me up."

Roland snapped at a servant passing by, telling her to also bring a Sazerac and a mojito.

"Now that that's been sorted out…" he said to the crowd. "In a little while we will be serving our first course, roasted calamari with chickpeas and artichoke chutney."

III

"This is a really good mojito you've made here." Brandy told Roland. "Just thought you'd like to know."

"I appreciate the gratitude." he replied coldly before attending to the other guests.

"This really may be the best mojito I've had in a long, long time, though." she then told Olive.

"Oh yeah. Henry the chef really knows his way around a mojito." she said back. "Though they haven't been the same since Raúl got fired. *That* guy knew how to concoct a mojito, you know."

"Yeah, too bad I didn't get to have one of those. This one's more than alright, though. Like, if this was the last mojito I'd have before I got snuffed, y'know, I'd say like, 'fine', y'know, like, 'do me in, I got what I came for', y'know. Wouldn't bother me one bit, y'know."

"I'm really glad you like Henry's work, friend. I hope you enjoy his cooking as well."

Brandy slurped down some more of her drink.

"I see that dude over there got his fix, too." she said, pointing at the loud fellow from earlier, now enjoying a whiskey sour.

"That's Ernest Lafayette." said Olive. "He owns the Bopscot Corporation, have you heard of them?"

"Nope."

"Well, they pretty much own a monopoly on the world's rubber chicken industry. If you've ever owned a rubber chicken, it's almost definitely from them. He would be an immense asset as an investor in the project."

"Aw yeah, he was probably one of the first folks I shook hands with. He was the one with *really* sweaty hands, if I'm not mistaken. So how much you think he's gonna pledge?"

"Well, tens of millions, if we can manage to marinate him enough."

166

"Alright, so, heh, you're gonna get that bozo signing on in a drunken stupor?" Brandy jestingly blurted, swinging her glass around.

"Well, that's why we're hosting this banquette, right?" Olive replied with a straight serious face.

"That's your plan? Getting folks so sloshed they'll sign on to anything?" Brandy asked.

"What did you say, young lady?" asked the man sitting right next to her.

"What? What didja hear?" she asked back.

"Didn't you say we could sign on for slushies?" he said.

"Oh, uh, yeah, I mean, down at the Seven Eleven. They'd let you get, like, a subscription, of sorts, for slushies. Seven slushies a month, half price."

"Oh, I just need to check that up." the man said. "I love those slushies, you see. Perfect beverage for a hot summer day. My wife doesn't want me drinking the stuff, though. She says they're bad for my cholesterol."

"What was that, Howard?" asked his wife next to him.

"Nothing, darling. We were talking about, well, plushies. Plush rabbits, and such. Didn't your sister collect those?"

"Well, not so much anymore, after the diagnosis."

Soon thereafter, the first course arrived. A rectangular plate with a straight line of four sets of calamari tentacles pointing up like jester hats over a layer of orange molasses, scattered with chickpeas, rucola leaves, twigs of fresh thyme and little pink thyme flowers, and on the far right a pale green chutney shaped in a spiraled peak, capped with paper-thin beet slices. The dish was quite delicate in its presentation, and Brandy would a few weeks ago have started salivating at the sight, but unfortunately she had since the operation suffered a loss in appetite, only bothering to eat out of necessity. Even if she would enjoy each bite of a meal, she never felt any desire to take another.

"I hope you all have finished your drinks." Roland said. "The calamari will be paired with an unpasteurized Prosecco."

Then about twenty servants showed up, beginning to pour the wine into each of the guests' tall wine glasses. As soon as Brandy's glass was filled with cloudy sparkly white wine, she quickly proceeded to pick it up, before Roland sternly tapped her on the shoulder.

"Not yet." he told her. "Not before the official toast."

"I would like to raise a toast." Olive declared to the crowd. "A toast to good health and prosperity, and long living."

Everybody raised their glasses in unison.

"And with that, let the banquette dinner officially begin." she continued.
"Hear, hear." said some of the guests.

Brandy took a sip from her glass, assuming that was now in order, and then moved on to the food. By the time she had just barely poked a squid with her fork, she noticed Olive was already two fifths through her meal. The units of squid were each quite small. Probably no point carving into them with a knife, she thought, and put one into her mouth whole.

"So how do you like the calamari?" asked Olive immediately after having swallowed her third set.
"Hrmm?" mumbled Brandy with a few tentacles sticking out her mouth.
"Do you enjoy the food?"
"Or yrr." Brandy nodded, noticing Roland staring ominously at her. She quickly chewed her squid and swallowed it with some minor hardship, and sent him a disapproving glare of her own, at which point he turned to Olive.

"I do have some business to attend to, lady Olive. I must go now."
"That's fine. I'll see you later on." she said back.

Roland said nothing further, and just left.

When there was nothing left but scraps on Brandy's plate, she turned to Olive, who was likewise finished.

"How long till they serve the second course?" she asked.
"Oh, you're really hungry, aren't you?"
"No. Well, not 'no', but, yes, I am hungry, but it's just, do you think I have time to pop into the bathroom for a short moment?"
"Well, I'd assume so, but don't stall for too long. You don't want to miss the next dish, it's a Hatya Ke Prayaas."
"What?"
"That's a type of Indian dish. I haven't tried it before, honestly. Henry the chef told me it's magnificent, though."
"How many courses are there, precisely?"

"Oh, including dessert, there should be seven. The main course, as in the *main*-main course will be the fourth one."

"Good to know. I'll be back in half a jiffy." Brandy said hastily, getting herself up.

IV

A servant had directed Brandy upstairs, to the 'guests' bathroom', which was again much larger than her own apartment. The room had four faucets, three cubicle toilets, two bidets, and a bubble bath in the corner. Brandy took one of the glasses by the faucets, filled it with water, dug up the pill bottle from her purse, tossed the blue little tablet into her mouth, and washed it down. Then she remembered she had been drinking quite a bit throughout the evening. Then she dropped to the floor. Blackness.

V

"Excuse me, where is Brandy?" Olive asked a servant passing by.

"The lady to your right?"

"Yes. She was sitting here. Have you seen her?"

"No. Shall we serve the second course soon?"

"Well, no. Roland needs to announce it first."

"I've been informed he is excruciatingly busy at the moment."

"With what? He's said nothing to me."

"I don't know."

Olive moaned.

"Very well." she said. "I suppose *I* will have to announce the next course."

She tapped her spoon against her glass four times, to catch everybody's attention.

"Our next course will be a Hatya Ke Prayaas, a vegetarian lentil-and-tomato-based dish of Indian origins."

Some of the guests nodded approvingly.

Soon the servants arrived with the dish. It had a much more simplistic presentation than the last. One small pot of red stew garnished with a few fresh bay leaves.

169

"What beverage shall we serve with this course?" Olive asked the closest servant.

"I don't know. It's your choice."

"Oh. Then I suppose we can try the red Californian Syrah."

"Very well."

Soon enough, the wine had been served, and the dining could commence.

"Howard, this is quite too spicy for my taste." said the wife of the man sat next to Brandy's seat.

"Try not to be rude, dear." he replied.

"I'm not rude. I am only telling you my opinion."

Olive ignored the chatter around her and gorged avidly on the dish, a chunky rich stew of vegetables and spices, full of exotic flavors. Within seconds she noticed it was indeed quite spicy, extremely so. The swigs of wine she swallowed between mouthfuls did nothing to soothe the volcanic eruption the food caused inside her. It was searing, burning, tremendously painful, but so tasty and delicious all the same.

"Dear, I mean, ma'am, are you quite alright?" Howard asked.

He had noticed Olive's skin had changed to a deep carmine complexion, and pouring out sweat by the gallons.

"There you see, Howard." said his wife. "I'm not the only one who can't stand spicy food."

"I'm fine." Olive haphazardly mumbled through another big mouthful. "It's just a little hot."

As she fought her way through the remainder of her dish, she noticed to have caught the attention of several more people. Were they dissatisfied with her manners? Maybe she was making indelicate noises with her eating, she thought. Trying to quiet down, and ingesting smaller portions at a time, she noticed she was becoming quite light-headed. Perhaps it was the sweat, she thought. That was what bothered her guests. Sweating publically has always been deeply frowned upon, even if, as in this case, one cannot help it.

"I apologize for my severe perspiring." she said to the crowd. "It is unfortunately how my body naturally reacts to extraordinarily spicy cuisine."

Then she involuntarily dropped her fork. She found her sudden inability to control her arm perplexing. Blackness.

VI

Brandy gradually awoke on the mattress soft bathroom floor. Despite knowing this situation was far from optimal, she could feel nothing but serenity. For five solid minutes she did nothing but enjoy her double vision of the slowly rotating ceiling, as a vaguely memorized Simon and Garfunkel song played inside her head. After that, she had regained enough motor skills to make significant movements, such as lifting and bending her limbs, an ability she utilized to slowly crawl to the nearest bidet, which she hugged loosely while giggling moronically, until the door opened. In entered a middle-aged woman she almost certainly had greeted, looking quite distressed and distraught.

"Oh my." the woman said at the sight of Brandy on the floor. "Are you alright, dear?"

"Yeah, I'm super-duper fine and dandy." Brandy said, unable to pronounce the consonants properly.

"Oh, this is just great." the woman said sarcastically to herself while rubbing her temples. "Tell me, darling, do you have a caretaker?"

"I don't care about no care for the take… what?" Brandy blurted out, still minus most of the consonants.

The woman helped herself to a glass of water from the tap. "I can't handle this." she said, and withdrew a small fan from her purse, and started waving it frenetically in her face, breathing stressfully.

"I just can't handle incidents like these. My father died from a heart attack just this summer, you see. It was his third one in a year, and we thought he would pull through. It just wrecks my nerves whenever that happens to someone. The infarction, I mean, not the death part, necessarily. God, I hope that doesn't happen now."

"What happens?" Brandy asked, now starting to regain her diction a little bit.

"Oh, never mind that, poor you. We need to find your caretaker, and give them a real talking to for leaving you in the restroom all by yourself, because that is awfully irresponsible. People just don't have any labor morale these days."

This woman was radiating an aura of intense negativity, polluting Brandy's buzz with bad vibes. Her presence was beginning to fill her with fuzzy angst, and the room started shrinking. There was also something obviously worrisome in regards to what she was talking about, even if Brandy could not quite understand it.

VII

"We're gonna need re-enforcement here." the paramedic said upon observing Olive's empty bloodshot eyes. "We can't carry her out by ourselves."

"What is wrong with her?" a woman asked him.

"She's suffering through a heart attack. A minor one, though. We should be able to save her, possibly." the paramedic responded, and turned to his co-worker. "Have you called for back-up yet?"

"They're on their way." he responded.

"Problem is…" the paramedic returned to the woman. "… She's much bigger than any patient we've dealt with before. So not only will transport be more complicated, but I also have no idea how a body like this can cope with cardiac arrest." he continued, starting to perform CPR on Olive's chest. "Alien complications may arise, catching us off-guard. We don't know, though. I'm only telling you the truth, we're still optimistic about this, it's just that there are too many unknown factors to know for sure."

"Oh, is this to be taken as a cancellation of the event?" the woman asked the others around her.

"Excuse me…" the paramedic asked her. "Are you her mother, or…?"

"Oh no. I am just one of her guests. Frankly, I've never even met her mother. I believe she and her husband are vacating in Belize at the moment. Wasn't that what she told us, Howard?"

"Well, you should try and contact them as soon as possible." the paramedic noted.

VIII

Roland nervously trudged back and forth in the second floor hallway, constantly checking the watch. When he passed the guests' bathroom for the umpteenth time, the door opened to his surprise. He was certain it had been vacant this whole time. Out came one of the guests, Missus Violet Blomquist, whom he had greeted on a number of

172

occasions, carrying over her shoulder the arm of Miss Brandy Rabinow, who, barely able to stand on her feet, dragged her old splintery cane behind her.

"What is going on here, Missus Blomquist?" he asked.

"I am trying to help this poor girl, Roland." she replied. "I haven't been able to get out of her who her caretaker is, or where I might find them."

"Excuse me?" Roland said.

Brandy drooled and moaned, emitting a sequence of slurry noises that might have been conceived as sentences in her mind.

"And I must say, Roland, it was horribly irresponsible of you to allow the serving of alcohol to someone with cerebral palsy." Blomquist continued.

"Cerebral palsy?" Roland sniffed. "Is that what you think she has? This young lady isn't handicapped. She is merely pie-eyed. Roaring drunk."

"So that's what you think? How can you tell?"

"I spoke to her a little over an hour ago. She was normal, well, she was reasonably well-functioning back then, but drinking heavily. I suspect someone her age wouldn't have a particularly high tolerance either. Actually, has she made a mess in the bathroom?"

"No, she has not. But how do you explain her cane, then?"

"Her cane is simply to support her balance in the wake of her recent surgery."

"Surgery?"

"It is a long story. Regardless, right now I suggest we have her ejected from the perimeters."

"But she is barely conscious. If she really is that inebriated, I suggest she sleep the night through in one of the guest bedrooms."

"Certainly not. That arrogant ill-mannered *seaka* has nobody but herself to blame for such obscene consumption of liquor, and no one in this house should have to endure the indignity of cleaning the sheets of her vomit tomorrow."

"Roland, you really, really do lack the slightest hint of sympathy, don't you."

"Y'know, go fuck yourself, Roland." Brandy blurted, and then puked on the floor.

"Do you still believe *I* am the unsympathetic one here?" Roland asked Blomquist. "We will call for a taxi to bring her home to her own residence."

"That'll have to wait for the ambulances to leave, though."

"Ambulances? They've arrived? How is lady Olive?"

173

"Oh, I went up here before they even came. I can't stand situations like these. They just stress me out. My father died of a heart attack very recently, you see."

"Is something the matter with Olive?" Brandy barely managed to ask.

"I believe I have to go." said Roland. "And please do not leave. The banquette is far from cancelled."

Then he left.

"What is… what he said?" slurred Brandy. "What you said about Olive?"

Blomquist pulled a Kleenex out from her purse, and stared wiping vomit off her dress.

"Oh, dear, we'll get you in bed now, won't we." she said. "There's a guest bedroom right down this corridor. We'll go there, and let you rest for a while, wouldn't that be nice?"

"Where is Olive?" asked Brandy, as Blomquist began pulling her onwards. "She in trouble? Is she sick?"

IX

After having observed the swirling ceiling paintings for a solid hour, Brandy finally felt sober enough to stand up and move by her own authority. She was still fairly light-headed and intoxicated, but not to a point of impairment as before. She grabbed the cane by the bed, and walked out of the guests' bedroom barefoot, making her way downstairs, only stopping by the bathroom to wash her mouth and scrub some minor vomit stains off her dress.

After an excruciatingly slow walk down the stairs, she entered the living room, to which all the other guests had now been re-located, watching a PowerPoint presentation by Roland, presumably about the project. She sat down in the closest available seat, and turned to the man next to her.

"What happened to Olive?" she whispered to him.

"They took her to the hospital." he replied coldly.

"What was it?"

"What?"

"What was the matter with her?"

"I wouldn't know."

174

Brandy gave up asking and switched her attention to the presentation.

"Naturally, we will take advantage of the newest innovations within robotic technology to fulfill the needs of our citizens." Roland said. "Dressing, bathing, feeding, and moving. That will be taken care of by different types of robots, for as many citizens as we can financially manage. The rest will receive the same care by the hands of human servants."

"Is this proposed technology adequately advanced for the task yet?" asked a man close to the center.

Roland threw him an irritated look.

"Of course it is. Have you not read the latest scientific journals on the matter? Robotic innovations have reached the point where they can even improvise in difficult situations, and even predict one's wants and needs. They could even save someone's life without being asked."

"Then why haven't you already acquired such technology for this home? Surely that would have been useful for the incident just a moment ago."

"Well, of course you realize we have to save finances and resources for the project, making it necessary to skimp on personal expenses. Regardless, we must continue..."

A new slide appeared, showing the details of the project's budget.

"At the moment, we are still three billion dollars short of the required funding to complete the project. This is indeed an expensive endeavor. If you've paid attention so far, I'm certain you understand why. And I assure you, we truly have squeezed every single penny thus far."

"Are you sure?" asked the same man from before. "Did the mayor's office really need to be that costly? Seems excessively lavish in my opinion."

"We are not building a homeless shelter, sir." Roland retorted with repressed anger. "It is supposed to be slightly lavish."

"What does your chief accountant have to say about the mayor's office then? Has she approved this?"

"I am afraid that, due to unpredicted circumstances, our chief accountant had to leave and will be unavailable for the remainder of the evening."

"No she won't!" yelled the man next to Brandy. "She's sat right here."

The whole crowd turned their heads towards her, including a surprised Roland, who was rapidly developing a thick vein by his temple.

"Is that really the accountant?" "She looks mighty young." "I thought she was Lafayette's daughter." "I thought she was his mistress." "No, she's Miss D'Orleans' cousin, she told me." "I see the resemblance."

Brandy stiffened from the attention, pressing herself to wave shyly at the others.

"So tell us, Miss accountant…" said the man in the center. "What do you make of the mayor's office."

"I actually didn't see that part of the… I mean, if nothing has changed significantly since last time I checked, which was fairly recently, I mean, then yeah, that building checks out just fine. Like, it's perfect. I can't see a single area in which we could cut costs, unless we wanted this to be a really, like, lousy town, which we don't, y'know."

"I believe there isn't time to go into every detail right at this moment…" Roland said, trying to revert the attention back to himself. "But I assure you, we have meticulously run through every number, every single digit on this budget, and it has been double-checked and triple-checked by multiple accountants and consultants, and everything does indeed add up."

"Excuse me…" said a woman sat closely to Brandy. "What about the legality of this project? Is that in order? Is everything here in accordance with state law and federal law?"

"Yes, yes." said Roland. "Everything adds up. We have double-checked and triple-checked every single microscopic detail of every single aspect of this venture. We have gone to great lengths to make the project as risk-free as humanly possible."

He turned the monitor projection behind him off, and pulled out a notebook and a ballpoint pen from his breast pocket.

"Now then." he said. "I appreciate that you have questions, though I must say, the success of the project does depend on a level of mutual trust. Anyway, have any one of you decided to pledge investment? Or would you like a moment to think?"

"I'll give you a million!" Mister Lafayette drunkenly blurted out. "Two millions in fact!"

"Are you sure that is your final offer, Mister Lafayette?"

"Aw hell, I'll give ya three millions, and a coupon for…" he reached into his pocket. "Let's see… 'twenty-five percent off any sandwich at Quiznos'. You know, I'll be extra generous, three *and a half* million, plus the coupon, but that's all I can do."

"The goal for this fundraiser is at three billion, might I remind you."

"Three billions? I ain't got that kind of money. Or do I, Claire?" Lafayette turned to his wife, who just shrugged. "You know, you drive a hard bargain…" he continued. "… but I'll give ya half a billion. *One half* billion, and no coupon. That's my final offer."

"Fantastic, Mister Lafayette. Who else would want to jump aboard?"

The others only responded in hesitant murmuring.

"Maybe it would be best if we had a little moment to decide." said the woman who had asked about the legal matters.

Some agreeing murmuring followed from the rest.

"Very well." said Roland. "How does twenty minutes sound? Would that suffice?"

The crowd responded with more agreeing murmuring.

"Then I hope to receive some decisive answers within that time."

While the guests started chatting among each other, Roland left into the foyer and intended to drag Brandy along, only to find that she started following him quite voluntarily.

"Why are you still here?" he asked her in frustration.

"I just wanted to hear about Olive." she answered innocently.

"You're still clearly intoxicated." Roland observed. "Though I presumed you'd be bedridden for at least a week given the state I saw you in up there."

"Well, that was, y'know, some pill mishap. I take these pills, y'know. The recovery is pretty fast with those."

"Nonetheless, I must still insist you'd be escorted home this instance."

"What is going on with Olive?" Brandy interrupted.

"We can deal with that tomorrow. Right now you must go home and get some rest."

"Fuck no!" Brandy erupted. "Tell me what's the matter with her *now*!"

Roland cast a worried glance at the living room door, awaiting a reaction from within.

"If you simply *must* know…" he said through his clenched teeth. "Lady Olive has been escorted to the hospital due to a minor health complication."

"I thought I heard something about a heart attack!"

"I am unfamiliar with the details, I'm afraid."

"You're her personal, like, everything! How could you possibly not find out about the details?!"

"Now, this had been a tremendously busy evening for me, you see."

"Y'know, fuck it. What hospital did she go to?"

"As I said, the details were never conveyed to…"

"Just fucking tell me!"

Roland breathed heavily through his nose.

"Spiro Agnew Memorial Hospital." he finally said. "Down in Lower Rhodes."

"Alright. Wasn't that hard, now was it? Now either drive me down there, or at least order me a cab, right fucking now."

The increasingly prominent vein by Roland's temple looked ready to pop, and a similar one had materialized on the other side of his head. His eyes looked ready to shoot out their sockets.

X

At the Spiro Agnew Memorial Hospital, which was much more lavish than the one Brandy had stayed at, the receptionist continuously rejected her plea to pay Olive a visit.

"You have unfortunately come far past visiting hours." she said.

"Will she be alright, then?" asked Brandy.

"I really can't say. I only know it was a mighty chaos when she got here."

"Will she pull through, though?"

"I've got no clue, honestly. Come back tomorrow, though I can't promise she'll be in health for visitors."

"Alright, I'll try, but…" Brandy reached into her purse. "Could you just try and give her this?"

She handed the receptionist her copy of 'The Undying Man'.

"Y'know, I don't know if it'll be any use to her any time soon, but, well, it's just a gift."

"I'll try to have it directed to her room by tomorrow, okay."

"Super." Brandy said somberly with a raised thumb.

Exiting the hospital, she looked up past the building top at the full moon, where she caught a glimpse of a bird, a crow, looking peculiarly similar to Tucker.

It flew away.

CHAPTER FIFTEEN

Sat directly in the sun ray coming through the window, Brandy slowly equipped her armor of ravished wool and cotton, savoring each step of the process. Only after an evening of wearing someone else's dress did she appreciate the comfort and security her regular set of clothes brought her.

That evening. While there were individual pleasant moments along the way, the event as a whole gave her nothing but loathsome vibrations that lingered inside her still. She now required a strict re-enforcement of normality to get its twisted atmosphere out of her system.

On the positive side, it made everything in her daily life feel like a desirable confirmation that all was alright again. Even the Manson Asylum was now seeming more hospitable, with the smells, the noises, and the colors. When she had returned last night, a group of people on the same floor had been causing a wild ruckus, a cacophony of music, screaming, violence, and property damage; but it turned out as only familiar white noise to Brandy, who had effortlessly fallen into a serene slumber upon slumping into bed.

Having completely dressed herself, she received a text message. 'Good day, Miss Rabinow. This is Roland...' it started, to which she reacted with a frustrated groan. 'I hope you are in better shape and mood than yesterday. Regardless, tomorrow you will travel to Wyoming to evaluate and council the project's development, as is your duty as chief accountant. If you happen to have unfinished, urgent business in Riverside, I suggest you make sure to attend to it by then. You will be escorted to the airport from your home residence at 7 a.m. tomorrow morning, so be certain to have packed and prepared all you deem necessary by then.'

Brandy read through the message slowly, her pulse raising with each word, and then proceeded to write her reply: 'Fuck you fuck you fuck you fuck you fuck you fuck you, not gonna go, fuck off.'

Before sending it, however, her rage mildened enough that she could consider the consequences. She remembered what Mister Wilkes threatened to do with her if she ever came to disobey, or betray the project. Then again, there was no way she would voluntarily travel across the country on Roland's errand. The project had so far pulled her into enough unpleasant travesties as it was, with nothing in return except Olive's generosity. Only she had shown Brandy any form of respect and appreciation since her involvement, and in Brandy's opinion, only she deserved such in return. Brandy intended to pay her a visit later today, after her first pill coma, a few drinks, and lunch.

'I'm sorry,' she then wrote, 'I can't make the trip. I'm going back to Philly the same day to visit my dad in the hospital. It's very serious. You should have notified me earlier.'

She sent that message, confident that the white lie would set her free. She then dropped her morning pill, poured herself another glass of wine, and started playing her Talking Heads playlist on her phone.

II

When her pill high had weakened enough to allow her sentience and free movement, she crawled out of bed, and checked her phone. No reply from Roland. No news are good news, she thought.

"Come on now, Tucker." she said to nothing, grabbed her cane, and left.

III

After having sobered up at a coffee shop on Harmony Square, Brandy figured a solid drink was due. 'Yo, wanna drop by the O'Caiside?' she texted Imogen, only half-expecting a reply. She had during her pill high dropped by Barnstable & Kearney to look for a new book to replace 'The Undying Man', but had by this point forgotten what she bought. Details from these periods usually slipped her mind. What she dug up from the bag was in fact two books. Conway Twitty's autobiography, 'More Than a Twit: My Road to Success, Redemption and Wisdom', and a harlequin novel written in German,

181

'*Heißdampf unter den laken*'. Slightly disappointing, she thought. After finishing her chamomile tea, she went outside, heading for her favorite pub, to read about the life of her sixth favorite country singer.

IV

"Another mojito?" asked the bartender.

"You bet." Brandy answered. "Make it exactly like you always do, dark mint and everything."

She tapped her fingers rapidly against the counter, eagerly awaiting her drink. She then started scouting around the room, as she suddenly realized Mister Wilkes also frequented this place. He was nowhere to be seen. Maybe he went to Wyoming, she thought, hoped, intensely.

"Where's your little bird friend?" asked the bartender, stirring in the mint.

"He's, uh, not here. Staying at home, I think."

"You think?"

"Yeah, I… I think I… I think my grasp on reality is loosening."

"No better cure for that than a mojito, eh?"

"No better cure for anything."

As Brandy received her drink and slapped the money on the counter, she found her thankfully vacant seat in the far end booth. The bar had been getting more crowded lately. Perhaps more people were discovering it. Several of its patrons today had, however, brought in large shopping bags, so perhaps they just wanted a place to relax after some early Christmas shopping at the nearby mall. The bar itself was also ushering in the season with some modest Christmas decoration. There was even a little Santa Claus doll hooked to the candle light at Brandy's table. It looked a little like the Son of Sam having had his face dipped in cotton candy. She tossed the brick of an autobiography on the table, slurped down some mojito, realized she had not bought any peanuts, then realized she did not need to anymore, and sighed deeply.

"*Every little thing… is gonna be alright…*" she sang to the bird with the injured wing way back when. She was fourteen, he was God knows what age. He had an injured wing, had crashed into the kitchen window to the startling of her mother, and landed in the window box. Brandy took him inside, gave him a bath, sang.

182

Brandy stared blankly at the first page of the book, looking at the words but not thinking about them. There were quite a few things to think about, all of them more absorbing than Conway Twitty's childhood in Mississippi. She chugged down her mojito, and went to the bathroom, leaving the book behind.

V

The bathrooms at the O'Caiside had a jarringly steep drop in quality from the rest of the establishment. Wet floors, green buzzing fluorescent lights, an overfilled trashcan, and only one out of three faucets working. Brandy wondered what the men's room was like. Could it be worse? Maybe it resembled the Manson Asylum hallways. In the toilet cubicle she sat, there was a blue urinal cake stuck to the ceiling above her. It was attracting flies.

As she sat there urinating, she saw someone had written 'BEWARE THE COCK' on the cubicle door, carved with a knife, accentuated with ballpoint ink.

The entrance door opened, and footsteps sounded from outside, getting closer to Brandy's cubicle. A body knocked against the door, the body of a person giving no regard to anyone who might sit inside, no care that they might want to get out. Or, perhaps this person *wanted* them to stay within.

"How do you do, Brandy?" said the slivering voice of Mister Wilkes.

Brandy's heart dropped to the pit of her stomach at the sound.

"Shit." she said under her breath.

"Is that why you're here?" asked Wilkes.

"What? I mean, why are *you* here? Get out. You're not allowed in here. Go to the boys' room."

"I've been many places to which I was not permitted."

"Well, I'm gonna fucking tell on ya if you don't leave right fucking now."

"You will report me *now*? For *this*? This is your breaking point of acceptable behavior?"

"Well, you'll definitely get in *some* trouble if someone else walks in here."

"Oh, I'm quite used to getting into a little trouble. Believe me."

Brandy quickly wiped and then pulled up her pants for safety's sake. She put the toilet seat down, and climbed onto it, sitting there crouched with her cane tightly gripped like a weapon, ready to strike the man if he dared to open that door, even if it was locked from her side.

"So again, why the fuck are you here?" she asked.

"Oh, just wanted to offer my condolences for your poor father. What was it that ailed him again?"

'Fucking bullshit' Brandy thought.

"You're gonna do that in here? Couldn't fucking wait two minutes outside?" she said.

"I understand you are under a lot of distress because of this. Now what did you say his problem was?"

'Ugh, fucking leech' Brandy thought.

"Uh, cancer." she said.

"*Uh*, cancer, yes. What type of cancer, if you don't mind me asking?"

"It was, uh, it is lung cancer."

"Ah yes, that dastardly old lung cancer. Was your father a heavy smoker, then?"

"Uh, yeah. He smoked. Two packs a day."

"Ah yes. It seems those pesky cigarettes have claimed another victim, then. Now, what was your father's name again?"

"What? Like fuck I'm telling you that."

"Why? Is there something about him you wish to conceal?"

"You know what?" Brandy raised the cane above her shoulder in defense. "You've been stalking me around, commanding me around, threatening me with murder and torture, and now you're not even gonna let me piss by myself. And you know what? I've fucking tolerated all of that shit. I've played along. I've been goddamn fucking nice, and done as you wanted me to the whole time. But fucking seriously, if you're gonna rope my fucking family into this, you know what, fuck you! Like, fucking fuck you, asshole!"

The volume and pitch of her voice raised with every syllable.

"I'm beginning to sense that there are details to your father's situation you don't want me to know."

"The fuck it is! Have you ever heard of fucking privacy, you fucking pervert?! It's been kind of a big deal through fucking all of human civilization!"

Wilkes sighed.

184

"I does not really matter." he said. "All I can tell you is that we will see you outside your home tomorrow, at seven o'clock sharp. If not… I hope you're not too sentimental about your eyelids. That's the first step, you see. People just can't enjoy my artistry if they keep shutting their eyes."

Then he went and washed his hands. Then he activated the hot air dryer, dried his hands for ten seconds. Then he stepped outside.

Brandy sat still for a little while, remaining in her defense position. Soon she realized she needed to use the toilet some more.

CHAPTER SIXTEEN

Brandy had most likely gone to bed at six AM more often than she had gotten up at that hour. It felt wrong to her, it messed with her brain and body, everything felt alien and off. Having only slept a total of twenty minutes before the alarm clock went off did not help matters either.

After having spent half an hour squirming around in bed, she finally accumulated the strength and willpower to get up and dress. She left her apartment ten minutes before the appointed time, her hair even messier than normal and with icky menthol toothpaste lingering in her mouth.

Outside, the snow had mostly melted, making it look more like a dreary late November morning than mid-December. Due to the hectic string of recent events, Brandy had been unable to return home to join her family for Thanksgiving, and now she had also missed half of Hanukkah, and would also miss the rest. Not that those celebrations had much personal significance to her anymore, but their absence now stingingly reminded her how lonesome she had become during this fall.

Very soon, a car rode up to the Manson Asylum entrance. It was a shiny black Oldsmobile circa nineteen fifty. Brandy inhaled deeply and went to open the back door.

In the back seat sat Roland staring gloomily at her as she went inside.

"You're not gonna drive this time?" she asked him.

"No. Why, is that all I am to you? A chauffeur? A servant?"

"Hey, I didn't mean to offend ya, man."

The car drove off before Brandy could even properly attach her seatbelt.

"I have been forced to do some dirty work under the D'Orleans' employ, I shall admit." Roland sniffed and coughed. "These later years in particular I've been forced to perform some quite lowery tasks in the care of lady Olive, but only because all others in our staff lack the competence to attend to her needs. She is a special case. Still, I am certainly more than a simple servant. I function rather as manager of the estate."

"Is that what they call butlers now-a-days?"

"I've never cared much for the term 'butler'. It has too much of a submissive tone to it, in my own opinion."

"I s'pose. How's Olive, by the way?"

"Still recovering, little by little."

"Yeah, I was gonna go see her yesterday, but they just said she wasn't in shape for visitors yet. Have you been to see her?"

"I've been told the infarction was a relatively mild one."

"Yeah? That's good, I s'pose."

II

After a forty minute drive out from Riverside city limits, they arrived at a vast flat area fenced off with barbed wire. It was the D'Orleans Private Airport, with two parallel strips and rows of hangars rooming a double digit amount of aircrafts, one of which was currently placed outside, an obsidian black jet the size of a smaller short haul airliner, with the D'Orleans Industries logo printed in large silver letters on its sides. A staircase was being pushed towards its opened entrance as the car parked a few dozen feet away.

A vicious wind blew Brandy in the face as she exited the car. It was very cold out here, much colder than back in the city. Holding tightly on to her beret, she pushed herself against the wind towards the plane.

The plane's interior was quite luxurious, with cream-colored walls and comfy leather seats catching Brandy's eyes upon entry, and that was just the first room in a chain of four, disregarding the cockpit. Going further back, she found a room with a forty inch television and a minibar opposite a white sofa, and after that a bedroom with four full-sized water beds, one of which she eagerly dropped into, ready to fall asleep.

"We need to strap in for take-off, Miss Rabinow." said Roland, having followed her into the bedroom. "It is only twenty minutes."

"Can you wake me up in twenty minutes, then?" asked Brandy, already drowsing off.

"No. Get up now, and come to the front section."

Brandy quietly growled to herself in frustration as she pulled herself back up.

III

Around thirty thousand feet in the air, gliding over a blanket of clouds concealing the terrain of rural Wisconsin, Brandy was mixing herself a Cuba Libre while idly scanning through the Blu-ray collection. Roland sat in the sofa, fervently working on his laptop.

"Will you please come look at this spread sheet?" he soon asked her.

"Look, I'm honestly not in the mood for numbers and math and all that shit at this hour, alright. It's like, the crack of dawn."

"It's half past nine."

"Yeah, exactly. And I'm woozy as fuck. Like, I barely even slept last night."

"And you believe the solution to wooziness to drink like that? Isn't that your third alcoholic beverage this morning?"

"Nah, second. Unless you count that little can of Pabst. Look, I've got like, not fear of flying per se, it's just that I'm not super comfortable with it either, so, like, just really need something to calm my nerves, y'know."

"It seems then like you have a lot of nerve trouble in general."

"Aw yeah, I have genuine issues with anxiety. Like, I haven't been diagnosed with anything, but y'know, I get nervous a whole fucking lot."

Every time she impulsively cursed, she immediately feared Roland would come to slap her again, although he did seem much calmer now than during their last encounter, almost a little jaded.

"Well, when you've calmed your precious nerves, could you *then* please take a look at this?" he asked with a hint of frustration.

"I thought I'd just watch a movie, actually. Like, wow, you got the Buster Keaton collection here."

Brandy popped the DVD in, grabbed the remote, and slumped into the sofa, barely averting spilling coke and rum all over. Roland sighed and put the laptop away.

"Want a drink?" Brandy asked him.

He gave her a perplexed look.

"I will fetch myself a bottle of mineral water, thank you." he said, and did just that.

"Don't want a beer or nothing?"

"No, I am a teetotaler."

"What, are you Muslim or something?"

"It has nothing to do with religious conviction." he replied sitting back down. "I simply prefer to keep my thoughts clear at all times."

"Like, you never feel like kicking back a little? Relax a bit?"

"I'll admit I do allow myself once per month to indulge in a single alcoholic beverage. Sometimes I've shared a drink with lady Olive, other times I've enjoyed one after she's gone to bed. A small glass of liqueur perhaps, not too much, though. I can't risk intoxicating myself while on duty, which, given lady Olive's condition, is every hour of every day."

"Alright, so, have you had your monthly drink yet, then?"

"No, I shall wait till Christmas. Every year, on Christmas Eve, after everyone's gone to sleep, and I've placed the presents under the tree, I have made it my own holiday tradition to sit back with a glass of port in front of the fireplace. Of course I didn't get the time for that last year, but it didn't bother me much. Fortunately I value aspects of life other than hedonistic indulgences."

Brandy swallowed the rest of her Cuba Libre, and started chewing on an ice cube.

"Well, you know what, buddy?" she said. "I think you should make up for that missed beverage. Like, do we have any port on this flight?"

"I doubt it. And I wouldn't need to have a glass regardless."

"Aw, c'mon, you gotta enjoy yourself just a little bit." Brandy stood up and approached the minibar again. "Like, what if I find a decent substitution 'round here?"

"I am perfectly fine, thank you."

"Aw, lookie here!" Brandy said discovering the separate wine storage next to the minibar.

She withdrew from it a curvy bottle of red, a Georgian Saperavi.

"How about a glass of this little thing? It's got funny writing on it and everything, so it's just gotta be good, y'know."

"No."

"C'mon, just to make up for the one ya missed out on last December."

189

She twisted the cap off the bottle. All the wine bottles had twist-off caps.

"It's not even brunch time."

"Well, right now, we're not in the same time zone as when we took off, y'know."

Brandy already began pouring the wine into two glasses.

"And So?" asked Roland.

"So, you can't just live according to one time zone. That'd just be impractical for everyone."

"Well, is there maybe a special occasion? To justify this?"

"Special occasion? Well, duh, it's the fifth day of Hanukkah."

"I am Catholic."

Brandy handed him his glass.

"Doesn't matter, we're all human, y'know. And all humans should really just celebrate as many holidays as possible, regardless of nationality, or religion, or culture, or any of that shit. Just celebrate everything, y'know. 'Cos we need celebrations. We need these predictable festivities to look forward to, these ritualistic periods of fun, 'cos, y'know, everything else in this world is so unpredictable, and so much of it is just miserable. We need these, y'know, these scheduled little interludes of joy between all the chaotic bullshit that is life, and as many of those as possible."

Roland took a tiny sip from his glass.

"What if…" he said. "…I promise you to partake in some minor hedonism this once, and then you promise me to take the project a little more seriously, and actually put in a significant effort to make certain it succeeds?"

Brandy sipped from her glass likewise.

"That seems like a good deal to me."

She reached out to toast Roland, and he somewhat reluctantly obliged her. "This really was a good wine, though." she said as their glasses clinked. "Much better than that cheap shit you get at Market Basket."

She selected 'The General' from the DVD menu, and the film began playing.

"Have you seen it before?" she asked. "Have you seen 'The General'?"

"I'm afraid I am not particularly acquainted with cinema." answered Roland. "I have never found it extraordinarily intriguing."

"Really?" Brandy took another swig. "Well, it's really good though. This one, it's really good. I watched it with my dad when I was a little yout. 'Bout twelve years old. It's really funny."

IV

"So, uh, about this, uh, what was it called, the country? Agaradaddy-stan?" Brandy asked.

"Do you mean Ugratistan?"

"Yeah, that one. What's like, what's the deal with that?"

"What do you want to know, specifically?"

"Another helping?"

Brandy poured Roland's glass halfway to the brim before he could answer, just like the previous times.

"Well, y'know..." she then said. "... it's just, like for one thing, I don't think I've ever even heard of that country before, y'know. I don't think they ever mentioned that one in geography class, y'know."

"Well, first I'd like to say this country's educational system is severely flawed. And I take it you went to public school?"

"Yeah."

"Yes, so simply saying you did not learn something at school is by no means any evidence against its credibility."

"Alright, but, well, where is it, then?"

"It is located in the Caucasus, by the Caspian sea. The problem is, its autonomy is still a matter of dispute. In fact, most nations, including the US, recognize it as just an oblast of the Russian Federation. Ugratistan itself, however, remains adamant regarding their status of absolute sovereignty, as they have since the end of the Cold War."

"Kinda like the same deal as with Chechnya?"

"Ugratistan could, in layman's terms, be regarded as the lesser known cousin of Chechnya, indeed. Their conflict with Russia has been much quieter in nature, but as a result, has made much less progress. The two still remain bitter enemies, to be frank. That is why we were forced to conduct business with the Ugrati government so discreetly. We

191

wouldn't want Russia to know an American-based company is in trade with a country they're currently attempting to isolate into submission."

"Like, they're seriously doing that?"

"Well, yes. Any international trade attempted by the Ugrati government or companies based within their borders is technically considered illegal by Russia as they refuse to pay Russian taxes, and conduct business in the guise of a separate nation."

"So why do *you* guys conduct business with them?"

"Because they expressed interest in the project. Their president did. I am not certain why, but we are currently not in a position to decline offers of financial support."

"So, is the president, uh, Zurba-Durba or whatever his name is…?"

"Dzargonin Dzarban."

"Yeah, that dude. Is he like super fat, then?"

"Not to any discernable degree from the few pictures I've seen."

Brandy sat back in the sofa, sinking into its back cushion while swirling the wine around under her nose.

"Smells really good, this wine." she said.

"It does have a rich bouquet." replied Roland, also sniffing at the wine.

"Too bad you don't drink more often. I mean, considering you got access to all this super extravagant booze, y'know. Like, wines from all over the world, fine spirits. That rum I got back at the banquette."

"I believe that was cognac."

"No, after that. That bottle Olive had in her bed stand."

Roland nearly coughed up his latest swig and became at once sternly interrogative.

"Did you raid lady Olive's bed stand?" he asked.

"She treated me. I don't go around stealing shit. She offered me some rum, and I said yes."

"If you say so." Roland calmed down again. "I'll have to ask lady Olive herself for confirmation, though."

"Fine." Brandy exhaled exasperatedly. "Also, what was the deal with that gun she's got?"

"So you *did* look inside her bed stand?"

"Well, yeah…"

"You *did* raid her bed stand!"

"What, no! She was the one who made me. I had to actually fetch the bottle. Olive couldn't do that herself. You weren't around, and I couldn't push her. I'm weak as a kitten."

"Really, now?"

"Yeah! Me and Olive were alone, she offered me some rum, I said yes, she told me to go fetch it. You think I'd, like, not only steal shit from you guys but also just casually admit it?"

"Fine." Roland exhaled exasperatedly.

"But yeah, what *was* the deal with that gun?"

"Did you ask her?"

"Yeah, she just said she got it from her grandpa. Which is like, fine, I s'pose. It's just that it was a bit of an odd place to put it, if you ask me. I mean, she's not like, suicidal or anything, is she?"

Roland moaned.

"Like, I know that kind of is a bit of a touchy subject, y'know." Brandy said. "It's just, like, well, fuck it, y'know. I won't ask. Not gonna be a little clingy leech getting up in your panties about personal shit like that. I'm sorry. I'll just drop it."

Roland emptied his glass, and reached it out to Brandy for a refill, which he received.

"She is not suicidal, at least not in the regular sense." he said. "The problem is that her lifestyle, which is her choice and nobody else's, might increase the risk of certain health issues."

'No shit!' thought Brandy, sealing her mouth to avoid blurting it out.

"Of course, she and I do not discuss those matter." Roland continued. "But rest assured, we are both very aware, and we are both quite worried, Olive in particular. She does not show it, and in fact, she hopes to be able to deny it away, but come night, it's all she can think about. So many nights have I needed to comfort her away from impending panic attacks caused by the prospect of diabetes and other related diseases. It is her biggest fear, that her lifestyle, her eating habits in particular, would come to cause a sickness, one that would prevent her from continuing to live the way she currently does.

193

She cannot imagine any other way to live, you understand. She has always been something of a gourmand."

"So what, she's gonna, like, snuff herself if she gets diagnosed with diabetes?"

"Or something akin to diabetes. I assume by 'snuff' you mean…"

"Yeah. That."

Brandy poured the last few drips into her glass, and swallowed them.

"That's kinda… don't have a good word for it." she said. "Can't she just get, like, weight loss surgery or something?"

"We've tried. No doctor would allow it unless she lost weight by herself first. And of course we've tried. We've offered ample compensation for the doctors to ignore a few fine prints in the hospital policies, believe me."

"You've tried bribery?"

"I think 'bribery' is such a crass word."

"Well, it's a crass thing to do."

"And may I assume you have been perfectly law-abiding your entire life?"

"Oh, I've been crass. I've been awful crass a number of times. Doesn't mean I can't call other folks crass too."

"I suppose that would be fair." Roland sighed deeply. "I honestly believed getting employed at the D'Orleans estate would be the end of my unlawful days."

"Do you want to pop another bottle?" Brandy stood up.

"We've drunk a *whole* bottle?" Roland seemed quite surprised.

"A '*whole*' bottle? Jeez, man, it wasn't a bottle of moonshine. I drink a whole bottle of wine by myself several times a week. Ain't that big of a deal, y'know. You wanna pop another one or what?"

"I really should take time to process what I've already consumed, actually."

"No you don't. Half a bottle? What's that? You'd get a stronger buzz from smelling your own socks. Just let me find a good one."

Brandy picked up another bottle from the storage.

"Like this one. It's a…" she read the inscription on the label. "It's an Arizonan Syrah. And whaddya know, it was made by that guy from Tool. That's cool. Quite an eclectic taste whoever selected these wines got, I'd say."

"I really should not have any more."

"Sure you do. You've got thousands of sober nights to make up for."

Brandy twisted off the cap and immediately started pouring Roland's glass full.

"That was by no means consensual." Roland said.

"Neither was, well, I won't be crass." Brandy said and poured herself a glass, and sat down.

"So, then…" Roland took a sip of his wine, looking a tad discontent. "What was I talking about, again?"

"Didn't you say something about being employed by the D'Orleans' or something?"

"Well, yes. I remember the day the D'Orleans estate employed me. It felt like quite an achievement to be hired by the wealthiest institution in New Hampshire. I was younger then, more naïve. I remember when I first came to this country, having emigrated from Botswana in nineteen sixty six. Of course, that was before they gained their independence, so I arrived in America with a British passport. I remember the customs suspected me of having faked my passport, because of my skin's color."

"Boy, that must've been, like, you must've had a trip, y'know."

"I remember having difficulties accustoming myself to the American culture. I am not certain I even have yet."

"Like how?"

"It is difficult to explain. People react differently than you expect, they expect you to react differently in return. The big differences I learned reasonably fast. I learned how to adjust to those. The small ones, however, the tiny nuances in behavior and expectations, those could be terrifyingly confusing."

"I s'pose."

"I certainly must say…" Roland took a swig and began paying attention to the film. "… I don't understand why these films have to promote such an irresponsible disregard for safety. You cannot ride a train on the side like that. He could fall off and get pulverized on the rails."

"It's supposed to be a comedy."

"What's comedic about toying with death like that?"

"Well, this sure ain't the worst thing he'll do through this movie."

"He will continue to tease his own mortality in this manner? For our entertainment? Is this one of those films Mister Wilkes talks about making?"

195

"It's just a movie."

"It's a perverted one."

Brandy subtly rolled her eyes.

"Can I ask you what it is you do for entertainment? Or recreation?"

"Normally my work is my entertainment, and my recreation. Sometimes I partake in the D'Orleans' recreational activities, such as tennis or golf, if my assistance is required or desired."

"So you never feel the need to have a break and get your mind off of things?"

"I cannot stop thinking. The human brain doesn't have the ability to deactivate itself."

"No, I meant like, y'know, fuck it. Don't bother."

Brandy drank up her glass, and stood up.

"Well, I don't exactly *need* to watch this movie one more time. You clearly don't enjoy watching it. How long till we arrive?"

"I would estimate at least an hour and a half still, but I can consult the pilot."

"Don't bother. I'll just go take my pill and have a nap."

"Very well."

And with that Brandy left into the bedroom.

V

Brandy awoke perfectly sobered up to the sensation of the plane's rapid decrease in altitude. That combined with the consistency of the waterbed mattress made her feel like being right in the eye of a fatal sea storm, which was what she dreamt the last few minutes before waking up. It was at this point she remembered how ill prolonged periods in a waterbed made her feel. She wanted to leave the bed and lie down simultaneously, conflicted about which would best nurture her nausea.

"You better come to the front now, Miss Rabinow." Roland burst in to say. "We are about to land."

VI

After a bumpy but tolerable landing on a strip surrounded by snow coated forest, Brandy stumbled out of the front exit, her cane in the left hand, a can of Pabst in the right, and her backpack over one shoulder. The clouds above gradually dissolved to reveal a sharp

196

blue sky. The freezing air was quite welcomingly refreshing to her face and lungs. The last time she was this happy to be cold was back in her late teens, after she accidently got locked inside that sauna on a trip to New York, something she was grateful happened in January and not during summer.

This strip was barred off with the same barbed wire fence as the one near Riverside, though this one was bigger and more ravished, easily mistakable for an abandoned military base. Maybe it was.

"The construction site is an hour's drive form here." Roland said. "Our ride should arrive shortly."

Minutes later, a large pick-up truck with a variety of rust colorations appeared through the woods. It wobbled from side to side, failing to drive in a straight line, produced a series of tiny explosions and other worrisome noises, and left a thick black fog in its trail.

"Is that it?" Brandy asked jokingly, expecting the vehicle to be driven by some random disoriented hillbilly.

The truck parked ten feet away, and Roland approached it. The driver rolled down his window, and reached out to shake his hand.

"Come on, now." Roland said to Brandy.

"No, wait, what, seriously?" asked Brandy. "*That's* the ride? An hour's drive in *that* thing?"

"Yes. Or shall I order a Hummer limousine for you instead?" Roland replied sarcastically.

Brandy moaned quietly and approached the car. With Roland now already sat inside in the middle, she took the right window seat. The truck was of that old kind without discernable seats but instead one solid row, in brown leather, with spring heels and chunks of rubber foam sticking out through various little tears. There were no seatbelts to be found.

The driver was a small skinny figure, balding and unwashed, his wide grin revealing roughly every second tooth to be missing on each row, one gap being used to hold his cigarette in place. The man was severely underdressed for the weather with only a holey old t-shirt and dungarees.

"How do you do, Dorek?" Roland asked him.

197

"Very good, very good." he responded with a thick foreign accent. "I do very good, all day."

"That's swell. Now be sure to drive carefully. It's more important to get there alive than to get there fast."

"I drive very good. Very fast."

"Yes, but not too fast, now."

"I not drive very too fast. Only fast, not too."

Then Dorek took a swig from the tin flask he held around the staring wheel, pressed the pedal down with all his might, drove down the strip and took a sharp U-turn at the end, before thundering back into the woods. Brandy dropped the quarter-full beer can to the floor, which was already covered in garbage, and gripped tightly around the top of the seatback and the door handle, as the truck raced haphazardly down the unpaved bumpy road. 'If I survive this, I'll totally kiss Roland' she thought. 'Kiss him straight on the lips, then I'll kill the driver, knock the rest of his teeth out then punch his Adam's apple till he stops breathing'.

CHAPTER SEVENTEEN

After significantly less than an hour, they finally arrived at the drop-off point. Brandy carefully stepped out, and when her feet hit the ground, that gloriously safe soil, her legs trembled uncontrollably from the fear-induced adrenaline. For a long while all she could do was look down on the earth beneath her while waiting for her heartrate to normalize.

"So, what do you think of it? Are you impressed?" asked Roland, getting out behind her.

"What? The driver? Was I impressed by him?"

"No, no, no. The site. Do you see any potential?"

Brandy looked up, and saw before her a massive flattened area, a construction site stretching to the horizon. And in the distance, about a mile away, a grand construction resembling a mushroom cloud.

"Holy shit." she said.

"Construction has just barely started on this end." said Roland. "Further in, however, you will see some significant progress. The district around Main Street is in fact fairly near completion."

"What's that big thing over there?" asked Brandy, referring to the mushroom building.

"We call it the Martini Tower. It contains the President's office. Or the 'mayor's office' as we called it at the banquette. It was the first thing we built. It is also where we'll be living the coming week."

"The coming *week*? We're gonna stay here that long?"

"Well, yes. What did you think? A few days? The weekend? A week should be an adequate amount of time to properly assess the situation."

Brandy sighed.

199

"Okay." she said.

"Also, I'm afraid we need to walk there. Private vehicles are still forbidden on the site, even for us. Do you think your handicap will make that too difficult?"

"Whaddya mean 'handicap'? It's just a little post-surgery fatigue."

"My question was, will you be able to walk that far?"

"How far?"

"Roughly a mile and a half."

"I can do that no problem."

"That is good."

'Fucking handicap, you say I'm fucking handicapped, you fucking dipshit' thought Brandy as they began walking. 'Calling me a cripple all casually, walking around all high and mighty like a snooty fuckface'.

II

Up close, the Martini Tower did indeed resemble a giant martini glass in its shape. It was a dizzyingly tall building in typical art deco architecture with a glass entrance door big enough to fit two elephants and a giraffe.

The art deco motif continued on the inside, the reception being a glossy area the size of a stadium, with burgundy wall-to-wall carpet and gilded walls, the center or the room featuring a large bronze fountain with a statue of a boteroesqe naked woman on top, and a single large Peter Paul Rubens painting had been hung on the wall, with the presumed intention of hanging more ones later. The whole area was completely desolate, with not a single person present besides Brandy and Roland.

"Shall we take the elevator?" asked Roland.

"Yeah, thanks. I don't really feel like taking the stairs right now."

"There are no stairs here. There are no stairs in the entirety of this city. Apart from the ones the workers use."

And so they went into the first of the six elevators, and it was an unusually roomy one, about the size of Brandy's whole apartment. Roland pressed the button for the second highest floor, and up they went.

"So, is, like, Olive gonna be the president here?" asked Brandy.

"Initially, that was the idea." answered Roland. "I am not certain, however, if the lady would be capable of the task after her recent health complication."

"You don't think she'll recuperate?"

"We can only speculate. But at this point, I doubt she'll be able to handle a job of such daunting responsibility. I fear the stress would be greatly detrimental."

"So, like, are you gonna call the shots 'round here, or...?"

"If it comes to that, I will accept the responsibility."

Soon they reached their floor.

III

The second highest floor seemed to consist of a luxurious apartment, with a combined living room and kitchen meeting Brandy upon leaving the elevator. Out the windows was a view of the whole city-in-progress and the surrounding Wyoming forests, similar to the view from the D'Orleans tower.

"You can have the bedroom on the left." said Roland.

Brandy did enter through the door on the left, to find a large bedroom, again bigger than her own whole apartment. Was her apartment just abnormally small? She threw her backpack up against the bed, as there was nothing of significance to unpack at this moment, and then she flumped into the king-size bed and rolled herself into the silk duvet to make a big Brandy burrito. Drained of most mental stamina, she now drifted into a shallow slumber.

"When you are done unpacking, we need to get to work." Roland said in the doorway.

"What? No. I'm gonna sleep."

"You had your nap on the flight over. Now we need to look over the charts."

"Fuck off."

"Miss Rabinow, are you going to cooperate at all?"

"Yeah, after I get my nap. I'm fucking exhausted."

"How about this. You will come out in an hour. One hour. Sixty minutes, zero seconds. If you do not by that time, there will be consequences. Dire consequences. Understand?"

"Yeah, yeah, fuck off now."

Roland closed the door slowly, straining to fight his primal urge to slam it shut with all his might. Brandy snorted and buried her head inside her duvet wrap, starting to imagine herself as a little fetus inside a womb.

IV

"As you can see, the available funding doesn't stretch to meet our current budget. We may need to cut back on certain areas, but the uncertainty lies in where to cut without compromising the ideal behind the project. That, I think, is our currently biggest challenge." said Roland.

Brandy's eyes idly scanned over the charts on the computer screen as Roland's speaking filled up the background noise.

"Do you have any ideas?" he asked her.

"Yeah, sure."

"What, then?"

"What?"

"What are your ideas?"

"Ideas? Uh, I dunno. Do we, like, need to build the whole city at once? Aren't most cities, like, don't they just start off as small towns, then they grow into cities? Can't we just build part of the city to completion, then take it from there?"

"Did you not pay attention?"

"Attention to what?"

"What I just told you."

"Well, yeah, sure, we need to, like, find out where to cut, without making it shit."

"That was the last bit, yes, but I also told you about all the people who have already applied for residence in the state, and have been accepted. They've even paid for their homes. The numbers are in the area of fifty thousand so far. Fifty thousand accepted residents, all having paid. Do you think we can afford to let them all down?"

"Well, we could put some of them on hold, maybe? Tell them to wait a little?"

"For how long? Years?"

"Maybe?"

"They have all been promised residence by the end of July. *Maybe* we can stretch it to August or September for some of them, but I dare not consider the lawsuits should we disappoint too many."

"Well, that's all I got." Brandy stood up. "I didn't make this fucking logistical mess. Why the fuck should I be the one to solve it all?"

"You *are* the chief accountant, after all."

"And who the fuck decided that? Not me. I didn't apply for this job. I didn't decide shit."

Brandy left the dinner table where they sat, and went straight to the kitchen's liquor cabinet, while Roland rubbed the bridge of his nose with squinting eyes.

"Where's the Kahlua?" Brandy asked with a vodka bottle in her hand.

"Why, oh why?" Roland asked himself.

"Espresso Bohême?" Brandy observed with said bottle in her hand. "Alright, I guess."

"You are aware that we can easily fire you, are you not?" asked Roland.

"Well, I didn't actually apply for this job, and I... Do I even get paid for this? I haven't gotten a single check yet."

"We paid for your surgery, did we not?"

"Oh, so you took that out of my salary?"

"Your salary is not my business. Yet. Lady Olive is still technically your employer."

"And yet you can fire me?"

"I can tell lady Olive she has no choice if she wants the project to succeed. She will hopefully be rational enough to understand."

Brandy pulled out a carton of whole cream from the fridge.

"Well, you know what? I take it you're a man who values human life, right?" she said pouring the cream into her glass of coffee liqueur and vodka and ice. "So the thing is, if you fire me, that Wilkes motherfucker, he's gonna fucking snuff me."

"I am aware of his unorthodox methods of conviction."

"Yeah, and you don't think that son of a bitch is fucking smack dab crazy? You usually only see creeps like him on '*Unsolved Mysteries*'."

"I personally have never taken the man's threats particularly seriously."

"Yeah, well, if that fish-lipped freak ever fucking touches me, that's on your conscience. I fucking mean that."

"Well, I will not allow you to wallow in unrestrained sloth and procrastination just because you've been intimidated by an uncharismatic co-worker."

"And what if you're wrong? What if he really wants to fuck me up?"

"Then I suppose I am wrong. I consider myself to have good judgment, but I have made mistakes before, and I accept that I can make mistakes again."

"Yeah, that'll be all the fucking consequences, right? If you're wrong, you'll have to admit that you're wrong? Never mind that I'll be some loony sadist's rape slave until I die. That's not important."

Roland looked back down on the charts.

"I *will* have a talk with lady Olive about your uppity behavior. You simply cannot continue with this lack of work ethics."

Brandy said nothing, and went surly back to her bedroom with her drink in hand.

V

Stripped down to her panties and a tank top, Brandy sat in an enormous bean bag chair and sipped from her drink, gazing out to the horizon, meditating on the tranquilly slow spins of the tower cranes. How did she end up here, she thought. She had never before in her life been this far west. She was going to travel to California on that road trip back when, but those plans were cancelled when they reached Missouri, and one of the others got hepatitis from bad shrimp, and they all had to return home. The absolutely furthest west she had been, however, was that one time she had gone with her family to Texas, to visit some distant relatives she could no longer even remember the names of, who lived in a tiny fishing village which struggled financially on account of being nowhere near water. She did not remember much from that trip, it was pretty eventless.

Her phone started ringing. She put her drink on the floor and proceeded to dig it up from the pile of clothes she had left in the corner. It was Olive ringing. Had Roland spoken with her?

"Yo girl, how ya doing?" Brandy said in the phone.

"Hey, friend." sounded Olive's weakened voice from the other side. "I'm okay. Still recovering."

"That's great. I've been kinda afraid for ya, y'know."

"Oh, thank you."

"Didja get the book I left you?"

"Yes. I haven't had the strength to read much of it, though."

"That's alright. You can have it, y'know. Just take as much time as you'd like. It's like, I'm sorry I couldn't give you anything else. Maybe I should've bought some flowers or something, I dunno. I think I'll look for, like, a proper gift some time soon."

"Oh, but you don't need to do that, friend."

"Well, yeah, after you paid for the who procedure I went through and everything, of course I gotta give ya something in return, y'know."

"Brandy, dear, your friendship is more than enough."

"Uh, yeah, I'll still try to look for something, though."

"Oh, Brandy, you sweet little thing, you. You're the kindest person I've ever met in my whole life."

"Well, gee, thanks, I guess."

"The doctor said I'll be good enough to go home by Sunday. I'll try to make it over to Wyoming as quickly as possible after that."

"Aw no, really? Don't you think you should rest a bit?"

"Resting is all I've been doing here. The food was terrible too. I had to get Mister Wilkes to bring me all my meals. It's been a lot of McDonald's and KFC lately, I can tell you that."

"Like, really?"

"Oh yes. I thought I'd get tired of those family buckets from the Colonel, but they're just simply addictive, you know."

"And the doctor lets you eat all that?"

"Oh, he started complaining at first, like he always does, but Mister Wilkes dear got him to quiet down. I really shouldn't have any much stress around me right now."

"But, like, is it really good for you to eat that kinda stuff, like, right after a heart attack?"

"Oh, Jiminy flip, Brandy, not you too."

"Not me too what?"

"Everyone keeps telling me I need to eat less, and less greasy, and all that, because of my heart, but it's gotten nothing to do with that. It's hogwash. I just have a heart condition, you know. I have high blood pressure, always have had. There's nothing to do about that."

"Yeah, but you don't think cutting down on deep-fried food would…"

"Stop saying that." Olive wheezed, seemingly attempting to shout. "It's not my fault. Stop blaming me for everything bad that happens to me."

"Alright, alright. I'm sorry. I just… I'm not a doctor, alright. I don't know about how this works."

"Well, the doctors don't seem to know much either. It's just a giant echo-chamber of just giving the obese the blame for all their plights. 'It's your fault', 'just eat less' and all that nonsense."

"Yeah, I s'pose."

"I honestly thought you understood, though."

"Hey, look, don't be like that. I'm not blaming you for anything. I'm just… I don't know anything about this shit, I'm not a heart expert."

"Then maybe you should not talk about it either. Maybe you shouldn't regurgitate ancient thin people propaganda about issues you don't understand."

"Look, I am sorry. Like, honestly, I apologize."

"Honest?"

"Honest to God almighty."

What followed was a long stretch of heavy breathing from Olive's end.

"Olive? Are you alright?"

"… Yes. Just please promise you don't say something stupid like that again."

"I promise."

"… Good. You are my best friend."

Then Olive hung up.

CHAPTER EIGHTEEN

The streets of Obesiana had no car lanes. They instead consisted solely of wide flat walking areas with travelator belts being constructed or planned for construction close to the edges. It was Monday, and Sebastian Kenutsen had arrived to tour the city's more complete areas with Brandy for evaluation. They had to walk.

"How long has it been since they started construction, really?" asked Brandy.

"It began officially in mid-October." answered Kenutsen.

"Well, that's impressive, then. If they've built this much in such a short time, then, y'know, that's a ton. That's amazing."

"Well, I do retain some skepticism regarding the quality of the workers' craft. Very few of these buildings actually have electricity."

Brandy soon became heavy at breath.

"Hold on." she said, and sat down at a nearby bench.

"Is anything the matter?" Kenutsen asked, more demandingly than concerned.

"My legs ain't what they used to be." Brandy said mocking the speech of an elderly person. "No, but seriously, that surgery really fucking did me in. That's why I got this cane, y'know. I'm not a paraplegic or nothing, just a little weakened still."

"Well, we're still on a very tight schedule today, and I would like to reach Dom DeLuise Avenue before lunchtime."

"I'm sorry, I'll just need a couple seconds to catch my breath."

At that point she noticed two laborers attempting to run towards them, dragging a third one along the asphalt by the arms. He seemingly struggled to escape. As they arrived they tossed him to the ground by Kenutsen's feet.

"What is going on here?" Kenutsen demanded to know.

"This man, boss…" said one of the two laborers. "He try to escape. We catch him."

"Is that so?" asked Kenutsen.

"No, no. Not escape." said the man on the ground. He grabbed around Kenutsen's legs in a begging fashion. "I am loyal. Very loyal." he desperately continued, teary eyed and out of breath.

"What is your name?" Kenutsen asked him.

"He is Kokhir, boss." said one of the other two. "Kokhir Kurban. He try escape many time."

"No, is lie. I never escape. Very loyal. So much!" Kokhir pleaded.

"Stop staining my pants." Kenutsen barked and shook him off.

Brandy urged to intervene, but had no clue what to say.

"Now you two, what are your names?"

"I am Tarek." said one of the two.

"I am Anbaris." said the other.

"And how many times has he tried this before?"

"Two time." said Tarek.

"No, is lie. No time."

"You shut up."

"Yo, 'scuse me, Seb, but is this how you fucking treat your employees?" Brandy asked.

"This is none of your business." Kenutsen hissed back.

"Alright, but, like, what the fuck? Is this like a fucking Russian gulag around here?"

"Russia?" asked Anbaris.

"This is a management issue, young lady. It is by no means within your field." Kenutsen turned back to the laborers. "How did he try to escape?"

"I *no* escape!" cried Kokhir.

"*You* shut up now."

"He take car, say he need get supplies." Anbaris explained.

"What kind of supplies were those, Kokhir?"

"I need cement. Much cement, no cement for need build where is."

"There was not enough cement left, you mean?"

"Yes. Not cement where is."

"You do realize we receive all our resources from contractors, do you not? We don't make regular laborers venture off to buy their materials. You would have to drive for almost half a day before reaching the nearest town."

Kokhir looked confusedly at Kenutsen, hardly grasping much of his speech.

"And even then, how would you pay for the cement? With your own funds?"

Tarek translated everything to Ugrat for Kokhir. He looked more desperate to respond by the syllable.

"Please, please. I have money. I pay. I do no wrong. I go out, get cement, go back. All is very good."

"I will say this…" Kenutsen removed his glasses to clear them. "Under normal circumstances, I would have fired you. However, since we are not in a financial position to cut down on labor, I believe a different type of penalty would be necessary."

"Just let him go, man." Brandy said. "Just let him get back to work, and forget all about it."

"I'm afraid we still cannot allow grave misconduct here." retorted Kenutsen. "Were all you three working on the same unit?"

"Yes." said Tarek. "We are all in Unit Twenty Eight K in Oedipus District."

"Well, that's quite convenient. As a reward, you two will go unpunished, the rest of the unit, including you, Kokhir, will be reported to Ugrati authorities, and then they will deal with you accordingly upon your eventual homecoming."

"What? Seriously?" said Brandy.

"Do all three of you understand?"

Tarek nodded.

"Good enough. Now get back to work, and don't forget to relay my verdict to the rest of the unit."

Tarek and Anbaris then attempted to lift Kokhir from the ground, but he resisted, begging Kenutsen in Ugrat with his hands intertwined. Eventually they got him up on his feet, and pulled him away.

"What the hell was that?" Brandy exclaimed.

"Just ordinary discipline." Kenutsen said. "Part of the job."

"Is this fucking turning into North Korea? You can't treat your workers like that?"

"Of course I can. They are not even here legally."

209

"Yeah, I suspected that, but still, like, what are these Ugratistan authorities gonna do about them when they return?"

"Oh, a prison sentence would be expectable. I doubt they'd be executed, though. Don't worry your messy little head about that."

"You '*doubt*' they'll get *snuffed*? Like, there's a fucking chance of that?"

Kenutsen shrugged nonchalantly.

"Like, what kind of rights have they got back there?"

"Oh, I don't take much interest in social politics. Now then, shall we get back to work ourselves? I certainly hope these travelators can endure the ensuing weight of the citizens."

II

It was finally dinner time at the Martini Tower. Roland had prepared a pork stew with black beans, bell pepper, and shallots, garnished with orange zest and fresh cilantro. He himself only paired it with a glass of water, but Brandy had instead opted for a bottle of Chilean Zinfandel from the apartment minibar. The two of them ate their dinner on opposite sides of the dinner table, with chairs for four people between them. Initially, Kenutsen, who had taken residence a few floors beneath them, was invited to join, but declined upon figuring his work was more expansive than first thought, requiring his full attention for the rest of the day.

"So, how did the evaluation of the city go?" asked Roland in the manner of a father querying about his child's day at school.

"It was pretty damn exhausting, actually." Brandy sighed.

"I will have no cursing at the dinner table." Roland said sternly.

"Alright. Well, like I said, I think we made it through, like, four districts or something, on foot no less, and Seb had to make notes on everything."

"Yes, that was the intention."

"Yeah, but couldn't we have had a little car? Like a golf cart or something? I kept looking at those travelators, and I was like, 'couldn't these… things… start working soon', like, it was such a tease to have them stand there and do nothing, like, I'm starting to think my muscles are actually deteriorating. I actually think I feel a bit worse now than when I left the hospital. It's like, I know it could just be 'cos I'm exhausted, but shouldn't there be like, some improvements, y'know? Shouldn't I have gotten a bit stronger after a week?"

"Yes." Roland responded dismissively and disinterested.

Brandy poured herself another glass of wine.

"You have not eaten much." noted Roland. "Is the food not to your liking?"

"Oh, it's, I mean, the craftsmanship is just excellent. It's, um, really, my appetite's just been kind of dulled lately."

"I understand."

Brandy had never enjoyed pork much. Her family did not eat it, and the taste had not appealed much to her either. The only exception was one hotdog she bought from a street vendor when she was fourteen. It was the best thing she had ever tasted, and gave her a newfound appreciation for life. Her throat was sore and her back hurt that day, but that hotdog made everything alright.

"Man, I used to be so depressed back in the day." Brandy thought out loud.

"Pardon?" said Roland.

"Nothing." Brandy looked down and continued digging around in her stew. "Um, have you heard anything more from Olive?"

"I did phone lady Olive to relay my displeasure with your work ethics, although she was quite alarmingly nonchalant about it. Either only she understands the extents of your alleged talents, or that infarction has had an impairing effect on her judgment."

"Did she seem alright?"

"Well, she insisted she was in decent health, sufficiently so to visit us in person on Monday."

"Do *you* think she's ready for that by then?"

"It is hard to say what she can or cannot endure at this point. To be brutally frank, her body has already been pushed to a ridiculous extreme."

"Yeah, it kinda worries me too, y'know. Didja hear what she's been eating at the hospital?"

"She did tell me, yes."

"Man, what if she get, like, another heart attack? That could happen, y'know."

"Well, fortunately, I doubt it would cause any significant damage to the project."

211

"Well, yeah, I wasn't worried about that. I'm sure you guys could handle it. I'm just, like, Olive, y'know, I just hope she maybe turns around soon. Maybe we could get her to eat some more veggies or something."

"I highly doubt she would be easily convinced."

"Yeah, she got like super aggressive when I brought up her eating habits, and, well, not even brought up, just reacted when she mentioned eating deep fried chicken right after a heart attack."

"Yes, she became quite defensive about her lifestyle after the Closet endeavor."

"What was that about?"

"Oh, never mind. Not a suitable topic for a dinner conversation. Thinking of it, neither is a person's health. I suggest we switch to discussing something more appropriate."

The remainder of the dinner proceeded in total silence from both parties.

III

Many, many nights ago, years in fact, Brandy had an extraordinarily vivid dream of being an old woman in a desert. It looked like no desert she had been to in real life, and, to her memory, not seen at all. But there she was, in the middle of this vast dry terrain that never existed but in her mind, and it felt so authentic. She felt the heat, the grains of sand blowing into her skin. And she was an old woman, in a pale blue night gown, and she was all alone. Unlike most of her dreams, this one was not another rapid-fire sequence of vaguely related nonsense tossing her from one setting to another. This one was a shaped experience. It consisted of one singular event, and it felt realistic, absolutely realistic. And in it she had separate memories, of a non-existent past. She remembered a whole life of people and events and places that never really were. And now she wandered aimlessly through the desert, walking past a peculiar construction, a building of sorts built into the wall of a massive cliff. A building of dark metal, with circular window, three on each side. And through one of them, someone flashed a tiny light straight in her eyes. Someone who wanted her to visit, or go away, or neither. But the building was so far away, miles possibly, it was hard to tell. All she knew was she could not move away, or come closer, for she could only walk when not deciding to.

When she woke up, she wanted to go back to sleep immediately, to continue her dream, but when she did, she just dreamt the same type of frantic inanity as always. It had bothered her ever since that she never found out who was in that building, even if she knew that was idiotic to think. It felt so real.

CHAPTER NINETEEN

On Monday afternoon, Brandy decided to, instead of a shower, take a proper bath, something she normally did very rarely. Her family did own a bath tub, but her father forbade everyone from filling it up to more than an inch. He was quite adamant about saving water.

So she lay stretched out in the tub with a bottle of Heineken in her hand and a warm wet cloth over her eyes; boiling water filled to the brim with rose scented bath salt creating a terrain of bubbly white mountains across its surface. A small disc player mounted to the wall was playing a CD of calming whale noises. The beer was reacting to the chemical remnants of the pill she took a few hours ago, just enough to make her comfortably lax, but with nowhere near the tranquilizing effects of pairing the two directly.

Since she had arrived in Obesiana, Roland had woken her up at nine every morning for breakfast. She then took her morning pill a little before ten, usually without pairing it with any alcohol, and discovered it to under those circumstances have no outwardly effect on her.

At this point it did not matter much that she was thousands of miles from home, in the middle of the uncivilized wilderness, in a city the government probably did not know about, working on a project she did not understand, contributing with skills she did not possess. Perhaps it did matter somewhat, but she could still put it aside for now and focus on her own thoughts, free from Roland's nagging and Kenutsen's whining. Right now she was completely alone inside her own little bubble, her little sanctuary, and it mattered none whether that sanctuary was in Wyoming, Riverside, Philadelphia, or Abu Dhabi.

After a long while, up towards an hour, the foam had flattened, and the whale CD had reached the end. Brandy sat with her elbows on the tub edges submerging the empty beer bottle into the now tepid water, watching it emit a stream of bubbles until completely filled up, then she poured the water out again, and repeated the process.

Then she started to notice a wild commotion outside, probably in the living room. It was hard to hear properly, as her private bathroom and the living room had her bedroom between them, but there was definitely a ruckus out there, people talking, quarrelling. The loudest voice clearly belonged to Roland. The other was a meek feminine one. Brandy crawled out of the tub as fast as her body would allow, and grabbed her cane and a towel.

II

Attired in a pink bathrobe and matching slippers, Brandy stormed out into the living room, or at least tried to, it was more like a sloppy limp, but she did push the sliding door aside very quickly, and it slammed loudly into the wall.

In the living room, by the elevator, stood Roland conversing with Olive.

"Olive!" Brandy exclaimed.

Olive turned to discover Brandy, and her face lit up upon the sight.

"Brandy!" she said. "How are you doing?"

"I'm reasonably alright, thank you very much."

"I see you found your custom-made bathrobe."

"Custom-made?" Brandy looked down to scan her robe.

"It has your initials on it and everything." Olive noted.

Brandy noticed the robe had the letters 'RR' written in bronze curly cursive over the left side of the chest.

"Pretty neat, right?"

"Yeah, it's great, though I s'pose I have to change my name to Randy now." Brandy chuckled.

"Oh, does that say 'RR'? The boys must have misread."

"Well, I'm not complaining. I've never had a bathrobe custom-made for me."

"Well, we couldn't give you any of the regular robes we have here. They would all be way too big."

215

Roland, who was indeed still standing there, cleared his throat.

"We will finish this discussion later, my lady." he said sternly to Olive, and went into the elevator.

"Never mind him." Olive said flapping her hand dismissively in his direction. "He's been such a grump lately."

"Tell me about it."

Brandy noticed the contraption Olive was sitting in, a far cry from her regular wheelchair.

"What's with the new wheels?" she asked.

"Oh yeah, guess what, there really *were* electric wheelchairs for my size. Or something akin to a wheelchair, at least. Way better than a wheelchair, in fact, this thing can fold down to a bed."

The contraption was a four-wheeled motorized vehicle similar in appearance to a space rover, with a black leather queen size bed on top currently bent up to a sitting position. She operated the whole thing with the foldable armrests on each side, the right one with a large joystick for maneuvering, the left with an array of buttons for the various settings.

"Well, that's awesome." said Brandy.

"Oh, and while we're on the topic." Olive grabbed her cane from its holster behind her. "This is yours now."

"What?"

Olive pointed the handle end of her cane towards Brandy.

"I don't need a cane anymore, you see. I have this thing to get around with now."

"You don't need your cane as, like, even a safety measure?"

"Of course not. This thing is sturdy as heck. And it drives uphill no problem. Drives up really steep ramps, barely even slowing down. It can even drive through rough terrain, I've been told. Can't see what I'd need a cane for."

"What if you fall out?"

"Can't you see I'm strapped in like a baby here?"

Olive did have a seatbelt around her waist.

"Besides…" she continued. "… If I fall out, you'd think a *cane* could help me back up? Last time I fell on my butt, we had to call the fire department to help me up. I think there were three guys. It was kind of fun actually, being touched by three guys at once. Has that ever happened to you?"

'I once had two guys inside me' Brandy thought.

"Not that I can recall." Brandy said.

"It was pretty sweet." Olive shook her cane a bit. "Well, take it, then."

Brandy grabbed the cane by the silver handle.

"I mean, no offense, but look at that crummy little twig you already have." Olive referred to Brandy's old cane. "How many splinters have you gotten from that thing already?"

"None." Brandy lied.

"Well, I bet it's diseased with something or other. Most things from pawn shops are. It has probably got the Aids."

Brandy dropped her wooden cane, and gripped around the rabbit ear handle, which felt like molded for her palm. She stomped the cane into the ground, leaning on it, trying to get a feeling for it. It was taller than her previous one, reaching a few inches above her hip. It also felt sturdier and more solid, not wobbling in the slightest, no matter how much weight she pressured it with. Pure compact ebony, always reliable, never wobbly, no splinters.

"Thank you." Brandy said. "I don't know many people who've been so generous. I don't even think my own parents would do this. I mean, they don't even have the resources, but still, I mean, I dunno. Would they have given me this much even if they could?"

"Parents are so overrated." Olive huffed. "You know, just because they tell you they love you, that doesn't mean they do."

Brandy walked over to the nearest seat, a white designer sofa shaped like a tidal wave. Olive drove after.

"So, anyway…" Brandy said. "You look really well. I mean, better than me, like, my looks just went way south after my stay at the hospital. You look well maintained though. You're a little bit paler than before, but for someone who's been through a fucking heart attack you look just great."

217

"Thanks. I suppose I should spend more time in the sun. Too bad there won't be much of that for about half a year."

"Yeah, it's gonna be pretty dark for a while."

Olive drove over to the window, gazing out at the city beneath her.

"What do you think, then? About the city?" she asked.

"Well, it is a work in progress, of course, but I s'pose I see the potential here."

"Have you figured out some more clever ways to save funding, then? I mean, without compromising anything?"

"Well, *some* things will have to be compromised in some way, theoretically."

"You know what I mean." Olive's tone switched from jovial to very serious. "It was your job to find loop holes and cheats."

"You mean like tax evasion?"

"Oh no, of course not."

"Well, then…"

"We've gotten that covered ages ago. All funding has been filtered through a company in the Bahamas. We pay literally zero cents in taxes. Of course we don't pay any taxes. Do you think the government would accept taxes from a project they wouldn't even approve of?"

"Well, I guess that makes sense. So, um… we got that cleared out, I guess… But um… Y'know, honestly, I don't think I got a perfectly clear picture of the entirety of the budget. Like, seriously, there's so much about this project I don't understand, like how things work, where they come from, where they go to, how they get there. And, like, every time I find something out, it seems to be more illegal shit. Like, another facet of a bigger crime."

"I've been very clear about the project being at odds with the ideals of the government, given that they and I are severely ideologically differing."

"Yeah, but there's a difference between ideology and… like, you can't just not pay your taxes just because you disagree with The Man, y'know."

"Of course you can. My family's always been cheating on their taxes. Although, I suppose that's not so much of a political thing, my father always voted Republican, I don't think he was that much opposed to the feds, he just didn't want them to have his money."

"Well, um… well, regardless, I don't have much yet, so just give me a bit more time to get a good overview of this whole shebang, before I can figure out a way to cheat it and whatever."

"You have had a good amount of time already, don't you think?"

"Well, another day or two should do it, I think."

Brandy stood up, and approached the liquor cabinet in the kitchen area.

"Do you want something?" she asked. "Some wine, maybe? Wine thins out your blood, y'know. Might do you some good."

Olive looked somberly out the window, not reacting.

"Hello?" said Brandy and waved for attention.

Olive turned her vehicle slowly around, creating a tense dramatic effect.

"Some wine would be lovely, yeah." She said, suddenly switching back to her jovial self, and drove over to the kitchen.

"Well, whaddya like to have, girl?" Brandy asked her as if she held ownership of the selection.

"Oh, I'm not sure. *Whaddya* recommend, *girl*?"

"Um, well, we got this really good one from Georgia, which I had some of on the plane." she said. "Bet it's even better on the ground."

"I didn't know they even made wine in the south."

"No, Georgia as in the *country*, y'know."

"Georgia is its own country now?"

"You know what? We have this other one here, from Arizona. The label says the dude from Tool made it, and it was actually pretty damn excellent. Wanna try?"

"Well, you're the expert. You seem to know a lot about liquor."

"Oh, well, I do have nearly a decade of experience, y'know."

Brandy twisted off the cap and poured them both a glass each. They toasted.

III

A couple of bottles down, Brandy had dropped back into the sofa, where she finished her glass and then checked the time. It was half past two.

"Do you want something more?" she asked Olive.

"Oh, no more wine, please." she responded. "I'm starting to get a craving for some food, actually. How long is it till dinner?"

"Fuck if I know. I reckon at least three hours."

"Three hours, that's… have they opened any restaurants in town yet?"

"Well, less than a quarter of the city is even finished, and in those parts that sort of are, about an tenth have electricity. And we don't really have any residents yet, so…"

"So no?"

"Well, don't we have the food we need right here?"

"Are you good at cooking, then? I'm not supposed to deal with kitchen utensils, at least not the sharp ones. Or the electric stuff."

"I s'pose we have to wait for Roland to cook us something then. Unless you want my cooking, which is… like, I could maybe offer you a bowl of cereal, but that's really it."

Olive groaned and rubbed her stomach like a feeble animal.

"But I'm hungry *now*." she quavered.

Brandy looked at her watch again, and started counting the hours backwards in her head.

"Say, are you on any meds at the moment?"

"What does that have to do with food?"

"Just asking."

"Well, I weren't prescribed anything."

"Alright, because, y'know, we've had this wine here, and as I said, wine really is a great blood thinner. But I got prescribed with these amazing anti-bloodcurdling pills. And, like, I need to take about three of them every day, throughout the day. And if you're impatient for dinner, y'know, these bad boys really, really helps time fly by."

"Are you gonna take one of those pills right now?"

"I thought so, yeah. Wanna join in? Have a pill? It can only help ya, y'know. Help with the blood pressure and shit."

"Are there any side-effects?"

"Only happiness."

"Really? They make you happier?"

"They make *me* happier, at least."

Brandy got herself up, and walked into her bedroom, waving for Olive to follow, which she did.

"Here they are, girl." Brandy grabbed the bottle from her night stand. "The '*Nequam Intergalactic*' or whatever. They're good, *and* good for ya. One pill is all it takes. Or... I dunno about you. *Maybe* you should take two. I dunno. Do you usually double the recommended dosages on your meds?"

"I just take as much as Roland tells me to whenever I need to take anything."

Brandy reached inside the bed stand cupboard and withdrew a small bottle of bourbon she had nicked from the liquor cabinet the day before. She went into the bathroom and found a pair of glasses that she each filled with a small quantity of the spirit.

"Swallow down with this." she told Olive handing her one of the glasses.

She then took back the pill bottle and opened it, dropped a pill in her palm and ate it, flushing it down with her glass. Then she gave the bottle back to Olive.

"Take two, just to be sure." she said.

Olive obliged, and swallowed one pill in the same manner as Brandy, flushed it down with a portion of the bourbon, then repeated the process with another pill.

"Set your thingy there, your wheelchair machine thing, set it to lie-down bed mode. Like flat." Brandy instructed while lying down in bed.

Olive pressed and held a button on her armrest, and with a blaring vibration noise her chair slowly folded down to a flat bed.

"Now what?" she asked.

"Now what, what?"

"What should I do now?"

Blackness.

IV

Since coming to Obesiana, the more lucid second phase of Brandy's Nequam highs had become more boring. Not less delightful, only less stimulating. The Martini Tower apartment was a cramped little place where there was very little to do, and its ultra-modern interior design looked more sterile and inhospitable by the day.

Should her motor skills be reliable enough to handle the remote, she would try to watch television, only to be insufferably annoyed and turn it off again. No amount of alcohol or narcotics could help her tolerate daytime television, and she had been subjected to its horror more than enough on her hospital stay.

This time she had forgotten to turn on music before commencing the pill coma, having been distracted by instructing Olive. Her phone lay on the bed stand. Pressing one button on the side unlocked it. Then she pressed the music icon from the main menu, and started whatever playlist was already selected. The Nequam high still impaired her too much to let her perform more complex actions on her phone.

She had been searching on the internet for '*While We're in Paradise*' ever since she first heard it, but could find no audio of the song, and very little information about it besides a brief mentioning on The Winged Lieutenants Wikipedia page, which was shorter than a haiku.

The voice of Melanie Safka distortedly beamed out from the limited capacity of the phone speakers, a song of hers which Brandy did not recognize, perhaps a cover tune.

Olive still lay unconscious and motionless like a humongous dome of blubber on her bed devise, still breathing slowly and heavily, even more so than usual. Brandy started wondering if it really was that smart to subject her to this. Could she survive her dose without complications or repercussions? As Brandy's heartrate began raising, she figured it best to avoid such loaded concerns while in this condition. Pills and alcohol made her mind too irrational and clouded to be trusted with serious matters. Once she sobered up, she thought, she would go on to verifying that Olive was indeed alive and well, beyond the risk of overdose. What would even be an overdose for a body weighing just south of a metric ton? Two pills and some alcohol? Hardly, Brandy thought.

V

The back label of the Nequam bottle only listed the same rare side effects that Doctor Walker mentioned, but Brandy had started to worry that the mixing with alcohol might have created new ones. Long term side effects, sneaking up on her, developing too gradually to notice before it was too late.

Already her new habit seemed to have vitiated her digestive system, she thought, as she now sat on the toilet, straining all her muscles trying to push out solidified excrement. Big nuggets of rock hard black turds with a subtle red tint scraping her anus with their edges as they passed through. She had not been sweating this much on the toilet since visiting Florida. That was the last time she got food poisoning.

Fatigued but relieved, she exited the bathroom all sobered up, and checked her watch. It was already half past four. She walked over to Olive, still unconscious. She moved her ear close to her mouth to check if she was still breathing. Olive emitted a mild snort. She had fallen asleep.

"Yo, wake up, girl." Brandy said to Olive lightly slapping her cheek.

No response.

"Yo, Olive! Wake up, it's dinner time!" Brandy shouted and slapped her harder.

Olive's eyes started flickering, and soon opened halfway.

"HEEEEEY…" she blurted at Brandy. "What is going on, girl?"

Her tone was quite slurry and wavy.

"You fell asleep." Brandy said.

"Yeah, it was amazing. I dreamt about clouds."

"Looks like you haven't really gotten all those chemicals outta your system yet, y'know. Want some water, maybe?"

"Yeah, I'm thirsty. Give me some water."

"Well, you'll have to sit up straight if you're gonna drink it."

"No problem."

Olive waved her arm in the general direction of her left armrest and finally landed on the keypad, which she patted aimlessly with her palm.

"Need any help?" Brandy asked.

"No, no. I have done this so many times."

Brandy looked at the layout of the keypad.

"Is this the button you're looking for?" she asked and pressed an arrow-shaped blue one, causing Olive's bed to jerk upwards a little bit. Olive giggled at the sensation.

"Should I hold it in, maybe?" Brandy asked.

She pressed and held the button, and Olive's bed gradually ascended up to a sitting position, with Olive giggling through the whole process.

"Ooh my, this strap thingy is way too tight, we need to let go of that." Olive said about her seat belt, trying to unfasten it.

"No, don't do that, buddy." Brandy stopped Olive by grabbing her arms. "We don't need another accident now. Can't risk sending you to the hospital again."

"Aw, come on, buddy. It's suffocating me."

Brandy went to fetch Olive a glass of water as quickly as her body let her.

"No, it's not." she said. "And drink up. We need to clear up your head some more."

Then entered Roland, with wrinkles around his frown.

"Are you doing alright, lady Olive?" he asked.

"She's alright, alright. Just a bit dehydrated, y'know, like, y'know how heart attacks can do ya in. High blood pressure makes ya need a lot of liquid." Brandy said, helping Olive to drink her water.

"I was asking lady Olive, miss."

"Alright, whaddya say, *lady* Olive? Feeling alright?"

Olive swallowed her water.

"I'm feeling *so* super. Super-*duper*, in fact. Super-duper."

"Is the lady inebriated, Miss Rabinow?" asked Roland sternly.

"No, no, no. Just a tad light-headed from the whole heart incident, y'know. She's totally sober."

"Well, I had intended to hold a meeting regarding the project before dinner, and naturally you will both need to participate."

"You feeling up for that, buddy?" Brandy asked Olive. "Like, business shit?"

"Yeah, absolutely, friend. Let's grind this town into a thriving little metropolis, *y'know*."

"I will be awaiting you both at the dinner table." said Roland. "I presume it will not take long."

VI

The three of them sat around the end of the dinner table, Roland in the middle, with the two ladies on each side.

"Now, since I do not know a better way to introduce this meeting, I will skip straight to the matters." Roland said. "As you both already know, many of the pledges from the fundraising banquette, all of them in fact, have been retracted. Most detrimentally, Mister Lafayette retracted his only a couple of days after, which is frankly

224

not uncharacteristic of him, as he tends to retract most of his overly generous offers after having sobered up."

"When did they say this?" Brandy asked. "That they didn't want to support us anymore?"

"Almost immediately, or, to be more precise, over the span of about a week."

"Well, why didn't you tell me?"

"I did. Several times, in fact."

"No, you didn't."

"Yes, I most certainly did. I suspect you may not have paid attention, but *I* can hardly be faulted for that."

"Well, I surely never heard anything about it."

"That, miss, only proves your total lack of investment in the project. You clearly haven't been paying close enough attention."

"Yo, Olive. When did you hear about the whole fundraising flop thing?"

"The what?" Olive asked.

She was almost falling asleep again.

"The fundraising flop. All the rich folks at the banquette who retracted their pledges. That thing. When did you hear about it? How long ago?"

"They… what did you say? They retracted their pledges?"

"Yeah, ain't that right, Roland? All their pledges?"

"Yes, miss. Every single one of them. One after the other. A bit of a bandwagon effect, in my opinion. They all frightened each other into abandoning the project."

"They did?" asked Olive mournfully.

"They did, yes." said Roland.

"See, Roland, I wasn't the only one not to know. Pretty sure you just forgot to tell people. Nothing to do with me." Brandy said smugly.

"They all retracted their pledges?" Olive repeated. "*All* of them? Every single one?"

"I am afraid so, lady Olive."

"Yeah, y'know, Rolly-boy, you've done a pretty shit job communicating that to us all, y'know." Brandy continued on. "I mean, and then you just pin it all on us? Like, fucking doody, man. Take a little responsibility, y'know."

Roland's eyes pierced into Brandy's.

"Silence, miss." he said. "You speak only when spoken to."

225

"Well, now you're speaking to me, so…"

Roland slammed his fist in the table.

"Not another word from you, miss, unless I explicitly request it. Understand?"

Brandy looked at him in silence for a while.

"Was that a request, or…?"

Roland slammed his fist in the table again.

"If it was *explicit*, you would not have needed to ask." he said.

"They *all* abandoned us?" repeated Olive once more. "After we stood treat for dinner? They still just abandoned us?"

"Yes, lady Olive, I am afraid so." Roland said.

"How much money do we have left?" Olive asked.

"Of the current budget?"

"Yes."

"My latest estimate lands at around a little less than a billion."

"Well, that's quite a hefty pile." said Brandy.

"I am quite certain it is more money than you have ever seen in your poor life, but in the context of building an entire city, I assure you it won't suffice."

"But… their donations were just a small part, right?" asked Olive. "We still have President Dzarban's contributions. Right?"

"If he approves of the project's progress so far, yes."

"Well, I think it's pretty impressive so far, what you've made out of this." Brandy said. "I mean, as I said, I certainly see the potential."

"Thank you, friend." Olive said.

"Yeah, and maybe he'll come over here and have a little look-see himself, y'know. I'm sure he'll be impressed."

"I am afraid that, due to complicated relations between his country and the United States, that would be quite improbable." said Roland.

"Alright, so how does he keep himself updated on this thing?"

"Mister Kenutsen will continually update him through the dark net we've established through the Helping Hand Company. You may not have heard of that organization, but they are the only way in which we can safely communicate with the president without

226

alerting authorities. They may admittedly work slowly, which is why this process takes so long, but rest assured they are a quite reliable group."

"Roland…" Olive said dingily. "Do you believe we will be able to pull this through?"

"Frankly, lady Olive, it is hard to say at the moment."

"Do you believe?" Olive repeated.

"I do hope, my lady. It's important to hold an optimistic outlook."

"I said, do you *believe*?"

"I… do believe, still, lady Olive. I believe the project can be completed."

Olive then drove away, into the elevator.

"Remember…" she said. "… We haven't come this far only to fail. Not now. That can't happen."

She pressed a button, and the elevator closed.

"Where's she going?" Brandy asked.

"To the Presidential suite." answered Roland. "She will be back in half an hour, though, for dinner. I'll be preparing some spaghetti carbonara. Several gallons, of course. I hope you enjoy that. Most people do."

"Hey, uh… do you, like, really think we'll pull this through?"

"I believe something substantial can come of this, yes. The only issue is that we have a few retardant factors that honestly should have been taken care of a long time ago."

"Yeah, that old 'do-it-tomorrow' attitude coming back to bite ya behind again. Been struggling with that, myself."

"Yes. I believe you on that."

CHAPTER TWENTY

Morale had plummeted into a deep pit for all of Unit Twenty Eight K. The news had just arrived that Enver, one of the unit's most efficient workers and a close friend to many of them, had been knocked dead by a hammer dropped from atop the shopping center he worked on by an unknown colleague who never dared accept blame. Enver did not wear a hardhat, for there were only enough of those for half of the unit, and so they had to switch every day. Today Enver had handed his helmet over to Anbaris, who used it to cover his eyes from the daylight while he napped behind the nearby post office.

Then there was the fact that the whole unit was to, when construction was finished, be put on trial in their home country, meaning they would, after a brief formality with a judge, be ruled guilty of treason and sent to the Gmerzh re-education facility, where they expected to survive for about a year or two.

"Men dvum edemilumiyim bilmayirma." said Ayberk, which translated to English as "I don't think I can keep going on anymore."

He was sitting in the barracks living room with six of his co-workers, all eating their bowls of Farmer Willy ltd. brand imitation gruel for dinner (Farmer Willy ltd. is a daughter company of D'Orleans Industries). It was eight PM, and they had collectively decided to call it an early day, to mourn the newest victim of the construction site's haphazard safety measures. They did not do this every time someone died in an accident, but Enver was particularly popular, and they had additionally been informed of their own impending death penalty earlier the same day.

"I just don't see the point. I have no strength anymore."

"But you must remain strong." said Abdul, sat to Ayberk's right. "If not for the city, or for the rest of us or even for yourself, then at least for your family."

"Don't mention my family, Abdul. All that does is reminding me I'll never see them again. It's hopeless. Once we return they'll send us to Gmerzh. Doesn't matter if we even finish this job."

"I know it looks grim right now, my friend. I myself had to force myself to keep working, for there was no motivation. But we can't let ourselves get completely apathetic, that only harms us further."

"How can anything harm us further? If we don't die like Enver... you know what? Enver was lucky. I'll say it. He got away with a quick bump on the head. Meanwhile, the rest of us are doomed to a small eternity in Dzarban's death camps."

"Don't say that. A man's passing is never a blessing. Life in any form is a gift worthy of endless gratitude." Abdul proclaimed in a somewhat rehearsed tone.

"Let's hear you say that after a week in Gmerzh." Ayberk rubbed his hands up and down his face. "Can you believe it? We are going to die in Gmerzh, no matter what we do."

"But at least it's not our fault." said Urdnay, sat opposite the two. "No, Kokhir is the one to blame."

Kokhir had not joined them for dinner this evening. After his shift was over, he had just crawled into his bed, wallowing in shame and self-pity.

"You're right." Abdul said. "He was the disloyal one. He betrayed us for his fleeting dream of decadent freedom."

"Yes." Ayberk said. "Not only did he disrespectfully underestimate our American employers by thinking he could escape from work that easily, but even if he succeeded, he would only damn the rest of us. He betrayed our employers, and he betrayed us."

"Naturally he has to be taken care of the same way we take care of all traitors." Urdnay declared.

"Are you suggesting...?" wondered Ayberk.

"Killing him." Abdul guessed.

"Correct." said Urdnay.

"That sounds like a fitting fate for a traitor." said Abdul.

"But... we can't do that. Kenutsen will punish us. A dead laborer is no better than an escaped one."

"But you said it yourself, Ayberk. How can we possibly be punished further?"

"And *you* just said that every life is a gift worthy of eternal gratitude."

"I only meant you should respect your own life, and the lives of the innocent. Kokhir, however, has written his own fate in blood. He chose to betray us, thus he chose to resign his right to live."

"But we've already lost one life today." Ayberk argued. "What does it help to take another?"

"May I offer a new perspective on the matter?" said Dorek, sat to Urdnay's left.

"Of course." said Abdul, having always been deeply respectful of Dorek's wisdom and intelligence. "Now listen, Ayberk, to what Dorek has to say."

"The thing is…" Dorek began. "… the way I see it, Kokhir is not entirely the one at fault here."

"What?!" exclaimed Abdul.

"Yes. For you see, who was it that turned him in? Tarek and Anbaris."

"They only did what they were duty-bound to do." Abdul said.

"And at no cost. When they return home they will, unlike the rest of us, walk free, return to their families. They gave up everyone else's liberty just to turn an alleged escapee, who we, frankly, don't even know if is guilty."

"Of course he is guilty." Abdul said. "Did you hear him deny it?"

"I did. Many times, first to Tarek and Anbaris, then to Kenutsen."

"They all claim to be innocent."

"And that means they're guilty?"

"I firmly believe he's guilty, no matter what you say."

"Well, we can debate until the goats die whether he is guilty or not. My point is, you can believe Kokhir is guilty *or* innocent, but you know that Tarek and Anbaris did what they did."

"They did nothing wrong."

"And yet they doomed us to a lifetime in Gmerzh?"

"So what is your suggestion, Dorek?" asked Ayberk. "That we kill Tarek and Anbaris instead?"

"What I'm trying to say is that Kokhir is damned the same as us, while those two are not."

"That's because, unlike Kokhir, they did the right thing." insisted Abdul.

"Then why did we get punished? Did we do anything wrong?"

"It's how the system works, and Kokhir knew that well."

"So did Tarek and Anbaris. And yet they chose to turn him in, fully knowing they did it to the detriment of all their colleagues."

"Are you actually saying that respecting their duties was a crime?"

"Not a crime, but I do think it was highly immoral."

"What is the point of all of this?" said Ayberk, very annoyed. "We're only discussing whether we should kill one or two men. What is the point of that. I'm not sure I want to kill anyone."

"The discussion may have drifted away in the wrong direction." Dorek said. "But my point is not to kill anyone. My point is that if one of us commits a crime or even a slight misdemeanor, we all get collectively punished. However, if we *all* do it, then what? What if, say, this whole unit refused to work? What if we dropped our tools, and left?"

"I assume they would punish all who remain? All the units."

"Then what if all the units did it? Who then is there left to punish?"

"And you suggest we just ask all the other units to rebel?"

"I know for a fact that at least roughly half of them have been penalized same as us. They have nothing to lose. The rest would then be more at risk if they didn't join. And unlike back home, these people, our American employers, they don't have police or guns or an army."

"Are you sure they don't?" asked Ayberk.

"Have you seen a single gun or uniformed man around? They have nothing but the authority of Dzarban's legal system to threaten us with."

"This seems completely ludicrous." said Urdnay.

"It seems treacherous to me." said Abdul.

"I am not saying you have to. All I'm saying is, if you want a little bit of final satisfaction before we're sent home to die, don't go after one poor little man who may have made a mistake. Go after the system who made those mistakes so devastating."

"I still must say I have some qualms about all this." said Ayberk. "What do you even mean we do? Go and say 'we don't want to work anymore' and leave. To where? We're in the middle of no-man's land. When they said we were going to America, I imagined New York, not this uncivilized wasteland."

"Oh, no, we won't leave. What we'll do is something called in the English tongue a 'strike'. We put down our tools, stand still with our chins high, and call out our demands to the employers."

"What demands?"

"Oh, I'm not sure. Maybe 'not going to Gmerzh' would be a nice start? The thing is, they need us much, much more than we need them. I've seen these people bickering and stressing around. They need to finish this city very soon. And if we refuse to work, that would be to *their* detriment."

The whole table had stopped chatting in order to listen to Dorek. When he finished, they were all totally silent, some with doubtful eyes, others cautiously nodding agreeingly.

"Maybe you should all be sleeping on it." Dorek followed. "Tomorrow, when we're more well-rested, we can make up our minds about this."

The room stayed silent for a while longer. Nobody said a word, some did not even breathe.

Ayberk tossed his plastic spoon into the now empty bowl of gruel. He stood up.

"I'll say this…" he said. "I haven't taken many hard decisions in my life. In fact, I haven't taken many easy ones either."

It was true that in Ugratistan, unusually many of people's personal decisions were taken for them by the authorities.

"However…" he continued. "I figure that if there ever was a time in my life to do something drastic, something extreme, something foolish, this would be it. It may seem like a hard decision, but the more thought I give it the easier it becomes. We have literally nothing to lose. I stand with you, Dorek."

Dorek smiled.

"This is *treason*." barked Abdul. "This type of attitude is why they installed the re-educational facilities in the first place."

A man at the very end of the table then stood up. His name was Blagoy.

"I stand with you too, Dorek." he said.

Soon more people stood up, all repeating the phrase over each other. After a while, every one of them stood with Dorek, expect Dorek himself, and also Abdul, whose face looked more frustrated by each new erection.

232

Everybody looked at Abdul, anticipating him to join them, especially Dorek, who sat with his feet on the table and a smug grin on his face.

After a few seconds of awkward silence, Abdul did finally stand up, only to leave the table.

"My mother didn't raise me to become a filthy rebel." he said facing the floor.

He flipped up his pack of Lucky Strike, and went outside.

II

There were times when one could feel movement in the Martini Tower, the sensation of it swaying gently from side to side. The wind could, at the altitude of the top floors, be vicious and forceful enough to slightly push the construction along. The building was after all a tall thin pillar with a gigantic wide bowl on top, a type of design severely vulnerable to wind, without proper counter measures, of which it had been installed with none.

There were times when Brandy had difficulties differentiating between her own intoxication and the wind. Both could throw her off her balance at unpredictable moments, but only the wind could do it to the rest of the room likewise. She wondered how this would affect the window washers. Actually, they did not seem to have been employed yet, for the windows were terribly dirty on closer inspection. On some sides of the apartment, they were in fact hard to properly see through, although, the view was practically identical on all sides, a vast stretch of unfinished city, then lush pine forest until the horizon, and it had at this point become an insufferably boring view to Brandy. She had for the past few days been secluded to this tower staring out at the financial and legal mess beneath her. There was no point going down to explore the city either, for what fun was there to look at street upon street of empty half-finished concrete buildings? The whole city was so egregiously homogenous too, nothing like Philadelphia or Riverside, or any other town she had been to. There was no finesse or variety to the architecture, each new street was indistinguishable from the last. It was the work of an obsessive compulsive child with an endless supply of Lego.

"Yo, Roland!" Brandy shouted from the kitchen area. "Have we got any more limes? Can't find the rest of the limes, I thought we had a ton of those."

Nobody answered.

233

"Hey, where you at, Roland?!" she yelled, still to no reply.

Since Olive had shown up, Roland had spent plenty of time on the floor above, her apartment and apparent office, the 'Presidential suite'. Brandy did appreciate the alone-time, but she also now needed lime for juice and garnish for the day's first mojito, and had no idea where to look. Having already checked all the cupboards she could reach, and every corner of the fridge, she saw no other option but to ask Roland, and so went into the elevator, hoping she would not disturb important work, or catch the two in an awkward position.

She had been to Olive's suite before, near exactly identical to her and Roland's, only bigger. She had, however, not yet been in the office. That door was always locked, whether Olive was inside or not. Brandy hoped the latter was the case, or at least that Roland was not in there with her.

Just like her luck, he was. As she stepped out of the elevator she heard his voice from within the tall redwood double door, but not a clear word of what he was saying.

She knocked five times.

"Yo, Roland, are ya in there?" she asked.

A short silence followed.

"We're quite busy, if you don't mind." Roland shouted back.

"Just wanted to know where you keep all the limes."

"I don't have time for this. Disturb me later, please."

And so Brandy returned to the elevator, prepared to have her mojito without lime, not nearly as enjoyable.

III

For dinner, Roland had prepared another stew, this time a thick beef stew with lentils and shiitake mushrooms, served on buttery fettucine noodles, paired with an aged South African Pinotage.

"This is pretty good, Roland." said Olive, having almost finished her second helping by the time Brandy was halfway through her first. "You have really improved as a cook lately."

"Thank you, my lady." Roland responded dryly.

234

"Although, it's not the same as chef Henry's dishes. Maybe we should have him sent over."

"It won't be long before we return home." said Roland.

"Home, yes. I'm actually starting to think of this as my home now. I feel so... in my right element here. It's like I'm in my own world."

"Yes, yes." Roland said trying to end the conversation.

"So, Brandy..." Olive said to Brandy. "... Do you um... I've read the book you borrowed me. Parts of it. The beginning at least."

"Oh, no. you didn't borrow it." Brandy said. "You can keep it for the rest of your life."

"Oh, you'll get it back soon."

"No, it's yours to keep, alright."

"Well, anyway, I read the first few chapters, and I really liked it."

"It doesn't really get there until about halfway through though."

"No, I thought it was really good already. I really feel like I can empathize with the main character, you know, because I always used to be really afraid of death. Actually, he has a lot of the exact same thoughts I remember having back in the day."

"Huh. That's something, I s'pose."

"Of course, I'm not afraid of that anymore. There are lots of worse things in life than death."

"I s'pose there are."

"Took me many years to come to terms with death. Like, how it's just inevitable, and natural."

Olive then swallowed the last piece of noodle.

"More please." she said, and Roland approached her with the two casseroles, and served her another big heap. "Anyway..." she continued. "... now I'm a *lot* more comfortable with my own mortality. It's just the way things are, you know. I mean, what's so great about living forever? I'd rather have an awesome and short life than an elongated bore of an existence. You think like that too, don't you?"

"I dunno." Brandy said taking a sip of her wine. "It wasn't that long since I was really close to die. So I just like to appreciate every second God'll allow me."

"Oh, but me too. The doctor said I was minutes away from dying at the hospital. He told me it was a total miracle that I survived. But at least I could say I had a good run up until

235

that point, with a few bumps of course, but at least if I died at that point, I could've said I've had a decent life. It wouldn't have been a terrible point to die."

"You're so not old enough to die yet, buddy."

"I mean, I'm glad I didn't die then, but I don't think I'd be sad right now if I did either. Of course I wouldn't be."

"What about your parents?"

"What about them?"

"Would they be sad?"

Roland cleared his throat.

"Ladies…" he said. "… should we perhaps find a more suitable subject to discuss for dinner? This conversation has turned most horrendously morbid, and it falls especially inappropriate over a meal."

"So what do you want to talk about, Roland?" Olive asked.

Just then, Sebastian Kenutsen slammed the door open, then behind him slammed it shut.

"Have you finally decided to join us for dinner, Mister Kenutsen?" asked Roland.

Kenutsen had in fact since his arrival only eaten his own self-cooked meals by himself.

"I'm afraid dinner will have to wait." Kenutsen said. "First I have some news to convey regarding the development of the project."

"Please tell." Olive said intrigued.

"I am afraid the course of the project has developed not necessarily to our advantage."

"Why?" asked Roland.

"It seems all our laborers have gone on strike. And I mean *all of them*. They refuse to work.

Olive coughed up a roll of pasta she almost got stuck in her throat. Roland did the same.

"What on earth do you mean they've gone on strike?!" exclaimed Roland.

"It was just as baffling to me. I honestly didn't know they even knew of that concept. As far as I know, there is no Ugrat term for 'strike', so where they got that from, I don't know. It makes no sense."

"So are you telling me they are rioting in the streets?"

"No, it's far calmer than that, remarkably. They've just laid down their tools and are now just standing there, unflinching."

"Then what do they want?"

"Well, there is this issue of communication, you see. They don't speak English all that well. None of them. And I don't speak any Ugrat other than a couple of simple phrases."

Olive got increasingly restless in her body language.

"Can't you just make them start working again?" she asked Kenutsen.

"How?"

"Just tell them to."

"Don't you think I have tried that? Several times? Hundreds of times?"

"Well, just make them work again."

"How?"

"That's your responsibility."

Kenutsen sighed heavily.

"Uh, 'scuse me…" Brandy said. "… how long have you… like… in what way have you tried to negotiate with those workers?"

"I have tried for as long as my language could reach." said Kenutsen. "The problem is, that's not very far in regards to these cretins. They can't by any means understand the nuances fo my reasoning, for they can barely understand a simple road direction."

"And you never bothered to learn *their* language?" Brandy asked.

"Why would I learn that? Ugrat is only spoken by about a million, all inbreeds and none with a driver's license."

"Well, y'know, maybe that type of attitude is why they started striking in the first place."

Everybody went quiet for a few seconds.

"Young lady, what exactly do you think this is?" Kenutsen asked coldly.

"I mean, just maybe show the poor guys a tiny bit respect, y'know. That's all I'm saying."

"Frankly we have shown them more respect than they deserve." Kenutsen replied. "Far more."

"Well, seems to me like you treat them like cattle, frankly. This is actually, to be honest, bordering on fucking slavery. You should really only expect this kind of reaction from those Ugrati folks. It's what you get for being a total dick for so long."

Kenutsen's face turned a sharp carmine.

"Why, you ungrateful little tramp. You punk slut!"

"What was that? Whaddya call me?"

 Roland stood up.

"I must say, this conversation has turned quite uncivilized." he said. "Apologize immediately. Both of you. I won't tolerate such lewdness at the dinner table."

Olive parked backwards, then drove away from the table.

"Yo, where're you going, Olive?" Brandy asked.

Olive drove onwards, not responding. She left the room without a word.

CHAPTER TWENTY ONE

Brandy had found some limes in a bag in the cupboard reserved for light bulbs and batteries and detergents, about ten pounds of them. She squeezed their juices into her mojitos, then chopped off a wheel and tread it down the glass edge. It was not an authentic mojito without that, she thought. She brought her drink to her bedroom, where she sat on the bed, looking out at the scene of a city stuck in progress. The tower cranes had stopped turning, they stood frozen. Little swarms of people gathered throughout the streets, like black little grains of sand that looked like ants. They did nothing yet, only stood around.

It was a decent view to Brandy, a decent landscape. The lack of activity calmed her, even if she knew it did the opposite to her friend, Olive. She figured a mojito would be necessary before she approached the girl, something to ease off the edge before she could consolidate her, during what must have been to her fantastically troubling times.

She drank the last half of her drink in the elevator, and tossed the ice cubes and mint leaves in the sink of Olive's apartment, before knocking on the office door.

"Hey. Olive. You in there?" she said.

"Yes." said Olive's voice.

"Mind if I come in?"

A long moment of silence followed.

"… The door is open."

Brandy opened the door slowly. She went inside, to find Olive behind her desk fervently scanning through a stack of papers with a laptop by her side.

"How's it going?" Brandy said.

"Not good." said Olive. "Not good, not good at all. It all just… this is atrocious."

"Alright?" Brandy said sitting down on her chair. "What's the issue?"

Olive took the currently uppermost paper from the stack and shoved it in Brandy's face.

"Look at this!" she said. "Can you make any sense of this?"

Brandy looked over the sheet, a massive maze of numbers and signs in the thousands, combined in no way she could understand.

"I... well... it's... it seems to be in order... well... I'm gonna be dead honest with you, I have no fucking clue what this means." she said.

"Really?" Olive asked.

"Honestly."

"Are you absolutely serious?"

"I'm 'fraid so."

Olive looked up in the ceiling for a second.

"Well, that proves it." she said. "If not even *you* can understand it, it clearly makes no sense. I'll tell Mister Kenutsen to revise it."

She flipped the paper aside.

"So, how are things going?" Brandy asked. "Are you doing alright?"

"It's terrible. Absolutely horrific." Olive wiped her forehead. "My whole dream has screeched to a halt."

"You talking about the strike?"

"For one, yes. I have no clue how to deal with that."

"Well, shit, you don't have any... um, I just hate myself for saying this, but don't you have any cops to deal with this?"

"No, I never thought police would be necessary in Obesiana. If everyone is content, then nobody would have any incentive to commit any crime. Right?"

"You thought everyone would be content here?"

"Of course they would. This was going to be my perfect society, you know, without bullying or exclusion or any of that petty cruelty we have in the rest of the world."

"Well, it's your design. You're the one who's got the overview over all this shit."

"Yes..." Olive sighed. "Now I'm not so sure anymore, though."

"Come on now, buddy." Brand said.

240

She got up and moved in behind Olive, beginning to massage her jelly-like shoulders.

"Keep your chins up now. Chin. Keep you chin up. We've just hit a little bump, alright. All projects do that, y'know. Up to several times."

"Even the successful ones?"

"Especially the successful ones. Ever heard of the French revolution? Or '*Apocalypse Now*'? Or Susan Sontag's career?"

"I hope you're right." Olive moaned in delight from the massage. "Ooh, I really needed that. I've become so tight lately."

Brandy moved on to massaging through the flab collar around Olive's neck.

"You shouldn't stress out so much, girl." she said. "You've been through one heart attack already."

"I know. 'Don't stress, don't overwork, avoid fatty and spicy food'. I don't really think I can do the last one, though. I mean, I don't need overly spicy food. I like flavor and a little heat, but to be honest, that Indian dish was *way* too much for me."

"Yeah, it sure was."

"No, I mean, I didn't like it. Well, I liked it a little bit, but it really was far too spicy for me. And it made no sense to serve it either. None of the other guests liked it, and it completely crashed with the gastronomic theme for that evening."

"Was there a theme?"

"Yes. We were trying to go for a Balkan cuisine experience. India's not in Balkan, or the Balkans, Balkan-land, what do you call it?"

"Uh, 'The Balkans', I think."

"Yes, the Balkans. India's quite a way away from that, is it not? Isn't that down in Africa, somewhere, or right next to Africa, between Africa and Iraq?"

"It's in south-east Asia."

"Yeah, that's pretty far from the Balkan, right. In fact, the second course was originally going to be chicken liver dolma with lemon zest. Then suddenly the day before, there was apparently a change to the menu. It just happened. Henry just informed me that it already had happened. It was completely without my consent, and it couldn't be changed for some reason."

"Just try to relax, sweetheart."

"Thanks, friend, but I really can't."

Brandy started rubbing harder.

"Sure you can." she said. "That Kenutsen dude will sort this strike clusterfuck out in no time. Just wait, don't stress, don't strain your heart."

"I still have budgetary concerns to attend to."

"Can't that wait?"

"Not really. I don't want the IRS on my neck. I like what *you* are doing to my neck, though."

"You don't want them figuring out about your tax evasion?"

"I don't want them figuring out about anything. *Ooh*, right there, yeah. But I just want no authorities sticking their noses in this project at all."

"So what is the problem, precisely?"

"It's... I may be wrong, I hope I am, maybe I should get Kenutsen to look over it when he's got the time, but it seem we are actually running out of money."

"Didn't we have, like, a couple billions or something?"

"It's actually substantially less than that now."

"Ya got an exact figure?"

"We're currently at around half a billion. Tomorrow we may have only half of that."

"No, we mayn't. That makes no sense. What are we even losing money on, if there is no progress in construction or anything?"

"Well, that's pretty credible logic, but really, we don't have money to... *ooh*... to finish the city as planned."

"Can't you just finish parts of it? Then tell some of those peeps that've bought property here they need to wait for a while?"

"Maybe..."

"Yeah, maybe. Maybe indeed, y'know."

There was no joint fluid left in Brandy's fingers as she let go of Olive's neck, and they hurt tremendously from the excessive blubber rubbing.

"I need to take a break now." Brandy said. "Too tired to keep going."

"That's okay. You were great. You really have some talent in the massage... when it comes to massage, it's... you're really good at it." Olive said and stretched her arms. "Do you want to come have some drinks in the living room?"

"I'd love to." Brandy replied with an eager grin.

II

Kenutsen had found himself a car with a roof window large enough for him to stick his body through. It was an old dark gray Subaru, its frame rusty around the wheels, and with a cripplingly dirty windshield. It would suffice, he thought, for the purpose of confronting the strikers. He would of course never approach them on his own feet, when they could turn violent at the drop of a hat. He had dealt with protestors before. One mistake, one little wrong nuance in one's speech or body language, and they would wreak total mayhem, cause an eruption of vandalism and chaos, uncontrollable anarchic havoc. Eighty percent chance of it normally, and now even more considering these were foreigners from a far less civilized country. The extent to which they could be reasoned with was severely limited on account of their cultural handicap, Kenutsen thought.

He had stopped the car with the engine running in the middle of Hitchcock Plaza, where the Ugrati strikers soon marched towards him, to his surprise right on schedule. They were just as angry as he was scared, but he would of course not show that. He had to appear authoritarian, and angry too. They were the ones who were in the wrong, and he needed to show them that in every aspect of his behavior.

The strikers, with Dorek in the front, stood tall and straight, all of them tightening every muscle in their bodies, looking towards the dweeby little man peaking up from the roof of the old Subaru.

"What is it you want?!" Kenutsen said into his megaphone.

"We want no go Gmerzh!" yelled Dorek back.

"What?!"

"We no go Gmerzh. You no make us go!"

"What are you even talking about?! What does 'Gah-merge' mean in English?!"

"You hear we say no Gmerzh!" Ayberk yelled from the crowd. "We live normal when Ugratistan return!"

"If you all paid better attention at the English course, we could have actually begun to discuss the matters! As it is now, I have no idea what any of you are saying!"

Kenutsen hoped his response had not come off as too aggravating.

"No fair! We see family again! Not Gmerzh, old life!" Dorek shouted.

"How about this?! You go back to work immediately, and we will actually continue to feed you until you're done here!"

Dorek took one step forwards, and the rest followed suit. Soon all the strikers started marching towards Kenutsen and his Subaru.

'Mother Mary fiddley-fuck' thought Kenutsen, and ducked down into his car, and put it in reverse. The game was up. Negotiation had failed. The riots had commenced. These striker wanted only blood now.

Kenutsen backed the car far down the road, only to be stopped by a separate crowd of strikers that had marched down to the plaza from the opposite end of town. In their front line stood Abdul, with Tarek by his side.

"Stop this now, Dorek!" Abdul yelled in Ugrat. "This is treason!"
"This is justice, you slimy coward!" Dorek yelled back.
"Justice?! You call betraying the trust of your fatherland 'justice'?!"
"Our fatherland's government are swine!" shouted Ayberk, who was peaking out from behind Dorek. "They've abused and oppressed and hurt us since the fall of the Soviet, and now our American bosses are doing the same!"
"Nonsense!" screamed Tarek. "Grand President Dzarban has protected us from the oppression of the Russian Federation!"
"You've eaten up the war propaganda like a baby!"
"You've eaten your own propaganda!"
"What kind of sense does that make?!"

Soon other Ugratis on both sides joined in on the political shouting battle, with Kenutsen's car trapped in the middle. A young man from Abdul's crowd suddenly jumped up on the car's roof and tossed an empty beer bottle at Dorek's chest. It did not burst from the impact, as he expected, but it still hurt a bit. Provoked by the aggression, Ayberk charged towards the little man, butted his head in his chest, and pushed him off the roof down to the ground. Abdul, who held a wrench in his hand, charged towards the unarmed Ayberk. In a matter of seconds, everybody attacked each other, while Kenutsen sat with his head between his knees, his car violently tilting from side to side. He was desperately praying to the Virgin Mary for rescue.

III

"I used to not understand father's obsession with guns." said Olive out of the blue, looking out the window from her living room to the dead city, sipping from the White Russian that Brandy had mixed for them both. "I mean, he loved his gun collection, it was his most priced possession. He owned maybe a thousand fire arms. Modern, vintage, antique, all sorts. He always showed them to his business partners, and pretty much any guests we had over. He was so proud of them."

"Yeah, I guess." said Brandy.

"And like I said, I never really understood what was so great about them. Then again, he never understood any of my interests either."

"I s'pose not."

"Now, he gave me a gun a while back. A Smith & Wesson."

"Yeah, I've seen it."

"What, you did? When?"

"At the banquette, remember? You told me everything about it."

"I don't recall that."

"Well, I s'pose we were both a bit tipsy at that point. Do you get really forgetful when you drink? I don't. I know some people do, but not me."

The two of them took a sip in unison, as they stared blankly out to the forest.

"Father always wanted to take me to his shooting range. I never went, didn't want to. He always wanted to make me learn how to use guns, and practice shooting. I never wanted to. When I was a child, I remember him talking about taking me to Kenya one day, and hunt lions with him. He often went to Kenya alone."

Brandy idly shook the cream coated ice cubes in her emptied glass.

"What another drink?" she asked.

"I still have a bit left." Olive answered. "This was really tasty, though. You absolutely have a little genius when it comes to making drinks. I've had this type of drink many times before, but none of them were this good."

"Well, I use Espresso Bohême instead of Kahlua. And Russian Standard vodka, and whole cream." Brandy said pulling out a bottle of Heineken from the fridge. "You should try one of my mojitos, though. I really think I've learned to nail the technique since I came here."

She popped the beer and sat down again.

"Y'know..." she said. "... My dad was always really on about cars. He was really into the automobiles. He tried to get Brendan to take over his repair shop at first, I remember, but Brendan only wanted to study sociology for some reason. And Brad, y'know, he couldn't tell the sides of a screw apart, like, you couldn't let someone like that run a repair shop, or any kind of business, really. I mean, I love that son of a bitch, he was always the nicest one to me, but he really was too much of a doofus to be in charge of anything, y'know. He wasn't very book smart, or street smart, or any kind of intelligent. And, well, what I was saying was that eventually dad wanted me to take over, y'know, or at least start working there and see how I turned out. And, uh, that never really went anywhere, y'know. I don't think he appreciated my efforts."

She looked over at Olive, who did not seem to pay much attention to her anecdote, but rather to something down in the city.

"Is that a building on fire?" she asked, scowling at a glowing point down in the streets.

Brandy looked down and saw a tiny little spot in the distance that seemed to be burning.

"Whaddya think that is? The rioters?"

"Maybe... " said Olive. "Maybe the rioters have begun burning down the city."

IV

Kenutsen's car had been tipped on its head, and he now lay crouched on the ceiling. Some of the strikers had engineered Molotov cocktails, and others had gathered demolition material, such as C4 and nitroglycerin, all of which they eagerly utilized in the raging havoc. For the first time in thirty four years, Kenutsen cried, big pellets of tears streaming down his snotty red face. God had forsaken him this time too. God had forsaken him every night at the casino, and every time he bought a lottery ticket, and now, in his most needing moment, God had forsaken him yet again. God had given up. It no longer mattered to God whether Kenutsen lived or died. Was it his fault? Should he have converted to Presbyterianism like his uncle?

A striker kicked against the windshield repeatedly, broke it. Two other strikers reached their boney arms inside and pulled Kenutsen out.

Kenutsen lay on his back, whimpering, trying to compress into a fetal position. One striker placed his booth on his throat. He stopped moving.

"What do you want?" he gasped at the man.

Dorek sat down besides his head, bruised and cut on every second inch of his skin. He held in his hand a big sturdy hammer, and started bashing it into Kenutsen's skull, repeatedly, over and over again, till there was a massive deep bloody crater where his forehead used to be, his brains mashed into porridge.

V

The riots had raged on far into the night. In the living room of Olive's apartment, Roland marched nervously back and forth trying repeatedly to call Kenutsen for updates on the situation, but received no response. Soon he angrily stuffed his cell phone back in his pocket, and went to call for Olive, who had been preoccupied with paperwork in her office.

"Would you like to join us, lady Olive?" he asked through the door. "I'm sure those spread sheets can wait till tomorrow."

"I just need to sort out a few expendable cutbacks." sounded Olive from within.

"That can wait, dear. If you come out I'll make you some hot cocoa, and we can listen to some Vivaldi while this whole silly thing outside blows over."

Brandy sat by the window still, covered in a thick fleece blanket, with a cup of hot cocoa with whipped cream and whiskey in her hand, looking out at the troublingly brightening city, while making clicking sounds with her tongue to the rhythm of an old reggae song she did not know the title of or lyrics to. Her head was occupied with a million thoughts, but none of any substance or direction. Ideas, worries, scenes from old movies and her own past, all cruised by as her brain failed to grab any of them. A reminder to take her next Nequam kept emerging, peaking its head up from her passive memory, sometimes inexplicably accompanied by a taunting reminder to breathe manually.

"Come out soon then, my lady. Your papers will not disappear overnight." said Roland to the office door.

"Just a second…" sounded Olive.

The elevator opened. In walked Mister Wilkes, rubbing his knuckles against his chest.

"What is the matter, Mister Wilkes?" asked Roland.

Brandy heard Roland's namedrop, and turned around to face the smug revolting lips that had haunted a number of her dreams.

"What are you doing here?" she asked Wilkes sourly.

"Well, work of course." he replied. "Same as you, I presume."

"When did you get here?" Brandy asked, no more hospitably.

"Oh, I understand you haven't seen my face much, but I came her alongside lady Olive. Maybe it was a little rude to not announce my arrival, but, you see, I've been quite busy, just as I imagine you have been."

"Please, what is it you have to report?" Roland asked insistently.

"Oh, yes, of course. Sorry we got carried away with the chatter. Now then, I just came to tell you that you unfortunately will have to hire a new project manager. Sebastian Kenutsen died in the riots recently."

Roland stood quiet for a bit, silently flapping his mouth.

"Wh-what... what are you telling me?" he finally asked.

"I said Mister Kenutsen just died, about thirty minutes ago. One of the rioters killed him, and, might I add, it was tremendously brutal. You should have seen it, actually. His head looked like a bowl of Texas chili. Just needed a dollop of crème fraiche and some chives, and you could have served it at Denny's. I wouldn't recommend an open casket funeral, to be honest, even if he was a Catholic."

"I... that is quite tragic." said Roland. "Terribly tragic."

"It's a bit of a bummer, yeah." Brandy added.

"Lady Olive..." Roland knocked on the office door again. "Did you hear? Did you hear what Mister Wilkes said?"

"What?" Olive said.

"Awful news, my lady. I am afraid Mister Sebastian Kenutsen is dead."

"Oh..."

Olive gave no further response.

"I understand it is hard to take in. It always is when someone dies." said Roland. "Would you like to come out now?"

No sound came from the office.

"I say we have a minute of silence, to mourn our colleague." Roland said to the other two. "And it would be appreciable if you could join us, lady Olive." he then said back to the door.

There was still no response.

"Very well. I understand if you need to process this some more. Now then, the rest of you, let us gather in a circle now."

Wilkes and Brandy did as told. Soon the three stood in a triangle, all staring at their bellybuttons for a rough minute, during which Brandy thought to herself 'You're now breathing manually again, dumbass', followed by 'fuck you, brain'.

CHAPTER TWENTY TWO

Watching the situation down on the streets seemingly worsening by the minute for a very long time made Brandy's yawning also worsening by the minute. The riots went from troubling her to boring her as her eyelids grew heavier.

"You guys, think I'll just drop my pill and hit the hay. Wake me if something more shitty happens, or it gets dangerous to be here, or whatever."

She did consider that it might already be quite dangerous in the tower, with Wilkes hanging around. She figured the presence of Roland would protect her in some sense, and if not, if Wilkes did get his horrifying ways with her, at least that naively trusting Roland would get serious egg on his face, and learn a valuable lesson in not trusting gore-obsessed sex criminals just because they wear business suits.

Brandy found some slices of smoked salmon in the fridge, which she ate straight from the package, washing it down with a bottle of Heineken. After that she went into the bathroom to fetch her bottle of Nequam, only to not find it anywhere, which annoyed her greatly, for not only did the Nequam guarantee her a blood-curdling free night, but it also made her sleep a lot better with the assistance of alcohol. Also, the Nequam had that magical effect of erasing any potential hangover that said alcohol could cause. It would have been a dream drug was it not for the abominable taste.

Thinking back, Brandy did recall taking her last pill while hanging out at Olive's place. She had asked Olive to join her, but she refused this time, saying her first time gave her insidious nightmares throughout her coma. Brandy did not remember dreaming anything during her Nequam comas, although one time she did experience an hallucination of James Dean with a poncho and a sombrero and a pair of six-shooters during the waking phase of the high, though that might have had something to do with combining the pill with cheap tequila and cheaper pizza with jalapeños and pepperoni.

She decided to go back upstairs.

II

"You guys seen my pills?" Brandy asked immediately upon leaving the elevator.

"They're kinda important, y'know."

"What did they look like?" asked Roland, now in the kitchen area.

"What're you doing?"

"I've decided to go prepare lady Olive a nightcap. She loathes going to bed hungry."

"She's coming out?"

"I honestly have no idea. She has made no further signal yet." Roland said cutting up a zucchini. "Now then, what exactly did you ask me about again, miss?"

"Oh, uh, my pills. Y'know, big blue pills in this little bottle, like a small plastic pickle jar. Called 'Nequam Inter-yadda-yadda-something-Latin'. Like, I doubt there are many like it around here, shouldn't be that hard to find. Y'know, you seen me with it several times already, I'm sure."

"I'm afraid I haven't seen anything like that lately." Roland said. "Not on this floor at least. Are you sure haven't lost it downstairs? I've seen the total mess you've created in your bedroom."

"I'll have a looksie around anyway."

Brandy started ransacking the apartment, opening cupboards and flipping sofa cushions.

"Where did Wilkes go, by the way?" she asked while scanning the terrain under a commode.

"He went downstairs, to his own apartment in the tower's middle section." Roland answered.

"He's been living right beneath us this whole time?"

"Yes. And why exactly is that so alarming to you?"

"Didn't I tell you all about the…"

"Oh, don't let yourself get intimidated by his demeanor. He only has a unique way of communicating his needs."

251

"He's got some pretty unique needs as well, y'know."

"Now don't be prejudiced, young lady."

Brandy said nothing in return. After a few more minutes of searching in vain under the furniture, she decided to knock on the office door.

"Yo, Olive. I think you got my pills. I don't know for sure, but can I just take a look inside?"

"It's no use, miss Rabinow." said Roland. "I think she took Mister Kenutsen's death very hard. She's always been sensitive about death, you see. I think she will need some more time alone."

"Yo, Olive!" Brandy kept knocking on the door. "Mind if I just pop in for a short sec? Don't need to talk or nothing, just wanna look around for my pills."

There was no response. Brandy pressed her ear against the door to listen for subtle sobbing, or other kinds of noises. Nothing.

"Is this door locked?" she asked Roland.

"Yes, as always. And it is quite sturdy at that. That may be wood on the outside, but that's only for aesthetic purposes. This door has a solid steel core, and the lock itself is in fact the latest in home security technology, fit to survive a nuclear explosion at ground zero, or so the advertisement proclaims at least. Nevertheless, there is no way to penetrate it without the help of the national guard, and I assume even they would struggle. Naturally we would do our best to protect lady Olive in the event of an invasion or a disaster."

Brandy turned the handle of the door and opened it and went inside.

"Youth…" Roland snorted. "No manners at all."

He continued to cut the zucchini.

III

Inside, Olive sat with her back turned, looking up at the painting behind her.

"You feeling alright, Olive?" Brandy asked walking in. "Y'know, it's fine if you don't wanna talk right now. I just came looking for my pills. We can talk tomorrow, right?"

She then noticed that Olive held in her hands her revolver. That gun looked so huge back in the drawer, yet so tiny between Olive's mighty paws.

252

"Shit, Olive." Brandy muttered. "Is there anything you, like, need to talk about?" There was no response.

"Because, well, if this is like, shit, fuck, don't you do anything stupid, ya hear."

She thought of grabbing the gun from her hands, then refrained when considering the risk. Touching Olive in any way could in fact be pose a risk right now, she thought.

"Look, listen, Olive, friend..." Brandy tried to look straight into Olive's watery numb eyes. "I understand what... well, I won't claim I understand, actually, I don't know shit, alright, I don't wanna say I know what you're going through or how you feel, 'cos we all have different, like, fuck it, just listen, alright. I've had some bad times too, y'know, like, actually, one really dark day a long time ago, like several years, I, y'know, I went up to this big tree on a hill, and uh, hey, are you like, listening?"

Olive did not look like she was. She just examined her gun like it was an alien artifact, a really uninteresting one. She seemed utterly disinterested in her surroundings, including Brandy.

"Hey, yo, look at me, buddy." Brandy impulsively started snapping her fingers in Olive's face.

Olive let go of the gun, letting it rest on her stomach.

"Yeah, yeah. That's good, friend." Brandy carefully picked up the gun by the barrel. "Alright, so, uh, would you like to talk about something, or... it's alright if you don't, right now, just be like, um, would you like a hotdog, maybe? I could make you a hotdog."

Olive did not respond. She did not breathe, as evident by the stillness of her stomach and the silence. Olive's breath had always been audible from at least within arm's reach.

"Yo, Olive, are you alright? Like, physically?"

At that point, Brandy finally found her bottle of pills, behind a tall stack of paper on the desk. It was empty.

"Oh fucking God." gasped Brandy, shaking the bottle upside down, as if expecting it to still contain a few blue pellets, even if it was a transparent bottle.

She turned to Olive.

253

"Shit, shit, shit." she said. "Olive, buddy dearest. Did you… please, friend, don't tell me… shit fuck, did you fucking *swallow* these?! Like, fucking all of them?!"

She scanned through the label, reading everything twice or thrice in her panicked haze. 'For adults eighteen and up', 'Recommended dosage: three pills a day, spread evenly throughout', 'Overdose: Two pills simultaneously, or more than three pills in one day', 'Lethal Overdose: Three pills or more simultaneously, or more than five pills in one day'.

"Shit fucker cunt piss! Assfuck up the shitter!"

Brandy looked over at Olive, who sat there unmoving. She checked the label again for anything about weight. Surely that would have to be a relevant factor. For once, Olive's fatness could actually save her life.

"Fuck, fuck, fuck, holy mac 'n cheese enema. Please, something."

There was not a single word to be found on the subject. Still, though, weight should by any logic play some part in this.

"*YO, ROLAND!*" Brandy screamed at the top of her lungs. "*ROLAND, ARE YOU THERE?!*"

Roland entered with a cleaver in his hand.

"You could approach me to a normal conversation distance, and address me with your indoor voice." he said.

"Yo, Roland, you gotta call an ambulance. Olive's Oh-Dee'ing on my pills!"
"What?!" Roland dropped the knife and rushed over to Olive.
"I don't know how lethal it is, or how much time she's got, but if we could try and get her pumped she could probably make it, like I dunno, but I hope, is what I'm saying…" Brandy babbled.
"Why on earth didn't you tell me before, you buffoon?!" Roland barked trying to check for Olive's pulse.
"I just found out, alright! Fucking don't get mad at me! I fucking am like, fucking trying to save the poor girl!"
"Stop yammering, you dumb bimbo, and go find the defibrillator in the cupboard above the kitchen sink!"

'Dumb bimbo' was the crudest English explicative Roland had used in well over a decade.

Brandy promptly limped to the kitchen, trying to build up a light jog with her cane. Soon she hastily returned with the defibrillator, clumsily dropping it on the floor.

"I'm sorry, I'm sorry, I'll pick it up." she stammered.

"Get away from it!" Roland hissed and picked it up for her. "I can't find any pulse on her. It's difficult with all her layers of fat, but it is still usually more doable than it is now." Roland started untangling all the machine's cables. "I don't need you anymore. Go outside and try not to cause any more trouble."

"I'll call nine-one-one." Brandy said whipping up her phone.

"For what?"

"For… whaddya mean 'for what'?"

"There aren't any ambulances around here until several dozen miles away. No roads for them to reach us either."

"Alright, I'll fucking ask them for a helicopter. What're the coordinates around here?"

"Forget it! Do as I say and just wait outside! We cannot send an ambulance here! Not yet! It's far too risky!"

"Excuse me, are we fucking trying to save a life here or what?!"

"I can do that myself, thank you very much!"

"How?! She needs to get pumped! You got equipment for that 'round here?!"

"*GO WAIT OUTSIDE, YOU FILTHY YIDD WHORE!*" Roland roared.

'Filthy yidd whore' was the crudest English explicative Roland had used since 'dumb bimbo'.

Brandy walked outside with clenched teeth and wet eyes.

IV

In a fit of frustration, Brandy had pulled out several cups and plates from the cupboard and smashed them in the ground. She had done the same to the turntable and a gaudy lamp that actually deserved it anyway for its dreary design. Sat curled up in a ball in the sofa, devastated and exhausted, she listened intently to the sounds of the defibrillator from the office, repeating over and over. She hoped Roland was right, that he actually could save Olive, but her skepticism seared in the membrane, telling her to just accept what had happened. 'Please God, please save her' she thought, considering whether she should start praying properly, if that helped any.

After a minor eternity, Roland stepped outside with a reserved frown, paying no attention to Brandy's destruction.

"I did all I could, but..." he sighed deeply. "... I am afraid lady Olive has passed away."

Brandy sat motionless, holding her breath, staring into the floor. She then pulled herself up, limped over to Roland, shivering, quivering, unable to blink.

"You goddamn fucking impotent Uncle Tom asswipe!" she shouted furiously at him. "You motherfucking son of an Aids-ridden whorehouse sample pussy! You fucked it up! You let her fucking die, you worthless lump of wet dick puss! Shit-eating... piece of... fuck! Fucker! Fucker! Fucker!"

Roland said nothing, and instead pulled Brandy into his chest, and hugged her tightly. It did take long before her eyes moistened up again, and she started weeping. Soon they both wept indiscreetly.

CHAPTER TWENTY THREE

The night Olive died, Brandy had laid in bed wide awake until sunrise, staring into the ceiling, thinking about nothing. When Roland had knocked on her door to invite her to breakfast, she refrained from answering, and refrained from moving.

First in the afternoon, terribly thirsty and no longer able to hold her bladder, she got out of bed, but had still no desire to leave her room. For the rest of the day, until sunset, she had been sitting around on various chairs, limped back and forth, and idly examined objects like they were alien artifacts.

As the day passed, the riots outside gradually calmed down. There was only so long an overworked and undernourished crowd could keep fighting and vandalizing without sleep.

When they sky darkened outside, Brandy felt her belly rumbling, and decided to go out to the fridge.

On her way there, she noticed Wilkes sitting in the sofa, looking at her, which in itself surprised her only slightly, but it was his face that now made her skip a heart beat. He looked mournful, actually hurt. She had never before seen any expression on his face besides condescending smugness and malevolent glee.

"How do you do?" he asked somberly, a tone just as jarring with him as his face.
"I... just wanted to get a snack." Brandy replied in confusion.
"Do you want to sit down and talk?" Wilkes asked.

Under any other circumstances, Brandy would have rejected him on the spot, or at least wanted to do that, to tell him straight in his fishlike face to leave her alone, which she would gladly had done without hesitation were it not for the prospect of abduction

257

and torture. Right now, however, the emotional atmosphere was different, greatly so. Furthermore, Wilkes sounded completely sincere for once, genuine in his attitude.

"Alright…" Brandy said, to her own surprise.

She sat down next to Wilkes, whose eyes for once wandered elsewhere. His left knee shook rapidly, seemingly beyond his will.

"So, how exactly do you feel?" he soon asked.

"Well, hard to say. A bit… depressed, maybe. Exhausted, mentally. A little… scared, to be honest. Don't feel like I'm in my right element anymore."

"I am in a very similar mood, myself, to be honest."

"Are *you* sad that Olive is gone?"

"Her death did make an impact on me, certainly."

"I thought you were more like a, y'know, 'don't-give-a-fuck-about-snuffing' kinda guy, like, remember how you talked about Seb when *he* died?"

"What did I say?"

"What did you *say*? That was like, yesterday."

"I don't bother to catalog every sentence I've spoken."

"Well, you seemed to take his death pretty lightly, to be frank."

"I've never had any personal relationship with *him*, though. He was a bit of a bore, to be honest. Only occasionally conversed with him. Only discussed business."

"Still, y'know, that's a fucking life getting ended. Fucking gruesomely too, from the way you talked about it."

"I don't care much about human lives in general. They will all perish at some point. I only care about the ones that make some kind of impact on me personally."

"And Olive did?"

"Yes. She very much did."

Wilkes visibly strained himself to hold back tears. An absurd sight to Brandy.

"Olive was *quite* unique." he said. "To me, at least, she was a bona fide one in a trillion type of person. A little diamond in a world of coal. She was so lonely though. One easily becomes lonely when being so special. And she was truly special. She always tried to be positive about things, but I saw how she spiraled into depression. Every day all of society tried to beat her into submission. And she tried to just counteract all that cruelty with love and tolerance. And that worked for her, mostly, for a while. Though I suppose

258

everybody have their breaking point. Olive had hers, and so she created this. This city. Quite impressive, in my opinion."

"Yeah, she was a great bud, actually. I mean, maybe this is just the moment speaking, like, the post-tragedy period, but I actually think she might have been my best friend ever. At least close. At least my best human friend."

"Yes, that's what I hoped. That's why I brought you two together."

"Actually, I was just hired as an accountant. And we kinda just, y'know…"

"I know. I was the one who hired you."

"Well, yeah, I remember you tried to… like… I'd say 'persuade' me, but it wasn't like I had much of a choice, really. Wouldn't it say it was that smart of a move either, like, you really didn't get the most qualified person."

"But I'm surprised you didn't get that yet. I didn't bring you onboard because of any professional qualifications. I didn't even expect you to do anything expect play the part. To be honest, all the accounting on the project has been conducted by a team of actual economists over in Riverside. People who know what they're actually doing."

Brandy threw Wilkes a confused glance with one eyebrow raised high.

"What?" she asked in mild vexation.

"No, the only reason I brought you into this was because I wanted Olive to have a real friend. A real homosocial relationship with someone of the same generation. I found you, and, miraculously, you also looked a lot like her. Did you know that people who are physically similar are more likely to befriend each other?"

"So… this was like, what, all just a ruse, sort of?"

"Well, I wouldn't call it a 'ruse', exactly. Just a minor manipulation of the truth for the sake of a greater good. You've told a little white lie once in a while too, haven't you?"

"And why exactly didn't you tell me this in advance?"

"I figured you'd play your part more authentically if you did so cluelessly. Isn't that obvious?"

Brandy rubbed her temples with one hand.

"So… this is a load to take in. I was a Ponzi, of sorts? Is that the correct term here? You just used me?"

"I tried. I thought a good friendship would be healthy for Olive. Help her develop. But now, it's… where do I start?"

259

He looked at Brandy again, with pink moist eyes.

"Oh God. Every time I look at you… you look just like her." he said. "Same azure eyes. Same nose, same lips… eyebrows a bit bushier, but similar shape on them at least."

"Yeah, I s'pose, and maybe we're a few pounds apart as well."

"Oh, well, naturally. Her size was another way in which she was unique. And now, since the surgery, you've practically reached the other extreme. You're unhealthily skinny now."

"Yeah, I've always been really skinny."

"Oh, I remember you being a bit pudgier the first times I saw you."

"I was not."

"You certainly had some freshman chub."

"No I didn't. I was skinny as… I was skinny back then too."

"You had a bit of a pot belly poking out."

"Shut up. I was fine."

Wilkes' condescending grin started to return, albeit in a slightly warmer form. Brandy was indifferent to his mood and his person now. Perhaps it was the revelation of his more sensitive facet, or maybe she was just emotionally numbed, but she did not find him frightening anymore. He was only another loser in a universe of losers, several billions of broken pathetic lumps of jelly hiding behind a variety of different façades.

Wilkes and Brandy shared a awkward ambivalent chuckle. After the laughter had faded, they shared an even more awkward silence. Brandy had nothing she wanted to say. If Wilkes wanted to continue this conversation, he would have to take the initiative. That was what she usually thought during dead air in social situations.

Wilkes stood up.

"I have business to attend to." he said, referring to probably nothing, and then left the room.

Brandy sat alone in the sofa, only now remembering how famished she was. For the first time since her operation, her regular appetite had returned.

II

"How do you feel?" Roland asked Brandy in a therapeutic tone, while she sat with her bowl of scrambled eggs in the reclining chair, idly watching an old episode of '*St. Elsewhere*' on television. "Are you sure you don't want to join me at the breakfast table?"

"I'm fine." she answered. "Just still need some time to, y'know, I really, uh, this whole thing is just really, really heavy, y'know."

"I understand. I too take the lady's passing very heavily."

"Yeah, shit, I... can we talk about this later." Brandy murmured and splatted some more Tabasco on her eggs.

"Tell me when you're ready." Roland said nodding, and returned to his own breakfast.

The weight that had slightly eased by the time Brandy went to bed last night, had once again rushed back with full force when she awoke this morning. Her appetite had also faded again. All progress was lost with six hours of sleep.

III

Around lunchtime, Brandy approached Roland in Olive's apartment, which had now begun to stink viciously.

"Is she, like, still in there?" she asked reluctantly.

"I am afraid so. I cannot remove her by my own power, naturally. Wilkes managed to acquire a particularly desperate moving company in the 'area', relatively speaking, but they won't arrive until at least tomorrow. We re still uncertain on how to handle the funeral."

Just able to keep herself from gagging, Brandy pulled her shirt over her mouth and nose.

"I'm starting to get fucking sick here." she complained. "What are you even doing here?"

"Doing some paperwork, some accounting, nothing you would be interested in."

"Yeah, but here?"

"I thought it'd be best if neither of us were to be disturbed."

"Still, though, fucking here? Isn't this smell fucking bothering you?"

261

"I've never objected to the lady's bodily scents."

Brandy could to think of no response, and so headed for the elevator.

"What was it you wanted to ask?" asked Roland.

"It was nothing, really. Nothing important. I just wanted to ask if I could, like, maybe go home soon…"

As the elevator door opened, Roland stood up and went inside after Brandy.

"Home?" he asked with a level of surprise.

"I just wanna see my family again, y'know. Family and friends."

"Will you then appear at the lady's funeral?"

"Yeah, well, won't it be in Riverside? Will it be here?"

"I believe she would wish to be buried here in this city, yes. Her own creation."

The elevator stopped and Brandy left into her own apartment. Roland followed after.

"Perhaps it would be more practical if you waited until then?" he continued.

"Maybe you can just send me back once we get there, or… I dunno, I just wanna go back, really."

"Are you not happy here?"

Brandy poured some simple syrup into a glass on the kitchen counter, and started crushing a few mint leaves into it.

"To be honest, this whole place is starting to make me queasy. I dunno, it's… don't take it personally or anything, but I just hate it here. It's such a depressing place."

"Do you mean this tower, or the city as a whole?"

"Both, actually. But yeah, the city's pretty damn dreary. Really uninspired, monotonous, samey, lame, hate it. Fucking hate it."

She whipped up a bottle of white rum from the liquor cabinet, and started pouring it into the syrup.

"It will only be about a week." Roland said.

"That's a week too long. I wanna go home today, really." Brandy said pouring crushed ice into the mixture.

"I understand." Roland said. "Unfortunately, this city never really lived up to its potential. Things got out of control quite fast. I will admit we lost perspective of the project. It was perhaps far too broad of an endeavor."

262

Brandy squeezed in the juice of half a lime, and cut a wheel off the other half and thread that onto the glass edge as garnish along with a couple whole mint leaves.

"I hoped to turn this city around, though." Roland continued. "I want to use the lady's design as merely a catalyst for something much more profitable. This could perhaps be the next Las Vegas, although I am personally not particularly found of the hedonistic decadence that has defined *that* city's image. To tell the truth, ideally I would want Obesiana to become a kind of haven for high culture. Art museums, operas, libraries, theaters, just imagine how we could excel at all of those. We could create this... new little free state for the world's intellectuals."

"And call it Obesiana?" Brandy asked sipping from her mojito.

"Well, naturally, the name would have to change. Many little details would have to change. Big broad details too, actually. But it could be done. I was thinking... I was thinking ever since this project gained traction in its infancy of how, in the case that something should happen to the lady, it could live on, but in another direction, more in accordance with ideals of enlightenment and intellectualism."

"Isn't that kinda disrespectful to Olive, y'know? Like, perverting her work into something else?"

Roland went to sit down in the sofa.

"Let me be quite honest." he said. "With all due respect to the late lady, her plan was admittedly quite infantile, naïve, horribly disconnected from reality, which, frankly, is not too surprising given her devastatingly isolated life. She did come far, though, on account of her family's great fortune, in addition to her own keen sense of business conduction, and her natural charisma. However, it wouldn't take too long before the project would fall apart under her lead. Sooner or later she would have to step back, and *then*, only then could this city actually reach its potential."

"You don't say..." Brandy said leaning over the kitchen counter, clutching her drink.

"Yes. Unfortunately, it would turn out to be much too late, and of course under much too tragic circumstances. I was hoping that at some point the pressure of all the responsibility would force her to voluntarily resign, but it seems her spirit was far more resilient. It is in fact quite admirable how tenacious the lady has been. She would not give up until pushed to the absolute threshold."

Brandy looked into her glass, gently swaying it in a circle.

"Are you sad that she's gone?" she asked.

"Why, what?" Roland responded chokingly. "Why, of course. I mourn the lady more than I did my own mother. Granted, she and I had a very turbulent relationship."

"What, Olive or your mom?"

"The latter, of course. Several nasty episodes. But I digress. The lady's passing is, naturally, a disastrous event, a deeply tragic and saddening incident. She was far too young, far too... vivid. I may be disciplined enough to not let my mourning sabotage my work or my dignity, but let me assure you it is quite active."

Brandy then finished her drink in one big gulp.

"Y'know, I don't know what's gonna happen to this place, but I assume you won't need me anymore regardless."

"Mister Wilkes told you about your actual purpose?"

"Yeah. I kinda had a feeling all along, y'know, it all seemed a bit off."

"Oh yes, I remember being quite baffled by your presence. To be fair, Mister Wilkes' methods have always been very eccentric, often infuriatingly so."

"Yeah, I know... When did you find out about the truth, regarding me?"

"The same day as Olive's passing. A bit earlier that day. I was far less shocked than I probably should be."

"Yeah, same here, or, well, not sure."

A short silence followed.

"But, anyway..." said Brandy. "I just really want to go home now."

"You really do?"

"Please."

Roland sighed.

"You do know that should the authorities ever catch us, I'd have no choice but to inform them of your involvement."

"You gonna snitch on me?"

"I am afraid they will demand full disclosure, and it would then only be harmful for me to resist."

"Do ya think that's likely, though?"

"I think I should be able to avert any undesired attention in the same manner as before. But there is always a possibility."

264

Brandy sighed.

"I understand." she said. "I guess I have *some* kind of responsibility here. Or, I dunno, I guess I deserve a little slap on the wrist or something. Maybe. But still, could you just send me home? I promise I'll try to make the funeral, even if I have to pay the travel expenses myself."

"I will not force you to attend."

"Yeah, but, y'know, Olive. Still, do you think you can get me home?"

Roland stood up.

"I can call for a flight to pick you up. They could be here as early as seven PM if I call now. Is that what you want?"

"Yeah, totally. Get me home."

"Do you by 'home' mean Riverside, or your native Philadelphia?"

"Philly. Philly all the way. All the stuff I got in Riverside I can do without. Get me to the City of Brotherly Love. Don't know what that's like with the airport and shit, but…"

"That will not be a hassle." Roland whipped up a cell phone, and started scrolling through his contact list. "Are you certain, though?"

"Dead fucking certain."

IV

Fluffy dots of powder snow descended upon the road as Roland drove Brandy to the landing strip. As they exited the car, said strip was covered in an inch-deep white layer, rendering it nearly invisible from the sky, probably.

"There is a chance they will be a might late." Roland said as his watch struck seven. "There has been some nasty wind over the mid-west these past hours." he continued.

Looking up at the snowy sky, Brandy noticed a little black crow taking off from a nearby pine tree, flying into the distance.

She then removed her beret to shake of a layer of snow that had accumulated on it in a matter of minutes, while also shaking some out of her hair, which had a notorious habit of absorbing snow like a sponge and inflict her with a cold. Her nose had gotten a little snotty already, though that could be from the low temperature, not a virus.

265

Right next to the strip was a hill the size of a small house with a large dead pine tree atop, which attracted Brandy's attention, soon making her approach it. Despite her weakened body, she braved up the steep hill, and sat down to soak her butt in the fresh snow by the tree's root, scouting out through the area. Her cold fingers, not protected by the wool gauntlets, she squeezed between her armpits. The strip was not very well-lit, just enough to find one's way around on foot, but still much dimmer than a regular airport.

Brandy thought to herself that some day she would finally release the pressure, let go, move on, and laugh at these past few months.

The End.